MAKING YOUR MIND UP

Jill Mansell

making your
mind up

headline
review

First published in 2006
by REVIEW

An imprint of Headline Book Publishing

1

Cataloguing in Publication Data is
available from the British Library

ISBN 0 7553 0489 6 (hardback)
ISBN 0 7553 0490 X (trade paperback)

Typeset in Bembo by
Palimpsest Book Production Limited,
Polmont, Stirlingshire
Printed and bound in Great Britain by
Mackays of Chatham plc, Chatham, Kent

Headline's policy is to use papers that are natural, renewable and
recyclable products and made from wood grown in sustainable products.
The logging and manufacturing processes are expected to conform to
the environmental regulations of the country of origin.

HEADLINE BOOK PUBLISHING
A division of Hodder Headline
338 Euston Road
LONDON NW1 3BH
www.reviewbooks.co.uk
www.hodderheadline.com

In memory of
my beloved mum.

Acknowledgements

I've never used this page to thank my agent and editor before, as it always seemed a bit of a teacher's pet thing to do. But after so many books the time has definitely come to thank Jane Judd, my agent, and Marion Donaldson, my editor, for all their wonderful help, advice and hard work on my behalf. And while I'm at it, everyone else at Headline too. You're all fantastic and an absolute joy to work with. So thanks again; you've changed my life.

Chapter 1

'You maaaaake me feeeeel,' Lottie Carlyle warbled soulfully at the top of her voice, 'like a natural womaaaaan.'

Oh yes, the great thing about singing when your ears were underwater was that it made you sound *so* much better than in real life. Not super-fantastic like Joss Stone or Barbra Streisand, obviously – the words silk purse and sow's ear sprang to mind – but not so alarmingly bad that small children burst into tears and hid under tables whenever you opened your mouth to sing. Which had been known to happen on dry land.

Which was why she was enjoying herself so much now, in Hestacombe Lake. It was a blisteringly hot day in August, her afternoon off, and she was floating on her back in the water gazing up at a cloudless, cobalt-blue sky.

Well, nearly cloudless. When it was four o'clock in the afternoon and you were the mother of two children there was always that one small bothersome cloud hovering on the horizon:

What to cook for dinner.

Something, preferably, that didn't take ages to make but sounded like a proper meal. Something that contained the odd vitamin. Something, furthermore, that both Nat and Ruby would deign to eat.

Ha.

Pasta, perhaps?

But Nat, who was seven, would only consent to eat pasta with olives and mint sauce, and Lottie knew there were no olives left in the fridge.

OK, maybe bacon and mushroom risotto. But Ruby would pick out the mushrooms, accusing them of being slimy like snails, and refuse to eat the bacon because bacon was – bleurgh – *pig*.

Vegetable stir-fry? Now she really was wandering into the realms of fantasy. In her nine years Ruby had never knowingly eaten a vegetable. Most babies' first words were Mama or Dada. Ruby's, upon being confronted with a broccoli floret, had been *yuk*.

Lottie sighed and closed her eyes. As the cool water of the lake lapped around her temples she lazily twitched away an insect that had landed on

1

her wrist. Cooking for such an unappreciative clientele really was the pits. Maybe if she stayed out here long enough someone would eventually call social services and a battleaxe child protection officer would turn up. Ruby and Nat would be whisked away to some echoing Dickensian children's home, forced to eat liver with pipes in and cold turnip soup. And after a couple of weeks of that, *then* they might finally appreciate what a rotten thankless task she had, endlessly having to think what to give her finicky children for dinner.

Freddie Masterson stood at the drawing room window of Hestacombe House and experienced that familiar lift to his spirits as he surveyed the view. As far as he was concerned, it was the most glorious in the whole of the Cotswolds. Across the valley the hills rose up dotted with trees, houses, sheep and cows. Below, the reed-fringed lake glittered in the afternoon sunlight. And closer to hand, his own garden was in full bloom, the freshly mown emerald lawn sloping down towards the lake, the fuchsia bushes bobbing as bumble bees swooped greedily from one fragile flower to the next. A pair of woodpeckers, energetically digging in the grass for worms, glanced over their shoulders and flew off in disgust as a human made its way down the narrow path towards them.

This could be it, then. Watching as Tyler Klein reached the summerhouse and paused to admire the view himself, Freddie knew the American was equally impressed. Their meeting had gone well; Tyler undoubtedly had a fine brain and they had got on with each other from the outset. He had the money to buy the business. And, so far, he appeared to like what he saw.

Well, how could he not?

Tyler Klein was now heading for the side gate that led out into the lane. With his dark blue suit jacket casually slung over one shoulder and his lilac shirt loosened at the neck, he moved easily, more like an athlete than a businessman. Clark Gable hair, thought Freddie, that was what Tyler Klein had, with most of it slicked back but that one dark lock falling uncontrollably into his eyes. Or Errol Flynn. His beloved wife Mary had always had a bit of a thing for Clark Gable and Errol Flynn. Ruefully, Freddie ran a hand over his own sparsely covered head. And to think the poor darling had ended up with him instead.

Glimpsing a flash of brilliant turquoise out of the corner of his eye, he thought for a split second that a kingfisher was darting across the surface of the lake. Then he smiled, because once his vision had had time to adjust he saw that it was Lottie, wearing a new turquoise bikini, rolling lazily over in the water like a sun-seeking porpoise. If he were to tell her that he'd mistaken her for a kingfisher, Lottie would say teasingly, 'Freddie, time to get your eyes tested.'

He hadn't told her that he already had.

And the rest.

The lane that ran alongside the garden of Hestacombe House was narrow and banked high on both sides with poppies, cow parsley and blackberry bushes. Turning left, Tyler Klein worked out, would lead you back up to the village of Hestacombe. Turning right took you down to the lake. As he took the right turn, Tyler heard the sound of running feet and giggling.

Rounding the first bend in the lane, he saw two small children twenty or thirty yards away, clambering over a stile. Dressed in shorts, T-shirts and baseball caps, the one in front was carrying a rolled-up yellow and white striped towel, whilst his companion clutched a haphazard bundle of clothes. Glancing up the lane and spotting Tyler, they giggled again and leapt down from the stile into the cornfield beyond. By the time he reached the stile they'd scurried out of sight, no doubt having taken some short cut back to the village following their dip in the lake.

The lane opened out into a sandy clearing that sloped down to meet a small artificial beach. Freddie Masterson had had this constructed several years ago, chiefly for the benefit of visitors to his lakeside holiday cottages, but also — as Tyler had just witnessed — to be enjoyed by the inhabitants of Hestacombe. Shielding his eyes from the glare of the afternoon sun as it bounced off the lake, Tyler saw a girl in a bright turquoise bikini floating lazily on her back in the water. There was a faint unearthly wailing sound coming from somewhere he couldn't quite place. Then the noise — was it singing? — stopped. Moments later, as Tyler watched, the girl turned onto her front and began to swim slowly back to shore.

It could almost be that scene from *Dr No*, where Sean Connery observes Ursula Andress emerging goddess-like from a tropical sea. Except he wasn't hiding in the bushes and he had all his own hair. And this girl didn't have a large knife strapped to her thigh.

She wasn't blonde either. Her long dark hair was a riot of snaky curls plastered to her shoulders, her body curvy and deeply tanned. Impressed — because an encounter like this was the last thing he'd been expecting — Tyler nodded in a friendly fashion as she paused to wring water from her dripping hair and said, 'Good swim?'

The girl surveyed him steadily, then looked around the tiny beach. Finally she said, 'Where's my stuff?'

Stuff. Taken aback, Tyler gazed around too, even though he had no idea what he was meant to be looking for. For one bizarre moment he wondered if she had arranged to meet a drug dealer here. That was what people said, wasn't it, when they met up with their dealer?

'What stuff?'

'The usual stuff you leave out of the water when you go for a swim. Clothes. Towel. Diamond earrings.'

Tyler said, 'Where did you put them?'

'Right there where you're standing. Right *there*,' the girl repeated, pointing at his polished black shoes. She narrowed her eyes at him. 'Is this a joke?'

'I guess it is. But I'm not the one playing it.' Half turning, Tyler indicated the narrow lane behind him. 'I passed a couple of kids back there, carrying off stuff.'

She had her hands on her hips now, and was surveying him with growing disbelief. 'And it didn't occur to you to stop them?'

'I thought it was their stuff.' This was ridiculous, he'd never said the word *stuff* so many times before in his life. 'I guess I just thought they'd been swimming down here in this lake.'

'You thought the size twelve pink halter-necked dress and size five silver sandals belonged to them.' The sarcasm – that particularly British form of sarcasm – was evident in her voice.

'The sandals were wrapped up in something pink. I didn't actually get a close look at the labels. I was thirty yards away.'

'But you thought they'd been swimming.' Gazing at him intently, the girl said, 'Tell me something. Were they . . . *wet?*'

Shit. The kids hadn't been wet. He'd make a lousy private eye. Unwilling to concede defeat, Tyler said, 'They could have come down for a paddle. Look, did you really leave diamond earrings with your clothes?'

'Do I look completely stupid? No, of course I didn't. Diamonds don't dissolve in water.' Impatiently she shook back her hair to show him the studs glittering in her earlobes. 'Right, what did these kids look like?'

'Like kids. I don't know.' Tyler shrugged. 'They were wearing T-shirts, I guess. And, um, shorts . . .'

The girl raised her eyebrows. 'That's incredible. Your powers of observation are dazzling. OK, was it a boy and a girl?'

'Maybe.' He'd assumed they were boys, but one had had longer hair than the other. 'Like I said, I only saw them from a distance. They were climbing over a stile.'

'Dark hair? Thin and wiry?' the girl persisted. 'Did they look like a couple of gypsies?'

'Yes.' Tyler was instantly on the alert; when Freddie Masterson had been singing the praises of Hestacombe he hadn't mentioned any gypsies. 'Are they a problem around here?'

'Damn right they're a problem around here. They're my children.' Intercepting the look of horror on his face, the girl broke into a mischievous smile. 'Relax, they're not really gypsies. You haven't just mortally offended me.'

4

'Well,' said Tyler, 'I'm glad about that.'

'I didn't see a thing, little sods. They must have crawled through the bushes and sneaked off with my stuff when I wasn't looking. That's what happens when you have kids who are hellbent on joining the SAS. But this isn't funny.' No longer amused, the girl said impatiently, 'I can't believe they'd do something so stupid. They don't *think*, do they? Because now I'm stuck here with *no* clothes—'

'You're welcome to borrow my jacket.'

'And *no* shoes.'

'I'm not lending you my shoes,' Tyler drawled. 'You'd look ridiculous. Plus, that'd leave me with nothing to put on my feet.'

'Wuss.' Thinking hard, the girl said, 'OK, look, can you do me a favour? Go back up to the village, past the pub, and my house is three doors down on the right. Piper's Cottage. The doorbell's broken so you'll have to bang on the door. Tell Ruby and Nat to give you my clothes. Then you can bring them back down to me. How does that sound?'

Water from her hair was dripping into her clear hazel eyes, glistening on her tanned skin. She had excellent white teeth and a persuasive manner. Tyler frowned.

'What if the kids aren't there?'

'Right, now I know this isn't ideal, but you have an honest face so I'm going to have to trust you. If they aren't there, you'll just have to take the front door key out from under the tub of geraniums by the porch and let yourself into the house. My bedroom's on the left at the top of the stairs. Just grab something from the wardrobe.' Her mouth twitching the girl said, 'And no snooping in my knicker drawer while you're there. Just pick out a dress and some shoes then let yourself out of the house. You can be back here in ten minutes.'

'I can't do this.' Tyler shook his head. 'You don't even know me. I'm not going to let myself into a strange house. And if your kids are there . . . well, that's even worse.'

'Hi.' Seizing his hand, she enthusiastically shook it. 'I'm Lottie Carlyle. There, now I've introduced myself. And my house really isn't that strange. A bit untidy perhaps, but that's allowed. And you are?'

'Tyler. Tyler Klein. Still not doing it.'

'Well, you're a big help. I'm going to look a right wally walking through the village like this.'

'I told you, you can borrow my jacket.' Seeing as she was dripping wet and his suit jacket was silk-lined and seriously expensive, he felt this was a pretty generous offer. Lottie Carlyle, however, seemed unimpressed.

'I'd still look stupid. You could lend me your shirt,' she wheedled. 'That'd be better.'

Tyler was here on business. He had no intention of removing his shirt. Firmly he said, 'I don't think so. It's the jacket or nothing.'

Realising when she was beaten, Lottie Carlyle took the jacket from him and put it on. 'You drive a hard bargain. There, do I look completely ridiculous?'

'Yes.'

'You're too kind.' She looked sadly down at her bare feet. 'Any chance of a piggy back?'

Tyler looked amused. 'Don't push your luck.'

'Are you saying I'm fat?'

'I'm thinking of my street cred.'

Interested, Lottie said, 'What are you doing here, anyway? In your smart city suit and shiny shoes?'

There clearly wasn't much call for city suits here in Hestacombe. As they turned to leave, Tyler glanced back at the lake, where iridescent dragonflies were darting over the surface of the water and a family of ducks had just swum into view. Casually he said, 'Just visiting.'

Gingerly picking her way along the stony, uneven lane, Lottie winced and said meaningfully, 'Ouch, my feet.'

Lottie Carlyle attracted a fair amount of attention as they made their way through Hestacombe. Something told Tyler that irrespective of what she was wearing, she always would. Passing motorists grinned in recognition and tooted their horns, villagers out in their gardens waved and made teasing comments, and Lottie in turn told them exactly what she was going to do with Ruby and Nat when she got her hands on them.

As they approached Piper's Cottage they spotted the children playing with a watering can in the front garden, taking it in turns to spin around holding the watering can at arm's length and spray each other with water.

'Viewers of a nervous disposition may wish to look away now,' said Lottie. 'This is where I go into scary mother mode.' Raising her voice, she called out, 'Hey, you two. Put that watering can *down*.'

The children looked at their mother, promptly abandoned the watering can and, giggling wildly, shot up into the branches of the apple tree overhanging the front wall.

'I know what you did.' Reaching the garden, Lottie peered up into the tree. 'And trust me, you're in *big* trouble.'

From the depths of the leafy branches, an innocent voice said, 'We were just watering the flowers. Otherwise they'd die.'

'I'm talking about my clothes. That wasn't funny, Nat. Running off with someone's clothes is no joke.'

'We didn't do it,' Nat said immediately.

6

Ruby chimed in, 'It wasn't us.'

Tyler looked over at Lottie Carlyle. Maybe he'd made a mistake. Catching his concerned expression, she rolled her eyes. 'Please don't believe them. They always say that. You can catch Nat with a mouthful of chocolate and he'll still swear blind he hasn't had any.'

'But it *wasn't* us,' Nat repeated.

'We didn't do it,' said Ruby, 'and that's the *truth*.'

'The more guilty they are, the more they deny it.' Lottie sensed Tyler's unease. 'Last week they were playing with a catapult in the bathroom and the bathroom mirror happened to get broken. But guess what? Neither of them did that either.'

'Mum, this time we really didn't take your clothes,' said Ruby.

'No? Well, this man here says you did. Because he saw you,' Lottie explained, 'and unlike you two, he doesn't tell lies. So you can climb down from there and go and get my clothes this minute.'

'We don't know where they are!' Ruby let out a wail of outrage.

Without a word, Lottie disappeared inside the cottage. Through the open windows they heard the banging and crashing of cupboards and wardrobes being opened and shut. Finally, triumphantly, she re-emerged carrying a scrunched-up pink dress, a pair of flat silver sandals and a yellow and white striped bathtowel.

'It wasn't us,' Nat blurted out.

'Really. Funny how they happened to be in the back garden then, isn't it?' As she spoke, Lottie was shrugging off the miles-too-big suit jacket, handing it back to Tyler and wriggling into her crumpled sundress. 'Now listen, taking my clothes was bad enough. Telling lies and denying it is even worse. So you can forget about going to the balloon festival this weekend and you won't be getting any pocket money either.'

'But it was somebody else,' squealed Ruby.

'This man says it was you. And out of the three of you, funnily enough, I believe him. So get down out of that tree, get into the house and start tidying your bedrooms. I mean it,' said Lottie. 'This minute. Or I'll stop your pocket money for the next six weeks.'

First Ruby, then Nat dropped down from the branches. Dark eyes narrowed in disgust, they glared at Tyler. As Ruby stalked past him she muttered, '*You're* the big liar.'

'Ruby. Stop that.'

Nat, with bits of twig caught in his hair, looked up at Tyler and said with a scowl, 'I'm going to tell my dad on you.'

'Ooh, he's so scared.' Lottie deftly swept him past Tyler. 'Inside. Now.'

Nat and Ruby disappeared into the house. By this time feeling terrible, Tyler said, 'Listen, maybe I did make a mistake.'

7

'They're children, it's their job to get up to mischief.' Knowingly, Lottie said, 'I'm guessing you don't have any of your own.'

Tyler shook his head. 'No.'

'Look, they hate you for grassing them up.' Lottie's eyes sparkled. 'They're doing their best to make you feel bad. But you never have to see them again, do you, so what does it matter?' As she spoke, someone inside the cottage burst into noisy heaving sobs. 'That'll be Nat, standing by the window to make completely sure we can hear him. I'm surprised he didn't tell me an eagle flew off with my clothes then dropped them in our back garden. Anyway I'd better go. Thanks for the jacket. I hope it isn't too damp.' She paused, raking her fingers through her wet hair, then broke into a dazzling smile. 'It was kind of nice to meet you.'

'Waaaaahhhh,' bawled Nat, evidently inconsolable.

'Kind of nice to meet you too.' Tyler had to raise his voice to be heard over the heartbreaking noise.

'Hurh-hurh-hurrhh-waaAAAHHH!'

'Well, thanks again.' Lottie paused as a thought occurred to her. 'Um . . . did you hear me singing earlier?'

'That was you?' He grinned. 'More to the point, that was *singing*?'

Her dark eyes danced with mischief. 'I sound a lot better underwater.'

As a fresh round of sobbing broke out inside the cottage, Tyler said, 'I'll take your word for it.'

Chapter 2

Changed into a lime-green vest top and white jeans, Lottie made her way out onto the broad terrace behind Hestacombe House, where Freddie was sitting at the table levering open a bottle of wine.

'There you are. Good, good. Have a seat,' said Freddie, thrusting a glass into her hand, 'and get some of this down you. You're going to need it.'

'Why?' Lottie had been wondering why he'd asked her to come over to the house this evening. Not normally reticent, Freddie had been out and about a lot recently without letting on what he was up to. Tonight, in his white polo shirt and pressed khaki trousers, he was looking tanned and fit, maybe even a little trimmer than usual. Don't say he'd found himself a lady friend at last.

'Cheers.' Freddie clinked his glass against hers. There was definitely a secret in there, waiting to burst out.

'Cheers. Don't tell me.' Delighted for her employer, Lottie held up her free hand to stop him in his tracks. 'I think I've already guessed!'

'Actually, you probably haven't.' But Freddie was leaning back, smiling at her as he lit a cigar. 'But fire away. Tell me what you think.'

'I *thiiiiiink*,' Lottie drew out the word, 'that love could be in the air.' Playfully, mystically, she wiggled her fingers. 'I do believe we could be talking romance here.'

'Lottie, I'm too old for you.'

She pulled a face at him. 'I meant with someone your own age. Am I wrong then?'

'Just a bit.' Freddie was puffing away on his cigar, his signet ring glinting in the sunlight.

'You should, you know. Find someone lovely.' Since Mary's death, Freddie hadn't so much as looked at another woman, yet if the right one were to come along Lottie knew he could be happy again. It was what he deserved.

'Well, that's not going to happen. Are you drinking that or letting it evaporate?'

Lottie obediently took a couple of giant gulps.

'Like it?' Freddie surveyed her with amusement.

'What kind of a question is that? It's red, it's warm, it's not corked. Of course I like it.'

'Good, seeing as it's a Chateau Margaux nineteen eighty-eight.'

Lottie, who was to fine wines what Johnny Vegas was to tightrope walking, nodded knowledgeably and said, 'Ah yes, thought so.'

His eyes sparkling, Freddie said, 'Two fifty a bottle.'

'Hey, excellent. Is that one of those half-price offers in the supermarket?'

'Two hundred and fifty pounds a bottle, you philistine.'

'Jesus, are you joking?' Spluttering and almost spilling the rest of the wine on her jeans, Lottie clunked the glass onto the table. Seeing that he wasn't joking she wailed, 'What are you doing, giving me stuff like that to drink? That's the stupidest thing I ever heard!'

'Why?'

'Because you *know* I'm a philistine, so it's just a complete *waste*.'

'You said you liked it,' Freddie pointed out.

'But I didn't *appreciate* it, did I? I just guzzled it down like Tizer, because you told me to! Well, you can finish my glass.' Lottie pushed it across the table towards him. 'Because I'm not touching another drop.'

'Sweetheart, I bought this wine ten years ago,' said Freddie. 'It's been in the cellar all this time, waiting for a special occasion.'

Lottie rolled her eyes in despair. 'It's certainly a special occasion now. The day your assistant spattered Chateau Margaux-whatever-it-is all over your terrace. You'd have been better leaving it in the cellar for another ten years.'

'Yes, well. Maybe I don't want to. Anyway, you haven't asked me yet why this is a special occasion.'

'Go on then, tell me.'

Freddie sat back and blew a perfect, practised smoke ring. 'I'm selling the business.'

Startled, Lottie said, 'Is this another joke?'

'No.' He shook his head.

'But why?'

'I'm sixty-four. People retire at my age, don't they? It's time to hand over and do the kind of things I want to do. Plus, the right buyer happened to come along. Don't worry, your job's safe.' His eyes twinkling, Freddie said, 'In fact, I think the two of you might get on extremely well.'

Since this was Hestacombe and not some bustling city metropolis, it didn't take a genius to work it out.

'The American guy,' said Lottie, exhaling slowly. 'The one in the suit.'

'The very same.' Nodding, Freddie said slyly, 'Don't try and pretend you can't remember his name.'

10

'Tyler Klein.' Freddie was right; when strangers were that good-looking, their names simply didn't slip your mind. 'We met down at the lake this afternoon.'

'He did happen to mention it.' Entertained, Freddie took another puff of his cigar. 'Interesting encounter, by the sound of things.'

'You could say that. So what's going to happen, exactly? Is he buying everything? Are you moving away? Oh Freddie, I can't imagine this place without you.'

Lottie meant it. Freddie and Mary Masterson had moved to Hestacombe House twenty-two years ago. Freddie had caught her stealing apples from his orchard when she was nine years old, the same age Ruby was now. He was part of the village and they would all miss him if he was no longer around.

Plus, he was a great boss.

'I'm not selling this house. Just the business.'

Relieved, Lottie said, 'Oh well, that's not so bad then. So you'll still be here. It won't really be that different after all.'

Hestacombe Holiday Cottages had been built up by Freddie and Mary into a successful concern over the years; eight original properties, painstakingly renovated, were either dotted around the lakeside or, for greater seclusion, tucked away in the woods. Guests, many of them devoted regulars, rented the ravishingly pretty homes for anything between a couple of nights and a month at a time, safe in the knowledge that their every whim would be catered for while they enjoyed their break away from it all in the heart of the Cotswolds.

'Here, drink your drink.' Freddie pushed the glass back across the table towards her. 'Tyler Klein's a good man. Everything'll be fine.' With a twinkle in his eye he added, 'You'll be in safe hands.'

Now there was a mental image to conjure with.

This time, taking a girlie sip, Lottie did her utmost to appreciate the expensiveness of the Chateau Margaux. It was nice, of course it was, but she'd still never have known. 'So where will he be living?'

'Fox Cottage. We only have to rejig a few bookings. As long as the guests are moved into something better they won't mind.'

Fox Cottage, their most recent acquisition, had spent the last three months being extensively redesigned. By some miracle the work had been completed ahead of schedule. It was one of their smaller properties, the first floor now knocked through to make just one huge bedroom with floor-to-ceiling windows affording a stupendous view over the lake.

'Not very big.' Innocently Lottie said, 'Won't his wife find it a bit cramped?'

11

Freddie grinned. 'I think what you're trying to ask is, is he married?'

So much for being subtle. Kicking off her sandals and tucking her feet under her on the padded chair, she said, 'And?'

'He's single.'

Excellent, Lottie thought happily. Although having met Nat and Ruby she'd probably already succeeded in putting him off her for life.

But something else was still puzzling her. 'Where did you find him, then? You didn't even tell me you were thinking of selling the business.'

'Fate.' Freddie shrugged and refilled their glasses. 'Remember Marcia and Walter?'

Of course. Marcia and Walter Klein, from New York. For the past five years the Kleins had been coming to Hestacombe every Easter without fail, using one of the cottages as a base while they explored, with typically American enthusiasm, Stratford-upon-Avon, Bath, Cheltenham – all the usual tourist traps.

'They're his parents.' Lottie realised that the son Marcia had been boasting about all these years was in fact Tyler. 'But he's some kind of hotshot Wall Street banker type, isn't he? Whyever would he want to give that up and move over here? That's like Michael Schumacher giving up Formula One to drive a milk float.'

'Tyler wants a change. I'm sure he'll tell you his reasons for doing it. Anyway, Marcia rang a couple of weeks ago to arrange their booking for next Easter and we got chatting about retirement,' said Freddie. 'I happened to mention that I was thinking of selling up. Two days later she rang back and said she'd mentioned it to her son, who was interested. He'd had a good look at the website. Of course he'd already heard about us from Marcia and Walter – bless 'em, they were praising us to the skies. So then Tyler rang me. I told him what I was asking for the business and put him in touch with my accountant so he could go through the figures. Last night he flew into Heathrow and came to see the place for himself. And two hours ago he made me a fair offer.'

Just like that.

'Which you accepted,' said Lottie.

'Which I accepted.'

'Are you sure this is the right thing to do?' Was it her imagination, or was Freddie not quite as happy with the situation as he was pretending to be?

'Absolutely sure.' Freddie nodded.

Oh well then. He was entitled to a bit of fun. 'In that case, congratulations. Here's to a long and happy retirement.' Raising her glass and clinking it against his, Lottie said encouragingly, 'You'll have a fantastic time. Think of all the brilliant things you'll be able to do.' Teasingly, because Freddie loathed the game with a passion, she added, 'Who knows, you might even take up golf.'

This time Freddie's smile didn't quite reach his eyes. 'There's something else.'

'Oh God. Not Morris dancing.'

'Actually, it's worse than Morris dancing.' His fingers tightening around the stem of his glass, Freddie said simply, 'I have a brain tumour.'

Chapter 3

Lottie looked at him. This couldn't possibly be a joke. But it had to be. How was Freddie able to just sit there and say something like that? She felt her heart begin to thud loudly, like a drum. How could it be *true*?

'Oh Freddie.'

'I know, bit of a conversation-stopper. Sorry about that.' Evidently relieved to have it out in the open, Freddie added, 'Although I must say, I never thought I'd see you at a loss for words.'

Lottie gathered her wits. 'Well, it's a *shock*. But the doctors can do so much now, it'll be fine, they just whip them out these days, don't they? You wait, you'll be as good as new in no time.'

It was what she wanted to believe, but even as the words were tumbling out, Lottie knew the situation was far worse than that. This wasn't like cradling a child with a grazed knee, sticking a Disney plaster on and reassuring them that it would stop hurting in a minute.

This wasn't something she could kiss better.

'Right, I'm telling you this but I'd appreciate it if you don't pass it on to anyone else,' said Freddie. 'The tumour is inoperable so the surgeons can't whip it out. Chemo and radiotherapy won't cure me, but they might buy me a little more time. Well, funnily enough I wasn't tempted by that so I said thanks but no thanks.'

'But—'

'I'd also appreciate it if you didn't interrupt,' Freddie said calmly. 'Now that I've started I'd quite like to finish. So anyway, I decided pretty much straightaway that if I don't have long to live, I'd rather live it on my own terms. We both know what Mary went through.' He looked at Lottie. 'Two years of surgery, endless nightmare treatments. All that pain. She spent months feeling like death and what good did it do? At the end of it all, she died anyway. So I'm going to give that a miss. According to my consultant, I have maybe a year. Well, that's fine. I'll make the most of it, see how things go. He warned me that the last few months might not be pretty, so I told him that in that case I'd probably give them a miss too.'

It was all too much to take in. Lottie, her hands trembling, reached for her glass and knocked it onto its side. Five minutes ago she would have thrown herself across the table and licked up the spilled wine rather than waste it. Now she simply poured herself some more, right up to the brim.

'Am I allowed to ask questions yet?'

Freddie nodded graciously. 'Fire away.'

'How long have you known?'

'A fortnight.' His smile was crooked. 'Of course it was a shock at first. But it's surprising how fast you get used to it.'

'I didn't even know you were ill. Why didn't you say something before?'

'That's just it, I don't *feel* ill.' Freddie spread his hands. 'Headaches, that was all it was. I thought I probably needed new reading glasses, so I saw my optician . . . and when she looked into my eyes with that light instrument of hers, she was able to see that I had a problem. Next thing I knew, I was being referred to a neurologist, having scans and all manner of tests. Then, boom, that was it. Diagnosis. Lottie, if you're crying I'll throw my drink over you. Stop it at once.'

Hastily Lottie blinked the tears back into her eyes, sniffed loudly and ordered herself to get a grip. Freddie was confiding in her because he thought he could trust her not to dissolve in a heap. She wasn't the crying type.

'Right. Done.' She sniffed again, took a gulp of wine and said defensively, 'Sorry, but it's just not fair. You don't deserve this.'

'I know, I'm marvellous.' Stubbing out his cigar, Freddie said, 'Practically a saint.'

'Especially not after what happened to Mary.' Lottie's throat tightened; she couldn't bear it.

'Sweetheart, don't get angry on my behalf. Mary isn't here any more.' Reaching across the table, Freddie took her hand between both of his and gave it an encouraging squeeze. 'Don't you see? That makes it *easier*. Finding out about this thing in my head isn't the most terrible thing that's ever happened to me. Not even close. Losing Mary and having to carry on without her beats this tumour of mine hands down.'

Now Lottie really was in danger of bursting into tears. 'That's the most romantic thing I've ever heard in my life.'

'Romantic.' Freddie repeated the word and chuckled. 'Know what's ironic? That's how her nickname for me came about. Mary always said I was about as romantic as a string vest. Oh, she knew how much she meant to me, but it was easier for us to tease each other. All that lovey-dovey hearts and flowers stuff was never our thing.'

Lottie remembered. The two of them had always been gloriously happy together, theirs had truly been a marriage to aspire to. Their verbal sparring had been endlessly inventive, as entertaining as any TV double act.

15

She couldn't imagine how desperately Freddie must have missed his beloved wife.

So that was why Mary had always called him 'String'.

The unfairness of what was happening hit Lottie all over again. 'Oh Freddie. Why does this have to happen to you?'

'Or there's the other way of looking at it, telling yourself you're lucky it didn't happen forty years ago,' said Freddie. 'Now that would have pissed me off. But I've made it to sixty-four and that's not so bad.' Counting off on his fingers, he went on, 'When I was seven, I fell out of a tree and broke my arm. I *could* have landed on my head and died. When I was sixteen I was knocked off my pushbike by a lorry and cracked a few ribs. But I could have been killed then too. And there's the time Mary and I were on holiday in Geneva. We got so plastered with a group of friends on our last night that we missed our flight home. And what happened? The plane crashed.'

He was getting carried away now. Lottie had heard this story before.

'It didn't crash,' she corrected Freddie. 'One of the wheels came off and it tipped over on the runway. Nobody was killed.'

'But we could have been. People were injured.'

'Bumps and bruises.' Lottie wasn't to be swayed; there was a principle at stake. 'Bumps and bruises don't count.'

'Depends how bad they are.' Freddie eyed her with amusement. 'Are we bickering?'

'No.' Ashamed of herself, Lottie instantly backed down. Bickering with a dying man; how could she stoop so low?

Evidently reading her mind, Freddie said, 'Yes we are, and don't you dare start giving in. If you won't bicker with me any more I'll find someone else who will. I only told you what's going on because I thought I could rely on you to handle it. I don't want the kid-glove treatment, OK?'

'You don't want any treatment at all,' Lottie retaliated heatedly. 'The thing is, maybe radiotherapy and chemo *would* work.'

'You're allowed to bicker,' Freddie said firmly, 'but you definitely aren't allowed to nag. Or I shall have to sack you.'

'You're selling the business.'

'Ah, but I could sack you now. Sweetheart, I'm a grown-up. I've made my decision. If I've got six good months left on this earth, then I want to make the most of them, do what I want to do. In fact, that's where you come in.' He was more relaxed now, casually swatting away a hovering wasp as he spoke. 'There's something I'm going to need a hand with, Lottie. And I'd like you to help me out.'

For an appalling moment Lottie thought he meant help with doing away with himself when the time came. Jolted, she said, 'In what way?'

'Good grief, not that kind of help.' Yet again reading her mind – or more likely the look of absolute horror on her face – Freddie gave a shout of laughter. 'I've seen you clay-pigeon shooting. The only thing you managed to hit was a tree. If I need putting down when the time comes, I'll ask a damn sight better shot than you.'

'Don't joke about it.' Lottie glared at him. 'It's not funny.'

'Sorry.' Freddie was unrepentant. 'But the thought of being aimed at by you and a twelve-bore is. Look, I'm dealing with this in my own way,' he went on, his tone consoling. 'We all have to go some time, don't we? I could have a heart attack and drop dead tomorrow. Compared with that, being given six months' notice is a luxury. And that's why I'm not going to waste it.'

Lottie braced herself. He'd said he needed her help. 'So what will you do?'

'Well, I've given this a lot of thought. And it's actually not as easy as you'd imagine.' Freddie pulled a face. 'I mean, what would you do? If money was no object.'

This was surreal. Morbid and surreal. But if Freddie could do it, so could she. Lottie said, 'OK, it's a cliché, but I suppose I'd take the kids to Disneyland.'

'Exactly.' Looking pleased, Freddie nodded vigorously. 'Because you know it's what *they'd* love more than anything.'

Defensively Lottie said, 'I'd love it too!'

'Of course you would. But if the kids couldn't make it, would you go along by yourself?'

The penny dropped. Feeling terrible all over again, Lottie longed to hug him. Instead she said, 'No, I suppose not,' and took another gulp of wine.

'You see? My point exactly.' Freddie sat forward, his elbows on the table. 'Years ago, before she got ill, Mary and I used to dream of retiring one day and travelling the world. She wanted to walk the Great Wall of China, visit the Victoria Falls and explore the lost city of Peru. Top of my list was a fortnight at the Gritti Palace in Venice, followed by trips to New Zealand and Polynesia. Then we'd start arguing because I said when the travelling was out of our system we should buy ourselves a little villa in Tuscany and Mary insisted that if she was going to be old anywhere, she'd rather be old in Paris.'

He paused, gazing for a moment at the almost empty bottle of Chateau Margaux. 'But that's the thing, isn't it? The whole plan was that we'd be old *together*. Now I can afford to go anywhere I want in the world, but there's no point any more because where's the fun in going on my own, or with a bunch of strangers? I only wanted to see those places with Mary.'

17

Lottie pictured him in front of some spectacular view with no one he cared about to share it with. It was how she would feel, sitting all alone in a carriage on one of the rollercoaster rides in Disneyland. Without Nat and Ruby there at her side, how could she possibly enjoy it?

'Travelling's out, then.'

Freddie nodded. 'And I've decided to give the dangerous sports a miss. Doing a parachute jump, abseiling, whitewater rafting.' His mouth twitched. 'Not really my scene.'

How *could* he be this cheerful? Mystified Lottie said, 'So what *are* you going to do?'

'Well, that's why I'm asking you to help me.' Freddie looked pleased with himself. 'You see, I have a plan.'

Chapter 4

Nat and Ruby had been despatched to their father's house for the evening. When Lottie arrived at nine o'clock to pick them up, she was greeted at the door by Nat who threw himself into her arms and said, 'We've been having *fun.*'

'Hooray.' After the last couple of traumatic hours digesting Freddie's news, Lottie gave him an extra-fierce hug.

'Ow, Mum, let go. Dad's told us all about VD.'

'Has he?' She blinked. Had Mario gone completely mad?

'It's great. I love it.' Wriggling free and dragging Lottie through to the kitchen, Nat exclaimed, 'I'm going to do loads and loads. VD's my favourite thing.'

'Not veedee, you plank.' Ruby rolled her eyes with nine-year-old superiority. 'It's voodoo.'

'I'm not a plank. You're the plank.'

'Anyway, VD's something completely different. It's to do with—'

'So, voodoo,' Lottie hastily interjected. 'Why's Daddy been telling you about that, then?'

'We told him about the horrible man. Didn't we, Daddy?' As Mario entered the kitchen, Nat turned to him eagerly. 'The one who told the lies about us this afternoon. And Dad said what we needed was to get our own back and we should try VD.'

From the doorway, Mario grinned. 'I find it generally does the trick.'

'*Voodoo,*' Lottie emphasised.

'Voodoo. So Dad told us how you make models of people you don't like and stick pins in them. So that's what we've been doing!' Triumphantly, Nat rushed over to the kitchen table and brandished a plasticine figure bristling with cocktail sticks. 'This is the man, see? And every time you stick a stick in him, he gets a real pain in the place where you've stuck it. Like *this,*' he continued with relish, jabbing another cocktail stick into the plasticine figure's left leg. 'In real life he's hopping around now, going OW!'

Lottie looked at her ex-husband. 'Just remind me again, how old are you?'

19

'Don't get your knickers in a twist.' Mario was grinning broadly. 'It's just a bit of fun.'

'And *this*.' Nat gleefully stabbed the plasticine figure in the stomach. 'Ha, that'll teach him to tell lies about *us*.'

A bit of fun. Wonderful. Lottie wondered sometimes if Mario had an ounce of common sense in his head. Exasperated, she said, 'You can't teach them to do things like that. It's irresponsible.'

'No it isn't, it's great.' Ruby was happily prodding her own voodoo doll with cocktail sticks. 'Anyway, we didn't take your clothes so that horrible man deserves it.'

'That horrible man is going to be my new boss,' Lottie sighed. 'So you're just going to have to get used to him.'

'See? Even you think he's horrible.' Interestedly, Nat studied her face. 'Is that why you've been crying?'

'I haven't been crying. It's just hay fever.' Pulling herself together, Lottie realised how hard it was going to be, keeping the news of Freddie's illness to herself. 'Come on, you two, time to take you home.'

'No need to rush off. Give them ten minutes in the garden.' Mario, shooing them out through the back door, steered Lottie gently onto a kitchen chair and said, 'You look as if you could do with a drink. I'll get us both a lager.'

Chateau Margaux one minute, a can of Heineken the next. Oh well, why not? Kicking off her sandals and leaning back in the chair, Lottie watched him fetch the cans from the fridge then reach up to the wall cabinet for glasses. She loved being divorced from Mario, but it was still possible to admire his good looks and effortlessly toned body. In fact it was probably easier now, without the associated emotional ties and that perpetual sense of anxiety in the pit of her stomach that he might be sharing his body with someone else on the quiet.

Which, in the end, was exactly what had happened, although needless to say it hadn't been Mario's fault.

But then, nothing ever was.

'There you go. Cheers.' Having poured the Heineken into two glass tumblers, Mario handed one over and surveyed her over the rim of the other. 'So are you going to tell me why you've been crying?'

No.

Lottie shook her head. 'It's nothing. Freddie and I were just talking about Mary. It got a bit emotional, that's all.' Reaching across the table for the plasticine voodoo dolls, she began pulling out the cocktail sticks. 'He misses her so much. We can't imagine what it must be like.'

'And there was me thinking you were upset because today's our wedding anniversary,' Mario teased.

20

Heavens, was it? August the sixth. Crikey, it was too. How weird not to have remembered. Weirder still that Mario had.

'It isn't our wedding anniversary. It would have been,' Lottie corrected him, 'if we'd stayed married.'

'Ah, but you left me. You broke my heart.' Mario looked convincingly bereft.

'Excuse me, I left you because you were a cheating weasel.'

'Ten years ago today.' His expression softened at the memory. 'That was such a great day, wasn't it?'

Actually, it had been. Lottie smiled. She had been twenty years old – far too young really – and Mario had been twenty-three. Mario's Italian mother had invited hordes of her excitable relations over from Sicily for the occasion and Lottie's girlfriends had been entranced by the male cousins' smouldering dark looks and Godfather-ish glamour. Everyone had mingled joyfully together, the weather had been glorious and the dancing had carried on until dawn. Lottie, all in white and only slightly pregnant, had wondered if it was possible to be happier than this. She had Mario and a baby on the way; things really couldn't be better. Her life was officially perfect.

And to be fair, it had been pretty perfect for the first few years. Mario was charming, irresistible, never boring and never bored. He was also a fantastic father who adored his children and – especially good, this – didn't shy away from changing nappies.

But Mario's legendary capacity to charm was coupled with flirtatiousness and after a while Lottie had begun to experience the downside of being married to a man who enjoyed being the centre of attention. Other girls made their interest in him only too blindingly obvious. Lottie, no shrinking violet herself, told Mario the flirting had to stop. But it simply wasn't in his nature. That was when the arguments had begun. It was crushing to realise that you'd married a man who, essentially, wasn't the marrying kind. At least, not marrying and monogamous. Jealousy was a pointless emotion and one that Lottie had never suffered from. She had too much self-esteem for that. If Mario couldn't be faithful to her, then he didn't deserve her. Staying with someone you were unable to trust wasn't something she could countenance; sooner or later she knew they would begin to hate each other.

Either that or she would end up stabbing him with something far bigger than a cocktail stick.

For the sake of Nat and Ruby and before the hatred and bitterness could take hold, Lottie announced to Mario that their marriage was over. Mario was devastated and did his best to persuade her to change her mind, but Lottie stood firm. It was the only way, if they were to remain friends.

21

'But I love you,' Mario protested.

He did; she knew that.

'I love you too.' It was more of a struggle than she let on to be brave and go through with it. 'But you're having an affair with your receptionist.'

'No I'm not!' Shocked, Mario insisted, 'It's not an *affair*. Jennifer? She means nothing to me!'

That last bit was probably true as well.

'Maybe, but you mean everything to her. She phoned me in tears last night to tell me just how much. For an *hour*.' Lottie sighed. 'And don't tell me you'll change, because we both know that would be a big lie. It's better this way, trust me. Now, why don't we sit down and decide who's going to live where?'

Mercifully money wasn't an issue. Mario was the manager of a glossy car dealership in Cheltenham and, it went without saying, a superlative salesman with an income to match. They agreed that Lottie and the children should stay at Piper's Cottage, while Mario would buy one of the new houses on the other side of the village. It hadn't occurred to either of them that they wouldn't both stay in Hestacombe. Nat and Ruby would still be able to see Mario whenever they wanted, and he would be able to continue to be a proper father to them.

It had all worked out incredibly well. Ending a marriage was never without pain and sadness, but Lottie had taken care to keep hers well hidden. And before long she had known she'd made the right decision. It was like moving into the shallows after far too long frantically treading water. Mario Carlyle may have been a less than ideal husband but you couldn't ask for a better ex.

Apart from when he thoughtlessly taught his children to stick pins in plasticine effigies of her new boss.

Chapter 5

'Hello? You're miles away.' Mario was waving his hand in front of her face.

'Sorry.' Brought back to the present with a bump, Lottie said, 'I was just thinking how much nicer it is, not being married to you any more.'

'Not being married to anyone, you mean.' Mario enjoyed mickey-taking about her lack of love life. 'You want to watch yourself – won't be long now before you turn into a born-again spinster. It's called getting set in your ways. In ten years the kids'll be off and there you'll be, all alone, stuck in your rocking chair, yelling at the TV and refusing to let anyone from the gas board into the house to read the meter because they might be *male*.'

Lottie lobbed her rolled-up ball of plasticine at him. 'In ten years' time I'll be forty.'

Undeterred, Mario said, 'And shaking your walking stick at any man who dares to come within half a mile of you. You'll be the scary old woman with a houseful of dollies. You'll make little lacy outfits for them and give them names and send them cards on their birthdays.'

'Not when I'm forty. I wasn't planning on doing that until I'm at least fifty-six,' Lottie protested. 'Anyway, I don't need to rush out and grab the nearest man. I'm fine on my own. In fact I'm enjoying the rest.' Beaming at him, she said, 'You should try it some time.'

Since this was like suggesting he might want to climb the Matterhorn in ballet shoes, Mario ignored her. 'I'm serious. Since we split up you've been out on *one date*.' He held up one finger in case she was unable to comprehend the shameful *singleness* of the number. 'And look how *that* turned out. Lottie, it's just not normal.'

Wasn't it? Maybe not, but she genuinely didn't let it worry her. Far easier to be free and single, Lottie felt, than have to force yourself to go out on dates like her disastrous one last year. She'd only agreed to have dinner with Melv the Twitch because he'd already asked her three times and she hadn't had the heart to turn him down again. Besides, he was a sweet, eager to please man, the kind who would never treat a woman badly. And it was only dinner, after all. What could possibly go wrong?

23

Sadly, lots. Melvyn's nerves may have played a part, but it was hard to enjoy yourself in the company of a man – OK, a VAT inspector – who had a distressing nervous tic and spent the first hour of the date giving a lecture on tax returns. Lottie, who had been up most of the previous night with Nat (tummy bug, not pleasant), had almost dislocated her jaw in an effort not to yawn throughout Melvyn's convoluted explanations of the lengths some people foolishly went to in their attempts to avoid paying tax. When their starters had been cleared away, desperate for a proper unin-terrupted yawn, she had excused herself from the table and escaped to the loo.

Where, overcome with exhaustion, she had promptly fallen asleep.

Waking up in the cubicle and realising that ninety minutes had passed had been bad enough. Returning to the restaurant and discovering that Melvyn had paid the bill and left had been worse. Assuming that she'd legged it because he was so boring, he hadn't even sent a waitress into the ladies' loo to see if she was still in there.

'He kept saying it was his own fault,' the waitress had chattily informed Lottie, 'because he'd been talking about work again. Between you and me, I reckon he's had girls do a runner on him before. Poor chap, I did feel sorry for him. He looked gutted. But I told him straight, a bloke can't expect to bowl a girl over while droning on and on about interest rates and VAT.'

The final humiliation had come when Lottie, discovering she didn't have enough cash on her for a taxi, had been forced to ring Mario and ask him to drive into Cheltenham and pick her up. Ravenously hungry, she had ended up letting him buy her a Burger King triple cheeseburger and fries to eat in the car on the way home.

How he'd laughed at her that night.

Oh well, at least Melvyn hadn't asked her out again. Sometimes you just had to be grateful for small mercies.

'One lousy date,' Mario repeated, still grinning, 'with Melv the Twitch. Not even a whole date, more like half of one. Honestly, you're a lost cause.'

'I blame being married to you. It's scarred me for life,' Lottie said comfortably.

'You're too picky, that's your problem.'

'Unlike you. You're the opposite of picky.'

'Thanks a lot. I'll tell Amber you said that. In fact,' Mario turned his head at the sound of a car pulling into the drive, 'I'll tell her right now.'

'Apart from Amber,' said Lottie. In the three years since she and Mario had separated, a constant stream of girlfriends had passed through Mario's life. Which would have been fine as far as Lottie was concerned – it was allowed, he was a free agent now – but for the fact that there was Nat and Ruby to consider. Most of these girlfriends had been wildly unsuitable. Lottie didn't want to come across as the Wicked Witch of the West or as some jealous ex-wife hellbent on breaking up every new relationship her husband dared to enter into, but how could she pretend to be delighted to meet them when there was even an outside chance they might end up becoming involved in her children's lives?

Not that these girls were bad, cruel or deliberately unkind, nothing like that. They were just thoughtless, careless or simply not up to the task. Invariably they pretended to adore Ruby and Nat because they were so keen to impress Mario. In order to court popularity and win their friendship they were always buying them sweets and ice creams. One ditsy blonde had offered to highlight Ruby's hair – cue tears and tantrums when Lottie had swiftly informed Ruby that *that* wasn't going to happen. Another girl had bought Nat an industrial-strength catapult. Last year, without thinking to consult Lottie or Mario first, a chirpy brunette called Babs had promised Ruby *faithfully* that on her ninth birthday she would take her in to Cheltenham to have her belly button pierced.

After that it had been bye-bye Babs. God knows what she might have had planned as an encore. Sneaking Nat off to a tattoo parlour, possibly, for an Action Man tattoo.

But Amber was the longest lasting girlfriend to date, and Amber was different. She genuinely liked Mario's children and Lottie in turn liked her. A lot, in fact. If she could organise everyone's lives – God, wouldn't that be *great*? – she would choose Amber to settle down with Mario, tame him, marry him and become stepmother to Ruby and Nat. Of course she might also have to arrange for Mario to be neutered like a dog, but what the hell. Anything to keep him on the straight and narrow.

Still, she could certainly do her bit to encourage the relationship. Anything to prevent another Babs wiggling onto the scene and becoming the next Mrs Carlyle.

The front door opened and banged shut, and Amber appeared in the kitchen. Blonde and petite, with a perky smile and a penchant for short skirts and vertiginously high heels, she wouldn't immediately strike anyone as ideal stepmother material, but beneath the low-cut tops beat a heart of gold. Amber was feisty, hard-working and addicted to sparkly jewellery. She and Mario had been seeing each other for seven months now and she wasn't the type to put up with any nonsense. So far, he'd managed to keep himself in check. For her own sake, Lottie could only hope he'd continue to do so.

'Hi there. Monsters in the garden?'

'Don't worry, I'm taking them home now.' Lottie offered her the lager she'd barely touched. 'We'll leave you in peace. Good day?'

Amber ran her own busy hairdressing salon in Tetbury, employed four part-time stylists and had earned herself a wide-ranging and devoted clientele.

'Interesting day. I've been offered a free holiday in the south of France.'

Mario said, 'That's nothing. When I opened my post this morning I was offered twenty-five grand and a trip to Australia. Sweetheart, it's called junk mail. They don't really give you all this stuff for free.'

'You're hilarious. This is a genuine offer.' Her many bracelets jangling as she delved into her pink diamanté-studded rucksack, Amber produced a travel brochure and pulled up a chair next to Lottie. 'Come on, I'll show you. One of my clients booked a fortnight in St Tropez for herself and her boyfriend, but they broke up last week. She asked me if I'd be interested instead. Here we go, page thirty-seven. It looks fantastic, there's a private pool and everything, and it's only five minutes from the harbour where all the billionaires moor their yachts.'

'Wow. Flash apartment too.' Lottie was poring over the photographs in the brochure. 'And how about that view over the bay?'

Interested now, Mario leaned across to take a look. 'I've never been to St Tropez. When's it booked for?'

'The beginning of September. Apparently it's heaving in July and August, so that's a better time to visit.'

'All the women go topless on the beaches.' Lottie glanced sympathetically at Mario. 'You'd hate it.'

'Actually,' Amber began, but Mario had pulled the brochure towards him.

'You know, I could manage a fortnight then. I've still got three weeks to take before Christmas. Could be just what we need.' He looked at Amber. 'I'll have to brush up on my French before we get there. *Voulez vous coucher avec moi, mon ange, ma petite, mon petit chou . . .*'

'*Mon petit chou.*' Lottie pulled a face. 'You know, I've never understood that. If someone called me a cabbage I'd box their ears.'

'Actually,' Amber broke in hurriedly, 'she invited just me, not you.'

Mario looked confused. 'But you said—'

'Mandy broke up with her boyfriend, but she's still taking the holiday. She asked me if I'd like to go with her in his place.'

'Oh. Right.' Crestfallen, Mario shrugged. 'And she's just one of your clients?'

'Well, yes, but she's a friend too. Mandy's been coming to the salon every week for the last three years. We never run out of things to talk about. The holiday's all booked and paid for and she's been looking forward to it for months. But she doesn't want to go on her own and none of her other friends can take time off work at such short notice. So she asked me,' Amber said brightly. 'And I thought crikey, free holiday, why not?'

Mario looked taken aback. 'So you've already said yes.'

'I have.' Amber nodded, her long silver earrings dancing around her shoulders. 'Well, I'd be mad to turn down an offer like that, wouldn't I? Patsy and Liz are going to work extra hours in the salon. There's no reason not to go. God, I'm excited already!'

Lottie was pleased for Amber, who worked her socks off and deserved a break, but she could think of a reason why she shouldn't go. If Mario was to be abandoned, left to his own devices for an entire fortnight, who knew what he might get up to? Without realising it, Amber could be putting their whole relationship at risk.

But much as Lottie didn't want that to happen, it wasn't her place to interfere. She could hardly tell Amber that if she wanted to make sure Mario remained faithful to her she should cancel the holiday. Or arrange to have him arrested and slung in jail for that fortnight – so long as there wouldn't be any female prison warders.

'Eeeurgh, yuk, *monsters!*' Feigning horror and disgust, Amber shielded herself with the holiday brochure as Nat and Ruby exploded into the kitchen. 'Urrgh, don't let them near me, they're so *ugly.*'

'You like us really.' Nat beamed and leaned against her chair. 'You promised to play Uno next time you came over.'

'I did. But sadly your mum has to take you home now. Phew, what a relief,' said Amber. 'I mean, oh dear what a tragedy, I'm *sooo* disappointed.'

'We can play it next time. Did you bring us any sweets?'

'No I did not. Sweets make all your teeth go rotten and fall out. You're scary enough as it is.' Amber began to tickle him in the ribs, expertly reducing Nat to a shrieking, giggling heap then clapped her hands and exclaimed to Ruby, 'Oh, you'll never guess who came into the salon today.'

'Buffy the Vampire Slayer.'

'Not quite. We don't tend to get too many vampires in Tetbury. No, this lady happened to mention that she taught at Oaklea Primary School. And I said crikey, poor you, I know a couple of monsters who go there.'

Ruby said excitedly, 'Who was it?'

In a conspiratorial voice, Amber whispered, 'Mrs Ashton.'

'Mrs Ashton? She's my form teacher!'

'I know! She told me she was your teacher! I said you'd spent the whole of the summer holidays doing homework and practising your tables.'

Ruby giggled. 'Did she believe you?'

'Not for a minute. She said I must be talking about a different Ruby Carlyle.'

Entranced, Ruby said, 'What did you do to her hair?'

'Well it took ages to dye it bright pink. Then I had to put in about a million white-blonde extensions. I crimped some of them and braided others,' Amber explained, 'and by the end of the afternoon she looked fantastic, just like Christina Aguilera in *Moulin Rouge*. But she made another appointment for two weeks' time because it all has to go before school starts again. When you see Mrs Ashton next time she'll be back to normal, short brown hair and a fringe. Just as if it had never happened.'

Ruby and Nat looked at each other, torn between delight and disbelief. 'Really?' said Ruby.

'What, you don't believe me?' Amber's eyes widened. 'All the teachers do it. They have to have ordinary teacherish hair during term time. But when it comes to the school holidays, let me tell you, they go completely mad.'

'Mr Overton can't go mad,' Nat pointed out. 'He hasn't got any hair.'

'Ah, but you should see his holiday wigs.'

Watching the three of them interacting so effortlessly, Lottie felt her heart expand with love. All she wanted in the world was for her children to be happy. If she were to die and Ruby and Nat were living full-time with Mario, she couldn't ask for a better potential stepmother than Amber.

God, please don't let Mario mess everything up. Maybe she should consider breaking both his legs, forcing him to spend the fortnight flat on his back in traction while Amber was away.

Chapter 6

How to lose friends and really annoy people, thought Cressida, her skin prickling with embarrassment at what she could be about to do.

On the other hand, she'd clearly be doing this man a favour. Plus there was something about him that made her want to fall into conversation with him, even if he was sounding pretty frazzled just now.

So long as he didn't think she was some kind of deranged madwoman. Hastily running her hands over her flyaway light brown hair – yes, even here in Hestacombe village shop it was making a valiant attempt to fly away – Cressida mentally rehearsed what she would say.

Ted, who ran the shop, was busy serving someone at the counter, ringing up items on the till and grumbling good-naturedly about the latest cricket scores. At the back of the shop, the man Cressida was currently stalking sifted dispiritedly, yet again, through the collection of greetings cards on sale and murmured to his son, 'It's no good, there's nothing here. We'll have to drive into Stroud, find something decent.'

The boy looked distraught. For the second time he whined, 'But Dad, we're supposed to be fishing. You *promised*.'

'I know, but we just have to do this first. It's Gran's birthday tomorrow and you know what she's like when it comes to cards.'

The boy, who was about eleven, said frustratedly, 'Well, get her that one then,' and whipped a card from the rickety carousel.

From the corner of her eye, Cressida saw that the card he'd chosen featured a cuddly overweight bunny clutching a bunch of flowers. The boy's father said flatly, 'Gran would hate it. She'd think I couldn't be bothered to choose her something decent. Look, if we drive into Stroud now, we can be back by midday.'

'Dad, we won't be though, will we?' The boy rolled his eyes in disbelief. 'You always say things'll be quick and they end up taking ages, and then you'll say it's not worth going fishing because it's too late now—'

'Ahem.' Clearing her throat and double-checking that Ted was still otherwise occupied at the far end of the shop, Cressida said in a low voice, 'I might be able to help you out.'

This was it, then. The point of no return. She'd just approached a complete stranger in a public place and shamelessly solicited her wares.

The man and his son both turned, clearly startled. The man said, 'Excuse me?'

Oh dear, bit loud. Pulling a keep-your-voice-down face, Cressida moved a couple of steps closer.

'Sorry, I shouldn't be doing this, bit of a cheek. But if you like I could make you a card.'

The boy said, *'What?'*

Now they really did think she was barking. The door clanged as the other customer left the shop. Lurking back here furtively whispering together like a couple of secret agents was bound to rouse Ted's suspicions.

'Making greetings cards is what I do.' Faintly annoyed by the boy's manner, Cressida said, 'I live just up the road. I'll be out of here in two minutes if you're interested. Otherwise, no problem. There are plenty of good card shops in Stroud.'

Ugh, now she felt disloyal to Ted and embarrassed for herself. Aware that her cheeks were burning, Cressida grabbed a bottle of washing-up liquid from the shelf and slipped away from them. Reaching the chill cabinet she helped herself to milk and butter then moved towards the counter.

'Bloody holidaymakers,' grumbled Ted as the door jangled shut behind the man and his son. To come into the shop and leave without buying anything he regarded as a personal affront.

Cressida reminded herself that there was really no need to feel racked with guilt; the man hadn't been about to buy one of the sad little collection of cards on the carousel anyway.

But her conscience wasn't about to let her off that easily.

'I know, they're a pain, aren't they? I'll have a packet of fruit gums as well, Ted.'

'And a walnut cake? Fresh in this morning.' Nodding encouragingly, Ted was already reaching for a patisserie box.

'Go on then.' Cressida caved in; resisting sales patter was another of her weaknesses. 'And a walnut cake.'

Outside in the sunshine the man and his son were loitering awkwardly some twenty yards away from the shop. Joining them, Cressida said, 'Sorry, I know you must have thought I was a bit strange, but I promise you I'm not. That's my house just up there, overlooking the village green.'

'Well, this is all very MI5.' The man made a feeble stab at humour as Cressida glanced both ways before unlocking her emerald-green front door.

'Ted can be a bit touchy. I'd hate to be banned for life from the only shop in the village. Come on through, my workroom's at the end of the hall.' Cressida showed them into the large sunny ex-dining room, painted yellow and white and cluttered with piled-up boxes. Against one wall was a desk containing her computer; thanks to the internet, this was how she attracted most of her business. Next to it, the work she was currently making a start on was spread out over a ten-foot long table.

'Right, I won't keep you long, I know you're in a hurry to go fishing.' Cressida glanced at the boy, who was shuffling his feet, evidently counting every second under his breath. 'But if you tell me what your mother would like, I can do you a card right away. I make them to order.'

The man moved towards the table, the vibration from his footsteps on the wooden floor causing the computer screen to shimmer into life. Having taken in the sheets of heavy card, the reels of silk and velvet ribbons, the bowls of dried petals, feathers and coloured glass beads, he looked again at the VDU and read, 'Cressida Forbes Cards. Is that your name?'

'That's me.' In an attempt to do what any self-respecting business-woman would do, Cressida said in a too-jolly voice, 'Perfect cards for every occasion!'

The boy, whom she was fast beginning to dislike, gave the kind of under-his-breath snort that clearly translated as: you are *such* a dork.

'Cressida. Nice name.' His father valiantly attempted to make amends.

'Not when you're at school and everyone calls you Watercress.' Cressida spoke with feeling.

Another snort reached their ears. With a smirk the boy said, 'Or Mustard and Cress.'

'Oh yes. That too. *Anyway.*' Grasping the mouse, she clicked from her website's home page onto a sample of greetings cards and rapidly scrolled through them. 'I can make any of these and personalise it for you.'

The boy looked dismayed. 'How long's *that* going to take?'

'Not long. Because I'm very clever. Less than half an hour,' said Cressida to wind him up.

'Half an *hour*!'

'I like this one.' The man was pointing to a lilac card with an impressionistic garden design composed of pale green iridescent gauze, rose quartz beads, silver ribbon and drawn-in metallic green trees. Turning to Cressida he said, 'And could you put "Mum, have a wonderful 70th birthday" on the front?'

'Of course I can.' Did he think she couldn't write? 'Anything you want.'

'Half an *hour*!'

'Here.' Reaching past the grumpy boy, Cressida took a ready folded A5 sheet of lilac card and matching envelope from one of the stacked trays on her desk. Opening out the card, she handed his father a black fountain pen and said, 'Write inside it and address the envelope. Go off and do your fishing. I'll have the card finished and in the post by lunchtime.'

'Yeah, but how do we know you'll send it?'

This was a boy sorely in need of a slap. With a sweet smile Cressida said, 'When you ring your grandmother tomorrow to wish her a happy birthday, you could ask her if she likes her card.'

'Donny, behave yourself. I do apologise.' Having finished writing inside the card and addressing the envelope, the man pulled out his wallet. 'This is very kind. And my mother will love it. Now, how much do I owe you?'

Cressida watched from the window as the two of them made their way down the High Street, climbed into their dark blue Volvo and drove off. The card Donny's father had chosen sold for four pounds but, embarrassed at having practically hijacked him and frogmarched him into her house, she had asked for two pounds. And on top of that she had to supply the first class stamp and walk down to the postbox herself.

Let's face it, she was never going to have to worry about becoming a tycoon and being forced to go and live in tax exile.

Still, he'd seemed like a nice man. Even if she hadn't even found out his name. All she knew was that his mother was Mrs E. Turner, that she lived in Sussex and that tomorrow she would be seventy.

Oh, and that her grandson was a sulky spoiled brat.

Glimpsing her own reflection in the window, Cressida saw that her hair was doing its Worzel Gummidge thing again. Locating a couple of tortoiseshell combs in her skirt pocket she gathered it into a twist and fastened it away from her face. Then, pushing up the sleeves of her white shirt, she sat down to put together Mrs E. Turner's card. It wouldn't do to miss the post.

Chapter 7

The doorbell went at seven o'clock that evening. Halfway through a chicken Madras on a tray in front of the television, Cressida guessed it was Lottie popping in for a drink and a chat.

'Oh!' Horribly conscious that her breath must reek of curry, she took a surprised step back when she saw that it wasn't Lottie at all.

'You undercharged me this morning. And I didn't get the chance to introduce myself.' The son of Mrs E. Turner was back on her doorstep, sunburned and smiling and wearing a clean blue shirt. He was also holding a wrapped bunch of freesias. 'Tom Turner.'

Ever since a traumatising incident in her teens ('Oh, how lovely, are those for me?' 'No, they're to go on my nan's grave') the sight of men bearing flowers had caused Cressida to fly into a mini panic. Flustered, she said, 'Tom, how nice to see you again. I'm Cressida Forbes.'

Tom Turner inclined his head. 'I already know that.'

'God, of course you do, I'd forgotten. Um . . . I posted your mother's card.'

He was smiling now. 'I knew you'd do that too. You have an honest face.'

Cressida didn't know about honest. It was certainly red. Still trying desperately not to look at the freesias she said, 'Maybe now isn't the time to tell you I rob banks.'

'Here.' At last he held the wrapped flowers towards her. 'I thought you might like these. My way of saying thank you for helping me out this morning.'

'Oh. Gosh!' Pretending to have just spotted them for the first time, Cressida took the freesias and enthusiastically inhaled their scent. 'They're beautiful. Thank you so much. You really didn't have to do this.'

'As I said, you undercharged me. I saw the prices on your website.' Tom smiled. 'I also wanted to apologise for Donny's behaviour. He wasn't at his most charming, I'm afraid.'

You could say that again. Peering over Tom's shoulder, Cressida said, 'Well, he's at that age. Is he waiting in the car?'

'No. I've left him at the cottage, hunched over his GameBoy.'

There was a pause. Tom was still standing there, making no move to leave. Conscious that she might have curry breath but keen to cover the awkward silence, Cressida said brightly, 'So, did you catch anything?'

Tom looked startled. 'Excuse me?'

Oh marvellous, now he thought she was quizzing him about sexually transmitted diseases. 'You were going fishing,' Cressida said hurriedly. 'I meant did you catch any fish?'

'Oh, right, sorry. Yes, yes, we managed to—'

'Come in for a drink!' Out of the corner of her eye, Cressida had glimpsed Ted from the village shop ambling down the High Street towards them on his way to the Flying Pheasant for his customary six pints of Guinness and a good old moan about the state of the country, bloody supermarkets taking over the world and that damn fool gaggle of amateurs calling themselves the England cricket team.

Cressida was startled to realise that without even thinking about it she had reached out, unceremoniously yanked Tom Turner into her hallway and slammed the front door shut behind him.

But something told her he really didn't mind too much.

Amused, he said, 'I thought you'd never ask.'

'Sorry. Ted, from the shop. Come on through.' Flinging open windows in the kitchen and chucking away the plastic container her microwaveable Madras had come in — at least she'd bothered to tip the food onto a plate after heating it — Cressida said, 'Sorry about the smell of curry. Now, let me just put these in something. Tea, coffee or a glass of wine?'

Tom looked at the freesias she was busy unwrapping. 'I think they'd probably prefer water.'

'OK.' Cressida nodded, realising she'd been gabbling again. 'Water for the flowers. And we'll have the wine. It's only cheap, I'm afraid.'

Tom smiled. 'Stop apologising.'

They sat outside on the patio and Cressida learned that Tom and his son were from Newcastle, staying down here in one of Freddie's holiday cottages. They were three days into a fortnight's holiday and plenty more fishing was planned. This afternoon they had caught six trout and five perch.

'Which cheered Donny up no end,' said Tom. 'That was another reason I wanted to see you again, I suppose. To let you know that Donny isn't always as stroppy as he was this morning. He's a good lad really. The last couple of years have been tough for him.'

'You got divorced?' It was an educated guess; father and son holidaying alone together. No wedding ring in sight.

Tom nodded. 'My wife ran off with another man.'

'Oh God. I'm so sorry.'

He acknowledged this with a shrug. 'It hit Donny hard. We hadn't any idea. She just walked out one morning and that was that. Left a note, didn't even say goodbye. She's living in Norfolk now with her new chap. Poor Donny, it's just the two of us now. I do my best and we muddle through. But it's not the same, is it?'

'It's not the same.' Cressida nodded sympathetically, feeling terrible for having decided earlier that Donny would benefit from a slap. Her heart went out to the man sitting opposite her. 'But it must have been awful for you too.'

'What can I say?' Tom shook his head. 'You just have to carry on, pick up the pieces. I'm forty-two years old and a single parent. Never imagined that happening, but it has. God, listen to me.' He grimaced, then broke into a smile. 'Now it's my turn to apologise. Talk about cheerful! Let's turn this conversation around, shall we? Tell me about you instead.'

Something fluttered in the depths of Cressida's stomach. He was a nice man with a friendly open face and an easy manner. She had inadvertently picked him up this morning in Ted's shop and now here he was, drinking wine on her patio and asking her to tell him all about herself. In her disastrous experiences with men, they'd invariably been far more interested in talking about themselves.

Then again, she'd always had an extra-special talent for getting involved with breathtakingly selfish members of the opposite sex.

What a shame this one lived in Newcastle-upon-Tyne.

'Well, I'm thirty-nine. And divorced.' Oh Lord, now she sounded like a lonely hearts advert. Dismissing the last bit with a wave of her hand, Cressida said, 'But that was years ago. And I love living here in Hestacombe, running my own little business. It started as a hobby while I was working as a legal secretary, but then I stupidly got myself into a relationship with my boss. Of course it came to a messy end after a few months and things were pretty awkward at work after that.' Pretty awkward was putting it mildly, but Cressida spared him the grim details of how it felt when your boss dumped you and took up with the nineteen-year-old office tart instead. 'So I jacked in the job and decided to give the card thing a go. The first few months were scary – I was travelling around begging shops and businesses to stock my work – but gradually it began to take off. And now . . . well, it's great. I'll never be rich, but I make a living and the hours are flexible. If I want to take a day off to go bungee jumping, I can. Other times, I'll be up all night making fifty wedding invitations or birth announcements. You never know what you'll be asked to do next and I love it.'

There, that was cheerful and positive, wasn't it? Tom couldn't think she was a sad sack now. She sounded wild and free, spontaneous and impulsive . . .

'Bungee jumping?'

'Why not?' Still feeling wonderfully wild and free – it possibly had to do with the wine – Cressida flashed a dazzling smile and casually tossed her hair back from her face. Click-click-clung went the tortoiseshell combs as they flew out of her hair, bounced off the back of the chair and hit the patio.

'OK.' Cressida gave up; she clearly wasn't cut out to be wild and free. 'Maybe not bungee jumping. But if I feel like it, I can take a day off and go shopping.'

'Nothing wrong with that.' Tom nodded in agreement. 'As far as my ex-wife was concerned, a week without new shoes was a week wasted.'

'Was she incredibly glamorous?' She'd always longed to be glamorous herself but Cressida knew it was never going to happen. Glamour was beyond her. No matter how many times she set out determined to buy something tailored and chic, she always seemed to end up being inexorably drawn to long gypsyish skirts, billowing cotton shirts trimmed with velvet and lace, and embroidered jackets.

'Glamorous? Not especially.' Tom considered this. 'Angie just liked to have lots of everything in every colour. She was always smart, though. Well,' he added, 'I daresay she still is.'

Something else I'll never be, thought Cressida. Smart implied being acquainted with a steam iron and she wasn't. Could a man who'd been married to a well turned out woman ever be interested in someone who didn't own an ironing board?

Oh dear, now she was definitely getting too carried away. The poor fellow had only come round to thank her for helping him out.

'Not that Donny appreciated it,' Tom continued easily. 'Angie was always trying to get him to dress smartly too, and all he ever wanted to wear was holey sweatshirts and camouflage combats. These days I just let him wear anything he likes. Kids have their own ideas of how they want to look, don't they? You must find the same.'

'Well, um—'

'Sorry.' Seeing that she was taken aback, Tom said, 'I couldn't help noticing the photos in the kitchen of you and your daughter. That's how I knew you'd understand about Donny, being a single parent yourself.'

All she had to do was laugh it off. Ridiculously, though, Cressida felt a surge of pride mixed with sadness because the pain might be hidden but it never really went away. Somehow the words were stuck in her throat and all she could do was take another sip of wine.

'What's her name?' said Tom.

This she could manage. 'Jojo.'

'Jojo.' He nodded. 'And she's what, roughly the same age as Donny?'

It was no big deal. She didn't have to tell him the whole story. Crikey, she might never set eyes on him again after tonight.

'Jojo's twelve. And I love her to bits.' Forcing herself to smile, conscious of the roughness of the sun-warmed paving stones beneath her bare feet, Cressida said, 'But she isn't my daughter. I just look after her a lot.'

Chapter 8

Tyler Klein saw them as he was driving into Hestacombe the next morning. Two children, emerging from a modern house on the outskirts of the village, wearing shorts, T-shirts and baseball caps. He couldn't swear they were the ones but he could soon find out. Tyler braked and pulled up alongside them.

The heat hit him as he stepped out of the air-conditioned hire car. The flash of recognition in their eyes told Tyler all he needed to know. One had longer hair than the other, but he'd been right about it being two boys.

'Hi there.' Tyler smiled easily. 'Was it you two I saw a couple of days ago, down by the lake?'

They regarded him warily. Finally the taller boy said, 'No.'

'Sure about that? Running off with someone else's clothes?'

'That wasn't us.'

'Look. You're not in trouble, I promise. I just really need to know the truth.'

The younger boy said earnestly, 'We didn't take any clothes.'

Déjà vu. Only this time Tyler knew he was right.

'Fine. Well, there are tests that can be done to find out who did. DNA,' said Tyler. 'Fingerprints.'

Behind the boys, their mother had appeared in the doorway of the house, young and plump and carrying an even plumper baby on her hip. She watched impassively as her youngest son blurted out, 'But we didn't steal them, she got them back. We threw them over the wall into her garden.'

'I know.' Tyler nodded. 'But thanks for confirming it.'

'Ow,' cried the boy as his brother elbowed him painfully in the ribs.

'You big *stupid*, you *told* him.'

'That hurt!'

Catching their mother's eye, Tyler said, 'Sorry about this.'

'Don't be sorry. Little buggers, I'll give them something to be sorry about. Whose clothes did they take?'

38

Tyler shook his head. 'It doesn't matter.'

'Not to you maybe, but it does to me. Harry, Ben, get inside the house.' As the boys slid past their mother and the fat baby placidly watched, she clipped each of them smartly around the ear. The older of the two, clutching the side of his head, turned and glared at Tyler before disappearing into the hallway.

As far as the under-eleven population of Hestacombe was concerned, Tyler realised, he was undoubtedly Public Enemy Number One.

Off to a good start.

Lottie was hard at work on the computer in the office when she heard the crunch of tyres on gravel outside heralding Tyler Klein's arrival. Glad of the break from processing bookings, she picked up her bottle of Orangina and went outside to greet him.

'Giving the suit a miss today then.' Leaning against the open door of the annexe, just across the drive from Hestacombe House, she watched him emerge from the car. He was wearing a pink-striped shirt and faded jeans, and there was no denying that as new bosses went, he was pretty damn gorgeous.

Which could be fantastic, or it could turn out to be a complete disaster. Only time would tell.

'I hate suits. I've had to wear them for the last twelve years.' Tyler Klein's dark eyes glittered as he shook Lottie's hand. 'From now on, if you catch me in a suit you'll know I'm either on my way to a wedding or a funeral.'

Lottie winced at the mention of the word funeral. It wasn't his fault; he didn't know Freddie was ill. His handshake was firm, but not knuckle-crunchingly so. And there was that aftershave again, making you want to keep breathing it in, even when your lungs were telling you it was time to breathe out.

'So, looks like we're going to be working together. Freddie's spending the day in Cheltenham, but he said you wanted to see how things are run around here.' She checked her watch. 'Teacher's Cottage is being cleaned before the next guests arrive. Shall I show you what we do to get it ready?'

Tyler shrugged and nodded. 'You're the boss. Fire away.'

'Actually, you're the boss.' Lottie closed the door of the office behind her. 'And I just hope you don't fire me.'

Teacher's Cottage was a four-bedded Grade II listed property in its own magical gardens. Lottie introduced Tyler to Liz, the cleaner, as she was leaving, then showed him over the cottage.

'We leave fresh food in the fridge. And a homemade cake on the kitchen table to welcome the new arrivals. Fresh flowers in the living room and bedrooms. Magazines and books are always going walkabout so we replace them regularly.'

'Speaking of going walkabout, I guess I owe your two an apology.' Tyler pulled a face. 'I found out who made off with your clothes.'

'Don't worry about it. I finally believed them.' As she spoke Lottie was busily straightening pictures on the walls, plumping up cushions and re-angling the coffee table. The pictures were already straight and the cush-ions plumped but there was no harm in letting your new boss know how efficient and hardworking you were. 'Who did it?'

'Two young boys.' Tyler wasn't about to tell her their names. 'They won't be doing it again.'

'Ben and Harry Jenkins then.' Entertained by the expression on his face, Lottie said, 'This isn't New York. Everyone knows everyone. Their mum helps out here sometimes with the cleaning. Can I ask you a question?'

Tyler spread his hands. 'Anything you like.'

'Are you actually going to be living here, running the business your-self? Or will you be popping down here every couple of weeks to keep an eye on your investment?'

'Living right here running the business.' Keeping a straight face, evidently amused by the unfamiliar expression, Tyler said, 'Where would I be *popping* down here from?'

'I don't know. London, I suppose. Or New York. You work in banking.' Lottie hadn't been able to figure it out for the life of her. 'It's a bit of a switch, isn't it? I thought maybe you'd carry on doing that and just kind of dabble in this on your days off.'

'Because you don't think I could cope with it full time?'

'Because it's not going to be as lucrative as being a financial high-flyer, wheeler-dealing on the stock exchange, trading zillions of shares and buying companies and stuff.' Aware that her grasp of the financial markets was tenuous to say the least, Lottie hurriedly bent down to straighten the maga-zines, yet again, on the coffee table. 'And if you're rich enough to be able to afford to buy all these holiday homes, isn't it going to be a bit weird, living in Fox Cottage? I mean, you must be used to so much better, a penthouse apartment overlooking Central Park or something. And working here isn't going to be at all what you're used to.' Lottie felt obliged to warn him. 'What will you do when a guest rings you up at three o'clock in the morning to tell you that a pipe's burst and water's pouring through the ceiling? Or that one of the drains is blocked? Or when they've just found a mouse in the kitchen? You see? How are you going to deal with stuff like that?'

'OK, OK.' Tyler held up both hands. 'The thing about asking a million questions is you have to stop occasionally to let other people answer.'

'Sorry. I'm just nosy. And I talk too much.' To prove that she was, nevertheless, an exemplary employee, Lottie fiddled with the flower arrangement on the table, tweaking the sweet peas and artfully reorganising the ferns.

'And you think I'm some clueless wanker-banker type who wouldn't know a monkey wrench from a plunger. Look, leave those flowers alone, Freddie's already told me you're indispensable.' Leading the way through to the kitchen, Tyler began briskly inspecting the cupboards. 'But I'm not actually that hopeless. I'm not afraid of hard physical work either. Or mice. But if there are any emergencies I really can't handle myself, I'll do what any normal person would do and call in an expert.'

Had she offended him by suggesting, more or less, that he wasn't up to the job?

'I didn't think you were a namby-pamby wanker-banker,' Lottie protested. 'I'm just wondering why you don't want to *be* a banker any more.'

Having thoroughly investigated the kitchen, Tyler leaned back against the granite worktop, hands thrust casually into his jeans pockets.

'OK. Let me tell you what it's like. We're talking high-pressure lifestyle here. Up at five every morning, off to the gym before work, then twelve hours in the office. Non-stop meetings, business rivals stabbing you in the back, having to make decisions that could make or break people's businesses – even their lives. Then wondering if you've made the right decision, dealing with the fallout when it all goes wrong. I'm telling you, it takes over your world. You think you're thriving on the pressure, but you're not. Nothing matters except making the next deal, the next million. You turn into a machine.' He paused, then said flatly, 'And it can end up killing you.'

The look in his dark eyes was bleak. Oh Jesus, thought Lottie, not you too.

Chapter 9

'Shall I tell you what happened?' said Tyler.

Mutely Lottie nodded.

'It killed my best friend.'

Oh. That was OK then. Well, not *OK*, obviously . . .

'His name was Curtis Segal,' Tyler went on. 'We'd known each other since we were six years old, grew up in the same street. We were closer than brothers. During college vacations we worked together on a ranch in Wyoming. After college we ended up going into the same business. Curtis was on a roll, getting promotion after promotion at his company, raking the money in and never getting enough sleep. But he was a fit guy. You never think anything bad's going to happen, do you, when you're in your thirties? Until Curtis had a major presentation one day – not the biggest he'd ever handled, but still pretty important. And he told his secretary he had a pain in his left arm five minutes before the presentation was due to begin. She wanted to call the company doctor in to see him but Curtis wouldn't let her do it, because everyone was up there in the boardroom waiting for him to make that all-important presentation.'

Silence. Tyler was still leaning against the worktop, lost in thought. Finally he continued. 'So he went up there and made it. Well, half of it. Then he collapsed and died, right there on the floor of the boardroom. The paramedics worked on him for forty minutes, but it was no good. He was gone. And guess what happened after that?'

'What?' said Lottie.

'His company lost the account. The other guys decided they didn't want to do business with the kind of bank where their top executives keel over and drop dead on you. You know what else?'

'What?'

'The CEO couldn't even make the funeral. He had other potential clients to wine and dine, out on Long Island. Very important potential clients, of course. He wouldn't have missed Curtis's funeral for just any old kind. And as he pointed out when I spoke to him afterwards he had sent a three thousand dollar wreath.'

His eyes were narrowed with disgust. Lottie's heart went out to Tyler. But since she could hardly fling her arms round him she said, 'When did this happen?'

'Five months ago. That's when I realised it could have been me. More to the point, it could be me *next*. And I made my decision just like that.' Tyler clicked his fingers. 'The day after Curtis's funeral I handed in my notice. Everyone told me I was mad. But I knew I was doing the right thing, there had to be more to life than slogging your guts out on Wall Street. I flew out to Wyoming, visited the ranch where we'd worked years before and thought about doing that again. It's an incredible place: just mountains, wide-open spaces and sky. But it wasn't the same without Curtis.' Tyler paused. 'Then I went to visit my parents and they were showing me all their holiday photos. They're so in love with this place, you have no idea.' He relaxed visibly. 'My mother kept saying I should come over to England, take a long vacation and see the sights.'

'So you ended up coming over here and buying the sights. By the way,' Lottie added, 'I like your parents. They're great.'

Tyler nodded and smiled. 'Crazy as larks, the pair of them. Or heart-warmingly eccentric, as you Brits would say. But yes, I guess I am buying the sights. I knew I liked this country. A few years back I was over here working for the London-based branch of our bank. Pretty intensive and only for six months, but it was enough to make me realise that here was somewhere I'd be happy to live. Then I spoke to my mother a couple of weeks ago. She was telling me they'd booked one of the cottages here for next Easter and happened to mention that Freddie was thinking of selling the business. Then two minutes later she said wouldn't it be great if I bought it, because then she and my father could come and stay for free.'

As he shook his head with good-natured amusement, Lottie sensed his genuine fondness for his mother. 'Thank your lucky stars she didn't have her heart set on the Taj Mahal.'

'That's what I said. I asked her if she wouldn't prefer me to buy Blenheim Palace.' Tyler rolled his eyes. 'But that evening I took a look at your website, purely out of curiosity, and all of a sudden it occurred to me that I could do it, that it might be just the change I needed. It's a fantastic place – my parents had already vouched for that. And if the price was fair, there'd be no risk. With properties like these . . . well, you can't go wrong. That's when I picked up the phone and called Freddie.' He paused and shrugged. 'That was less than two weeks ago. And now here I am. Beats Wall Street hands down.'

Lottie marvelled at Tyler's ability to make such a life-changing decision and to act upon it. He'd bought eight holiday homes, just like that. She'd spent longer choosing a new winter coat.

Aloud she said, 'You make it all sound so easy. Didn't you have to be interrogated by immigration?'

Tyler said drily, 'The British Consulate couldn't wait to grant me the visa, once they heard how much money I was planning to invest.'

Crikey, he must be loaded. And if after a few years he got bored, presumably he'd just sell the business and move on again. Maybe try an Australian sheep farm next.

Curious, Lottie said, 'Are you sure Fox Cottage is going to be OK for you?'

'Hey, I'm no namby-pamby.' Tyler clearly found the unfamiliar expression hilarious. 'Besides, it's only for a few months. I can handle that.'

So, a few months. Disappointment settled over Lottie like a sheet over a parrot's cage. She gave herself a mental shake. 'And after that?'

'Didn't Freddie tell you? He's planning to move out of Hestacombe House after Christmas. If I'm interested, I can buy it from him then.'

This time Lottie's heart turned over. She still hadn't been able to come to terms with the thought that Freddie was dying. *Planning to move out.*

'You don't look exactly thrilled,' Tyler observed.

'No, it's not that.' He didn't know, he didn't know, and she couldn't tell him. 'I just hadn't—'

Lottie was saved from further awkwardness by the sound of a car pulling up outside. Relieved, she checked her watch. 'Oh, that'll be the Harrisons.'

Tyler sauntered after her out of the cottage. The doors of a maroon people carrier were flung open and Glynis and Duncan Harrison and their five boisterous children spilled out.

'Here she is, waiting to welcome us,' Glynis exclaimed with delight. The Harrisons had been coming to Teacher's Cottage for the last ten years. 'Hello, Lottie love, you're looking well!' She enveloped Lottie in a rib-crushing, violet-scented hug. 'Ooh, it's so lovely to be back.'

'It's lovely to have you back.' Lottie meant it, she'd grown fond of so many of her clients. 'Good journey?'

'Roadworks on the M5 and the kids trying to murder each other in the back seats, but we're used to that by now. And who's this then?' Releasing Lottie in order to give Tyler an appreciative once-over, Glynis said, 'Got yourself a new fellow at last, love? I say, well *done.*' Eager to be introduced, she stuck out her hand and beamed up at Tyler. 'I was only saying to Duncan on the way down – wasn't I, Duncan? – it's about time Lottie found herself a nice young man.'

Lottie opened her mouth to explain but Tyler beat her to it. Greeting Glynis with a warm handshake and a wicked smile, he drawled, 'Tyler Klein. Good to meet you. And I couldn't agree with you more about Lottie. It's definitely time she found herself the right man.'

Chapter 10

Cressida was running a bath when her mobile phone launched into its jaunty tune. Locating it under the pile of clothes she'd just discarded on the bed, she made her way back through to the bathroom to choose which bubble bath to add to the gushing water.

'Cressida? Hi, it's Sacha.'

'Hi, Sacha. How are you?' As if she didn't already know the answer to that question.

'Oh, busy busy. Rushed off my feet as usual. What's that noise in the background?'

'I'm running a bath.' Reaching over, Cressida selected the bottle of Marks and Spencer's Florentyna and shook a generous dollop under the taps. Then another dollop for good measure.

'Lucky you! Having a lovely relaxing bath at five o'clock in the afternoon,' Sacha exclaimed. 'I wish I could do that. Now listen, Robert's stuck in a meeting in Bristol and I'm up to my ears with clients. God only knows what time we're going to be able to get away. OK if Jojo comes over to you?'

It wasn't the first time Sacha had asked this. Not even the three hundredth time. Sacha appeared to spend her life bobbing around in a sea of clients, only the top half of her head visible – although, naturally, her neat blonde hair remained immaculate.

'No problem.' Cressida swirled the bathwater with her free hand, generating foam. 'That's fine. I'll give her something to eat and she can help me in the garden later. What time will you be over to pick her up?'

'Well, the thing is, I'm being pressured to take the new clients out to dinner so I don't know how late it might be. And Robert thinks he may not be back before midnight, so . . .'

'How about if Jojo stays the night with me? Would that be easier?' Cressida wondered what Sacha would do if she told her she wasn't able to take Jojo. One day she must try it, see what happened. Sacha would rather chop off her own arms than miss out on the opportunity to woo her precious clients and make yet another spectacular sale.

Actually, it might be fun.

'Cress, you're a star!' Having got what she needed, Sacha put on her I'm-in-*such*-a-hurry voice. 'That's great, I'll give Jojo a ring and let her know. Well, it's chaos here so—'

'You'd better get back to them,' Cressida said helpfully.

'I really must. And you can get back to your bath! *Ciao!*'

Cressida switched off the phone. Was it just her, or was everyone else driven nuts by the annoying way Sacha trilled *Ciao!* at the end of every phone conversation? Whatever possessed a woman who'd been born and bred in Bootle to say *Ciao?* Maybe it was something that was drummed into you on training courses when you were learning to become a hotshot, high-flying photocopier saleswoman.

Oh well, who cared? At least she had Jojo tonight. She'd put up with as many *Ciaos* as Sacha could throw at her for that.

Lying back in the bath, Cressida ran her hand lightly over the familiar silver scar traversing her stomach. How different might her life have been had that scar never needed to be made? She closed her eyes and imagined herself, twenty-three again and still happily married to Robert. Both of them had been so excited by the prospect of the baby that although they knew it was far too soon they had been unable to resist rushing out and buying all kinds of baby paraphernalia. It had been the most joyful shopping spree of Cressida's life. To be a mother was all she'd ever wanted.

Back at home that evening surrounded by babygros, tiny knitted hats, a satin-lined Moses basket and a musical mobile that played nursery rhymes, Cressida had begun to experience the first excruciating knife-like pains in her stomach. She had crawled on all fours to the phone, petrified and plunged into icy panic, and tried to contact Robert who was out playing cricket for his works team. Unable to reach him, she had been on the verge of dialling 999 when the pain had intensified and everything had turned black. When Robert finally arrived home at ten o'clock that night, he found her unconscious and barely breathing on the bathroom floor. An ambulance rushed Cressida to hospital where emergency surgery was carried out to save her life. The pregnancy had been ectopic and her fallopian tube had ruptured. The degree of haemorrhaging was so severe that a total hysterectomy had been the only option.

When Cressida woke up to find Robert weeping silently at her bedside she knew her life was over. Their longed-for child was gone and, along with it, any chance of motherhood.

Cressida wanted to die too. They had tempted fate and fate had been tempted. Would this have happened if they hadn't bought all those things for the baby?

It was a prospect too horrible to contemplate. The more people told her that of course she hadn't caused it to happen, the less Cressida believed them. Awash with self-recrimination and grief, she sank into a depression so deep it was as if all the happiness had been sucked out of the world. She was trapped at the bottom of a well, its sides slippery and black. Nobody could help her to feel better because there was nothing that could *make* her feel better. People talked encouragingly about adoption but Cressida wasn't ready to hear them. Everywhere she went, she saw pregnant women proudly displaying their bumps, parents out with their children, mothers holding newborn babies and fathers playing rumbustious games of football with their sons.

Sometimes she saw frazzled housewives losing their tempers and yelling at their toddlers. That was when the knife-like pain ripped through Cressida's stomach all over again and she had to rush away before she could do something stupid.

But at least, as everyone was forever telling her, she and Robert still had each other. Their marriage was rock-solid. Together they would gain strength and get through this.

In fact their marriage was so rock-solid that eleven months after the night their lives had changed forever, Robert changed them again and moved out of the house overlooking Hestacombe village green. He told Cressida he wanted a divorce and Cressida said fine. Compared with the loss of their baby, losing Robert paled into insignificance. It barely registered on the scale of her grief. Besides, how could she blame him? Why would any normal healthy man in his right mind want to stay married to a 24-year-old wife with no womb?

If she'd been physically capable of divorcing herself, she'd have done it too.

That's not to say she wasn't hurt by Robert's next action. But then again, men were thoughtless. Having by this time moved into a rented flat in Cheltenham, he embarked on a whirlwind romance with a fiercely ambitious young sales rep called Sacha, who had just moved down from Liverpool to join the company. Cressida and Robert's divorce went through and four months later Robert and Sacha were married. Six months after that, Robert arrived on Cressida's doorstep one day to tell her that he and Sacha had just put in an offer to buy one of the houses on the new estate on the edge of the village. Taken aback, Cressida said, 'What, you mean *this* village?'

'Why not?'

'But *why*?'

'Cress, my flat's too small. We need somewhere with more space. I like Hestacombe and this new house is perfect. OK, so we're divorced.' Robert shrugged and said reasonably, 'But we can still be civilised towards each other, can't we?'

Her heart heavy, Cressida said, 'I suppose so. Sorry. Yes, of course we can.' She felt ashamed of herself. Robert had been through the mill as well. She should be glad that at least one of them was managing to rebuild their lives.

Robert looked relieved. Then he said, 'Oh, and I suppose I should tell you that Sacha's pregnant. That's another reason for the move, so we'll have room for the baby and an au pair.'

Cressida felt as if she'd been plunged into a vat of dry ice. Her tongue was sticking to the roof of her mouth but she managed to stammer, 'G-gosh. C-congratulations.'

'Well, it wasn't exactly planned.' Robert's tone was rueful. 'Sacha really wanted to concentrate on her career for the next few years, but these things happen. I'm sure she'll cope. As Sacha's always saying, women can have it all these days, can't they?'

It was as if he was stabbing her with a long gleaming blade, over and over again. Struggling to breathe, Cressida somehow fixed a bright smile to her face. 'Absolutely. Having it all, that's what it's all about.'

Stab stab.

As if realising he might not have been too subtle, Robert shoved his hands into his pockets and said defensively, 'I'm sorry, but you can't expect me to go through life not having children, just because of what happened to you.'

You, Cressida noted. Not *us*.

'I don't expect you to do that.'

'I've met someone else. We're having a baby. Don't make me feel guilty, Cress. You know how much I wanted a proper family.'

She nodded, wanting him to leave. Badly needing to be alone. 'I do. It's OK, I'm f-fine.'

Relieved, Robert said, 'Good. That's that, then. Life goes on.'

Now, lying back in the bath, Cressida studied her orangey-pink painted toenails and gave them a wiggle. Life had indeed gone on. She had thrown herself into her work as a legal secretary and in her spare time had redecorated the entire house because any form of activity was better than sitting down and thinking about the family she had lost.

Five months later she heard that Sacha had given birth to a seven-pound baby, a girl. That had been a hard day. Robert and Sacha named their daughter Jojo and Cressida sent them a card she had made herself, to congratulate them.

Another milestone survived.

When Jojo was two months old, a nanny was hired and Sacha went back to work. Astrid, who was from Sweden and far more of a fresh-air fiend than Sacha, could be seen every day pushing Jojo in her Silver Cross pram around the village. Keen to practise her English, Astrid stopped to chat with everyone she saw, which was how Cressida, arriving home from work one afternoon, found herself trapped into discussing the weather.

'The clouds, up in the sky, they are like major white pillows, do you not think?' Having been instructed that all English people loved to talk about the weather, Astrid always made this her opening gambit.

'Well, yes. Like . . . um, *big* white pillows.' Cressida was lifting a supermarket carrier bag out of the car.

'But I believe there may be raindrops later.'

'Rain, yes, probably.'

'I am Astrid,' the girl said proudly. 'I am working as a nanny for Robert and Sacha Forbes.'

Cressida, who already knew this, tactfully didn't say, 'Hi, Astrid, I'm Cressida Forbes, Robert's first wife.' Instead she said, 'And I'm Cressida. It's very nice to meet you.'

Astrid beamed at her, then turned the pram round and said brightly, 'But I must not be forgetting my manners! I have also to introduce you to Jojo.'

Cressida held her breath and looked down at the baby lying in the pram. Jojo gazed inscrutably back at her. Waiting for the familiar stabbing pain in her stomach, Cressida was relieved when it didn't come. She'd been terrified that she'd resent this baby for not being hers. But now she was here she knew she couldn't possibly resent an eleven-week-old infant.

'She is so beautiful, don't you think?' Astrid spoke with pride, leaning forward to tickle Jojo's chin.

'Yes, she is.' Cressida's heart expanded as, in response to the tickling, Jojo broke into a gummy smile.

'Such a good baby, too. I am enjoying very much looking after her. And are you having children as well?'

There was the stabbing pain. She knew Astrid meant do you have children, but this time Cressida didn't correct her. Clutching the supermarket bag containing her lonely meal-for-one, a packet of biscuits and a single pint of milk she said, 'No, I'm not having children.'

'Ah well, never mind!' Astrid beamed at her. 'You are still young, lots of time to have fun and enjoy yourself first, eh? Like me! We can have our babies in a few years, can't we? Whenever we like!'

For eight months Astrid had been the perfect nanny. Cressida often thought afterwards that she owed practically her entire relationship with Jojo to a moment's carelessness on the part of Astrid's mother.

Cressida had been coming out of Ted's shop one morning with her newspaper and a naughty packet of Revels when she had seen Sacha's company car heading down the High Street towards her. Screeching to a halt, Sacha stuck her head out of the driver's window and said, 'Cressida, can you save my life?'

She was looking decidedly harassed. On the brief occasions they had met before, Cressida had been struck by Sacha's air of calm and super-efficiency. Her clothes were efficient. Even her hair — neat and short and expertly highlighted — was efficient. Today, by way of startling contrast, there were milk stains on Sacha's sweatshirt and her hair was uncombed. Strapped into her baby seat in the back of the car, Jojo was wearing a T-shirt and a bulging nappy and was screaming her head off.

'What's wrong?' Cressida was alarmed. 'Is Jojo ill?'

'Astrid's mother's in hospital with multiple fractures. Crashed her car last night into a bridge. Astrid's gone to Sweden to see her and she doesn't know when she'll be back because there's no one else to look after her little brother.' As the words came tumbling out, the volume of Jojo's wailing increased. Sacha's knuckles whitened as she gripped the steering wheel. 'And Robert's away on a bloody management training course in Edinburgh, and in two hours' time I'm due in Reading to pitch for the biggest account of my entire career. If I don't get there on time I don't know *what* I'll do—'

'Where are you going now?' Cressida cut in, because Sacha's voice was on an hysterical upward spiral.

'The health centre! I thought maybe one of the nurses would keep an eye on Jojo for me if I paid them enough. Unless you know anyone who could help? That's why I stopped,' Sacha gabbled on wildly, 'because you know more people in the village than I do. I went to every house in our road this morning but nobody would take her. Can you think of anyone around here who'd look after a baby for the day?'

As if Jojo was the school hamster. Lost for words, Cressida gaped at Sacha.

'*Well?*' demanded Sacha, increasingly frantically.

'Um . . . well, no.'

'Oh, for crying out *loud.*' Sacha looked as if she might actually burst into tears. '*Bloody* Astrid. What have I done to deserve this?'

Jojo was screaming and Sacha was stuck.

'Unless . . . I suppose I could take her,' Cressida offered hesitantly. 'If it would help. I mean, I'm not a qualified childminder but I've done lots of babysitting in my—'

'*You?*' Sacha's eyes widened in disbelief.

Cressida, who'd seen the film *The Hand that Rocks the Cradle*, understood completely.

'No, sorry, it was just a thought. Of course you wouldn't want—'

'Oh my God, are you kidding? I can't believe it! Don't you have to work?'

Taken aback, Cressida said, 'It's my day off.'

'But this is brilliant! Why didn't you say so before?' Reaching over and flinging open the passenger door, Sacha yelled, 'Quick, jump in.'

And that had been it. Back at Sacha and Robert's house, Cressida learned that Jojo was only bellowing at the top of her voice because she hadn't been fed or changed this morning. Normally, Sacha explained, she was a placid, cheerful baby. Sacha, having showered and dressed at warp speed, left Cressida with the keys to the house and a shouted promise over her shoulder that she'd be back by six.

Evidently she'd never watched *The Hand that Rocks the Cradle*.

Then again, if Cressida hadn't happened to come along when she did, Sacha might well have dumped Jojo into the unsuspecting arms of the health centre's receptionist.

Which didn't stop Cressida being absolutely petrified when she stopped to consider the situation in which she'd landed herself. For the next nine hours she was responsible for the well-being of her ex-husband's baby. What if something should happen to Jojo? What if she was sick and started to choke? What if a lorry smashed into the house? What if Jojo accidentally drank bleach or fell over and broke a leg or took a tumble downstairs? Cressida blanched at the thought. Oh God, everyone would think she was a deranged baby-batterer. She couldn't do this, she just couldn't.

Except she had to, because there wasn't actually anyone else around to take over the job.

Cressida looked at Jojo, who was sitting on the living room floor solemnly chewing a Farley's rusk. After several seconds, Jojo dropped the rusk and broke into a delighted grin, revealing two pearly white bottom teeth. Seemingly unconcerned at finding herself alone in the house with a virtual stranger, she held out her arms to Cressida.

'What is it, sweetheart?' Her heart melting, Cressida crouched down in front of her.

Still grinning, Jojo laboriously manoeuvred herself into a crawling position before clutching at Cressida's trouser leg in order to haul herself to her knees. Then she imperiously raised her arms again, like the Pope.

And Cressida picked her up.

Chapter 11

'Aunt Cress? It's me!'

The back door opened and banged shut, heralding Jojo's arrival. Cressida, in the kitchen putting together a mushroom risotto, called out, 'In here, sweetheart,' then turned and opened her arms wide, keeping them outstretched as Jojo bounced into the kitchen and gave her a kiss.

'Trying to fly?'

'Trying not to get onion and garlic smells all over you.' Cressida indicated the chopping board and waggled her fingers. 'Good day?'

'Brilliant. Swimming, tennis and making fairy cakes. I was going to bring you some but we ate them.' As they both worked full time, Sacha and Robert paid for Jojo to attend a summer holiday scheme run by one of the private schools in Cheltenham. Luckily Jojo enjoyed it. Watching her at the sink as she ran the cold tap and glugged down a glass of water, Cressida experienced a rush of love for the girl who had brought more happiness into her life than any other living person. Jojo was twelve now, with fine straggly dark hair, her mother's neat features and Robert's long legs. Today she was wearing denim shorts, the sea-green T-shirt from Tammy that Cressida had bought her last Christmas, and beneath it a padded pink bra she didn't need but had insisted on buying because when you were twelve everyone at school teased you if you didn't wear a bra.

'Are those from the garden?' Jojo had noticed the freesias in a vase on the kitchen table.

'No. Someone gave them to me.'

'Oo-er.' Jojo raised her eyebrows. 'Man or woman?'

'As it happens, a man.' Cressida tipped the chopped onions into the frying pan and turned up the heat to maximum.

'Aunt Cress! Is he your new boyfriend?'

'I made a card for his mother. He wanted to thank me, that's all.'

'But he brought you flowers. Proper ones, from a shop,' Jojo emphasised, 'and he didn't have to do that, did he? So does that mean he'd *like* to be your new boyfriend?'

52

Time to change the subject. Vigorously stirring the onions in the pan Cressida said, 'I shouldn't think so for one minute. Now are you going to give me a hand with these mushrooms?'

'That's what I call changing the subject.'

'OK then, no, he definitely doesn't want to be my new boyfriend. And it's just as well because he lives two hundred miles away. And these mushrooms still need to be chopped.'

'But—'

'You know, I had such a lovely time this afternoon,' said Cressida. 'I was thinking back to the very first time I looked after you. You were ten months old and you couldn't talk at all.'

'Ten months.' This time Jojo was diverted; she loved hearing about the antics she'd got up to as a baby. 'Could I walk then?'

'No, but you were an Olympic crawler. Like a little train. You were eleven months before you started to walk.'

After that first successful day, Sacha had known a soft touch when she'd seen one. Less than a fortnight later she had asked Cressida to babysit again and Cressida had been only too happy to oblige. A week after that, Sacha and Robert had been invited to a smart wedding in Berkshire and Jojo and Cressida had spent a glorious day together, culminating in Jojo taking a series of tottering steps across the living room floor before stumbling triumphantly into Cressida's arms. That evening when Sacha and Rob had arrived to pick her up, Cressida had remarked on how active she'd been. Sacha, smiling smugly, had said, 'Oh yes, she'll be walking before long. She's very advanced for her age.'

Astrid hadn't come back. She was replaced by a series of unsuitable nannies and even more wildly unsuitable au pairs. If Sacha had asked Cressida to give up her job in the solicitors' office and look after Jojo full time, Cressida would have done it in a heartbeat. But that had never happened. Maybe it would have been just too weird. Or maybe it had something to do with the fact that Jojo had once accidentally called Cressida Mummy. Whatever, Cressida carried on babysitting whenever she was asked and helped out during emergencies. It was a situation everyone was happy with.

'What's the worst thing I ever did when I was little?' Jojo was at last slicing the mushrooms.

'The most embarrassing, you mean? Probably the time you took your nappy off in the middle of the supermarket and left it in the rice and pasta aisle.' Cressida paused, then said, 'It wasn't a clean nappy.'

'Euww!' Shaking her head and laughing, Jojo said, 'Tell me the best thing I ever did.'

Cressida pulled a face. 'Can't think of any.'

'That's not true! Tell me!'

'Oh, sweetheart. The best thing?' Abandoning the sizzling onions, Cressida enveloped Jojo in a hug. 'I really couldn't say. There are too many to count.'

Chapter 12

As Tyler pulled up outside Piper's Cottage a sludgy white splat hit the windscreen of his hired car and a large bird, possibly smirking with satisfaction at having scored a direct hit, flew off over the rooftops of the houses opposite. The splat was huge and, typically, situated in the dusty fan-shaped space precisely where the car's windscreen wipers didn't reach.

Was this an omen?

Lottie came to the door looking pink and out of breath.

'Oh, hi!'

'Haven't interrupted anything, have I?' Tyler half smiled, although she was dressed in a sleeveless white top and jeans so anything too salacious seemed unlikely. 'If this is a bad time . . .'

Lottie gave him a look and opened the door more widely, allowing him to see the Dyson behind her.

'Chance would be a fine thing. You just caught me trying to cram six weeks' worth of housework into thirty minutes. The kids have been writing their names in the dust on the TV.' Wiping her forehead Lottie said, 'Sorry, come on in. Don't trip over the lead. Is this about work?'

She was gorgeous. Curvy, smart and bursting with vitality. Watching as she bent over to pick up a can of Lemon Pledge, a duster and a bottle of Cif spray, Tyler said, 'Actually, I was wondering if you'd have dinner with me tonight.'

'Oh.' Lottie looked surprised.

'If you're free, of course.'

'Well, I can ask Mario to have the kids. That shouldn't be a problem.' Clearly unsure as to the nature of the invitation she said, 'Would this be so we can talk about work?'

'We can talk about work if you like. We can talk about all sorts of things.' Tyler smiled. 'How about if I pick you up at eight?'

'OK. Fine.' Her eyes bright, Lottie said, 'Although I'd better just check with Mario, make sure he can take them. Give me two minutes.'

She disappeared through to the kitchen to make the call. Since eavesdropping on a telephone conversation between Lottie and her ex-husband wasn't really on, Tyler waited in the living room. His gaze fell on the grey crumpled rag she'd evidently been using in her cleaning blitz and had forgotten to pick up. Tyler took it from the window ledge and made his way out through the still-open front door.

It was garbage collection day in the village. Everyone had their black wheelie bins – God, he *loved* that quaint English expression – outside their front gates. When he'd finished wiping off what the bird had so offputtingly deposited on his windscreen, Tyler dropped the cloth into Lottie's wheelie bin and headed back inside the cottage.

'There you are,' said Lottie. 'I thought you'd chickened out and made a quick getaway.'

'I just went out to—' Tyler's mobile phone burst into life. 'Damn, sorry.' Apologetically he pulled it from his shirt pocket.

'No problem, Mario's taking the kids for the evening. I'll see you at eight o'clock.' Keen to get back to her thirty-minute cleaning frenzy, Lottie ushered him out. As he prepared to answer the business call, Tyler heard the Dyson being switched back on in the living room.

He smiled to himself, already looking forward to the evening ahead. In the space of a few days his life had changed beyond recognition and he'd met Lottie Carlyle, who was sexy and beautiful and like no girl he'd ever met before.

Oh yes, things were definitely looking up.

Tyler heard the noise even before he stepped out of the car at five to eight that evening. An unearthly wailing was coming from inside the cottage. Mildly alarmed – that couldn't be Lottie surely? – he made his way up the front path and rang the doorbell.

'Hi, you must be Tyler.' A tall male with an air of resignation opened the door and shook his hand. 'Mario. Sorry about the racket, we're having a bit of a crisis.'

So this was the ex-husband. Stepping over the threshold, Tyler followed Mario into the living room where a giant box of Lego had been upturned in the centre of the floor. Lottie, looking harassed and still wearing her white top and jeans, was sitting in one of the armchairs cradling her son on her lap. Nat was sobbing as if his heart would break and judging by the sodden state of Lottie's top had been doing so for some time. At the sight of Tyler he redoubled the volume of his howls and buried his face in Lottie's neck. At the other end of the room Mario was unzipping sofa cushions and searching inside them.

'What's happened?' Tyler wondered if someone had died.

From upstairs Ruby yelled down, 'It's definitely not in the airing cupboard.'

'Nat's lost his noonoo.' Struggling to brush her son's hair out of her own eyes, Lottie winced as his howls of grief rocketed to new levels in response to her words. 'Sshh, sshh now, sweetheart, it's all right.' She rocked him patiently and rubbed his back. 'We'll find it, don't you worry. It's here somewhere.'

Mystified, Tyler said, 'What's a noonoo?'

'It's like a comfort blanket. Nat's had it since he was a baby. He can't sleep without it.' Lottie checked her watch and grimaced. 'God, sorry about this. And I haven't even had time to get changed. Look, any minute now we'll find noonoo and I can be ready in five minutes, that's a promise.'

Ruby's voice floated down to them. 'It's definitely not in the bathroom.'

'Hey, no problem.' Holding up his hands, Tyler sensed an opportunity to gain some much-needed points in his favour. 'I'll help you look for it. A comfort blanket, you say. Well, it doesn't have legs so it can't have run off anywhere, can it?'

'We know it's in the house.' Lottie nodded firmly and shot Tyler a grateful smile. 'Noonoo always turns up in the end. Nat's just left it in a safe place somewhere and it's turned out to be a bit too safe.'

Right, a comfort blanket. Picturing a pale blue cashmere blanket with satin edges, Tyler said gently but efficiently, 'So, Nat, let's start the search party, shall we? And any clues you could give us would be great. Like, where do you remember seeing it last?'

Nat, his chest heaving, sobbed piteously, 'On th-the w-w-window ledge over th-th-there,' and pointed across the room.

Oh fuck.

Oh shit.

Surely not.

Feeling sick – Jesus, he *never* felt sick – Tyler said, 'And the . . . uh, blanket is what colour?'

Lottie, still attempting to soothe her distraught son, shrugged and said, 'No colour at all, really.'

'It h-hasn't got a c-c-colour,' Nat wailed. 'It's my noonoo.'

Oh seriously fuck.

'Not in here.' Mario had finished investigating the innards of all the sofa cushions. 'It's a piece of old stretchy cotton material,' he explained to Tyler, 'from a babygro Nat used to wear as a baby. About thirty centimetres square, kind of greyish and manky looking.'

'It's NOT MANKY!' roared Nat. 'It's my *noonoo*.'

Tyler prayed his face wouldn't give him away. He'd played poker often enough through college, but this was on another level altogether. He could feel his palms sweating and—

'You were here this afternoon,' Lottie said suddenly. 'You didn't happen to notice if it was on the window ledge then, did you?' Her eyes were full of hope.

It was no good, he couldn't deny it. He couldn't lie to her. But he couldn't bring himself to admit the truth in front of Nat either. His mouth dry, Tyler inclined his head fractionally in the direction of the living room door, indicating that Lottie should follow him.

Lottie left Nat curled up in a heartbroken ball on the armchair and joined Tyler out in the hallway. 'Look, I'm really sorry about this. I suppose you're worried we'll miss our table at the restaurant, but I just can't—'

'It was me. I took the noonoo.' The words – words he'd somehow never imagined hearing himself say in his lifetime – spilled out in a rush.

'What?'

'I thought it was an old cleaning rag. You'd been cleaning this morning and it looked like you forgot to take it out with you.'

'Where is it?' From her expression Lottie had already guessed there was no happy ending in sight.

'I used it to clean some bird sh— some bird stuff off the car.' Tyler kept his voice low. 'It was pretty messy. Your trash was out, so I threw it in there.'

'Oh no,' Lottie groaned, burying her face in her hands. 'I don't believe this. And now the bins have been emptied. Oh God, what are we going to do?'

'I'm sorry, I'm really sorry, it was an accident.' Struggling to explain, Tyler said, 'But how was I supposed to know it wasn't a cleaning rag?'

'But you just took it!' With a trace of exasperation Lottie shook her head. 'If you'd asked me first I could have stopped you. Or mentioned it afterwards, so I could have fished it out of the bin.'

'I meant to. I was going to, but my phone started to ring and you wanted to get on with your vacuuming. Look, I know Nat's upset right now, but he's seven years old. Maybe it's time he gave up this comfort blanket business anyway. I mean, he can't carry on indefinitely, can he? This could be just the opportunity you need to break the habit.'

'Oh God,' sighed Lottie. 'You really don't have any experience of children, do you?'

'But—'

'YOU STOLE NAT'S NOONOO!' shrieked a voice above their heads and Tyler's heart plummeted still further. The next moment Ruby came thundering down the staircase, an accusing finger pointed at his chest. 'You stole Nat's noonoo and threw it away! Nat, it was that man, the one who told the lies!' Deftly dodging round Lottie's outstretched arm, she shot into the living room and yelled, 'He says you're too old for a noonoo anyway, you're seven and only babies have noonoos, and now it's gone and you're never going to see it again *ever*!'

Hot on Ruby's heels, Lottie blurted out, 'Nat, he *didn't* say that. And it was an accident, OK?'

Tempting though it would have been to walk out of the front door, climb into his car and drive off, Tyler followed Lottie into the living room. He'd thought nothing could be worse than the sound of Nat's sobbing, but the stunned silence that now greeted him beat it hands down. The little boy, white-faced and trembling with shock, looked as if he'd forgotten how to breathe. In disbelief he stared up at Tyler and whispered, 'You threw it away?'

Tyler nodded and exhaled slowly. 'I'm so sorry.'

'In the wheelie bin!' Ruby made the pronouncement with relish.

'He didn't mean to,' said Lottie.

'But it didn't fall in by accident, did it?' Her dark eyes widening, Ruby blurted out passionately, 'And what's Nat going to do now without his noonoo? He'll just *die*!'

'He won't die,' Mario said flatly as Lottie scooped Nat back into her arms and attempted to console him.

Knowing even as he said it that it was the wrong thing to say, Tyler ventured, 'Could you not make another, er, noonoo? Like maybe a better one?'

Everyone gazed at him in horrified disbelief as if he'd just suggested they all cheer themselves up with a kitten-throwing competition.

'Maybe not.' Tyler's hand moved to his wallet instead. 'Look, could I at least give you something to make up for what happened? You could buy yourself—'

'There's no need to do that,' Mario cut in. 'Really. We can deal with this. Come on, Nat, let go of Mum now, she needs to get ready to go out.'

'Not with *him*.' Nat's body stiffened and his voice rose. 'Mummy, don't go with that man, I want you to stay here with me. I want my noonoo back!'

Lottie was clearly torn.

'Look, I think you should stay,' said Tyler. 'We'll have dinner another night. I wish there was something I could do to make things better, but I can't. I'll just leave you to it, OK?' It wouldn't have been the happiest of evenings anyway, under the circumstances. Keen to be out of the cottage, Tyler moved towards the door. 'And Nat, I really am sorry. If there's anything at all I can do—'

'G-go away,' Nat sobbed, his tear-stained face buried in Lottie's shoulder. 'Go h-home to America. And n-never come b-back.'

Chapter 13

'Computers are wonderful things,' said Freddie.

'They are.' Lottie nodded in agreement.

'But I hate using them.'

'I know you do. That's because you're too lazy to learn *how* to use them,' Lottie reminded him. 'If you'd just let me teach you—'

'No thanks.'

'But it's so—'

'Whoa, hold it right there.' Raising his hands and shaking his head, Freddie said firmly, 'All my life I've hated technical things. Machines of any kind. I don't know how my car works and I don't know how aeroplanes stay up in the air. But that's OK, because we have mechanics and pilots who do. Same with computers,' he went on before Lottie could interrupt him again. 'If I've got six months to live, the very last thing I'm going to waste my time on is learning how to fish the internet.'

'Surf.'

'I don't want to learn to surf either. Or waterski. I'm not bloody James Bond.'

'I meant—'

'No, let me explain,' said Freddie, leaving Lottie wondering if she was ever going to be allowed to finish a sentence again. 'I don't *want* to learn this computer malarkey and I'm not *going* to learn it, because you can do all that side of it for me. I'll ask the questions, you can find out the answers and then you give them to me. Simple.'

'Fine. I'll do my best. What kind of questions?' On the night Freddie had broken the news to her that he was dying, he'd mentioned that he had a plan but had refused to elaborate. Presumably this had something to do with it.

In reply, he drew a sheet of paper from his jacket pocket and unfolded it.

'I want to find these people.'

There were five names written in Freddie's distinctive scrawl. Lottie barely had time to glance at the first name on the list before he'd whisked it away again.

Finally she said, 'Am I allowed to ask why?'

'Because I want to see them again.'

'Who are they?'

'People who were important to me. People I liked.' Freddie half smiled. 'People who one way or another shaped my life. God, does that sound completely nauseating?'

'A bit. It's kind of like those schmaltzy soft-focus films you only ever get on daytime TV the week before Christmas.' Lottie secretly loved those kind of films.

'Well, if it's any consolation, I'm the one who wants to see them again,' said Freddie. 'There's no guarantee they're going to want to see me.'

'And do I get the back story? Are you going to tell me why they were so important?'

'Not yet.' Freddie looked amused. 'I thought I'd wait until you found them. That way, I know you'll be giving it your best shot.'

Lottie pulled a face; she was incurably nosy and he knew it. 'I'll need more details though. How old they are, where they've lived in the past, what kind of work they did.'

'I'll give you as much information as I can.'

'We still might not be able to track them down.'

'Let's see how we go, shall we?'

'If you don't tell me who they are,' Lottie said idly, 'I'll have to guess.'

Freddie grinned. 'Guess away, darling girl. You still won't get the truth until you've found them for me. Hey, cheer up. It might be easy.'

Lottie said frustratedly, 'It might be bloody hard.'

'Might be an idea to get cracking then. The sooner the better.' Amused, Freddie lit a cigar. 'You'll just have to hope I don't drop dead before you've finished.'

The first mystery person on the list was ridiculously easy to trace. It took less than five minutes. His name was Jeff Barrowcliffe and he owned and ran a motorcycle repair shop in Exmouth.

'That'll be him,' Freddie said confidently, peering over Lottie's shoulder at the computer screen. 'Jeff was always obsessed with motorbikes.'

In order to make sure, Lottie sent an email:

Dear Mr Barrowcliffe,
On behalf of a friend of mine who is trying to trace
someone with your name, may I ask if your date of birth is
26 December 1940 and if, many years ago, you lived in
Oxford?
Yours, L. Carlyle

Like magic, his reply popped into her inbox ninety seconds later:

Yes, that's me. Why?

'Old Jeff, knowing how to use a computer and send emails,' Freddie marvelled. 'Who'd have thought it?'

'Who'd have thought you wouldn't?' Lottie retorted. 'You big ignoramus.' She flexed her fingers like a pianist over the keys. 'Want me to tell him?'

'No. I'll give him a ring.' Freddie had already scribbled down the repair shop's phone number featured on the website. Walking out of the office, he added, 'In private.'

'Is he going to be pleased to hear from you?'

Freddie waggled his phone. 'That's what I'm about to find out.'

He was back ten minutes later, his expression infuriatingly enigmatic.

Fixing Freddie with a get-on-with-it look, Lottie said, '*So?*'

'So what?'

'Jeff Barrowcliffe. You have to tell me, remember? Are you going to meet him?'

Freddie nodded. 'I'm driving down to Exmouth this weekend.'

'You see?' Delighted, Lottie clapped her hands. 'So he was glad to hear from you! Why did you think he wouldn't be?'

'Because I took his motorbike,' said Freddie. 'His pride and joy.'

'Big deal.'

'And crashed it. Completely wrote it off.'

'Oo-er.'

'His girlfriend was on the back at the time. The one he was going to marry.'

'Freddie! Oh God, she didn't—?'

'No, Giselle didn't die. Cuts and bruises, that's all. Bloody lucky.'

Relieved, Lottie said, 'Well, that's all right then.'

'That's what Jeff thought. Until I stole her from him.' His smile crooked, Freddie looked at the stunned expression on Lottie's face. 'So there you go. And you always thought I was a nice person. Just goes to show, doesn't it? You never can tell.'

Out in the back garden of the Flying Pheasant, a game of boules was in progress. Making her way through the archway of honeysuckle, Lottie saw that Mario was on the boules court helping a girl with her throwing technique.

Lottie paused and watched them, unobserved, the ice cubes clinking in her orange juice. Having called into the pub on his way home from work, Mario was still wearing a smart white shirt open at the neck and his dark blue suit trousers. At a nearby table stood his pint of Guinness and car keys, while his suit jacket was flung over a chair. The girl he was currently assisting – slim and dark with her sunglasses perched on top of her head – was batting her mascaraed eyelashes and giggling like a seventeen-year-old as Mario showed her exactly how she should be throwing the silver boules. Giggling like a seventeen-year-old, Lottie observed, despite the fact that she was thirty if she was a day.

Honestly, what was it with Mario? Was the she's-a-female-so-I-must-flirt-with-her part of his brain destined to go through life never being switched off?

Actually, it probably wasn't in his brain. Taking a sip of her drink, noting the envious glances of the other girls in the group of boules players, Lottie made her way over to join them.

'Hey, Lottie.' Mario straightened up and greeted her with a cheery grin. The dark-haired girl turned to stare at her and Lottie found herself being instantly sized up as competition for Mario's attention.

Just for fun and to see the look on the girl's face, Lottie gave Mario a kiss on the cheek and said easily, 'Hi, darling. I'll play you next, shall I? You know you love it when I beat you.'

Mario laughed, quite aware of what she was doing.

The dark-haired girl said huffily, 'Who's she? Your girlfriend?'

'Actually,' said Lottie, 'I'm his wife.'

'*Actually*, ex-wife.' Mario rolled his eyes. 'Although she does still love to meddle in my life.'

'Someone has to.' Lottie was aware of the dark-haired girl's head swivelling between them like a Wimbledon umpire. 'Where's Amber?'

'Trekking through the Himalayas, where d'you think? Working at the salon,' said Mario. 'Some emergency came up and she won't be finished before eight, which is why I called in here for a quick drink. If that's all right with you.'

'Who's Amber?' The dark-haired girl's eyelashes were no longer batting.

Lottie looked at Mario, who sighed and said, 'My girlfriend.'

'Long-term girlfriend,' Lottie added helpfully.

'Thanks,' said Mario when the girl and her friends, all tossing their sleek hair like ponies, had abandoned the boules pit and disappeared inside the pub.

Happily, Lottie said, 'Don't mention it. We can have that game now if you like. Unless you're too scared I'll win.' Although having seen off the dark-haired girl she felt as if she'd already won.

'Too hot.' Mario reached for his drink. 'Anyway, I'm off after this one.'

'Just as well I came along. What would have happened with that girl if I hadn't turned up?'

'Nothing.' He looked wounded. 'She didn't know how to throw the boules, that was all. I was showing her how to do it properly.'

'What's that?' Lottie pointed skywards. 'Some kind of flying thing . . . ooh, look, it's got trotters.'

Mario shook his head. 'This is what I don't understand. You never used to nag me when we were married. But now that we *aren't* married any more, you take it up big-time. Where are the kids, anyway?'

'Karate Club until seven. And don't try and change the subject,' she ordered. 'They're the reason I'm nagging. Amber's no pushover, you know. You don't realise how lucky you are to have her. If you start messing her around, she'll chuck you. I *mean* it,' Lottie insisted, because the corners of Mario's mouth were beginning to curl up. 'You're not that irresistible.'

'You used to think I was.' His eyes had that wicked glint in them.

'Well, I was young and gullible then. And now we're divorced,' said Lottie. 'So what does that tell you?'

'That you're not so young any more, quite ancient in fact – ouch, don't *do* that.' Mario rubbed his shoulder. 'I haven't been messing around, OK? For your information, I've been completely faithful to Amber.'

So far, were the unspoken words that hung in the air.

'Well, just make sure you keep it that way. Because there's Nat and Ruby to consider,' said Lottie, 'and if you and Amber break up because she finds out you've been playing away, you'll have more than a thump on the shoulder to worry about. You have to think about them and—'

'I do think about them.' Mario looked hurt, although Lottie suspected that expecting him to stop flirting was like asking a cheetah to give up meat in favour of a lifetime of carrots and broccoli. 'I think about them all the time,' he went on. 'If you'd stop having a go at me and let me get a word in edgeways, I'd quite like to ask how Nat is.'

Nat and the noonoo. The noonoo that, tragically, was no more.

'Better.' Lottie sighed, because the last couple of days hadn't been easy and the first night had been positively traumatic, punctuated by Nat jerking awake at hourly intervals and breaking into heart-wrenching sobs. 'He's been more cheerful today. I told him Arnold Schwarzenegger lost his noonoo when he was seven.' She pulled a face. 'Now he wants to write to him because Arnie knows how he feels.'

Mario's expression softened. 'He'll be fine. Give him a couple of weeks and he'll be over it.'

'God, a couple of weeks.' Lottie envisaged the disturbed nights ahead.

'Hey, cheer up. I bet your new boss feels bad about it.'

'He flew back to the States this morning. Tying up loose ends. Won't be back until next week.'

Mario checked his watch and rose to his feet, abandoning his half-drunk

64

Guinness. 'Look, why don't the kids stay with me tonight? I'll pick them up from karate and take them home. We'll have pizza and play on the X-Box. How does that sound?'

Touched, Lottie said, 'Like maybe you're not all bad after all.'

'I have my moments.' Mario winked and jangled his car keys. 'I'll go now, and watch the karate class. No picking up strange men, OK? You have an early night.'

He could be wonderful when he wanted. Wildly infuriating at other times, of course, but generous and thoughtful when you most needed it. For a moment Lottie longed to be able to confide in him about Freddie's terrible illness but knew she mustn't, despite the fear that when news of it finally came out everyone would stare at her in disbelief and shout: 'But why didn't you *force* him to get treatment? What were you thinking of? You can't just stand back and let someone die!'

Anyway, she couldn't tell Mario. Freddie was adamant that he didn't want anyone to know before they absolutely had to and so far there were no outward physical signs that anything was amiss. In fact the prospect of meeting Jeff Barrowcliffe on Saturday had perked him up no end; he was—

'Are you all right?' Mario sounded concerned and Lottie realised she'd been gazing blankly at the boules pit where the central puck lay in the sand surrounded at varying distances by five silver boules. She gave herself a mental shake.

'I'm fine. Busy at work, that's all.'

'OK. Karate Club here I come. You take care of yourself.' Reaching across the wooden table, Mario planted a kiss on her cheek. 'I'm off.'

Chapter 14

It was Saturday lunchtime and Jojo was sunbathing in her Aunt Cress's back garden, reading the latest edition of *Phew!* magazine and listening to Avril Lavigne on her CD Walkman. Her parents were hosting a barbecue this afternoon and their house and garden were overrun with caterers, because it wasn't the kind of bash where you just invited all your friends and neighbours and had a jolly time, culminating in everyone doing the conga down the street. As usual, her mum and dad's party was an oppor-tunity to network and make important new business connections. Impressing potential clients would be the order of the day; actually enjoying yourself – heaven forbid! – simply didn't feature on the agenda. When Jojo had suggested coming over to Aunt Cress's house instead, her mother had heaved a visible sigh of relief and said, 'That's a wonderful idea, darling. It wouldn't be much fun for you here.'

Jojo had been glad to leave and Aunt Cress had been delighted to see her. The sun was out and once Jojo was settled on the sun lounger in her pale blue cropped top and blue and mauve striped shorts, Cressida had shot off to the supermarket for a speedy stock-up. She would be back by two o'clock, she had promised Jojo, with lemon meringue ice cream and chocolate popcorn and more raspberry freeze-pops than two humans could consume in a week. Although if their track record was anything to go by, the chances were they'd all be gone by tonight.

Jojo finished the article she was reading, about a girl who had a crush on her physics teacher. Avril Lavigne was getting repetitive and the rest of her CDs were in her bag in the kitchen. Chucking down the magazine and making her way into the house, it wasn't until Jojo unplugged herself from the Walkman that she heard the doorbell ringing.

By the time she opened the front door the callers had given up and were making their way down the street. Jojo, watching them from the doorstep, wondered if she should call out to them. Then, as if sensing she was there behind him, the man turned and saw her. He said something to the boy with him and came hurrying back, just as Jojo remembered she had opaque white sunblock across her nose. Hastily attempting to wipe it off only caused it to smear stickily all over the palms of her hands instead.

'Hi there.' The man's manner was friendly. 'We thought there was no one home. I was ringing the bell for ages.'

'Sorry, I was out in the garden.' Jojo pointed helpfully at her ears. 'Walkman.'

'Ah yes, my son's got one of those.' The man indicated the boy behind him, loitering by the gate. 'Mind you, he doesn't need to have it switched on to ignore me. Adam Ant.'

What? Puzzled, Jojo said, 'Is that his name?'

'No, no, I meant you looked like Adam Ant with that white stripe across your face.' The man shook his head. 'Sorry, you probably don't know who he is. Far too young to remember. Anyway, you must be Jojo. Is your . . . um, Cressida in?'

'She's gone shopping.' Since Aunt Cress didn't exactly have hordes of strange men hammering at her door, Jojo had a shrewd idea who this one might be. With renewed interest she said, 'Are you the flower man?'

It was his turn to look confused. 'Flower man?'

'The one who bought a card and gave Aunt Cress flowers the other day, to say thank you.'

'Oh right, of course.' His face cleared. 'Yes, that's me. So what time d'you think she might be back?'

'Around two-ish.' Eager to be helpful, Jojo said, 'Did you want to buy another card?'

'Well, not exactly.'

'What is it then? If you give me a message I'll make sure she gets it – hang on, there's a notepad by the phone.' Reaching for the pad and a purple felt-tip on the hall table, Jojo flipped over to a clean page and stood before him like a waitress. Expectantly she said, 'Fire away.'

'Um . . . maybe I'll just give her a ring later.' The man went a bit red and Jojo realised he was embarrassed. As he shuffled his feet and made a move to leave, it suddenly struck her that he'd come here to invite Aunt Cress out on a date. Crikey, she'd teased her about it after the incident with the flowers but she'd actually been right! Galvanised by this discovery – and by the problems page she'd just read in *Phew!* where a girl had written in miserably wanting to know why boys always said they'd ring you but never did – Jojo knew that whatever happened she mustn't let this one slip away.

'Or I could write down your number and Aunt Cress can ring you,' she said briskly, adopting the super-efficient tone her mother used on the phone whenever she had a major deal she was determined to clinch.

'Um . . .'

'Or we could fix a time for a meeting now. I know for a fact that Aunt Cress is free this evening.'

'Well . . .'

Desperate not to let him escape – even now, he was looking as if he might bottle out and make a dash for the gate – Jojo thrust the notebook and pen at his chest and blurted out, 'Here, just write down your name and phone number, then she'll—'

'Excuse me.' The man's son, still leaning against the front gate with his baseball cap pulled low over his eyes, drawled, 'Are you always this bossy?'

Jojo bristled.

His father turned and said, 'Donny, there's no need to be rude.'

'I'm not rude.' Donny shrugged sulkily. 'I just asked a reasonable question.'

'And I'm not bossy.' Jojo's jaw tightened.

He raised his eyebrows. 'Sure about that? Have you been listening to yourself?'

'Donny!'

Ignoring his father, Donny said, 'My dad came here to ask your aunt out on a date.'

'I know that,' Jojo retorted. 'I was just being helpful.'

'Helpful? You've scared the living daylights out of him. As if he wasn't finding it hard enough already.'

Bewildered, the boy's father looked at Jojo. 'You knew? *How* did you know?'

'Look.' Jojo heatedly addressed the boy at the gate. 'It's not my fault Aunt Cress isn't here. But what if your dad said he'd call back later and he didn't? All I was trying to do was get something organised, something he couldn't back out of.'

'My dad doesn't back out of anything, OK?'

'Except our garden path,' Jojo pointed out.

'Only because you were interrogating him.'

'Now, now.' Recovering himself, the boy's father clapped his hands. 'Stop it, you two.'

'She started it,' Donny muttered under his breath.

'Donny, please. Now let's start again.' Fixing Jojo with a look that was determined rather than panic-stricken the man said, 'Yes, I came round here to ask your Aunt Cress if she'd like to come out to dinner with me, but—'

'Tonight?'

'Whenever suits her best. But as she's not here, I'll call by later. And that's a promise.'

'Tonight would be fine.' Still determined to close the deal, Jojo said, 'In fact, tonight would be perfect. Do you know anywhere nice to eat around here?'

Bemused, the man said, 'Well, I daresay—'

'They do brilliant food at the Red Lion,' Jojo rattled on. 'In Gresham. It's only a couple of miles from here. I went there with my parents the other week. Wicked sticky toffee pudding. Shall I say you'll pick Aunt Cress up at seven o'clock?'

Stunned, the man said, 'But I haven't even asked her yet. She might not want to have dinner with me.'

'Oh, she will.' Jojo was confident on this score. 'Aunt Cress hasn't been out with anyone for ages. She doesn't have much luck with men.'

A flicker of a smile crossed his face. 'I'm sure she'd be thrilled to hear you saying that.'

'It's the truth.' Jojo decided he seemed nice. 'She always goes for the wrong kind. So, seven o'clock then. I'll make sure she's ready on time.'

He was definitely looking amused now. 'And what about you?'

'Me? Oh, I don't go for any kind at all. I'm only twelve.' Jojo's tone was matter-of-fact. 'Basically, all boys are dorks.'

At the gate, Donny snorted.

'I meant do you have anything planned for this evening, or would you like to join us?' The man briefly indicated Donny, who was now engrossed in picking clumps of moss off the garden wall. 'Make up the numbers. I'm sure Donny would enjoy having someone of his own age to chat to.'

Donny looked as though he'd enjoy it about as much as performing the Birdy Dance on stage during school assembly. Naked. Jojo couldn't imagine the dinner being much fun either. On the other hand, she was twelve years old which meant grown-ups being funny about leaving you on your own for longer than a couple of hours at a time. What if Aunt Cress refused to go out with Donny's dad because she didn't want to abandon her? The alternative would be going home and having to endure the barbeque from hell.

Really, there was no contest.

'OK, that'll be great. Thanks.' As Jojo beamed at him she heard another snort of derision emanating from Donny. 'We can be your chaperones.'

'That's settled then.' Looking a lot happier now, Donny's father said, 'I'll book the table for seven thirty.' Jovially he added, 'Sticky toffee puddings all round!'

'Tuh,' Donny muttered, scuffing his trainers against the pavement. 'Sticky toffee pudding's for *girls*.'

'You what?' Cressida dumped the supermarket carriers on the kitchen table and stared open-mouthed at Jojo.

'I've got you a date.' Jojo was looking unbelievably pleased with herself. *Aaarrgh.* 'Who with?'

'The man who brought you flowers.'

'What?'

'*Duh,* like they're queuing up.' Grinning, Jojo said, 'You know who I mean. And you're having dinner with him this evening at the Red Lion in Gresham.'

'*This* evening?' Aware that she was starting to sound like a parrot – and that her blood appeared to think her body was a Grand Prix circuit. Cressida slumped onto a kitchen chair. 'But . . . what about you? I can't just leave you here.'

'No need. I'm coming along too.' Jojo began unpacking the carriers, chucking bags of sweetcorn and potato rosti into the freezer.

Faintly, Cressida said, 'You are?'

'Me and Donny. The sulky brat, remember? We're coming along to keep an eye on you, make sure you two behave yourselves. Because even old people can get up to mischief, you know.' Jojo said this so airily she clearly didn't imagine for a moment that it could be true. 'Anyway, so that's what we're doing tonight. Isn't it great? I told you he fancied you. Can I have some of this ice cream?'

Cressida nodded, her mind a whirl. It was only a dinner date, for heaven's sake, and a foursome at that. But her foolish old heart was nevertheless skipping around like Bambi in her chest. Tom Turner had been in her thoughts far more than he should have been these past few days.

'Oh God, what shall I wear?' Cressida blurted out, realising that the more ancient and out of practice you were, the longer you needed in order to get ready for a date. 'My eyebrows need plucking and my hair's all horrible. If I put fake tan on my legs now, will they be brown in time?'

'In the olden days women used to put gravy browning on their legs because they couldn't afford stockings. We learned that at school.' Interestedly Jojo said, 'Did you used to do that?'

'That was during the war, you evil child. And I'm sure if I tried it I'd have dogs licking the stuff off my ankles. If I'm going out somewhere with a man,' Cressida protested, 'I'd prefer not to be chased by a slavering pack of hounds. Damn, and my white shirt's got a spaghetti stain on the front.'

Jojo had by this time abandoned the unpacking and was leaning against the fridge eating lemon meringue ice cream straight from the tub with a teaspoon. 'Aunt Cress, he's not exactly Johnny Depp. You'll be fine.'

'I know.' Cressida ran her fingers through her hair, which was badly in need of a cut. 'But I still don't want him to run away screaming.'

'He's not expecting a supermodel,' Jojo reasoned. 'Just do your best.'

So young, so cruel. So right.

'OK,' said Cressida.

'Anyway, don't panic. I've got just the thing.' Jojo looked pleased with herself. 'I'm going to lend you my copy of *Phew!*'

Chapter 15

Jojo's magazine contained a double-page spread entitled Top Twenty Megatastic Tips for that Hottest Ever Date!!! Having assiduously read it – with Jojo breathing over her shoulder – Cressida learned that when out with Tom she should wear a perky little cropped T-shirt to show off her flat stomach (if you've got it, flaunt it!!!), that she should pop her trainers in the washing machine the day before (because no one likes mingin' trainers!!!) and that she shouldn't give him a love bite. (Yeeurgh, sooo uncool!!!) She was also sternly instructed not to diss his mates, not to wear too much gloopy lipgloss (because no one wants to snog a girl and end up getting stuck to her!!!) and not to text other lush lads during the course of the date.

Then, of course, there was: Laugh at his jokes, but not *too* loudly (don't want him to think you're a hyena!!!); Make sure you keep any spare tampons safely tucked away in the bottom of your bag (so they don't accidentally fall out and roll across the floor – aaarrgh!!!); and finally, Ration those cans of fizzy Coke – whatever you do, don't burp in his face!!!

Well, thought Cressida, thank heavens for teenage magazines. Imagine the hideous faux pas she might have made if it wasn't for *Phew!*

'Now, drinks.' In the bar of the Red Lion, Tom rubbed his hands together and turned to Cressida. 'What'll you have?'

'A Coke please,' Cressida said innocently, catching Jojo's eye and making her shake her head in despair. 'Actually I won't. Do you know, I'd love a glass of white wine.'

She saw Jojo relax.

'Excellent idea. Donny?'

'Coke.'

'Jojo?'

'Thanks.' Jojo beamed at him. 'I'll have a Coke too.'

'What did you have to do that for?' Donny frowned. 'It's boring out here.'

Jojo rolled her eyes and wondered how he could be so thick. As soon as their drinks had arrived she had insisted on dragging Donny out into the pub garden. 'It's boring in there as well. Anyway, I was being subtle. If we sit in there with them, your dad will ask me if I'm enjoying school and what my favourite lessons are, blah blah, and Aunt Cress will try and talk to you about your hobbies and what you want to do when you leave school, because they'll feel obliged to make polite conversation. It's what grown-ups do when kids are around. But all they really want is to talk to each other, so why get in their way? If we're out here we can do what we want.'

'And we don't have to answer a load of dumb questions.' Donny nodded, reluctantly acknowledging that this made sense, then looked at her from under the peak of his baseball cap. 'But there isn't anything to do out here.' With a tinge of sarcasm he added, 'Unless you want to play on the kids' climbing frame.'

'No thanks. You might fall off and start crying.' Jojo took a glug of Coke. 'We could always talk to each other.'

He glowered. 'What about?'

'Well *I* don't know, do I? But surely it wouldn't kill you to make an effort.' Losing patience, Jojo said, 'I mean, you live in Newcastle. It's not as if any of your friends are going to turn up here and catch you talking to a girl.'

'I'm not scared of talking to girls.'

'No? You're not making a great job of it so far, are you?'

Donny's lip curled. 'Maybe it depends on the girl.'

Jojo was sorely tempted to guzzle down the rest of her Coke and burp in his face. God, was it any wonder she wasn't interested in boys if this is what they were like?

'Look,' she said crossly, 'I'm not trying to chat you up. I don't fancy you. I just thought we could give your dad and my aunt a bit of time alone together, that's all.'

'Yeah yeah.' Donny exhaled noisily. 'But really, what's the point? We're down here on holiday. Next week we'll be back in Newcastle.'

'So? They like each other. What's wrong with that?' Irritated by his attitude Jojo said, 'Haven't you ever heard of a holiday romance?'

The R-word caused Donny to flinch and avert his head in disgust as if she'd just spat at him. Which, right now, was quite a tempting idea.

'Look,' Jojo tried again, 'I know nothing's going to come of it because you live so far away, but there's no reason why they can't see each other a couple of times and leave it at that. Think of it as a practice run. Aunt Cress has had really bad luck with men, so it makes a change to see her with someone decent. And your dad's probably out of practice too.' She paused, then said, 'Or is that the problem? You don't want him to see anyone at all?'

73

Donny looked down at his trainers. Finally he said, 'It's not that. It just feels a bit funny, that's all. My mum walked out on us two years ago.'

'I know. Aunt Cress told me.'

'And I know he'll probably get married again one day, but what if he chooses someone I hate? I mean, it's not like I'll have any say in the matter, is it? My friend Greg's parents got divorced and they both remarried, and Greg can't stand his stepmother *or* his stepfather.'

Feeling sorry for him Jojo said, 'But your dad might marry someone you do like. It doesn't always have to be bad. I know it's the wrong way round, but my dad used to be married to Aunt Cress and I love her to bits.'

'Your dad used to be married to her? What, before you were born?' Donny frowned, working it out. 'That's weird.'

'It isn't weird. She's brilliant. I'm lucky,' Jojo insisted.

Donny picked at the loose threads around a rip in his baggy jeans. 'I bet I wouldn't be lucky, I'm never—'

'Smile!'

'What?' Looking up, he saw that Jojo was beaming at him like a lunatic. 'Look happy,' Jojo instructed, her beam unwavering. 'Aunt Cress is looking out of the window, checking up on us. Just make out we're fine.'

'Why?'

'Honestly, you're so thick. Because then they can relax and enjoy themselves without having to worry about us.'

'Jesus, I wish I'd brought my GameBoy,' Donny grumbled, although he did attempt something that from a distance would pass as a grin. 'You are seriously weird.'

'They're fine. Laughing and chatting away together like old friends,' Cressida cheerfully announced.

'Really?' Tom looked relieved.

'Getting on like a house on fire. There, you see? All that worry for nothing. They're probably far happier being out in the garden than stuck in here with the old fogeys. Not that you're an old fogey,' Cressida said hastily as Tom's eyebrows rose.

He smiled. 'Neither are you.'

'Although I'm sure Donny and Jojo think we are.'

'Oh well, goes without saying. As far as they're concerned anyone over twenty-five is over the hill.'

Cressida didn't think of herself as an old fogey, not *quite*, but it was still much nicer being inside the pub, sitting at a pretty table in the restaurant section where the lighting was shaded and flattering to the complexion. The candles flickering on the table between them cast a further romantic glow. As she settled herself back down she felt a matching warm glow in her stomach from the wine. Tom looked nicely unwrinkly too. In fact he looked nice full stop. And the cooking smells wafting through from the kitchen were mouth-watering.

'Well, I'm glad we came here. You made a good choice,' Cressida said happily.

'Don't thank me, thank Jojo. It was all her idea.' Tom grinned. 'Not backwards in coming forwards, that one. She told me what time to pick you up and where to bring you. I just did as I was told.'

'Then I'm glad about that too. Unless you're hating every minute.'

'Now why would I be doing that? I'm enjoying this holiday more than I ever imagined.' Leaning closer he confided, 'Just think, if it hadn't been my mother's birthday this week we'd never have met.'

Feeling deliciously reckless and the teeniest bit light-headed, Cressida raised her glass and almost landed the lacy sleeve of her shirt in the flickering red candle. 'In that case, here's to your mother.'

'My mother.' Clinking his glass against hers, Tom said warmly, 'And to you.'

'To me.' Cressida clinked again. 'And to *you*.' As she gazed into his eyes she wished with all her heart he didn't have to live so far away. Then she told herself that she really mustn't drink any more wine on an empty stomach, because this was definitely one of those occasions when you didn't want to make a prat of yourself. 'Do you think we should order some food? Then you can tell me all about Newcastle.'

Tom looked amused. 'It's not that exotic.'

It's got you, Cressida thought with the kind of squirly excitement she hadn't felt since she was a teenager. That's exotic enough for me.

'Here she comes,' said Jojo as Aunt Cress appeared in the garden, shielding her eyes from the setting sun and waving a couple of menus in greeting.

'At last,' Donny muttered. 'I'm starving. We've been out here an *hour*.'

'Stop your whingeing. And *smile*.' Jojo gave him a kick under the wooden table and promptly received a harder kick in return. 'Hi, Aunt Cress. How's it going?'

'Oh, we're fine, darling, just fine.' Beaming back at them, Aunt Cress handed each of them a menu. 'We're just ordering the food. And are you two OK?'

'Great!' Having visited the Red Lion before, Jojo said promptly, 'I'll have the chicken fajitas please. And sticky toffee pudding. How about you, Donny?'

He scanned the menu at the speed of light. 'Burger and fries, please.'

'Don't have that,' Jojo complained. 'It's boring. Have the chicken fajitas.'

'I like burger and fries. I can have what I want, can't I?'

'Of course you can.' Aunt Cress bent down and confided, 'Just ignore Jojo, she always thinks she knows best. And what pudding would you like? Sticky toffee?'

'Um . . .' Donny glanced at Jojo who was ostentatiously zipping her mouth shut. Finally he sighed and said, 'OK.'

'And could we eat out here?' said Jojo. 'Look, other people are. But you two can stay inside if you'd rather.'

'That's absolutely fine! I'll tell the waiter to bring yours out when it's ready. It's so nice,' Aunt Cress went on brightly, 'to see the two of you getting on so well. In fact,' she caught Donny's eye, 'your dad's suggested we might all go to Longleat tomorrow! How does that sound?'

Jojo gave a whoop of joy. Donny, next to her, grimaced slightly then nodded and forced a smile.

Clearly delighted, Aunt Cress said, 'That's all sorted then! Right, I'd better get back inside, put these orders in.'

'That's all I need,' muttered Donny when they were alone again. 'Playing happy families.'

'Better than playing unhappy families,' Jojo retorted. Then she gave him a nudge. 'Come on, cheer up. It'll be fun.'

'A stately home.' Donny let out a low groan. 'All day. With *you*.'

'Longleat's brilliant.' Enjoying teasing him − actually, enjoying *annoying* him − Jojo said, 'And the lions *love* it when stroppy teenage boys accidentally get pushed out of cars right in front of them.' She raised her arms high and spread her fingers like claws. 'Rrrraaaaagggh!'

Donny looked at her, his thin face expressionless. Then he lowered his forehead and slowly banged it three times against the surface of the wooden table. '*Oh God.*'

Chapter 16

Freddie set off down the M5 after breakfast on Sunday morning. If the traffic ran smoothly he'd reach Exmouth in a couple of hours. Buzzing down the car window, he lit a cigar and determinedly ignored the dull persistent headache that these days settled over him each morning like a lead helmet. Outside the car, the surrounding countryside was wreathed in mist and the sun was struggling to break through. He was looking forward to seeing Jeff again, but apprehensive as well. Jeff had been taciturn on the phone, clearly taken aback at hearing a voice from the past – and a not particularly welcome voice at that.

Well, that was understandable. But Freddie hoped they could overcome the awkwardness, put the bad bits behind them and recapture at least some semblance of their childhood friendship. Then, the bond between them had seemed unbreakable. That they wouldn't be close for the rest of their lives was out of the question. But one fateful night was all it had taken to slash that bond, and after that their lives had changed forever. Jeff had suffered then, without a doubt. But had he continued to suffer for the last forty years? Freddie didn't know the answer and deliberately hadn't asked the question during their brief conversation on the phone.

Michael Wood service station was coming up and Freddie briefly considered stopping for a coffee and a couple more Ibuprofen. No, he wanted to get on with the journey, reach Exmouth and see Jeff again. He hadn't asked the all-important question the other day, but he was about to find out.

Of course, Jeff had always had a hot temper. He might be about to find out the hard way.

Then again, Freddie thought, maybe I deserve it.

'He's drunk.' Giselle had gestured in disgust. 'Drunk as a skunk. He can't even walk, let alone ride that bike home tonight. But he needs it for work tomorrow, and if Derek gives Jeff a lift, that leaves the bike here and me with no way of getting home. It's eight *miles*,' she concluded despairingly. 'I can't walk all that way on my own.'

Poor Giselle, she was at the end of her tether and who could blame her?

Freddie knew only too well that this wasn't the first time Jeff had got blotto and caused problems. They had grown up living next door to each other in Oxford and were best friends, but Jeff didn't do himself any favours when he embarked without warning on one of his periodic drinking sprees.

Tonight they had all come out to a party in Abingdon, held at a pub with a reputation for lock-ins. Freddie had got a lift with Derek, five of them having crammed into Derek's black Morris Minor. Jeff and Giselle had arrived on Jeff's motorbike, his prized Norton 350.

And now Jeff was incapable of riding it home.

Freddie gazed at Giselle, in her cherry-red top and full red and white spotted skirt. Her dark hair was tied back in a high ponytail and she was looking worried, hardly surprisingly as he knew she too had to be at work tomorrow morning. What's more, it was gone midnight already and her parents were the anxious kind who waited up for their beloved eighteen-year-old daughter to come home. None of them had enough money to pay for a taxi.

Luckily a taxi wasn't needed.

'Jeff can go back with Derek and the others. I'll take his bike home and drop you off on the way. How about that?'

'Would you?' Giselle's eyes lit up with relief. 'Oh Freddie, that's great. My mum'd go mad if I was late. You've saved my life.'

Famous last words.

Jeff was duly carried out of the pub and poured into the passenger seat of Derek's Morris Minor.

'And don't you dare throw up in my car,' Derek ordered as Jeff's head lolled slackly against the headrest.

'Why does he do it?' Giselle said helplessly as the car's tail lights disappeared from view. 'He's so lovely the rest of the time. When he isn't drinking, he's perfect. Then every couple of months he just goes off on a complete bender. It's so stupid and pointless.'

It was, but Freddie couldn't bring himself to admit it. Jeff was Jeff and he wasn't going to be disloyal towards his best friend. Instead he said with forced cheerfulness, 'He'll be fine in the morning. Everyone has a few too many every now and again. Come on, let's get you home.'

They were heading back to Oxford along the deserted A34 when a fox darted into the road ahead of them. Braking violently and swerving to avoid the animal, Freddie felt the back wheel of the powerful Norton begin to slide sideways beneath him. After that it all seemed to happen in slow motion. Giselle's arms tightened convulsively round his waist, he heard her scream as he lost control of the bike and the next thing he knew they were careering towards a wall.

Impact was sudden, noisy and brutal. Giselle, catapulted off the back of the bike, landed with a sickening thud on the other side of the wall. By some miracle Freddie found himself flung sideways onto the grass verge. Pain shot through every inch of his body but he told himself that at least he could still feel pain, which was better than not feeling it. Stumbling to his feet, he made his way dazedly over to the drystone wall and croaked, 'Giselle? Are you all right?'

Nothing. Just an eerie silence punctuated by the hiss of steam escaping from the engine of the Norton. Somehow in the pitch darkness Freddie managed to clamber over the wall into the field where she lay. Finally he heard her gasp, followed by the rustle of her stiff taffeta petticoat as she struggled to sit up.

'Giselle! Oh God . . .'

'I'm OK. I think. I landed on some rocks. My leg hurts,' Giselle whispered, her breath catching in her throat. 'And my back.'

When Freddie touched her arm he found it sticky with blood and his heart turned over. He had almost killed the girl he loved, the girl who was engaged to be married to his closest friend. As he reached for her hand and squeezed it he felt the tiny engagement ring digging into his clammy palm. 'Oh God, what have I done?'

'Written off Jeff's bike by the sound of things.' Giselle murmured the words with difficulty as the ominous hissing noise intensified. 'He's not going to be thrilled with you.'

Shortly afterwards Freddie flagged down a passing motorist who took them both to the casualty department at the Radcliffe Infirmary. While they were waiting to be seen by the doctor, Giselle told Freddie over and over again that it wasn't his fault, he hadn't done anything wrong. With tears in his eyes Freddie shook his head and said, 'I couldn't bear it if anything happened to you.'

The next thing he knew, right there in the middle of the casualty department with blood trickling down her arms and her cherry-red top muddy and torn, Giselle was kissing him. When the kiss finally ended she held his face gently between her hands, saw the long-hidden truth in his eyes and whispered, 'Oh Freddie, don't you see? It already has.'

Then Giselle's anxious parents arrived and she introduced Freddie to them, explaining that he had swerved to avoid a fox and hadn't been to blame for the accident. Giselle's father, regarding Freddie grimly for several seconds, said curtly, 'And where's lover-boy?'

'He got a lift home with Derek.' Giselle's tone was calm.

'You mean he was off his trolley again.'

'Yes. And I'm not going to be marrying him either.' Glancing down at the blood-spattered cluster of diamond chips on her left hand, Giselle announced, 'The engagement's off.'

Her mother burst into tears of relief.

'Well, thank Christ for that,' her father retorted. 'He was never good enough for you.'

Giselle gazed up at Freddie and his heart expanded with love and the urge to protect her forever from idiots like Jeff. Then, turning to face her father, Giselle slipped her hand into Freddie's and said simply, 'No, he wasn't. But I know a man who is.'

That was how it had happened. Overnight Freddie's life had changed. Having done such an excellent job of concealing his true feelings for Giselle during the course of the last eight months, he now found himself faced with the prospect of announcing them to the world in general and Jeff in particular. As they were leaving the casualty department at three thirty that morning, stitched up and bandaged like a couple of mummies, Giselle said, 'I'll tell Jeff today, OK? That it's all over between us and from now on I'm with you.'

Freddie didn't like to wonder whether he was a man or a mouse, but he heard himself saying, 'Or maybe we should wait a bit.'

'Why?'

'Well, you know.' He gestured awkwardly. 'To spare Jeff's feelings.' Plus the fact that Jeff had a famously volatile temper.

'It's his own fault. He'll just have to put up with it.' Giselle had evidently made up her mind. 'I'm not going to lie to him, Freddie. That's not the kind of person I am.'

'Right.' Freddie nodded and swallowed hard. Tomorrow Jeff would find out that his fiancée had chucked him and that his beloved 1959 Norton Model 50 350 was a write-off.

He would also discover who Giselle had left him *for*.

Freddie didn't sleep terribly well that night.

Jerked out of his reverie by the looming blue motorway sign announcing that the next junction was the one he needed to turn off, Freddie indicated left and pulled in behind a swaying caravan. Exeter, then Exmouth, then Jeff's house on the road to Sandy Bay. He'd be there in thirty minutes.

Freddie touched his nose, wondering if Jeff still packed a bone-crunching left hook.

Chapter 17

Lottie was having a wonderful time in the supermarket revelling in the air-conditioning and filling her trolley with all manner of tempting food. The fifteen-minute drive from Hestacombe had been hot and sticky but in here the air was blissfully cool. Best of all, having forgone breakfast this morning in favour of an hour of paperwork in the office before setting out, the fact that her stomach was empty and she was ravenous had rendered practically everything in the store irresistible.

Well, apart from the cat food.

Now, lustfully eyeing trays of just-baked croissants and pain au chocolat, she was wondering how many of each to buy – would half a dozen be enough? – when out of the corner of her eye she became aware that she was being watched. Turning, Lottie saw a man gazing at her with undisguised amusement. He was tall and rangy, wearing a faded denim shirt over baggy khaki shorts and leaning against an empty trolley. His hair was surfer's blond, his teeth white and his bare feet shoved into a pair of battered turquoise flip-flops, yet the watch on his tanned wrist was unmistakably expensive.

Which probably meant he was a mugger.

Turning back, inwardly enjoying the attention, Lottie peeled open two bags and helped herself to three croissants and three . . . no, four . . . OK, five pains au chocolat. It made quite a change to see such a good-looking man in the bread section of the supermarket at eleven fifteen on a Sunday morning. Was he still looking at her? Why was his shopping trolley empty? Was he waiting for his wife and kids who were busy round the corner in fruit and veg?

Glad she was wearing her pink spindly-strapped dress and had bothered to brush her hair this morning, Lottie chucked the pastries into her trolley then super-casually swung it round so she could catch the good-looking blond stranger's eye again and maybe acknowledge his interest with a brief super-casual smile of her own.

Except he was gone; neither he nor his trolley anywhere in sight. The pair of them had vanished, which wasn't exactly flattering. So much for getting her hopes up.

Bugger.

Twenty minutes later Lottie was in the wines and spirits section engrossed in the labels on the special offers. The trouble was, the labels all tended to waffle on about fruity undertones this and refreshingly zesty that, when what you really wanted was one that said: OK, I know I'm only £2.99 but I promise I won't be bitter or manky or strip the top layer off your teeth.

But since none of them did say that, Lottie was in the process of narrowing them down by other methods. The one in her left hand claimed to be spicy, peppery and red, while the one in her right hand claimed to be crisp, summery and white. This one would probably win because it came in a cobalt-blue bottle with a pretty silver label, plus it had been reduced by an enticing £1.50 whereas the other was only down by—

'Don't do it,' said a voice behind her, and Lottie almost dropped both bottles. She knew at once who the voice belonged to.

When she swung round he was shaking his head at her. 'You deserve better than that.'

'I know.' Lottie tried not to breathe too quickly but it wasn't so easy when your heart was going this fast. 'The trouble is, my bank manager might not agree.'

'Cheap wine is a false economy. Better one decent bottle than three nasty ones.'

'I'll remember that when I've won the lottery.' She put the blue bottle with the silver label into her trolley and the other one back on the shelf. The man promptly reached past her and swapped them round.

'And never *ever* buy wine because it comes in a pretty bottle.' He looked pained. 'That means it's bound to be horrendous.'

'You've lost your trolley,' Lottie pointed out, having observed that he was unencumbered.

'It's very badly trained. Should really keep it on a lead.' He put his fingers in his mouth and whistled, startling the other customers in the vicinity.

Amused, Lottie said, 'Will it come to heel?'

'Oh, I should think so. Sooner or later, when it's finished chasing after all the other trolleys . . . ah, see what I mean?' He tilted his head as a trolley came skittering round the corner of the aisle, steered by a skinny Knightsbridge blonde in a crisp blue shirt with a turned-up collar, immaculately pressed jeans and full make-up.

Ah. Bugger again.

'Seb, there you are,' the blonde chided. 'We've already done this aisle. Now, just the cocktail sticks and we'll be finished. I promised Mummy we'd be back by twelve.'

Lottie was doing her best not to boggle at the trolley the blonde was pushing. There had to be sixty bottles of champagne in there. Precariously balanced on top of the bottles were packets and packets of smoked salmon and Parma ham, boxes of quails' eggs and half a dozen cartons of freshly squeezed orange juice.

'And this is bloody heavy,' the girl chirped, shoving the trolley at Seb. 'You can jolly well push.'

'Party,' Seb drawled, Lottie's boggling not having gone unnoticed. 'It's Tiffany's birthday today.'

Automatically Lottie said, 'Happy birthday.'

Tiffany heaved a harassed sigh. 'It will be, when we get out of this bloody place.'

'It's a Breakfast at Tiffany's party,' Seb went on, indicating the contents of the trolley. 'Only it doesn't start until three, so it's Breakfast at Tiffany's in the Afternoon.'

'Why not?' Lottie flashed them both a bright smile and prepared to move off.

'Actually,' Seb put out a hand to stop her, 'you could come along. If you're not doing anything else this afternoon, we'd love to—'

'Thanks, but I'm busy.' This was true, she would be swimming in the lake with Ruby and Nat, but the look of alarm in Tiffany's perfectly made-up eyes hadn't escaped Lottie. Briskly reversing her trolley and wishing it didn't contain cans of beans, cartoon pasta shapes in tomato sauce and a mega-pack of loo rolls she said, 'Have a good time anyway. Bye.'

And headed for the checkouts as casually as if being invited to a glam-orous party by a complete stranger in a supermarket was the kind of thing that happened to her all the time.

'Honestly, Seb, you're so bloody thoughtless. All you ever think about is yourself.' Tiffany's voice behind her was high-pitched, tinged with irri-tation and carried like nobody's business. 'It's *my* party, OK? You can't just go inviting people willy-nilly. I mean, who *is* she?'

Lottie slowed, she couldn't help herself.

'Not the foggiest.' Unperturbed Seb drawled, 'But she's got a sensational arse.'

As always, Lottie managed to choose the checkout that looked as if it would be the quickest but turned out to be the slowest. She was still packing her cans of Batman pasta shapes and packets of biscuits into carriers when she glanced up and saw Seb and Tiffany leaving the store, because of course couples like them always magically chose the right checkout. Tuh, they probably had a chauffeur-driven limo waiting outside to whisk them home.

'Got your saver card?' said the bored cashier.

'Hang on, yep, here it is.' Lottie bet that people like Seb and Tiffany didn't bother with saver cards either. When you were that posh, no doubt a platinum Amex did nicely.

Five minutes later she was out in the car park unloading her trolley when another car drew up behind her.

'Hey.'

Straightening up and thinking that he'd just been getting a peerless view of her sensational backside, Lottie turned to see Seb behind the wheel of a filthy green Volkswagen Golf with Tiffany next to him in the passenger seat.

So much for the chauffeur-driven limo.

'Hey.' Lottie wondered if he was planning to persuade her to change her mind and come along to the party after all. Her gaze flickered in the direction of Tiffany's left hand to see if there were any significant rings on view.

Spotting the glance, Seb said, 'She's my sister.'

'Worse luck.' Tiffany rolled her eyes.

Maybe for you, thought Lottie, inwardly fizzing with anticipation. It was no good, she still couldn't go to their party but he'd stopped his car which meant he was definitely interested. If he asked for her phone number, she could scribble it on the back of his hand with one of Ruby's felt-tip pens and then he could ring her and—

'Here. Don't drink that red crap.' Cutting into her excited thoughts, Seb thrust a bottle of Veuve Cliquot through the Golf's open window. 'Drink something decent for a change.'

Taken by surprise – and because he was dangling the bottle perilously by two fingers – Lottie reached out and grabbed it before it could slip to the ground. 'Why?'

'Because I like your eyes.'

'And my bum.'

He laughed. 'That too.'

'Well, thanks.' Lottie waited for him to ask for her number.

'My pleasure. Enjoy it. Bye.'

Flabbergasted, she watched the dusty Golf shoot out of the car park. He'd gone. *Gone!* This wasn't supposed to happen, unless . . .

Feverishly Lottie scrutinised the bottle, telling herself that of course he must have scribbled his phone number somewhere on the label so she could ring and thank him properly. But, unbelievably, he hadn't. There was nothing. He'd just handed over a bottle of rather expensive champagne and driven off, leaving her with no way of contacting him or even discovering who he was.

Why? Why would he do that?

More to the point, *bugger.*

Chapter 18

Jeff Barrowcliffe lived in a nineteen-thirties bungalow painted sky blue and adorned with bright hanging baskets and window boxes. As Freddie clicked open the front gate he saw Jeff on the driveway at the side of the bungalow, tinkering with the engine of a motorbike. It was ridiculous to say he hadn't changed a bit, but he was still instantly recognisable – albeit bald, wirier and more wrinkled.

Straightening up, Jeff wiped his hands on an oily rag and waited for Freddie to reach him. They'd never hugged each other in their lives – back in the fifties hugging was strictly for poofters – and Freddie wasn't sure he had the courage to give it a go now. Thankfully, by clutching the oily rag in front of him, Jeff ensured this wasn't an option.

'Jeff. It's good to see you again.'

'You too. Took me back the other day, hearing from you out of the blue like that.' Rubbing a grimy hand over his tanned head, Jeff said, 'Still don't know why you called.'

'Curiosity, I suppose. We're all getting on a bit now,' Freddie shrugged, 'and none of us is going to live forever. I just wanted to catch up with people from the past, find out what happened to my old friends.'

Jeff said drily, 'Lost touch with a fair few of them then, have you?'

Since he deserved the jibe, Freddie simply nodded. 'Yes.' Then he said, 'The other reason I'm here is to apologise.'

'The last time I saw you, you were flat on your back with blood running down your face. And I had bruised knuckles.' There was a glimmer of a smile on Jeff's own face as he recalled the occasion. 'Do I have to apologise as well?'

'No. I deserved it.' The memory of that day was etched indelibly in Freddie's mind. Giselle had told Jeff about the incident the night before, then had gone on to announce that their engagement was off and from now on she and Freddie were an item. Freddie, chain-smoking in his bedroom, had heard the sounds of arguing coming from Jeff's house next door. The next thing he knew, Jeff was hammering on his front door demanding to see him and threatening to punch his lights out, and Freddie had gone downstairs to face him. Under the circumstances, it had seemed the least he could do.

That was the last any of them had seen of Jeff. He had packed a ruck-sack, left Oxford that same night and joined the army.

In a way it had been a relief.

'Coming in for a cup of tea?' Jeff said now.

'I'd love that.' Freddie nodded. There was so much to catch up on, he barely knew where to start. Prompted by the abundance of hanging baskets he said, 'Are you married?'

'Oh yes. Thirty-three years, two daughters, four grandkids. The wife's not here today.' As he led the way into the bungalow Jeff said over his shoulder, 'Thought it best to keep her out of the way while you're around. Wouldn't want you running off with her.'

Freddie saw that he was joking and relaxed. 'Those days are long gone.'

'How about you then?' In the tidy, newly decorated green and white kitchen Jeff set about making a proper, old-fashioned pot of tea. 'Did you end up getting married too?'

'Yes.' Freddie nodded, then said drily, 'But not to Giselle.'

'So you got your nose broken for nothing.'

'We just weren't right for each other. Well, we were only kids. Twenty years old – everyone makes mistakes. Thanks.' Freddie took the cup of tea Jeff was offering him and reached for the sugar bowl.

'They do that right enough.' Nodding in agreement, Jeff lit a cigarette. 'And now we've got our kids making mistakes of their own. Still, nothing we can do to stop them, is there? That's what life's all about.'

'We didn't have children. It never happened.' Freddie found himself envying Jeff his family, wishing he could meet them. 'But I married the most wonderful girl. We were so very happy.' A lump materialised in his throat and he willed himself to get a grip. 'I was a lucky man. Almost forty years of marriage before she died. Couldn't have asked for a better wife.'

'So we ended up with the right ones in the end,' said Jeff. 'I'm sorry your wife died. How long ago?'

'Four years.'

'You've still got your own hair and teeth. Might meet someone else.'

'That won't happen.' Freddie had no intention of telling Jeff about his illness; the last thing he was here for was sympathy. But talking about Mary had affected him more than he'd expected. Damn, he was getting soft in his old age.

Evidently having noticed that he was struggling to control his emotions, Jeff said, 'How about a drop of brandy in that tea?'

Freddie nodded. 'Sorry. Sometimes it catches you off guard. Ridiculous.' Breathing out slowly, he watched as Jeff fetched a bottle of cognac from one of the kitchen cupboards and sloshed a generous measure into his cup. 'Aren't you having one?'

Jeff returned the bottle to the cupboard and sat back down.

'Not for me. I gave up the drink.'

'Good grief.' Freddie was instantly diverted; this was something he could never imagine doing. 'Really? When?'

'Two years after I last saw you. Mind you, I drank twenty years' worth in that time.' Jeff spoke with characteristic bluntness. 'Of course that was to get over the fact that Giselle had left me for you, and that she'd told me I drank too much. Ha, I thought, you reckon *this* is too much? I can drink *plenty* more than that.'

'In the army?'

'Bloody hell, especially in the army. Then I got myself another girl-friend and she ended up leaving me too. Said I was a drunken waste of space. Funnily enough, so did the next one and the one after that.' Pausing to drink his tea and take another drag on his cigarette, Jeff said, 'In the end, I suppose it just hit me one morning that they might be right. Then again, it may have helped that I'd woken up in a hedge in someone's garden with their dog peeing on my best coat.'

'So you stopped? Just like that?'

'There and then. Just like that. So, ironically, I don't even know what my last alcoholic drink was or where I drank it. But I realised I probably wouldn't see forty if I carried on the way I'd been going. So I stuck at it and managed to get myself sorted out. I'm not saying it was easy, but I did it in the end. And life's been good to me. I'm still here and I'm happy. Can't ask for more than that, can you?'

'And there was me, wondering if I'd ruined it.' For Freddie, the relief was tremendous.

'You weren't my favourite person for a while. To put it mildly. But that's all in the past now,' said Jeff.

'Good. You don't know how glad I am to hear it.' Closure, Freddie realised. This was what he'd so badly needed. Feeling better than he had in weeks, he smiled across the table at the friend he hadn't seen for so many years. 'Now, I hope you'll let me take you out to lunch.'

'It's been a great day.' Tired but happy, Freddie hadn't been able to resist calling into Piper's Cottage on his way home that evening. Lottie, who had just finished putting Nat and Ruby to bed, gave him a hug and opened the bottle of Veuve Cliquot. Eyeing it with astonishment he said, 'I say, look at this. Been shoplifting again, darling?'

Honestly, just because she'd once happened to walk out of Top Shop with a purple and black zebra-print bra and pants set hooked to the back

87

of her sweater. They hadn't even been her size, but it hadn't stopped Mario branding her the Naughty Knicker-nicker and gleefully warning everyone in Hestacombe to keep an eye on their credit cards.

'Shop-flirting, actually. I met this rather gorgeous chap in the super-market. Then he came up to me in the car park afterwards and I thought he was going to ask me out.' Frustratedly Lottie said, 'But he didn't! He gave me this bottle instead and just − *zoooom* − drove off.'

'His loss, darling. Our gain. Anyway, let me tell you about Jeff.'

Far too enthralled by his own successful day to be remotely interested in her anonymous champagne-wielding admirer, Freddie launched into how he and Jeff had gone to lunch together, talked non-stop about every-thing under the sun and caught up with each other's lives. Lottie learned about Jeff's alcoholism, about his beloved grandchildren and − more than she needed to know, frankly − about his motorcycle repair business. All in all, the reunion had been a stupendous success and the difference in Freddie was heart-warming.

When the champagne was finished, Lottie said, 'So who are we going to look for next?'

Freddie's eyes twinkled. 'Do you even have to ask?'

'Giselle?'

He nodded. 'Giselle.'

Consumed with curiosity − OK, downright *nosiness* − there was some-thing else Lottie was desperate to know. 'You were in love with her. But you broke up. Why?'

'Ah well. Something happened,' said Freddie.

Well, obviously it had.

'*What* happened?'

Freddie rose to his feet, collected his car keys and bent to kiss Lottie's cheek. 'I'm afraid I was a bad boy. Again.'

'If you don't tell me,' said Lottie, 'I won't find her for you.'

He smiled. 'I broke Giselle's heart. She thought I was about to propose, and I finished with her instead.'

'Why?'

Freddie turned in the doorway. 'Because I'd fallen head over heels in love with someone else.'

Chapter 19

It was September the first and Amber was off to St Tropez with her friend Mandy. Mario, who had driven over to Tetbury straight from work, sat on the bed in her tiny flat above the hairdressing salon and watched her pack.

'OK.' Ticking items off on her fingers Amber said, 'Bikinis. Sarongs. Silver flip-flops. Pink sandals. Hair stuff, suntan stuff, insect stuff, white trousers, books, hat.'

'Don't forget the condoms,' said Mario.

'Already packed.'

'They'd better not be.' He reached for Amber's wrist and pulled her onto his lap. 'You girls behave yourselves, you hear? No falling for oily French millionaires with bloody big yachts.'

Amber wound her arms round his neck and kissed him. 'Nor you.'

'It's been a while since any bloody big yachts sailed into Hestacombe.'

'You know what I mean. The first time I met you, I knew what you were like.'

'I've changed.' Mario gave her a look of injured innocence. 'I haven't been unfaithful to you.'

'Ah, but I want you to carry on not being unfaithful to me. Even when I'm not here. Because if you ever were,' Amber met his gaze and held it, 'that would be it for me. All over. I wouldn't want to be with you any more.'

'I'm not going to do anything,' Mario protested.

'Good.' Dropping a kiss on the tip of his nose, Amber clambered off him. 'Lecture over. Now, do you think I've packed enough tops?'

Mario watched her counting them, then adding a couple more to the case. He trusted Amber implicitly but he still wished she wasn't going off to France without him. He would miss her. So would Nat and Ruby. Maybe when Amber was back, they should talk about her moving in with him.

He checked his watch. 'It's seven fifteen. What time are you leaving?'

'Nine. I said I'd pick up Mandy at quarter past.' Amber had declined his offer of a lift to Bristol Airport, explaining that it was easier to leave her own car in the long-stay car park, then it would be there for them on their return. 'Why, are you hungry? I could pop out and pick us up a takeaway.'

Mario slid off the bed and drew her towards him, kissing her again. 'You stay here and finish your girlie packing. I'll go and pick up the takeaway. Then when we've eaten there's just one more thing we have to do.'

'Oh yes?' Amber's silver and turquoise earrings swung as she said playfully, 'And what would that be? The hoovering or the washing-up?'

She was smart and sparky and he was going to miss her more than she knew. Sliding his hands over the strip of bare midriff between her skirt and orange cropped vest, Mario murmured, 'We're going to say goodbye to each other properly. In bed.'

It was Thursday morning and Lottie was in the office dealing with a mountain of post when Tyler, back from New York, came through the door.

God, it was fantastic to see him again. In a white polo shirt and Levi's he was looking tanned, handsome and not remotely jet-lagged. There was no doubt about it, a boss who was this easy on the eye was a definite bonus. Although maybe she wouldn't mention this to Freddie. Lovely though he was, Freddie had never made her mouth go dry and her heart go *twaanng*.

'Hi there.' Tyler nodded at the pile of post. 'You look busy.'

'You're my new employer,' said Lottie. 'It's my job to make you think I'm busy.'

He grinned. 'You know what? I've missed you.'

Heavens, how was she supposed to respond to *that*? If he thought she was going to tell him she'd missed him too, he could think again.

'And now you're back,' Lottie said brightly, wondering what was in the glossy dark blue carrier bag at his feet.

'Oh, right.' Following her gaze, Tyler reached down and began to delve into it. 'Nearly forgot. Freddie warned me that you don't speak to anyone these days until they've given you a bottle of champagne.'

Honestly, men. Hadn't she already been humiliated enough? Did Freddie genuinely not realise that expecting to be asked out by a gorgeous stranger then *not* being asked out by him was something she'd prefer not to become common knowledge?

Then again, if Tyler was feeling the need to compete, it could only be a good sign. 'Really,' Lottie began, 'you didn't have to—'

'Sadly he only told me this five minutes ago,' Tyler continued. 'So I'm afraid I've had to improvise somewhat.' Straightening, he held up a can of Dr Pepper. 'Bit warm, I'm afraid. Will this do instead?'

'Thank you.' Graciously Lottie accepted the can and put it on the desk. 'Vintage, I presume.'

'Absolutely. It's been in the glove compartment of my car for the last six days. Should have matured nicely by now.'

'Perfect. I'll save it for a special occasion.'

'I also called into FAO Schwarz while I was over there. Picked up something for Nat, to make up for what happened last week.' Tyler pulled two lavishly gift-wrapped rectangular parcels from the carrier. 'Then I thought I couldn't bring something for Nat and have Ruby feeling left out, so I got her something too.'

Deeply touched, Lottie said, 'Oh, you didn't have to do that. They'll be thrilled.'

'Call it bribery.' He looked amused. 'If this is what it takes to get back into their good books, that's fine by me.'

Lottie didn't know about *back* into their good books; he'd never been within a hundred miles of them in the first place. But maybe this would be the turning point they all needed.

'Well, it's really nice of you to do it anyway.' Reaching out a hand for the bag she said, 'Shall I give them to them tonight?'

'Actually, I wondered if you were free this evening. Maybe we could go out for that dinner we missed last week. Then when I call round to pick you up, I could give Nat and Ruby their presents myself.'

Lottie thought for a nano-second then nodded. 'That'd be great.' In fact it was doubly great, because if Mario was looking after the kids he couldn't be out getting up to mischief elsewhere, which could only be a good thing.

'We'll do that then.' Tyler looked pleased. 'Say, seven thirty?'

Experiencing a warm glow in her stomach, Lottie realised she was glad meeting Seb had turned out to be such a non-event. When a man liked you, he asked you out to dinner and fixed a time and date. And it seemed that Tyler Klein really did like her, because he was wasting no time at all.

Which was excellent news, seeing as she really liked him too.

'Mum, I hate that man. Don't go out with him,' begged Nat when he discovered who Lottie was seeing that evening.

'Sweetheart, I told you, he's really very nice.' Lottie was juggling mascara, lipstick, powder and scent in one hand as she concentrated on doing her face in the bathroom mirror.

'He isn't nice, he's *cruel.*'

'OK.' Lottie sighed. 'I wasn't going to tell you this, but Tyler's bought you a present. Does that make you like him a bit more?'

Mercenary? Her son?

Nat's whole face lit up. 'What kind of present?'

'I don't know, he's bringing it over tonight. But if you hate him, maybe you shouldn't—'

'So Nat's getting a present from that man?' Ruby had been sitting on the edge of the bath experimenting with Lottie's violet eye shadow without the benefit of a mirror. Outraged by the unfairness of this revelation she said indignantly, 'But we're the ones who've had to put up with Nat crying all the time like a *baby*.'

'And Tyler knows that.' Lottie deftly reclaimed her eye shadow while there was still some left in the pot. 'Which is why he's bought something for you too.'

Mercenary? Her daughter?

'*Has* he?' Overjoyed, Ruby almost toppled backwards into the bath. 'What's he got me?'

'No idea. He just told me he'd been to this place in New York called Schwarz and—'

'Schwarz? FAO Schwarz?' Ruby leapt up, her eyes wide with delight. She turned to look at Nat, who gasped, 'FAO Schwarz on *Fifth Avenue*?'

Bemused, Lottie said, 'How do you know that?'

'Mum! It's like the best toy shop in the whole world *ever*,' Nat gabbled. 'We saw a programme about it on CBBC, it's *amazing*.'

'Better than Disneyland,' Ruby chimed in, 'and you can buy anything you want, it's bigger than Buckingham Palace and they sell *everything* . . .'

Stars were practically coming out of their eyes. Aware that they were envisaging Tyler pulling up outside the cottage in some kind of ribbon-strewn articulated truck loaded to the roof with extravagant gifts, Lottie said hastily, 'Listen, you're getting one present each. Although like I said before, if you think Tyler's so horrible, I wonder if you deserve them.'

'If he's brought them for us all the way from New York, I think we should let him give them to us,' said Ruby. 'Otherwise his feelings might be hurt.'

'And if he bought them at FAO Schwarz,' Nat added seriously, 'they'll be really brilliant presents that cost loads of money.'

Mercenary? Her children?

'So I'm allowed to go out to dinner with him?' said Lottie.

'I think you should.' Ruby nodded and Nat joined in.

'Well, hooray for that. And remember,' Lottie warned them, 'manners. Whatever he's bought you, make sure that you look really pleased and—'

Rolling their eyes, Nat and Ruby chorused, 'Say thank you.'

Chapter 20

The mercenaries were hanging out of Nat's bedroom window when Tyler pulled up outside the cottage. At the front door he murmured to Lottie, 'I think we've turned the corner. Nat and Ruby just waved to me. Didn't boo or throw stones or anything.'

Lottie's stomach muscles were taut with longing; she so wanted her children to overcome their antipathy towards Tyler. They had got off to an unfortunate start, but with luck that was behind them now. That the three of them could get to know and like each other mattered a lot.

With luck the presents would do the trick.

'Hey, you two,' Tyler greeted them easily as Nat and Ruby, looking suitably angelic, appeared at the top of the staircase. 'How are you doing?'

'OK.' Nat was wide-eyed, making a huge effort not to gaze at the gift-wrapped presents Tyler was holding.

'Very well thank you.' Ruby was being ultra-polite. 'Did you have a nice time in America?'

Evidently relieved by the transformation, Tyler said, 'I had a great time, but it's even better to be back. And guess what? I brought you a little something.'

Lottie hid a smile as Nat and Ruby pretended to spot the shiny, extravagantly wrapped parcels for the first time.

'This one's for you,' Tyler held the parcel in his right hand towards Ruby. 'And this one's for you,' he extended the other towards Nat.

Together they came clattering down the stairs, took their parcels and said courteously, 'Thank you, Mr Klein.'

'My pleasure.' Tyler looked as delighted as if he'd just won an Oscar. 'And please, call me Tyler.'

Lottie led them all into the living room and crossed her fingers behind her back as Ruby and Nat began tearing into the wrappings. This was all going so much better than she could have imagined a week ago, it was going to make so much of a difference to—

Oh no.

Oh God.

'Of course I had no idea what to get for you,' Tyler was telling Ruby, 'but there was this really helpful saleswoman and she said this would be just perfect.'

Act, Lottie silently begged, *act like you've never acted before.* She willed her thoughts to be transmitted to Ruby as her daughter gazed, seemingly frozen, at the perspex case containing a rosy-cheeked china doll in ornate Victorian clothes.

Some nine-year-old girls adored dolls, maybe some even liked the kind you kept in a perspex case and couldn't actually play with. The only dolls Ruby had ever shown the remotest interest in were the voodoo kind.

'It's lovely,' Ruby said bravely, her chin wobbling with the effort of concealing her disappointment. 'Look, her eyes open and close when you tip her up. Thank you, Mr Klein.'

'Tyler,' said Tyler, blithely unaware that he couldn't have chosen a worse present if he'd tried. 'I'm glad you like it.'

'She's beautiful,' Lottie blurted out before an awkward silence had a chance to develop. 'Look at her hair! And her shoes! Ruby, aren't you lucky? Now, how's Nat getting along?' Turning to her son who had been having more trouble with the expertly taped-down wrappings, she said brightly, 'What have you got in there?'

The last layer of paper tore open at last and Lottie's heart plummeted into her boots.

'Warhammer,' said Nat, his tone expressionless. 'Thank you, Mr Klein.'

Warhammer, oh God. Requiring super-honed concentration skills, nimble fingers and endless patience – qualities poor Nat simply didn't possess.

'The saleswoman told me they sell truckloads of this stuff every week. All the kids are just wild about it,' Tyler announced with pride. 'They spend hours glueing the little models together and painting them. She reckons that'll keep you busy for weeks.'

Nat really looked as if he might cry. Hurriedly Lottie said, 'Isn't that fantastic? You'll *love* making all those little models, won't you!'

Nat nodded, stroking the lid of the box to demonstrate how much he loved it. In a small wavering voice he said, 'Yes.'

'Hi, I'm here.' The front door swung open and Mario announced his arrival. 'Sorry I'm a bit late – Amber just rang. She's having a great time and sends her love. Crikey, what's going on here?' In the doorway he halted at the sight of Nat and Ruby miserably clutching their presents. 'I didn't know it was Christmas.'

'It's not.' Abandoning her present, Ruby ran into his arms. 'Daddy, can we climb trees tonight?'

'And hunt for snakes?' begged Nat.

94

'Right, we'll be off.' Eager to get away while the going was good, Lottie grabbed and kissed each of them in turn. 'Have a great time.'

'You too,' said Mario with a wink. 'Don't be late.'

Terrified that he might add, 'And if you can't be good, be careful' or something equally crass, Lottie rushed Tyler out of the house.

It was a great evening. The smart restaurant in Painswick had been an inspired choice. Over dinner, Lottie got to know Tyler better and was liking him more and more. Considering how shamefully out of practice she was on the dating front, she hadn't even felt nervous once.

By eleven o'clock they were heading back into Hestacombe. Nat and Ruby would be fast asleep, Mario could leave and she could invite Tyler in for coffee.

Just coffee, nothing else. He was her new boss and she didn't want him to think she was slutty. Well, maybe a kiss wouldn't hurt, but definitely no more than that.

Then the front door burst open, spilling light and children into the garden, and that was the end of that idea. Just as well she hadn't been planning anything slutty, Lottie thought with a rueful smile. If it was a natural contraceptive you were after, you couldn't do better than Ruby and Nat.

She glanced apologetically at Tyler. 'They're supposed to be asleep.'

'No problem. They're looking pretty pleased with themselves,' he observed indulgently. 'Maybe they've been painting the Warhammer models and want to show me what they've done.'

Hmm, and maybe their new favourite food was mustard and sprouts.

Jumping out of the car, Lottie said, 'It's late! Why aren't you two in bed?'

'Dad said we didn't have to because we don't go back to school until next week. We had the best time tonight,' Nat gabbled, throwing his arms round her waist and kangarooing up and down in his excitement. 'Mum, guess what happened? You'll never guess!'

Lottie loved it so much when he was overcome with enthusiasm that she couldn't be cross with Mario for letting them stay up. 'You'd better tell me then.'

'No, *guess*!'

'You brushed your teeth without being asked?'

Nat looked incredulous. 'No!'

'OK, I give up.' As Nat attempted to drag her into the cottage – it was like being hauled along by a small determined tractor – Lottie called over her shoulder to Tyler, 'Coming in for a bit?' Oops, that didn't sound quite right. 'I mean, for a coffee?'

'Just try and stop me.' He locked the car and followed them up the path. 'I want to know what's happened.'

'*Two* things,' Ruby joyfully cut in, squeezing Lottie's other arm. 'Two things happened tonight!'

'My God, could life get any more exciting?' Bundling both children ahead of her into the cottage, Lottie whispered, 'Sorry about this.'

'Don't be sorry.' Tyler's dark eyes met hers. 'I'm enjoying myself. I wouldn't miss it for the world.'

'Right,' Nat announced importantly when they were in the living room. 'The phone rang and Daddy picked it up and they said it was an overseas call from America.'

'Heavens.' Lottie looked at Mario on the sofa.

'And then Daddy gave the phone to me and said someone special wanted to speak to me, so I took the phone and said hello and this man said, "Hi there, little fella, am I speaking to Nat Carlyle?" and his voice was quite funny, like not really proper English, and I said, "Yes, what do you want?"'

Lottie raised her eyebrows at Mario, who shrugged.

'And then he said, "Do you know who I am, little fella?" and I said, "You sound like Arnold Schwarzenegger."' Almost bursting with exultation Nat exclaimed, 'And he said, "Ho ho ho, well, that is very lucky because I *am* Arnold Schwarzenegger." And it *was* him!' Barely able to contain his glee, Nat had gone quite pink. 'And I said, "How did you know my phone number?" and he said, "Well, Nat, I had an email passed on to me by my personal private secretary, from someone who wrote to tell me about how you lost your noonoo and saying how upset you were, and that maybe a call from me might cheer you up and make you feel a bit better."'

'Wow, that's . . . *unbelievable.*' Lottie checked Mario again for giveaway signs. Mario shook his head.

'And it really was him,' Ruby nodded vigorously, 'because I listened as well. It was definitely his voice, just exactly like in his films!'

Who else had been aware of the fib she'd told Nat about Arnold Schwarzenegger? In disbelief, Lottie turned her gaze on Tyler, beside her. Had he persuaded a soundalike to give Nat a call? Or — OK, she knew this was unthinkable — had he really arranged for Arnold to do it, as a way of making up for causing all the upset in the first place?

There was a hint of a smile around Tyler's mouth. Good grief, he'd just come back from America, he moved in well-connected circles — did he actually *know* Arnold Schwarzenegger? When you came to think about it, he was just the kind of person who would.

'Did you organise this?' gasped Lottie, overcome with admiration and gratitude.

96

'Sshh, don't interrupt.' Refusing to look at her, Tyler nodded at Nat. 'He hasn't finished yet. Carry on, Nat, what did he say next?'

Nat took another deep breath, ready to start again. Ask him to learn his four times table and you'd still be there at Christmas, but when it came to remembering something relevant it was a different matter; along with endless episodes of *The Simpsons*, Nat was able to recall every word of the phone conversation verbatim.

Proudly he announced, 'He said he knew just how I felt because when he was a boy he had a noonoo and when he was seven a cruel man threw it away and that was it, he never saw his noonoo again. He said, "Oh Nat, if you knew how much it hurt me. I loved my noonoo so much. I cried every night, wondering where my noonoo was now. Then one day I thought no, I must be a brave boy, strong and powerful like Superman, and I must learn to live without my noonoo, and I must grow big and build up my muscles so that nobody can ever take anything away from me again."' His eyes shining, Nat said, 'Then he told me that I had to be brave and strong too, and made me promise I would, and not cry any more either. So I promised him, and then he said he was very busy and had to go now, and then he said goodbye and put the phone down.'

'Well.' Flabbergasted and impressed – whether Tyler had arranged for Arnie himself or a talented soundalike to make the call scarcely mattered – Lottie swung Nat up into her arms and showered him with kisses. 'That is fantastic. You are such a lucky boy, do you realise that? Fancy getting a phone call from Arnold Schwarzenegger!'

'I know,' Nat said ecstatically. 'And he knows my name!'

Over the top of Nat's tousled head, Lottie looked at Tyler and silently conveyed her gratitude. What a thoughtful thing to have done. They exchanged a secret smile and she felt her heart expand like a balloon. This was the kind of man she could fall in—

'Mum, that's not the only thing that happened!' Ruby was tugging at her arm now, demanding her share of the attention. 'There's something else!'

Chapter 21

'What else, darling?' Beaming happily, Lottie stroked her excited daughter's cheek. God, it could be anything. Had Tyler arranged for Beyoncé to drop by this evening? Was Orlando Bloom at this very minute waiting outside in the back garden?

'It's another surprise,' Ruby gabbled, 'in the kitchen.'

Oh, wouldn't that be lovely, Orlando Bloom in the kitchen. Better still, Orlando Bloom doing the washing-up. 'I can't stand the suspense,' exclaimed Lottie. 'So are you going to show me, or—'

'Jesus Christ!' shouted Tyler, his leg kicking out. Startled, Lottie blinked and saw something dark whip past her field of vision. Before anyone could move, the object hit the opposite wall with a noise between a slap and a thud. Faster than the speed of light, Tyler reached out and grabbed Ruby and Nat, pushing them towards the door. 'OK, kids, get out of here, close the door and run upstairs.'

'What *is* it?' shouted Lottie, because whatever it was had slid down the wall and disappeared behind the bookcase.

'Oh fuck,' Mario sighed, raking his fingers through his hair and heading towards the bookcase.

'Daddy, Daddy, was that Bernard?' Ducking back under Tyler's arm, Ruby's voice reverberated with fear. Having rushed over to join Mario she began furiously hurling books willy-nilly from the shelves. 'Bernard, where are you? It's all right, you can come out now.'

'I don't believe this,' muttered Tyler. Lottie saw that he was pale beneath his tan.

Bewildered, but with an ominous sense of foreboding, Lottie said, 'Who's Bernard?'

'My surprise.' Ruby was too busy burrowing through the bookcase to look up. 'I was just going to show you him. We found him in the woods tonight and Dad said I could keep him . . . oh, why hasn't he come out? Bernard, where are you? It's OK, don't be scared.'

'Will somebody please tell me who Bernard *is*?' Lottie demanded.

'A snake.' Tyler shook his head. 'I felt something on my foot and when

I looked down I saw a snake. Kicking out like that was a reflex, I just had to get it away from me. When I was growing up we spent a lot of time in Wyoming – if you get bitten by a rattler you can die.'

'We don't have rattlers here,' Mario said evenly. 'Bernard's a slow-worm. Slow-worms are harmless,' he went on. 'They don't bite. In fact they're not even snakes, they're legless lizards that live in – ah.'

Lottie didn't need to ask what that *ah* meant. She knew. In disbelief she clutched Nat to her side as Mario reached behind the lowest shelf of the bookcase and slowly withdrew Bernard. The slow-worm, seaweed brown and twenty inches long, was clearly dead. Kneeling on the floor next to her father, tears sprang into Ruby's dark eyes and a cry of anguish escaped her lips. She reached for Bernard and cradled his limp body in her lap.

'Oh shit,' murmured Tyler, ashen now. 'Not again.'

Lottie couldn't bear it. Just when she'd thought everything was going to be all right, something else had to happen. Was she jinxed or what?

'Look, I'm sorry.' Tyler heaved a sigh. 'But when I looked down I wasn't expecting to see a snake on my foot.'

'He shouldn't have been on your foot,' Lottie declared. 'He was supposed to be in the kitchen. Why wasn't the kitchen door shut?'

'We put him in a cardboard box with straw in it.' Nat's bottom lip trembled. 'He wasn't supposed to climb out. I just opened the lid a tiny bit so he could breathe.'

'Ruby, I'm sorry.' Tyler tried again. 'I didn't mean to kill him.' In desperation he said, 'Do they sell snakes in pet shops in this country? Listen, I'll buy you another snake. Any kind you like.'

Tears were dripping from the end of Ruby's nose onto the dead slow-worm in her lap. With a huge sniff she turned to look at Tyler. 'I don't want you to buy me another snake. You'd probably buy a really horrible one with a china face and a lace bonnet on its head and old-fashioned clothes. And even if you bought me a real python I wouldn't want it because I hate you, and I hate that stupid doll you gave me *and* you killed Bernard. So I don't want you to come to our house ever, *ever* again.'

Tyler thought about this. Finally he nodded. 'You know, I don't think I want to either.' Turning, he murmured to Lottie, 'I'll see you at work tomorrow.'

Numbly, Lottie nodded.

'And I don't want you going out any more with my mum,' Ruby flung at him.

Tyler didn't reply.

'And Nat hated his Warhammer models too,' she bellowed after him as he headed for the door. 'But that's all right, because Dad says we can always sell them on eBay.'

Lottie didn't bother following Tyler out of the door. Tonight probably wasn't the night for that all-important first kiss.

At Ruby's insistence Bernard was buried in the back garden. Mario dug a very long, very narrow grave and the brief but emotionally charged candlelit ceremony was conducted by Ruby herself. If the neighbours were looking out of their bedroom window they'd wonder what the hell was going on. Then again, they'd had years of practice at living next door to the Carlyles. Interring a slow-worm at midnight barely registered on the scale of out of the ordinary goings-on.

Finally Nat and Ruby were put to bed and were asleep within seconds of hitting the pillow. It was time for Mario to leave.

But, being Mario, he couldn't resist getting a dig in first.

'Sure you want to work for that guy?'

Lottie bristled. 'Why wouldn't I?'

'Oh, come on, surely you've noticed. Can't say he isn't accident prone.' Mario's eyes glittered with amusement. 'Say the phone rings in the office when you're both there. You make a move to answer it. John Wayne there thinks you're reaching for your gun and with his lightning reflexes grabs his and shoots you first. Well, I can tell you now, he can be the one to dig your grave because you'll be needing a damn sight bigger one than Bernard.'

'It was an accident,' Lottie said impatiently. Compelled to defend Tyler, she said, 'He thought it was a snake and Americans are used to snakes being dangerous. Anyway, it was thoughtful of him to arrange the phone call.'

'From Arnie?' Mario's grin broadened. 'You don't think it was really Arnie on the other end, do you?'

'No, of course it wasn't. I know *that*.' Hastily Lottie deleted those few moments when her disbelief had been magically suspended. 'But it was still nice of him to think of doing something like that, wasn't it? And you can't say it didn't cheer Nat up.'

'Oh, it definitely did that.' Nodding in agreement, Mario reached for his keys.

'So why can't you admit that it was a good thing for Tyler to do?'

'Because I just can't, OK?'

'Exactly!' Lottie was triumphant. 'Because you're too proud, too stubborn, too damn *Italian* to cope with somebody else appearing on the scene and getting on with *your* children.'

One eyebrow went up. 'Getting on with them? Is that what he's doing?'

Frustratedly Lottie said, 'But he *would* be if things didn't keep going wrong. He's making the effort. And that's what's important, isn't it? It means a lot to me.'

'I think we can all see that,' Mario drawled. He opened the front door to let himself out then paused on the step and turned back to face her. 'Oh, just one more thing. What makes you so sure it was Tyler who arranged the call?'

Lottie's fingernails dug into her palms. Dammit, she hadn't known Mario for eleven years without learning what that particular tone of voice implied. Bugger, *bugger*. He might not be looking unbearably smug right now but she knew for certain he was feeling it. How could she have been so stupid, leaping to the wrong conclusion like that? Just because the call had purportedly come from America and Tyler had just returned from New York. Talk about gullible.

And she wouldn't be allowed to forget it.

'Eamonn, the new guy at work,' said Mario. 'He's great at voices. He can do anyone. I asked him to give Nat a call.' Straight-faced, he said, 'Wasn't that nice of me? Aren't you going to tell me how thoughtful and wonderful *I* am for making the effort?'

God, he was loving every minute of this.

'They're your children,' Lottie said flatly. 'You're their dad. You're supposed to do stuff like that. It doesn't make you a hero.'

'You thought it made Tyler Klein one.'

'He's not their father!'

'Thank God for that,' Mario retorted. 'Face it, he's nothing but a liability.'

Lottie remembered something else about Mario that drove her mad: he *loved* to win an argument, any argument. What's more, he clearly had no intention of giving up until he'd won this one.

'But I like him.'

'I know.' Mario's expression softened. 'And that's the problem. Since we broke up you haven't been out with anyone else. Now this guy's come along, not bad looking . . .'

'Excuse me. He's *good* looking.' Lottie couldn't allow this to pass.

'Absolutely loaded . . .'

'That's not why I like him!'

'But you can't say it doesn't help. Come on, be honest,' Mario chided. 'Money, no money – which one would any of us prefer? And he's shown a bit of interest in you, which is flattering, but what I'm saying is don't get too carried away. Tonight was your first proper date in years. You don't realise how out of practice you are.'

'Bloody cheek.' Now Lottie really wanted to slap him. 'So what I should have been doing all this time was putting myself about, sleeping with everyone I meet, no matter how unsuitable they might be. *Like you have.*'

'I'm not saying that. Besides, you aren't the sleep-around type. Which is a *compliment*,' Mario added, getting ready to duck. 'I just think you shouldn't jump in with both feet the minute someone rolls up and starts paying you some attention. I know it's flattering but it doesn't automatically make him the one who's going to change your life. Plus, there's the kids to think of. How are they going to feel if—'

'OK.' Lottie had had more than enough. 'Save your lectures, I'm not listening to any more of this.' Since she couldn't win the argument and stabbing her ex-husband would only result in prison and tedious visits from solicitors, she slammed the front door in Mario's face.

Through the closed door she heard him laughing. As Lottie fastened the safety chain Mario called out, 'That means you know I'm right.'

Chapter 22

Cressida had never forgotten the day she received her first Valentine card. She had been eleven years old and it was her first year at secondary school. The post had arrived as she was ploughing through her bowl of Weetabix and her mother, hearing it plop through the letterbox, had said, 'Go and get the letters, will you, love?'

Out in the hallway Cressida had experienced a toe-tingling surge of joy mingled with disbelief when she saw that one of the letters was in fact a card in a red envelope, addressed to her and with S.W.A.L.K. written across the back. With trembling fingers she had ripped open the envelope while her mother called out from the kitchen, 'Anything interesting?'

The card had a picture of a kitten on the front, smiling coyly and clutching a huge red heart. Inside, beneath the printed inscription 'You're my Purrfect Valentine', was written: 'To Cressida, I love you, will you be my Valentine? Love from . . . ? xxx'

Oh, the unimaginable thrill of reading those words! She hurriedly stuffed the card back into its envelope and tucked it into the waistband of her school skirt, pulling her jumper down to conceal it from view. Pink-cheeked, she wandered back into the kitchen and handed over the remainder of the post.

'Just bills,' sighed her mother. 'No Valentine's card for me from Engelbert Humperdinck then.'

'No,' Cressida mumbled, cramming the last of her Weetabix into her mouth and glugging down her glass of Ribena. 'Right, I'm off, don't want to miss the bus.'

It had been a glorious morning. Actually, a glorious week and possibly the start of a glorious new life. Cressida had spent hours secretly poring over her Valentine card, hugging it to her like the most marvellous secret. She had sniffed the ink, run her fingertips over the words and fantasised endlessly over who might have sent it. Because somebody loved her, really *loved* her and wanted her to be their Valentine. It was frustrating in one way that they hadn't signed the card, because if someone wanted you to be their Valentine it would help to know who they were. On the other hand, *not* knowing allowed her imagination more scope to run wild. It could have come from anyone, *anyone at all*, which was a lot more exciting than discovering that it had been sent by spotty, weedy Wayne Trapp who was always staring at her on the school bus.

Sometimes it was just better not to know.

Heavens, that had been almost thirty years ago. If she closed her eyes now, Cressida discovered, she could still picture every detail of that card. Was every woman able to do that, or was it just her? Well, why not, she thought indulgently. It had been an important part of her life, a defining moment. Even if she never had discovered who'd sent it and had long suspected that it had in fact come from her mother.

And now it was happening all over again, but this time she was almost certain her mother wasn't the perpetrator. For one thing, she was dead. But Cressida was pretty sure that even in the afterlife her mother would never have got to grips with the logistics of email.

Tom had sent her an email, though. And her toes were curling with pleasure just as they had curled thirty years ago when she had opened that gaudy Valentine's card. She was already reading his email for the fourth time and it had only arrived in her inbox a few minutes ago.

Hi Cressida,

Just a quick note to let you know how much my mother appreciated the card. She has been showing it off to everyone and it occupies pride of place on her mantelpiece. So thanks again for coming to the rescue.

It was great to meet you last week and I really enjoyed the time we spent together. I'm sure Donny did too, but he would of course rather amputate his own feet than admit it. Or throw himself to the lions, maybe?! Hope you and Jojo enjoyed the trip to Longleat as much as we did.

Well, I'm now back at work and wishing I wasn't. That's the trouble with holidays, isn't it? To add insult to injury, it's raining here in Newcastle. Maybe I should contact Freddie at Hestacombe House and see if the cottage is free for the next fortnight! [Reading this bit had caused Cressida's heart to give a foolish leap of hope.] Seriously, I hope we'll be able to book it for a week next Easter. [Cressida's heart plunged; next Easter was almost eight months away.] If we do, I very much hope we'll be able to meet up again then.

Better go now, work calls.

All the best,

Tom Turner.

Glimpsing her reflection in the computer's screen, Cressida saw that she was grinning like an idiot. It was so lovely to hear from Tom; the last week had dragged horribly now that he was no longer around. And he'd started off by saying 'Just a quick note', but it hadn't ended up being quick, had it? As quick emails went, it was actually quite lengthy. It hadn't even been necessary for him to write and thank her for his mother's card – he'd already done that in person.

So all in all, Cressida couldn't help feeling, it was a very promising sign, indicating that Tom didn't want to lose touch with her and that *maybe* he—

'Aunt Cress, someone wants to order some wedding cards.'

Cressida jumped a mile as the door flew open and Jojo came in waving the cordless phone. Heavens, she'd been so enthralled by Tom's email that she hadn't even heard it ringing in the kitchen. Hurriedly, guiltily, she clicked on the Back button to remove his words from the screen, took the phone from Jojo and forced herself to concentrate on the wedding plans of an over-excited prospective bride in Bournemouth.

When the call ended – and with Jojo safely back in the kitchen – Cressida returned Tom's email to the screen and read it again. The thought of losing it was so alarming that she switched on her printer and printed a copy out. There, that was better, it was a proper letter now, on real paper. She'd write back, of course, but not yet. Replying to a casual friendly email within minutes of receiving it would be far too keen. Which was fine, because it gave her plenty of time in which to painstakingly compose a suitably casual and friendly reply.

Then she could send it tonight.

The door opened again and Jojo, this time with flour on her nose and in her fringe, poked her head round. 'Good news?'

'Excellent news,' Cressida said happily.

'How many?'

'How many what?'

'Wedding invitations!'

'Oh! Um . . . twenty.'

Jojo frowned. 'That's not many.'

'I know, they're just having a tiny intimate wedding.'

'So why's that excellent news?'

'Because tiny weddings are so romantic.' Cressida slid Tom's printed-out email into a drawer. 'And . . . because she sounded so happy!'

'Sounded drunk to me.' Jojo gave her an odd look. 'Are you all right?'

'Me? Yes, fine, great!' Gosh, it was hard to concentrate when you were mentally composing a casual friendly email in your head. 'How are you getting on with those fairy cakes?'

'They're in the oven. Nine minutes to go. When I've done the icing, d'you want chocolate sprinkles or glacé cherries on top?'

Hi Tom, how lovely to hear from you! Never mind booking one of Freddie's cottages, why don't you come down this weekend and stay with us? Donny can have the spare bedroom and you can bunk up with me, how's that for an offer you can't—

'Aunt Cress?'

'Oh, um . . .' Snapping herself out of that fantasy, Cressida said recklessly, 'How about both?'

When Merry Watkins had taken over the Flying Pheasant in Hestacombe two years ago she had been determined to make a roaring success of the venture. With a clear vision of how a country inn should be, she had set about transforming it with vigour. And to the relief of the locals Merry had achieved it, thanks largely to her charm and can-do personality. Every visitor to the pub was welcomed like a long-lost friend. The refurbished, but still traditional, bars were a comforting haven from the world, the draught beers were sublime and the back garden was family-friendly. Cleverest of all, Merry had transformed the area in front of the pub from a haphazard car park into the coolest place to sit, with tubs of greenery and flowers, rustic tables and comfortable chairs and hidden lighting that illuminated the outside of the pub and gave the impression that those people drinking outside were on a stage, appearing in a play any passers-by would want to see.

Shamelessly, Merry made sure the most attractive customers occupied this position. Less-than-glamorous walking types, the kind with woolly beards and rucksacks, were served their drinks at the bar and strongly encouraged to take them through to the back garden. The farming locals preferred to stay inside anyway, in their murky corner of the bar. Anyone well dressed and physically appealing – basically those Merry termed *desirables* – were ushered out to the prized area at the front, in order to attract more passing trade and further boost the image of the Flying Pheasant. And it did. Merry had created her own version of the VIP enclosure and people loved to drive over to Hestacombe and be seen out in the coveted stage-lit area in front of the pub.

Picking up his drink and his change, Mario said, 'I'll just take this through to the back garden.'

'You bloody well will not.' Merry wasn't a woman to be trifled with. 'Get yourself out the front there this minute, you gorgeous creature, and bring me in some more business.'

Mario made his way outside, greeting and briefly chatting to people he knew before settling himself on a chair at the last empty table and pulling out his mobile. He rang Amber's number, reached voicemail and hung up. It was eight thirty: she and Mandy were probably in a restaurant with a no-phone rule. He'd try again later.

One week down, one to go. Putting his phone away, Mario realised how much he was missing Amber. It was like giving up smoking and suddenly not knowing what to do with your hands. He'd been good, though. On his best behaviour. When Jerry and the lads from work had announced they were off into Cheltenham for a night of beer and clubbing, they had urged him to join them and he had said no, prompting good-natured jeers and pronouncements that he'd be wearing a pinny next.

But he hadn't changed his mind, chiefly because his workmates were a seriously bad influence and, coupled with serious amounts of alcohol, Mario wasn't entirely sure he wouldn't succumb to temptation should it happen to come along. Knowing himself of old, it was safer to say no.

A voice to his left said hesitantly, 'Excuse me, are these seats taken?'

Looking up, Mario saw a fragile brunette in a sea-green summer dress, accompanied by a chic older woman who had to be her mother. Couldn't get safer than that.

Taking off his sunglasses and gesturing towards the empty chairs, Mario flashed them both an easy smile. 'Help yourself.'

'Just the two drinks this time?' Merry beadily enquired.

It was ten thirty and the third time Mario had come inside to order another round of drinks.

'Just the two,' Mario agreed. 'They're staying at one of the cottages. The mother's tired so she's gone back for an early night. Is that OK with you, Merry?'

She gave him a look. 'Fine by me, darling. Money in the till. Is it fine by Amber, that's what I'm wondering.'

Village life, didn't you just love it? 'I don't know. I'll give her a ring and ask her permission, shall I?' Pocketing his change and picking up the drinks, Mario said, 'Anyway, I'm not doing anything wrong. We're out there in full view of everyone. Her name's Karen, she broke up with her fiancé and she's been a bit down lately. Her mother booked one of the cottages for a week to give her a break and take her mind off the ex.'

'Hmm.' It was a *hmm* loaded with meaning.

'They've never visited this part of the country before,' Mario continued evenly. 'Today they went shopping in Bath, which is why Marilyn, the mother, is exhausted. Karen isn't exhausted, so she decided to stay for one more drink. We're not having sex out there, Merry.'

'Delighted to hear it,' said Merry. 'Seeing as we don't have a licence for that kind of thing.'

'We're just talking. Harmlessly. It's what people in pubs do. They were the ones who started the conversation, not me.'

'She's a pretty girl.'

'Yes, well.' Exasperated, Mario said, 'We have you to thank for that, don't we? Seeing as you won't allow any ugly ones to sit out the front.'

'Apart from that one in the orange trousers who looks like a horse.' Merry grimaced across the bar. 'But she's with the Ballantyne crowd so I couldn't stop her.'

'You're slipping.'

Merry said pointedly, 'So are you.'

'I'm just being sociable! Does Amber being away mean I'm not allowed to leave the house? Should I maybe handcuff myself to the sofa,' Mario raised an eyebrow, 'and sit there for a fortnight watching crap TV? Surviving on Cup-a-soups and not daring to pop out for a takeaway in case I accidentally hurl myself in a frenzy across the counter at the girl in the chip shop?'

Merry said, 'Now there's a mental image to treasure.'

'Well, I'm not doing that. I'm here, I'm behaving myself beautifully and I don't need keeping an eye on.'

'Off with you then, don't want her wondering where you've got to. You said that really well, by the way,' Merry called after him. Amused, she added, 'Almost as if you meant it.'

Chapter 23

Marilyn and Karen Crane were staying at Pound Cottage, down on the lakeside. Lottie, arriving at the cottage at ten o'clock in the morning with a fresh supply of towels, found mother and daughter sitting out on the deck enjoying breakfast in their expensive silk dressing gowns. Karen was throwing bits of croissant to the ducks and sipping freshly squeezed orange juice. Marilyn was flipping through the latest edition of *Cotswold Life*. The sun was blazing down and classical music drifted elegantly through the open windows. The scene could have come straight from a Ralph Lauren ad.

Feeling hot and busy and not very Ralph Laurenish at all, Lottie hoisted the fresh towels out of the car and climbed the wooden steps leading up to the deck. For breakfast she'd had Ruby's leftover strawberry milkshake and Nat's discarded toast crusts. In fact she wasn't that different from the ducks. How the other half lived.

Brightly she said, 'I've brought your towels.'

'Oh lovely. Just pop them inside, would you?' Marilyn greeted her with a warm smile and patted the empty chair beside her. 'Then come and sit down. We're planning a trip to Stratford today and we want to know what's worth seeing. Apart from the shops, obviously!'

Having deposited the towels in the bathroom Lottie joined them.

'Coffee?' Marilyn reached for a spare cup.

'Thanks.' Real coffee; it smelled heavenly. Wondering if she might be offered the last buttered croissant too, Lottie's hopes were dashed as Karen picked it up, tore it into flaky strips and began throwing them to the attention-seeking ducks. How about if she leapt up and intercepted a piece as it flew through the air, catching it in her mouth?

'Now, I've been looking through my guidebook but we don't want to waste time on anything boring. And we'd quite like to squeeze in a visit to Stow-on-the-Wold on the way back.' Marilyn combed her fabulously manicured fingernails through her dark brown fabulously cut hair. 'We'd also like to know where to eat. Somewhere special.' She looked expectant. 'With Michelin stars preferably.'

Stars, not star. Noting the plural, Lottie racked her brains. 'Well, there's Le Manoir aux Quat' Saisons just outside Oxford. But I can really recommend a place in Painswick. They don't open for lunch, but I had dinner there last week and—'

'Somewhere in Stratford. For lunch, not dinner.' Karen, speaking for the first time, said, 'I'm already going out this evening.'

'OK. What I can do is look up some restaurant review sites, see what sounds good in Stratford and draw up a—'

'Hello?' Cutting Lottie off in mid-flow again, Karen had snatched up her ringing phone. 'Oh, hi, Bea. Yeah, great, I'm just feeding the ducks. No, it's not as bad as I thought, the cottage is really sweet. Mummy's been buying me loads of stuff to cheer me up.'

Lottie whispered to Marilyn, '. . . draw up a shortlist. Then if you pop into the office before you set off, I can give you a printed-out copy.'

Marilyn looked disappointed. 'You can't personally recommend any?'

'No.' Lottie felt like reminding the woman that she had a job that kept her rushed off her feet and couldn't actually spare the time to schlep around England trying out every restaurant currently in business.

'Oh. It's just that I always think any five-star reviews have been posted by the owners. You can't trust them.' Pulling a face, Marilyn complained, 'We went to a place in Knightsbridge once that was supposed to be spectacular and their pineapple juice wasn't even freshly squeezed!'

Heaven forbid. Lottie drank her coffee and admired Marilyn's nails. Not real, obviously, but beautifully done.

'. . . and you'll never guess what, I've got a date tonight!' Tucking her bare legs beneath her and hugging her knees, Karen was still chattering away on the phone. 'I know, can you believe it? I met him last night! Mummy and I got chatting to him outside the local pub, then Mummy got tired and came back here and we stayed on for another couple of hours. I mean, I know I'm heartbroken over Jonty – the bastard – but this guy was just so much fun. Even Mummy thought he was charming and you know what she's like, she hates everyone!'

Finishing her coffee, Lottie half rose from her seat and said, 'Well, I suppose I'd better—'

'And get this, his name's Mario,' Karen trilled into the phone.

Lottie abruptly sat back down.

'I know, isn't it a scream? I asked him if he sold Cornettos!'

Feeling as if she'd been punched in the chest, Lottie picked up her cup and swallowed a mouthful of bitter, lukewarm coffee grounds.

'No, he *doesn't* sell Cornettos. He manages a car showroom. And he isn't an oily oik either,' giggled Karen. 'Look, I'll ring you tomorrow and tell you everything then. If you see Jonty, let him know I'm not missing him a bit, OK? Mention that I've found someone far better than him. And tell him I want my CD player back. OK, speak to you soon, bye, honey bunny.'

Lottie wanted to punch Mario in the chest. Thanks to him she had revolting coffee grounds clinging to her teeth and nowhere to spit them out. Slowly, unwillingly, she ran her tongue around the inside of her mouth and swallowed the acrid grains. Why was she even surprised that Mario was up to his old tricks?

And what could she do to stop him?

Aware that it was now or never – having finished her coffee she no longer had any reason to be sitting out here on their deck – Lottie cleared her throat. Yeurgh, those disgusting coffee grounds. Casually she said, 'So . . . you're seeing Mario tonight.'

Karen perked up at once. 'Oh, do you know him?'

Lottie nodded. 'Very well.'

'Of course. He lives here in the village. You probably do too.' When Lottie nodded again, Marilyn said jokily, 'Don't tell me he's a complete psychopath!'

'Well, nooo . . .' Lottie drew out the word long enough to indicate that *that* wasn't the problem.

Not slow on the uptake, Marilyn raised an eyebrow. 'What, then? Is he married?'

Now wasn't the time to mention her own connection with Mario; it wasn't relevant. 'He's not married,' Lottie said hesitantly, 'but he does have a girlfriend.'

'Live-in?' demanded Karen.

'Well, no, they don't actually *live* together . . .'

'That's all right then.' Karen relaxed. 'Phew, you had me worried there for a minute.'

Anxious to get her message across, Lottie said, 'But it's not just a casual relationship. They've been together for eight months. Her name's Amber and she's lovely.'

But Karen was shrugging, supremely unconcerned. 'If it was serious, he'd be living with her. He's not.'

'But they're a couple. They—'

'Not a *real* couple.' Karen rolled her eyes. 'I'm not going to feel guilty just because he's seeing someone. Jesus, it's hard enough finding men who aren't married or shacked up. Anyway, we'd better start getting ready if we're going to Stratford.' Chucking the last shreds of croissant at the quacking, squabbling ducks, she rose to her feet and headed inside.

Lottie watched her go. Marilyn, patting her hand, said consolingly, 'I'm

111

sure you meant well. Don't worry, it's just a harmless night out. Karen will be fine.'

She might be, thought Lottie. But what about Amber if she found out? How could Mario be so stupid?

Back at the office she rang him. 'Hi, it's me. What are you doing tonight?'

'Don't ask. Some boring business meeting.' Damn, he was good. The words tripped so easily off Mario's tongue it was scary. He was utterly believable.

'Liar.' Lottie wondered how many millions of lies he'd told her over the years. 'You're seeing Karen Crane.'

'Like I said, a boring business meeting.' Blithely Mario continued, 'She's interested in the new Audi Quattro.'

'And I'm Trevor McDonald. We both know what Karen's interested in.' At her desk, Lottie doodled a spiky, furious hedgehog on her notepad. 'And you must be out of your mind. For crying out loud, do you *want* Amber to dump you?'

Mario sighed. 'This is stupid. I suppose you've been talking to Merry.'

'No, but I jolly well will now.'

'Look, we got chatting last night. I was just being friendly. And no, I didn't kiss her. Nor am I planning to.'

'You asked her out tonight.'

'I didn't. She asked me. She just wants a bit of company,' Mario protested. 'Someone to talk to. So I said yes. Is that so terrible?'

Lottie's eyes narrowed. 'Where are you taking her?'

'We're meeting at the Pheasant. All above board.'

'And after that?'

'Maybe a pizza in Cheltenham. Maybe not. God, Lottie, will you trust me? This isn't any big deal. Just because she happens to be female,' said Mario. 'If it was a bloke, you wouldn't be giving me this grief.'

So *reasonable.*

'I suppose not. But you lied about who you were seeing tonight.'

'That's because I knew you'd nag. Look, I've got to go now – Jerry's trying to sell a Mazda MX-5 to some old dear of about ninety. I'll see you soon, OK? And I promise to behave myself tonight.'

Lottie didn't believe him for a second – it was like a girl eyeing up a plate of doughnuts, going, 'No I mustn't, I really mustn't, seriously, I'm on a diet . . . oh well, just the one then.'

'Trust me,' said Mario when she didn't speak. 'I'll be on my best behaviour.'

Hmm. Doodling a harpoon about to land on the hedgehog, Lottie said, 'Just make sure you are.'

Chapter 24

Tyler, now settled into Fox Cottage, was busy on the phone when Lottie arrived with the file of booking figures for next year. Signalling for her to stay, he carried on talking to his accountant, leaving Lottie free to explore the living room. She checked out his collections of CDs and DVDs, relieved to see that he wasn't an avid fan of country and western music and science fiction movies. Unless he loved those so much he kept them safely tucked away in a separate box upstairs.

Oh, please don't let that be true.

Since the living room didn't take long to investigate – Tyler evidently wasn't one for clutter – Lottie moved outside into the garden. Bees buzzed and hovered from one flower to the next, butterflies darted around like It-girls at a party and the scent of honeysuckle hung heavy in the air. The small lawn was studded with buttercups and daisies and a pair of chaffinches were hopping around in search of food. Burying her nose in a tall spear of hollyhock, Lottie almost inhaled a wasp and leapt back. Batting away the wasp, she whacked the hollyhock at the same time. The wasp flew off and the hollyhock promptly bounced back like a punchball, spraying the front of her shirt with bright yellow pollen.

Her pale pink shirt, naturally. *Nature.*

'Problem?' Phone call over, Tyler materialised in the garden behind her.

'Just doing battle with a vicious plant.'

Tyler said gravely, 'Looks like you lost.'

'Wait until I get my hands on a machete, then I'll get my own back.' Vigorously Lottie brushed herself down, only succeeding in squashing the pollen more indelibly into the thin cotton. 'I'll have to go home and change. The booking file's on your coffee table.'

'Thanks. Don't go yet.' Putting out a hand to stop her, Tyler said, 'Look, I know we haven't done very well so far, but what are you doing this evening? I thought maybe we could drive into Bath, go and see a—'

'I can't,' Lottie stopped him. 'There's something I have to do tonight.'

'OK.' Tyler paused. 'Is that a polite way of telling me to get lost?'

'No, *no*. I really do have something else to sort out.'

'Because I realise it isn't easy for you, what with your kids hating me so much, but I thought maybe if I steered clear of them for a while it might help.' Tyler's smile was crooked. 'In fact, make sure I don't see them at all. Then with a bit of luck they might get used to the situation and in time we can try again. How does that sound?'

Like banning certain types of food from your diet, thought Lottie, then reintroducing them to find out if you're allergic to them. The trouble was, the human body wasn't a sympathetic entity. It was unlikely to take pity on you and decide to change its mind about being allergic to red wine and chocolate just because it knew how much you liked them.

And neither were Nat and Ruby.

But she didn't have the heart to tell him this. Instead Lottie nodded and said, 'That sounds . . . fine.'

'Sure?' Tyler raised an eyebrow.

'Sure.'

'So how about tomorrow night?'

God, she'd love that, she *really* would. 'Um . . . could we leave it for a few days?' Dry-mouthed and willing herself to stay strong, Lottie said, 'It's just that I'm pretty tied up for the rest of this week.'

There, talk about noble. It felt like turning down a fabulous five-star holiday in Mauritius in favour of a week in a leaky caravan in Cleethorpes. Like saying, 'Oh no, *you* have the fillet steak and chips, I'll be fine with the cold porridge.' Like being given the choice between a brand new Porsche and a manky old moped . . .

'If this is you playing hard to get,' Tyler remarked, 'you're doing it very well.'

'I'm not.' Lottie almost blurted out that where he was concerned she would in fact be ridiculously, shamelessly easy to get. With a surge of longing she said, 'Next week would be great.'

'OK. So long as you aren't messing me around.' His smile held a hint of challenge. 'Next Monday, then?'

Relief flooded through her. Lottie nodded vigorously. 'Next Monday.'

'Come here, you've got pollen on your nose.'

Moving obediently closer, she allowed him to brush it off.

'And here.' Tyler gently rubbed her left eyebrow, causing her stomach to contract with pleasure.

'And a bit more here,' he went on, stroking her right cheekbone. This time her toes began to tingle. Heavens, wherever next?

'All gone now?' Lottie murmured.

'Not quite. Just one last . . .' He touched her mouth, lightly tracing the outline of her lips. Then, closing the small distance between them, he moved his fingers aside and kissed her. Lightly and thrillingly. Phew. Eyes closed, Lottie felt his hands move to the back of her head. Her own arms found their way round his neck. It had been years, *years* since she'd been kissed like this. She'd forgotten how glorious it could be.

'There, that's better.' Tyler pulled away in order to study her face. His mouth twitched at the corners. 'Well, it's a start anyway.'

Nodding, Lottie struggled to regain control of her breathing. It was a hell of a start. Behind her she heard branches swaying as squirrels leapt playfully from tree to tree. Birds sang overhead and a pair of tortoiseshell butterflies pirouetted in tandem across the grass. All of a sudden she was in the middle of a Disney movie; at any moment she half expected flower buds to explode into bloom and a family of rabbits to burst into a rousing chorus of—

'I've been wanting to do that for weeks,' said Tyler.

'Me too.' Lottie's heart was banging against her ribcage.

'And I can't think of anything nicer than carrying on doing it.' His grey eyes flashed. 'But I suppose we should try and be faintly professional about this.'

Lottie nodded vigorously, shaking herself out of the daze that had enveloped her like a goosedown duvet. 'Absolutely. Professional. Sensible.' She floundered; what was the word she was searching for? Ah yes. 'Businesslike.'

'I'll have to behave myself. Until next Monday,' said Tyler.

'Next Monday.' Lottie couldn't wait for him to misbehave.

'No Ruby, no Nat. Just me and you.'

'Yes.' Oops, now there was a bright yellow pollen stain on the front of his shirt from where she'd been pressed against him. Rubbing at it ineffectually, Lottie said, 'Look what I've done to you.'

Tyler's eyebrows lifted with amusement. 'That's the least of what you've done to me. But I suppose I'd better go and change my shirt. Bit of a giveaway otherwise.'

The goosedown duvet slid away. Was he ashamed of her?

'You don't want anyone else to know?'

'Touchy.' He sounded amused. 'Not at all. I just thought maybe you'd prefer it if Nat and Ruby didn't know. In case they give you a hard time.'

Lottie swallowed with relief. She nodded. 'That makes sense.'

Inside the cottage, Tyler's phone began to ring. 'I'd better get that.'

'Then change your shirt. And I must go and change mine.'

He gave her hand a brief squeeze, then headed into the house. Smiling to herself, Lottie made her way back along the path. They'd just shared their first kiss.

Roll on Monday night.

When she was out of sight, the branches of the sycamore tree quivered again as the Jenkins boys, Ben and Harry, nudged each other and sniggered quietly. Sometimes when they hid in trees nothing much exciting happened and they spent their time carving rude words into the trunk. Other times they amused themselves dropping twigs, leaves and insects onto the heads of hapless passers-by.

But this was great. Actually watching grown-ups kissing was tons better than dropping beetles on unsuspecting heads. And not just any old grown-ups either. This was the new bloke from America, ha, and Nat and Ruby Carlyle's mother, ha *ha.*

Double-checking that the coast was clear, Ben and Harry dropped from the tree like mini-Ninjas and scooted off through the undergrowth. When they reached the safety of their den they punched each other and collapsed laughing on the dusty ground.

'They were snogging!'

'Yeeurrgh, snogging!'

'If we hide there on Monday night we might see them *doing it.*'

'Doing what?'

'*It,* you pillock.' Harry wiggled his hips to demonstrate.

'Oh right.' Dancing, Ben realised. He might be only seven but he knew that girls kissed boys when they danced with them.

'This is fantastic.' Harry, whose mission in life was to get one over on their rivals, punched the air triumphantly. 'Wait until Nat and Ruby hear about this.'

Chapter 25

'Hi there!' Spotting Mario and Karen at a corner table, Lottie waved at them and threaded her way towards them.

Mario, instantly suspicious, said, 'What are you doing here?'

'Now there's a welcome. Just as well I've already bought myself a drink!' Waggling her fingers cheerily at Karen, Lottie pulled out the third chair and sat down. 'Don't mind if I join you, do you? How was Stratford, by the way? Buy anything nice?'

'Uh, well . . . yeah.' Clearly mystified by this intrusion into their privacy, Karen looked at Mario.

'Where are the kids?' asked Mario.

'Locked up in a police cell.' Lottie pulled a face at him, then beamed. 'Cressida's babysitting. I just really fancied a night out.'

Mario gave her a measured look. 'I'll bet you did.'

'Well, why not? It's a beautiful evening.' Taking a sip of her drink and sitting back, Lottie heaved a sigh of contentment. 'What could be nicer than being out here, the three of us?'

'Hang on. Excuse me.' Her shoulders very straight, Karen demanded, 'Are you Mario's girlfriend?'

'Girlfriend? Gosh no. I'm his wife.'

Karen's eyes bulged.

'Ex-wife,' Mario corrected wearily.

'Ex-wife and mother to his children. But we still get on well, don't we?' Lottie gave Mario a friendly nudge. 'Not in *that* sense of course, but in a just-good-friends kind of way. Like I get on well with Amber, his girlfriend. She's away on holiday at the moment, but she's lovely. If you met her, you'd like her too.'

'OK.' Mario held up his hands. 'You've made your point, said what you came here to say. But there's really no need. I already told you, I'm not doing anything wrong. Karen and I are just *friends*.'

Lottie, wondering just how much he hated her right now, nodded vigorously. 'I know! And I think it's great! That's why I thought I'd join you, so we can have a fun evening and all be friends together!'

117

He'd been outmanoeuvred. Recognising that there was no way out, Mario shrugged good-naturedly and said, 'Fine. We'll do that.'

'Good.' Lottie's smile was dazzling. 'Karen? You don't mind, do you?'

From the look on her face, Karen was about as thrilled as if Lottie had suggested tattooing a dear little moustache on her upper lip. But since Mario had already acquiesced, she was forced to shake her head and say, 'No, of course I don't mind.'

Lying through her gritted teeth, naturally, but Lottie didn't let that bother her. Warmly she said, 'That's *great*.'

'Oh!' As if she'd just remembered she had a Get Out of Jail Free card, Karen blurted out, 'We won't be able to stay for long though.' She pretended to look disappointed. 'We're going into Cheltenham.'

'For something to eat.' Lottie nodded enthusiastically. 'I know, Mario mentioned it earlier. You'll love Trigiani's, they do the *best* spaghetti marinara. That's why I haven't had anything to eat!'

Honestly, for a girl who'd been looking for companionship and good conversation, Karen had made surprisingly little effort in that department. Following their meal at Trigiani's, the journey back to Hestacombe was a subdued one. When they reached Piper's Cottage and Mario slowed the car down, Lottie leaned forward from the back seat and said, 'Actually, why don't we drop Karen off first?'

'We're here now.' In the rear-view mirror, Mario's gaze met hers. 'Plus, I'd like a private word with Karen.'

Quelle surprise.

'And I'd like a private word with you,' said Lottie. 'About Ruby and Nat. You don't mind being dropped off first, do you, Karen?'

By this time thoroughly fed up and keen to escape, Karen gestured with her Chanel clutchbag – unlike every other Chanel bag Lottie had ever seen, it was the genuine article rather than a knock-off. 'No, go ahead. Whatever.'

Lottie loved that expression: it signalled, 'You've won, I give up.' *Whaaateverrrr.*

Hilarious.

'Well done,' said Mario, pulling up outside Piper's Cottage for the second time.

Lottie's smile was serene. 'Don't mention it.'

'Pleased with yourself?'

'Delighted, thanks.'

'It wasn't necessary, you know. I didn't need a chaperone.'

'Of course you didn't.' Patting his arm, Lottie said, 'You wouldn't cheat on Amber.'

'So what made you do it?'

'Just making extra-sure. Turn off the ignition.'

Mario rolled his eyes. 'Why?'

'Because you're staying here tonight. With us.'

'Are you after my body?'

Lottie said, 'No, but I know a girl who is.'

'She's gone.'

'Ah, but she might ring you, persuade you against your better judgement to meet up with her again. As your chaperone, it's my duty to protect
you from wicked wanton women. In fact, I think you should stay with us
for the rest of the week. The kids would love it.'

'And?'

'And when Amber asks me if you've been behaving yourself, I'll be able
to tell her you have.'

Mario shook his head, half smiling at the look on her face. 'It really
means that much to you?'

'I want my children to be happy. That means more than anything to
me. And they love Amber to bits. The two of you being together makes
them happy. I just don't want you to mess things up for them.'

'OK, OK. If it's that important, I'll stay here for the rest of the week.'

Yay, victory! Jumping out of the car, Lottie danced round to the
driver's side. When Mario climbed out, tall and rangy in his dark blue
shirt and faded jeans, she slipped her arm through his and planted a
grateful kiss on his cheek as together they made their way up the path.
It was only ten o'clock, which meant the kids would still be up and
doubtless she and Mario would be dragooned into a marathon game of
Monopoly.

'One thing.' Mario paused before she opened the front door.

'What?'

'This big old sermon about me staying with Amber because the kids
love her and if I was with anyone else it'd ruin their lives and turn them
into glue-sniffing delinquents.'

'Yes?' If they were going to play Monopoly, Lottie wanted to be the
racing car. She always won when she was the racing car.

Mario gave her a speculative look. 'So how come it's all right for you
to go out with Tyler Klein?'

Mario was at work when an appreciative wolf whistle echoed through the
air-conditioned showroom. Looking up he saw the cause of it; Amber was
stepping through the automatic doors.

'You're a lucky sod.' Jerry, the perpetrator of the wolf whistle, stroked
his designer-stubbled chin and studied Amber like a hard-to-impress trainer

at a horse auction. 'If you ever decide you don't want her, I'll take her off your hands.'

'In your dreams,' said Mario, because Jerry weighed sixteen stone and liked to conceal his greying hair with liberal applications of Just For Men.

Furthermore, Mario had no intention of offloading Amber onto anyone. Watching her make her way across the showroom, he was struck by how fantastic she was looking in a sunflower-yellow silk top and flippy white skirt. Her hair was blonder and her tan deeper than ever. She glowed with vitality. Luckily there were no customers around.

'You're back.' It had been annoying at the time, but now he was glad Lottie had appointed herself his guardian. His conscience was clear; he hadn't done anything wrong and it felt great. Hugging Amber, breathing in the gorgeous smell of her skin, he gave her a kiss. 'I've missed you.'

'Really?' Turning to Mario's co-workers, Amber said playfully, 'Has he?'

'Not at all.' Jerry, ever-helpful, said, 'I'd dump him if I were you. Fancy going out with me instead?'

'Does she look desperate?' Reaching for her hand, Mario said, 'Let's go somewhere more private.'

'Two secs. Jerry, has my boyfriend been behaving himself?'

'Absolutely. He was polite to all the lap dancers, always asked their permission before tucking the twenties into their G-strings.' Guffawing at his own wit, Jerry went on, 'Always warmed his hands before—'

'Sacking his staff,' Mario suggested.

'Maybe I picked the wrong person to ask.' Amber's smile was rueful.

Mario gave her hand a squeeze. 'Come on. We can talk properly outside.'

Out in the car park behind the showroom, he kissed her again. 'What time did you get back? I wasn't expecting to see you until tonight.'

'The plane landed at one o'clock, we were home by two thirty. But I can't see you this evening. One of my regulars got desperate and tried to do her own highlights while I was away. Apparently she looks like Worzel Gummidge and is refusing to leave her house until I've sorted out the mess. That's why I'm here now.'

'But . . . you were coming over to *us*.' Mario couldn't believe it, he'd spent the last week practically counting down the hours. 'We've got all the food for a barbeque. The kids have been dying to see you.'

Amber searched his face. 'How about you?'

'Me too.' How could she even ask him that?

'Well, good. But Maisie's highlights are green. They're going to take hours to sort out, and I know I'm going to be shattered tonight. So I'll see you tomorrow instead.' Amber unlocked the boot of her turquoise Fiat and lifted out a box. 'And you can give these to Nat and Ruby, that'll cheer them up.'

Unlike Tyler Klein, Amber was an inspired present-chooser, always managing to find just the right gifts. As the box was plonked into his arms Mario said, 'They'd rather have you there.'

'And they will. Tomorrow.' Checking her watch, Amber leaned across and gave him a brief peck on the cheek. 'I'd better shoot off, I've got so much catching up to do. Bye, darling. Don't forget to give the monsters a big squidgy hug from me.'

Mario stood and watched the Fiat shoot out of the car park and bomb off down the road. If he didn't know better, he'd wonder if maybe she hadn't met someone else on holiday.

No. That was ridiculous. Amber would never do that.

But there was still something unnervingly different about her. Swallowing disappointment – and grimly ignoring the sense of unease in his chest – he headed back into the showroom.

All that anticipation for nothing.

'Wa-heyyy!' crowed Jerry. 'Here he is, back from his quickie in the car park. And, ladies and gentlemen, at one minute forty-three seconds that *was* quick . . .'

Mario treated Jerry's infantile attempt at humour with the contempt it deserved. Jesus, was it still only four o'clock?

So much for counting down the hours till Amber's return.

Chapter 26

'Tonight's the night . . . da da, de-da da.' Lottie sang the song quietly so that no one else could hear as she surveyed her reflection in the dressing table mirror. Her dress was dark red and shimmery and so was her mouth. Her hair, hanging loose tonight, was a mass of glossy black ringlets and her eyes were bright. Beneath the dress, her black silk bra and knickers were the kind you wore when you very much hoped they'd be seen. Also beneath the dress, her heart was racing like a hamster on a wheel as she reached for the mascara and finished her eyes. In ten minutes Mario and Amber would be arriving to pick up the kids. Nat and Ruby were spending the night at Mario's . . . oh yes, this was definitely going to be an evening to remember. Turning sideways in the mirror, Lottie critically surveyed her figure. Hearing the gentle slap-slap of flip-flops on the stairs she called out, 'Ruby? Come and tell me what you think. Does my bum look big in this dress?'

Ruby appeared in the bedroom doorway. 'Yes.'

'Excellent.' Lottie patted her shapely backside with satisfaction. If she said so herself, it was one of her finest assets. Then she saw the expression on Ruby's face. 'Rubes? What's wrong?'

'Nat's got a stomach ache. He's been sick and now he's crying.'

'Sick!' Alarmed, Lottie rushed to the door. 'Where?'

'Not on the carpet. In the loo. He says his stomach really hurts.'

Together they raced downstairs. Nat was lying on the sofa in the living room clutching his abdomen and whimpering with pain. Lottie knelt beside him and stroked his face. 'Oh, sweetheart. When did this start?'

'Not long. I felt ill at teatime but it's just got bad now.' Nat screwed up his face and gritted his teeth. 'Mummy, it hurts so much.'

Lottie was stroking his forehead. Perplexed, she said, 'Why are you all wet?'

'I washed my face after I was sick. And I pulled the flush to make it all go away.'

'You washed your face? *And* remembered to pull the flush?' To see if

122

she could make him smile Lottie said, 'It's like a double miracle!'

But Nat buried his face in her neck and wailed, 'Hug me, Mummy. Make me better. *Ow*, I feel sick again . . .'

Lottie experienced a horrid feeling of trepidation, one she wasn't remotely proud of. Nat was ill; he'd always been more prone to stomach upsets than Ruby. She'd nursed him through plenty of vomiting sessions over the years and invariably he recovered by the next day.

But tonight was *the* night, *her* night, and she didn't want this to be happening now. She was all dressed up, her hair done, her legs freshly shaved. Tyler was expecting her at Fox Cottage in less than thirty minutes. Short of tumbling down the stairs and breaking both legs, she hadn't imagined anything could happen to stop her being there.

Foolishly, she'd forgotten she was a mother.

'I've brought the washing-up bowl,' Ruby announced, 'for him to be sick in again if it comes up really fast.'

'Thanks.' As Nat clung to her like a limpet, Lottie sensed that this was how it would feel if your lottery numbers came up the one week you hadn't bought a ticket. 'But it helps if you take the washing-up out of it first.'

'Where's Amber?' Ruby demanded when Mario arrived minutes later.

'Busy. She can't come over tonight.' Mario eyed Nat and the washing-up bowl with trepidation. 'What's going on?'

Nat gave him a piteous look. 'I'm really ill.'

Mario visibly recoiled as if Nat might suddenly launch into projectile-vomit mode.

'He might not be sick again,' Lottie pleaded. 'He's just got a tummy ache.' In desperation she stroked Nat's face and said, 'Maybe you just need to go to sleep, sweetheart.'

'Noooo.' Nat shook his head and tightened his grip on her.

'Poor Mummy.' Ruby looked sympathetic. 'She's going to miss her important business meeting in Bath.'

'Business meeting?' Mario raised a sceptical eyebrow at the tight-fitting red shimmery dress.

'It's a Tourist Board do. Meeting first, dinner afterwards.' Lottie, who had been rehearsing the lie all day, said defensively, 'At the Pump Rooms. Everyone dresses up.'

Not that it mattered any more. They all knew she wasn't going anywhere. Unless by some miracle . . . 'Nat, why don't you let Daddy look after you, hmm? He'd—'

'*Noooooooooo.*' Throwing himself at her, Nat whimpered, 'I'm poorly. Don't go out, Mummy. I want you to stay with me.'

★　★　★

'You're going out *again*?' Ruby looked horrified.

'What do you mean, again?' Busy clearing the breakfast table, Lottie raised her eyebrows in retaliation. 'I haven't *been* anywhere yet.'

It was the morning after, and Nat had made a suspiciously swift recovery from his stomach upset. *Alleged* stomach upset. Having already polished off a mountain of Coco Pops at record speed, he had raced upstairs to get ready for school and could now be heard clumping down again, bellowing out the new Avril Lavigne single at the top of his voice.

Ruby, sitting at the table still ploughing through her own bowl of Crunchy Nut cornflakes – which always took forever because she refused to sully them with milk – looked at Nat as he burst into the kitchen and said meaningfully, 'She's going out again.'

Nat abruptly stopped singing. 'Why?'

'Because you're going over to your dad's house for a barbeque and I've decided to join an evening class in Cheltenham.' Pouring herself a strong coffee, Lottie said, 'That's allowed, isn't it?'

'What evening class?'

What indeed? Macramé? Russian for beginners? Knit-your-own chastity belt?

'Line dancing,' Lottie said firmly.

They gazed at her in disbelief. 'What?'

'It's fun.'

'Where they wear cowboy hats and pointy boots? And all dance in a line?' Nat clapped his hands over his mouth, smothering a giggle. 'That's *saaaad*.'

'You don't have to wear a hat and boots.'

'It's still sad. Mega-sad. Only nerdy durr-brains do stuff like that.'

Feeling defensive on behalf of line dancers everywhere – she'd never attempted it herself but it always looked rather jolly – Lottie said, 'But I'll be doing it and I'm not a nerdy durr-brain.' For good measure she added evenly, 'Nor's Arnold Schwarzenegger, and he's been line dancing for years.'

'That's a lie!' Outraged, Nat cried out, 'He has not!'

'It's *all* a lie.' Ruby was scornful. 'She isn't going to any evening class. She's just saying it so she can meet that man again.'

Nat stared at Lottie. 'Is that true?'

Lottie's heart sank. Why did life have to be so difficult?

'OK, I *was* going to join the line dancing class.' She spoke swiftly because lying was one thing; being caught lying was quite another. 'But I'm meeting Tyler afterwards.'

Ruby pushed aside her bowl of Crunchy Nut cornflakes. 'See?'

'No.' Nat shook his head. 'Mummy, don't.'

'Nat, it doesn't make any difference to you. You don't have to see him. He's a nice man,' Lottie said helplessly.

His lower lip stuck out. 'You mean *you* like him.'

'Yes, I do.' Lottie put down her coffee. 'Sweetheart, it's just one night out. With a friend.'

'And then another night out, and another, and another,' Ruby chanted, 'and he isn't a friend, he's a *boyfriend*.' She spat out the last word as if it was botulism. 'Mum, please don't go out with that man. He hates us.'

'He doesn't hate you! How can you even think that? OK.' Lottie held up her hands as they both opened their mouths. 'We don't have time for this now. It's half past eight. We'll talk about it properly after school.'

'Fine.' Ruby glowered and pushed back her chair as Lottie began searching for the car keys. 'That means you're still going to see him tonight.'

Was there seriously any reason why she shouldn't? Picking up the half-empty cereal bowl and feeling unfairly got at, Lottie said, 'Yes, I am. And I'm looking forward to it. Now go and brush your teeth.'

The run of spectacular weather came to an abrupt end that afternoon. Charcoal-grey storm clouds rolled in from the west and the first fat drops of rain, as big as pennies, thudded onto the windscreen of Lottie's car as she drove to Oaklea School to pick up Ruby and Nat. Typically, by the time she'd found somewhere to park, the spattering of raindrops had accelerated to a downpour. Even more typically, Lottie hadn't brought a jacket. Bracing herself for a sprint up the road, she leapt athletically from the car and heard an ominous *rrrrippp* as the modest, meant-to-be-there split at the front of her skirt became a decidedly immodest one reaching almost up to her knickers.

Oh well, she'd just have to skulk at the back of the playground, signal her presence to Nat and Ruby from a distance and make a hasty getaway. Clutching the split seams together and discovering this meant she could only totter along like a geisha girl, Lottie gave up and did her best to cover the split with both hands. Now she looked as if she was desperate for a wee.

Never mind, nearly there. Damn, why did it always have to rain just as school ended? Glancing down to check she was at least semi-decent skirt-wise, Lottie sucked in her breath at yet another unwelcome discovery: her white shirt was wet and sticking to her like clingfilm. Proudly revealing her lacy red bra.

Chapter 27

Feeling like a dirty old man – although if she were a dirty old man she'd surely have the luxury of a mac – Lottie lurked furtively among the trees at the back of the playground and waved to Nat and Ruby when they came spilling out of their classrooms. By the time they'd raced over to her, she was already sidling towards the gates.

'Come on, let's go, look what I've done to my skirt.' Hustling them ahead of her, she used Ruby as a kind of human shield. 'Nat? Hurry up, sweetheart, it's raining.'

'We can't go. Miss Batson wants to see you.'

Lottie stopped dead. Were any words designed to strike a greater sense of impending doom into the heart of any mother? She was no wimp, but Nat's teacher was truly terrifying. Miss Batson – *nobody* knew her first name, possibly not even her own mother – was in her late fifties. Her iron-grey hair matched her clothes, which in turn matched her manner. When she requested a meeting with some poor unsuspecting parent you knew it was time to be scared.

'OK. I'll ring and make an appointment.' A facelift without anaesthetic would be preferable, but there would be no escape until the deed was done.

'No. *Now*,' insisted Nat.

'Sweetheart, it's raining. And my skirt's torn. I can't see her today.' Lottie attempted to move him on but he dug his heels in.

'You have to. She said *now*.'

Lottie's insides churned. 'Why? What have you done?'

'Nothing.' His head dropping, Nat kicked at a stone.

'Then why does it have to be now?'

He mumbled, 'Just does.'

Pointing across the playground, Ruby said, 'She's there. Waiting.'

Oh God, so she was. Feeling sick, Lottie saw Miss Batson framed in the classroom doorway. Even at this distance she was looking grim. And scary. And not a bit as if she were about to launch into a rousing chorus of 'My Favourite Things'.

126

Probably one of her favourite things was chewing up and spitting out hapless parents for breakfast.

Clutching Nat's hand, Lottie made her way across the playground. The last time she'd been summoned by Miss Batson was when one of Nat's classmates had poked him in the leg with a blunt pencil and Nat had retaliated by poking him back with a sharp one. Lottie, subjected to a long lecture on how Violence Would Not Be Tolerated at Oaklea and made to feel like a Very Bad Parent for having raised a child with such antisocial tendencies, had begun to wish she had a sharp pencil to hand herself.

Now, somehow more drenched than ever, she blinked rain out of her eyes and took a couple of deep breaths. 'Hello, Miss Batson. You wanted to see me?'

'Ms Carlyle. Good afternoon. Indeed I did.'

'Mrs,' said Lottie. She hated being addressed as *Mzz*, it sounded like a wasp being squashed.

Ignoring this, Miss Batson ushered Nat and Ruby into the classroom and through the maze of desks. 'You two can wait for us in the hallway. Sit outside the secretary's office. *Ms* Carlyle?' With a sharp inclination of her Brillo head she directed Lottie towards one of the chairs in front of her own desk. 'Make yourself comfortable.'

Which had to be a joke, surely. The moulded plastic grey chair was designed for infant-sized pupils. Lottie's knees were higher than her bottom, her bottom was wider than the chair's seat and no matter how tightly she clamped her legs together the crotch-high split in her skirt meant Miss Batson could undoubtedly see her stripy pink knickers.

Plus she was dripping rain onto the floor and the cups of her red bra were glowing through her wet shirt like twin traffic lights.

'Sorry about my skirt.' Attempting to sound cheerful Lottie said, 'I ripped it getting out of the car. Typical!'

'Hmm. We're here to discuss Nat.' Miss Batson's tone was designed to make Lottie feel frivolous and stupid. 'I have to tell you, Ms Carlyle, that I'm extremely concerned about him.'

Her mouth dry, Lottie said, 'What's he done?'

'He borrowed a ruler from Charlotte West this morning. And refused to give it back.'

'Oh right. A ruler.' Relief flooded through Lottie like alcohol. 'Well, that's not so terrible, is it?' Catching the look in Miss Batson's beady eye she added hastily, 'Well, of course it *is* terrible, but I'll speak to him, explain he mustn't—'

'When I eventually retrieved the ruler, Nat refused to apologise. And when I sent him to the naughty corner he used a crayon in his pocket to write on the wall.'

'Oh. What did he write?'

'He wrote I HATE,' Miss Batson reported icily, 'before I took the crayon from him. Then, when I told him off for defacing school property, he burst into tears.'

'Right. OK. I'll have a word with him about that too.'

'I then spent the lunch break speaking privately to Nat to find out why he was being so disruptive. He's a very unhappy little boy, Ms Carlyle. He told me everything, the whole story. And I have to say, I find it very troubling. Very troubling indeed.'

Numb and incredulous, Lottie said, 'What whole story?'

'Your son is a victim of divorce, Ms Carlyle. That's a traumatic enough experience for any small child to have to deal with. But now you, a single parent, have embarked upon a relationship with another man. A man, furthermore, whom Nat does not like,' Miss Batson stated firmly.

'But—'

'And this is having a catastrophic effect on Nat,' the older woman continued, her mouth rigid with disapproval. 'He feels powerless. He's made his feelings abundantly clear to you, yet evidently you have chosen to ignore his pain.'

'But I—'

'Indeed, you have taken the frankly extraordinary decision to continue with this unsuitable liaison, without regard for your son's mental state. Which, I have to say, shocks me. Any mother who chooses her own happiness at the expense of her children's is displaying a lack of concern that I find quite breathtakingly selfish.'

Stunned into silence, Lottie gazed past Miss Batson and focused on the map of Africa on the wall behind her. Then Africa began to blur and she realised to her horror that her eyes were swimming with tears.

'You have to seriously consider your priorities here, Ms Carlyle. Who is more important to you? This man or your own son?' Miss Batson paused, driving the message home. 'Whom do you love more?'

Lottie had never felt so small in her life. Shame welled up and a single tear slid down one cheek. Miss Batson thought she was a disgrace, an unfit mother and no doubt a slapper to boot, with her high heels and her look-at-me bra and her split-to-the-limit skirt.

'Well?' Miss Batson was tapping her fingers, demanding an answer.

'I love my son more.' It came out as a whisper.

'Good. Delighted to hear that. So do I take it we won't be needing this?'

'What is it?' Lottie looked at the card with a telephone number written on it.

'The contact number for social services.'

'What?'

'Nat told me everything,' Miss Batson repeated coolly. 'About the mental cruelty inflicted upon him and his sister by this so-called boyfriend of yours. The things he's said and done over the course of the last few weeks – well, it certainly wasn't pleasant having to hear about them. If you're looking for a potential stepfather for your children, you have to consider their feelings, Ms Carlyle. They're the ones who matter. Well, we'll put this away. For now.' She folded the card in two and slid it into her desk drawer.

'Now wait a minute.' All the blood rushed to Lottie's cheeks as she realised what Miss Batson was implying. 'There hasn't been any mental cruelty! Tyler isn't a monster! He's done everything he can to get along with my children, he never meant to upset them! If they'd just give him another chance they'd realise how—'

'Maybe we'll be needing this number after all.' Miss Batson's bony fingers swooped back down to the desk drawer.

'No we won't!' Now Lottie really wanted to stab her with a sharp pencil. 'We *won't*, OK? But I'm just trying to explain to you that this has been blown out of all proportion!'

'And I'm trying to explain to you,' Miss Batson explained evenly, 'that I gave up my lunch hour to mop up the tears of a seven-year-old boy and listen to him pouring his heart out to me about how devastated he is by the unwanted arrival of this man in his life.'

'But—'

'That will be all, Ms Carlyle.' Rising to her feet, Miss Batson checked her watch. 'Needless to say, we shall all be keeping a close eye on Nat and Ruby in the weeks and months ahead. The staff here at Oaklea regard the happiness and well-being of our pupils as of prime importance.'

Stung, Lottie said, 'So do I.'

'Good. And once this gentleman friend of yours is out of the picture I'm sure we'll all see a marked improvement in Ruby and Nat's mental well-being. Thank you for your time.'

As Miss Batson opened the door to send her through to the hallway where Ruby and Nat were waiting, Lottie found herself saying dazedly, 'Thank you.'

Chapter 28

Hi Tom,

If I make lots of mistakes it's because I'm typing this with gluey fingers – for the last four hours I've been sticking tiny white marabou feathers onto christening cards and only realised when I'd finished that I've run out of acetone so can't clean it off! Up to my eyes this week with lots of repeat orders coming in, which is great – except there are weeds popping up outside and I haven't had time to deal with them so the garden's a mess. (Though somehow still have time to eat chocolate!)

Is Donny settling back at school OK? Jojo's started learning Russian this term and was over here earlier asking me to help her with her homework, which is way too much for my poor frazzled brain to cope with.

Did you watch that murder mystery on ITV last night? I was so sure the vicar was the baddie. Spent ages trying to remember what else the actress who played his wife has been in. Still can't remember and it's driving me nuts. When I went—

The doorbell rang, making Cressida jump. Since Tom's first stilted message they had both relaxed and were now corresponding on a daily basis. Every time she clicked onto her email account she experienced a little thrill of anticipation, wondering if there would be something from him. Which she encouraged shamelessly by always including a couple of questions that would give Tom a reason to reply. And if that was cheating, Cressida didn't care. So far it had worked a treat.

'Hi!' Opening the front door, she was delighted to find a drowned rat on the doorstep clutching two bottles of wine. Taking them from her, Cressida said, 'For me? Thank you so much! Goodbye!'

'Not so fast.' Lottie already had her foot in the door.

Cressida grinned. 'Come on in. You look terrible.'

'Thanks. So would you if you'd had a day like mine. Corkscrew,' Lottie demanded, making straight for the kitchen. 'Glasses. Your individual attention and lots and lots of sympathy, that's all I ask.'

'Oh, poor you. I'll be with you in two seconds.' Veering off to the office, Cressida rushed over to the computer and typed at lightning speed: 'Got to go now – my friend Lottie's just turned up and she's having a crisis. Red wine being opened as I speak. Love and hugs, Cress xxxx'.

Then she pressed Send and raced back to the kitchen where Lottie, too impatient to search the cupboards for proper wine glasses, was pouring inky-red Merlot into mugs.

'So what else could I do?' Half an hour had passed and the first bottle was well on its way to being emptied. Lottie had related the entire cringe-making lecture from Miss Batson practically verbatim. 'We got home and I had a long talk with Ruby and Nat. It turns out that Ben and Harry Jenkins saw me and Tyler together the other day. We were having a bit of a moment outside his cottage. Not *that* kind of moment,' she added defensively as Cressida's eyebrows shot up. 'Just a kiss. But bloody Ben and Harry were hiding up a tree and they heard Tyler saying something like he never wanted to see Nat and Ruby again, and it all blew up from there. Anyway, I packed the kids off to Mario's at seven and phoned Tyler to tell him we couldn't see each other again. Well, apart from at work. Obviously. So that's it. All done. This wine isn't bad, is it?' Sloshing the last couple of inches into their glasses, Lottie said, 'The more you drink, the better it gets.'

Cressida didn't know about that, but it was definitely making her shoulders go numb. 'What did Tyler say when you told him?'

'What could he say? He didn't fall on his knees and beg me to change my mind. Well, he was on the phone so I don't know about the knee bit.' Lottie heaved a sigh. 'Anyhow, he didn't beg. He just said it was a shame and he was sorry things had turned out this way, but he agreed that I had to put my kids first.'

'I suppose he's right. I mean, it's all you *can* do.' Cressida was sympathetic. 'It just seems so unfair, doesn't it? When you're fifteen and you go out with an eighteen-year-old bad boy, you expect your parents to stop you seeing him. But it never occurs to you that in years to come your own children might do the same thing.'

'It never occurred to me that I'd have children like Ruby and Nat.' Lottie's eyes abruptly filled with tears. 'Oh God, I love them so much. They're my whole life. I hate that bloody old witch Miss Batson, but in a way she was right. I just didn't realise what I was doing to them, I swear I didn't. Peanuts.'

'Sorry?'

'Peanuts. And chocolate. They'll make us feel better, cheer us up. Not that you look as if you need cheering up,' Lottie called as Cressida headed into the kitchen to mount a raid on the snack cupboard. 'In fact you're looking quite perky and sparkly.'

'I'm not.'

'You are.'

'I'm not!'

'Oh yes you *are*.' Lottie wiggled an accusing finger at her. 'All perky and sparkly and *zingy*, as if you're hiding some brilliant secret. And I need to know what it is, for the good of my health.'

Cressida, always hopeless at keeping secrets, went pink and felt her eyes flicker in the direction of the office where even now a new email from Tom could be waiting, tantalisingly unread, in her inbox.

'You've got a man,' Lottie crowed, spotting the flicker and almost knocking over her drink with excitement. 'A man, hiding in your office! You wanton harlot! Is he naked? Is it wild sex or true love?'

'It's Tom Turner,' Cressida blurted out, 'and he isn't hiding in my office. We're just emailing each other.' Pausing, she added, 'Every day.'

'Tom Turner! That's fantastic!' Lottie clapped her hands. 'So it could *become* love?'

Love. A squiggle of apprehension wormed its way through Cressida's stomach.

Oh God. *Love*.

Had she? Or hadn't she?

It was eleven o'clock, Lottie had just left and Cressida was in front of the computer, unable to ignore the niggling fear a minute longer. It was the exact feeling she had experienced after her maths GCSE exam when everyone else had complained about how hard it had been to answer all five parts of the last question and Cressida had realised to her horror that she'd thought you only had to answer one of them.

Except that had been a case of carelessly misreading something. This time she had the toe-curling suspicion she had miswritten something instead.

Business emails were fine. She ended them with Yours or Best wishes or Many thanks.

Following Tom's lead she carefully signed off her replies to him with All the best.

But when she was replying to the jokey, affectionate emails Jojo sent her on an almost daily basis she invariably wrote Love and hugs, Cress xxxx.

And now she had the most horrible feeling that in those few moments following Lottie's arrival when she had hurriedly dashed off the end of her message to Tom, she had unthinkingly put . . . oh God . . . Love and hugs, Cress xxxx.

Not having saved a copy of her email, she couldn't check.

Cheeks aflame, Cressida feverishly logged in and drummed her fingers on the table, waiting to see if Tom had replied.

He hadn't. She took a gulp of wine. She had no way of knowing whether his failure to respond meant he hadn't yet read it or that he had and was too startled by her brazen signal to know what to do next.

He might be sniggering to himself. Or filled with alarm. All the best was a long, *long* way from Love and hugs and a row of kisses.

Oh hell, what to do to redeem the situation?

Obviously she had to write back.

Dear Tom,
Not sure if I should be writing this (bit pissed) but I'm really sorry if I wrote Love and hugs at the end of my last email. Meant to put All the best but got confused – what's new? – and thought you were Jojo. Well, what I mean is I thought I was finishing an email to Jojo, not you, because obviously I wouldn't send you hugs and a row of kisses.

Tipping her head back, Cressida emptied her glass and wiped the spilled drops of wine from her chin. Right, carry on, get the job done.

Not that I don't like you, of course. You're a very nice man and I really *really* look forward to your emails, which is why I hope my last one didn't scare you off. Although if I didn't write Love and hugs I suppose it wouldn't. Anyway, just wanted to explain. Sorry again. Please write back soon and let me know you don't think I'm barking mad. Unless you do, in which case I'd rather not know.
All the best.
Cress.
See? No kisses.
(Yet.)

Was that OK? Friendly and casual. Explanatory but light-hearted. Oh yes, it'd be fine. Completely fine. Tom couldn't take offence, he'd probably just tease her about it and it would become a shared running joke between them, which would be fun.

He'd understand.

Feeling a lot happier, Cressida pressed Send.

There, done.

Time for bed.

Chapter 29

Was something the matter with Amber?

It was Lottie's morning off and she was in the salon having deep red lowlights in addition to a trim, in an effort to cheer herself up and stave off the prospect of eternal spinsterhood. Normally she loved coming to the salon with its buzzy, gossipy atmosphere and comforting hairdressery smells, but the other girls were off today which meant she and Amber were alone. And for the first time since Lottie could remember the conversation wasn't flowing naturally.

What's more, the silences between her attempts at conversation were becoming downright awkward.

After struggling on for another fifteen minutes, Lottie said, 'Amber? Is anything wrong?'

Behind her, in the mirror, Amber shrugged. 'I don't know. Is there?' She paused. 'You tell me.'

There was definitely something wrong. Lottie shook her head and the wedges of foil around her temples flapped like spaniel's ears. 'Tell you what?'

Amber put down the flat brush she'd been using to paint dye onto the separate sections of hair. 'About Mario.'

'Mario? He's fine. Honestly!' Lottie wondered if Amber had heard about Mario's brief flirtation with Karen Crane.

'I know he's fine.' Amber's gaze was steady in the mirror. 'I just want to know if he's been seeing someone else.'

Lottie shifted, her fingers twisting together beneath the dark blue cape draped over her shoulders. As convincingly as she could, she said, 'No, he hasn't.'

'I think he has.'

'Like who?'

Another pause. Then Amber said, 'Like you.'

Lottie was so relieved she burst out laughing.

'Is that what this is all about?' she said finally. 'You think there's something going on between me and Mario? Amber, I'd tell you if there was.

But there isn't. I *wouldn't*, not in a million years! And that's a promise.'

Amber exhaled slowly. Finally she nodded, her pink and silver earrings rattling as she reached for the pile of foil squares.

'OK. Sorry. I believe you. It's just . . . I called into the shop yesterday and Ted was really surprised to see me.'

'Well, that's because you've been away for a couple of weeks.'

'That's what I thought. Then he said he'd thought you and Mario were back together. Then some old dear chimed in with, "That's what I reckoned too, what with him spending every night at Piper's Cottage."'

Village gossips. Couldn't you just tie them up and throw them in the lake?

'He slept on the sofa,' said Lottie. Then she shifted again, guessing what was coming next.

'The sofa.' Amber nodded. 'That's fine. But what I'd really like to know,' she went on slowly, 'is whose idea it was that Mario should stay over in the first place.'

'Well, the kids *loved* having him there,' Lottie began brightly, but Amber quelled her with a look.

'It was you, wasn't it? You made Mario sleep at your cottage every night. Because you knew he couldn't be trusted and it was your way of keeping an eye on him, making sure he didn't get up to anything while I was away.'

Amber was nobody's fool. Lottie shrugged, signalling defeat. 'OK, I thought it wouldn't do any harm. You know what men are like, brains in their trousers. Mario wouldn't deliberately set out to do anything wrong, but let's face it, he's a good looking bloke. And some girls are shameless. I just thought he'd be safer with us than going out with the lads from work and—'

'Forgetting he has a girlfriend,' Amber said bluntly. 'Out of sight, out of mind. Or maybe what she doesn't find out about won't hurt her.'

'I'm sorry. I thought I was doing the right thing.' Lottie watched in the mirror as Amber deftly parcelled up the last of the foil packages and wiped her hands on a cloth. 'Should I have just left him to it?'

Amber sighed and flipped her sun-bleached fringe out of her eyes. 'Oh God, I don't know. Why *did* you do it?'

'Because I want you and Mario to be happy and stay together forever. I think you make a great couple,' said Lottie. 'And I don't want anything to jeopardise that.'

'For the sake of the monsters.' Amber's tone was dry. 'Because they like me.'

'They *love* you. And that's important,' Lottie admitted. 'Of course it is. I want them to be happy. I was just trying to help.'

Amber looked at her. 'And what about me? Do you want me to be happy?'

'Yes! That's the whole point!'

'No, it isn't.' Pulling up a stool on wheels Amber said steadily, 'The point is, could I ever really *be* happy with Mario? With someone I'm not sure I could ever trust?'

Lottie was alarmed. 'But you've been together for, what, eight months now. You always knew what he was like. Mario's a charmer and a flirt, but you've always taken it in your stride—'

'I haven't.' Amber shook her head. 'I just started off doing what millions of other girls do all the time. I thought that, deep down, I'd be the one to change him. I kidded myself that this time it'd be different, he'd learn from his past mistakes and realise that what we had was too special to risk messing up.' She paused and raised her eyebrows at Lottie. 'I expect you thought that too, didn't you? When you married him.'

Yes, well. Lottie knew she had, of course she had. But she'd been nineteen. When you were nineteen it didn't occur to you that you might not be able to change someone for the better.

Conceding this with a shrug, she pointed out, 'But he hasn't been unfaithful to you.'

'Thanks to you and the kids keeping him under house arrest.' Amber smiled faintly.

'He loves you.'

'I know. But does he love me enough?'

'So what's going to happen?' Lottie felt a stab of fear.

'I don't know. I'm still trying to decide.'

'But Nat and Ruby—'

'Lottie, I love them to bits.' Amber reached for a square of unused foil and began tearing it to shreds. 'You know I do. But you can't expect me to stay with a man who's going to make me miserable, just to keep his children happy.'

'And his ex-wife,' Lottie reminded her. 'You'd be keeping her happy too.'

Amber's mouth twitched. 'You are shameless.'

'I wish I was rich and shameless.' Ruefully Lottie said, 'If I had pots of money I could bribe you to stay.'

'Just as well you aren't then. Now, let's see how these are doing.' Scooting close on her stool, Amber began unfolding a foil parcel at the nape of Lottie's neck and carefully inspected the contents. 'Not ready yet. Coffee?'

'Thanks.' Lottie nodded, relieved that at least the strained atmosphere had dissipated. Now at least the problem was out in the open and maybe between the two of them they could deal with it. Pulling a face she said,

'Men, eh? Why can't they ever appreciate how lucky they are?'

Amber was busy spooning coffee into mugs. 'Some do.'

'I suppose. But it's more likely to be the man who plays away, isn't it? Or always thinks the grass might be greener.' Lottie waved her arm vaguely in the direction of wherever the greener grass might be. 'I mean, if I had a gorgeous man I'd never be tempted to lie or cheat. Neither would you. So why do—?'

'I have.'

'*Have* you?' Fascinated, Lottie said, 'What, you've actually cheated on a boyfriend? Who was that?'

Amber carefully poured boiling water into the mugs, added milk and stirred. 'Mario.'

Lottie was stunned; this wasn't what she'd been expecting at all. 'Seriously?'

'Oh yes, quite seriously. Sugar?'

'Two. My God, when did this happen?'

Amber said, 'On holiday.'

'I don't believe it! You met someone in France! Oh my *God*!'

'Actually I didn't.' Matter of factly, Amber handed over Lottie's mug and sat back down nursing her own. 'We went to France together.'

Lottie's brain was in a whirl; she felt as if she were at a fairground trapped on the Waltzers. 'But . . . you said . . .'

'I know. I told you I was going on holiday with my friend Mandy.' Cheerfully Amber said, 'And no, I'm not a lesbian. I didn't go away with Mandy. That was a lie.'

Blimey. Lottie had to put her coffee mug down before she scalded her legs. 'Who then?'

'His name's Quentin.'

Yikes. *Quentin?*

'OK, I know what you're thinking. As names go, it doesn't exactly conjure up a picture of the ultimate hunk. Men called Quentin don't generally have movie star looks and rippling biceps, do they?' Drily Amber said, 'And this one doesn't either. He's just ordinary. Nice, normal and ordinary. We went out together a couple of years ago for a few months. It was one of those easy relationships, you know? Quentin phoned when he said he'd phone. He turned up whenever he said he'd turn up. He was a lovely boyfriend. Bought me flowers. Looked after me when I had flu. He even queued up all night once to buy tickets to see Elton John in concert for my birthday.'

'Wow. Can't argue with that.' Lottie was openly envious, she'd have torn off her own arm for the chance to see Elton John. 'But you broke up. So what happened?'

Amber shrugged. 'I got a bit . . . bored, I suppose. When someone's that thoughtful you find yourself taking them for granted. There wasn't the adrenaline rush, you know? I thought I wanted more excitement, someone who'd make my heart race and my knees go weak every time I clapped eyes on them. So I told Quentin I didn't think we had a future, that he was too good for me.' Her expression wry, she went on, 'And Quentin said, "You want someone who's bad for you, is that it?" But being the gentleman he is, he didn't put pressure on me to change my mind. He said he hoped I found what I was looking for, and that I deserved to be happy. And the next thing I knew, he'd jacked in his job and moved to London.'

'And now he's back.' Lottie was simultaneously shocked and enthralled. She knew she shouldn't be riveted but she couldn't help it.

'He is.' Amber nodded. 'He dropped in here six weeks ago to say hi, but I was rushed off my feet so I arranged to meet him for a coffee after work. Just to chat and catch up. It was nice to see him again, that was all. Quentin told me about his work and what he'd been up to. I told him about Mario. He asked me if Mario was bad enough for me, and if I thought I'd found the one I'd been looking for. I said I didn't know but I was enjoying myself. And that was it. Twenty minutes in the café down the road.' Pausing to fiddle with her earrings, Amber went on, 'Then that night Mario and I went to a party and this girl spent the whole evening chatting him up. We were there as a couple but she just completely ignored me. I felt like Harry Potter under his invisibility cloak. And Mario was chatting away to her as if nothing was wrong. He really didn't seem to notice what she was doing. Which made me furious. And started me thinking. So when Quentin rang my doorbell the next evening, I invited him in for a drink.'

'Just a drink?' Lottie's tone was mischievous.

'Yes. He'd brought me a little bunch of freesias. Then he told me he still loved me. And I suddenly realised that there were worse things than being loved by a genuinely nice man.'

Lottie bridled on her ex-husband's behalf. 'Mario's a genuinely nice man too.'

'I know he is. But will he really make me happy? Or will he break my heart?' Amber shrugged. 'Because it matters. And I'm telling you now, Quentin never would.'

'So just how serious is this thing between you?' The back of Lottie's neck began to prickle with alarm.

'I haven't slept with him, if that's what you mean.' Her eyes bright, Amber said, 'Not this time, anyway.'

'But . . . but you've just been on holiday together! For a whole fortnight!'

'Separate bedrooms. The holiday was Quentin's idea. He knew how torn I was. I needed some time away from Mario before I could make up my mind.' Amber paused, lost in thought. 'So technically I suppose I haven't been unfaithful. Does it count when you go on holiday with another man but don't actually do the deed?'

Wild with impatience, Lottie said, 'And now? *Have* you made up your mind?'

'Nearly,' said Amber.

'*Nearly?* Tell me!' Lottie squealed.

'No. That wouldn't be fair. I have to tell them first.' Amber inspected Lottie's magenta lowlights again. 'You're ready. Come over to the basin.'

As the basin filled with discarded foils and warm water cascaded over her tilted-back head, Lottie said, 'I still can't believe you did it. You're worried that Mario might cheat on you so you go away for a fortnight with some other guy. Isn't that a bit . . . unfair?'

'Probably.' Energetically Amber began to massage almond-scented shampoo into Lottie's hair. 'But if Mario cheated on me he'd be doing it because he was flattered or bored or just fancied a bit of how's your father. I went away with Quentin because I need to make a decision that's going to change the rest of my life.'

'So you didn't sleep with Quentin. But you kissed him?'

'I did.' Standing behind Lottie, Amber sounded as if she was smiling. 'Lots of times. And I know what you're thinking. I'm a hypocritical bitch. But I wasn't just doing it for fun. So I do have an excellent reason for being a hypocritical bitch.'

Chapter 30

It was eleven o'clock in the morning. Cressida winced and clutched her aching head when she saw there was a new email from Tom waiting in her inbox. This was all Lottie's fault, coming over here last night with bottles of wine and getting her drunk. Then swanning off into the night, leaving her alone in a house with a computer connected to the world-wide web.

And that was another thing. She'd had the *whole world* to choose from, she could have sent embarrassing emails to people living in Alabama or Fiji or Tblisi or Tokyo, and they would have been complete strangers so it wouldn't have mattered one bit what lunacy she might have spouted.

But that hadn't happened, had it? She hadn't written to any of the other fifty trillion billion internet users on the planet – oh no, that would have been far too sensible. Instead she had sent her disinhibited outpourings of twaddle to the man she liked most in the world, the man she was *most* keen to impress and the man she *least* wanted to conclude that she was a complete wazzock.

Cressida mentally braced herself. Too late now to wish she hadn't done it. And what was the worst that could happen, anyway? Tom could be writing back to tell her that she was a sad deluded loser and he'd be obliged if she'd never darken his inbox again.

Then she could just go and quietly drown herself in Hestacombe Lake. OK. *Click.*

Hi Cress.
Well, it's only nine o'clock in the morning but you've already brightened my day. Your email was wonderful. You say you look forward to mine but I look forward to yours more, I promise you. No need at all to apologise for sending Love and hugs (which you did, by the way. Followed by several kisses). I'm flattered. And definitely no need to be embarrassed.

141

Oh, thank heavens for that. Cressida exhaled slowly, giddy with relief. No need to drown herself after all.

And there was more . . .

Now, a suggestion. Donny mentioned Jojo last night. Despite feigning indifference, I think he's quite fond of her. When I asked if he'd like to see her again he grunted and said Dunno, which for a thirteen-year-old boy is pretty positive. (If I asked Donny if he'd like Keira Knightley for his birthday, he'd grunt and say Dunno.)

So I was wondering if you and Jojo would like to come up to Newcastle next weekend. I could show you the sights and there's plenty here to keep the kids happy. Donny has never had a female friend before and I think it would be good for him to keep in touch with Jojo. She's such easy company and a genuinely nice girl.

Anyway, just a suggestion. I know it's a long way to travel but if you and Jojo are free next weekend and would like to visit, we'd love to see you again. Let me know what you think.

Love and hugs
Tom xxxxxx

Let him know what she thought? Let him know what she *thought*? It was all Cressida could do not to launch into a jig before throwing open the windows and bellowing *Yesssssss!* This must be how footballers felt when they scored a winning goal in the Cup Final. Tom had *liked* her email! He hadn't been scared witless by her initial faux pas and subsequent drunken ramblings. He'd even signed off with Love and hugs and . . . how many kisses? Six!

And he was inviting them to Newcastle next weekend – what could be more fantastic than that? Breathlessly Cressida pictured Jojo and herself travelling up together on the train, being met at the station by Tom and Donny, the four of them spending the next forty-eight hours in a whirl of fun and laughter, maybe even *love and hugs* . . .

OK, getting ahead of herself now. Talk about turning into a shameless hussy. But it would still be a brilliant weekend and Jojo would enjoy it too; she was always up for a jaunt.

In fact she'd leave a message on Jojo's mobile now, before finding out train times.

Next weekend. Fizzy with excitement, Cressida reached for the phone. Next weekend she'd be seeing Tom again. Yes!

An hour later Jojo texted her reply: 'Sounds great. Can't wait. Travel up on Friday night? Love J xxxx'.

Cressida kissed the phone. She'd known Jojo wouldn't let her down. *Oh yes!*

The rest of her life might not be going according to plan but Lottie was enjoying being a private detective. She hadn't been able to trace the second name on Freddie's list, Giselle Johnston, but since Johnston was her maiden name and she was now sixty-two, this was hardly a surprise. She had had more luck with the next name on the list. Fenella McEvoy.

'I've got her,' Lottie told Freddie, bursting into the living room of Hestacombe House and waving a sheet of paper in triumph. 'Now you have to tell me who she is.' As he reached for the sheet of paper she snatched it away. 'Before I give you this.'

Fenella. Freddie lit a cigar and smiled to himself. This was going to be interesting. 'First you have to tell me how you found her.'

'Well, I wrote to the address you gave me and the man who lives there now called me back. He and his wife bought the house from the McEvoys twenty years ago. The McEvoys moved abroad, to Spain. But he heard on the grapevine a couple of years ago that Fenella was back in Oxford, then last summer she walked past his house while he was out in the garden and they got chatting. She told him she was living in Hutton Court, an apartment block overlooking the river, and that she'd been divorced twice since leaving Carlton Avenue. *So,*' Lottie gaily announced, 'I Googled Hutton Court and found a web designer who lives there and works from home. I rang and asked him if he knew a Fenella and he said, "Oh, you mean Fenella Britton, she lives on the top floor." You know, I am brilliant.' Lottie looked suitably modest. 'If I say so myself, I'd make a fantastic international spy.'

'And now she's written back.' Freddie's eyes were on the letter Lottie was keeping tantalisingly out of reach.

'She has. Your turn,' Lottie prompted.

'Some people have a moment of madness.' Puffing on his cigar and picturing Fenella as she had looked all those years ago, Freddie settled back in his leather armchair. 'I had a month. I was with Giselle. Fenella was married. I couldn't help myself,' he went on. 'She was like a drug I couldn't resist. We had an affair.'

'And I thought young people had morals in those days.' Lottie tut-tutted as she handed over the letter. 'You know what, Freddie? You were a right little tinker. Who dumped who?'

'She dumped me. As you young people so charmingly put it.' Remembering how devastated he had been, Freddie smiled and tapped

143

the ash from his cigar. 'Fenella was a high-maintenance woman. She already had a successful husband. Basically I just wasn't rich enough.'

Unlike Jeff Barrowcliffe who had been initially cautious, Fenella was over-joyed to hear from him.

'A voice from the past!' she exclaimed with delight when he called her. 'Freddie, how wonderful, of *course* I'd love to see you again! Where are you living now? Near Cheltenham? Why, that's no distance at all! Do you want to pop up here or shall I come down to you?'

As easy as that.

Putting the phone down several minutes later, Freddie wondered why it couldn't have been that simple thirty-eight years ago.

The first time he had seen Fenella McEvoy she had been in a leather shop in the centre of Oxford, choosing a pair of gloves. Freddie, dropping in to pick up a repaired watch strap, observed her trying on one supple dove-grey kid glove and one satin-lined pale pink one. Aware that she was being watched, Fenella turned and waggled her fingers at him. 'Which do you think? To go with a white suit.'

She was stunning, as dark and elegant as Audrey Hepburn. Confidence emanated from her like French perfume.

'The pink ones,' Freddie replied at once, and she had flashed him a mesmerising smile before turning back to the assistant behind the counter.

'A gentleman of taste. I'll take them.'

Freddie was already captivated.

Somehow they had left the shop together. As it started to rain outside, Fenella said, 'Of course what I should have bought was an umbrella. I'm never going to find a taxi now.'

'My car's just over there.' Freddie pointed across the road. 'Where are you heading?'

'Not only a gentleman of taste.' Cheerfully, Fenella moved towards the car. 'A knight in shining armour too. And what a beautiful car.'

'Not that one.' Slightly shamefacedly, Freddie steered her away from the gleaming Bentley and unlocked the doors of his own less than gleaming Austin 7, parked behind it. 'Still want a lift?'

Fenella laughed at the dig. 'It's better than a bicycle made for two.'

He dropped her outside her house, an imposing Edwardian villa on leafy, upmarket Carlton Avenue. By this time he'd already learned that she was married to Cyril who was fifteen years older than her. Cyril, it tran-spired, was something big in textiles.

'We're holding a cocktail party this Saturday.' Fenella's catlike smile was hypnotic, her tone confiding. 'Seven o'clock. Would you like to come along?'

Freddie swallowed. He'd never attended a cocktail party in his life. But he wanted to now, more than anything.

'The thing is, I've got this . . . um, girlfriend.'

Fenella's smile broadened. 'Good for you. What's her name?'

'Giselle.'

'Pretty.'

'Yes, she is.'

'I meant her name.'

'Oh. Sorry.'

'But I'm sure she's jolly pretty too. I couldn't imagine you with an ugly girlfriend.' Touching his sleeve, Fenella said, 'Come along to our party, Freddie. Bring Giselle too, if that's what you want. I'd like to meet her.'

On Saturday night Freddie and Giselle had gone along to the McEvoys' cocktail party and spent the evening feeling uncomfortable. The other guests, all older and intimidatingly well-to-do, had been polite but uninterested in socialising with a young couple so clearly out of their depth.

'What are we doing here?' Giselle whispered.

'I don't know,' Freddie murmured back.

He found out twenty minutes later when, on his way back from the bathroom, he encountered Fenella on the staircase.

'She's not right for you.'

'Excuse me?' Startled, Freddie was nevertheless aware of how close her body was to his.

'I can always tell. What are you doing on Wednesday evening?'

'Seeing Giselle.'

'Make an excuse. Come and see me instead. Cyril's going to be away.'

Freddie began to perspire. 'I can't do that.'

'Of course you can. Eight o'clock. Oh, cheer up, Freddie.' Fenella regarded him with amusement. 'Don't look so shocked. You know you want to.'

And, hating himself but unable to help himself, Freddie discovered that he did.

Having thought that Giselle was the love of his life, the explosion of Fenella into his world came as a shock to Freddie. Giselle felt guilty about sex before marriage and their infrequent couplings were marred by that. Whereas Fenella, already married, had no such compunction. On Wednesday night she seduced Freddie expertly and repeatedly. The sex was mind-blowing. Luckily Cyril was often away on business trips. He was a good provider financially, Freddie learned, but something of a flop in bed.

Unlike himself.

'You're working too hard,' Giselle complained four weeks later when he told her, yet again, that he wouldn't be able to see her that night.

'I know, but the boss needs me to close the deal. It won't be forever,' Freddie promised. And he knew it wouldn't. He and Fenella were meant to be together. Life without her was unimaginable. Hours later, in bed, he told her so and asked her to leave Cyril.

'Darling, how sweet.' Fenella ran her toes playfully along his bare leg. 'But why on earth would I want to do that?'

'Because I love you!' Utterly bewitched, Freddie was taken aback by her failure to understand what was happening here. 'We can't just carry on like this. I'll finish with Giselle. You can tell Cyril about us.'

Fenella giggled. '*What?*'

'You have to divorce him.'

'Heavens, he'll be furious!'

'This isn't about him,' Freddie said urgently. 'It's about us. I want to marry you.'

'And keep me in the manner to which I'm accustomed?' Gesturing around the vast tastefully furnished master bedroom, encompassing the wardrobes bursting with expensive clothes and shoes, Fenella said, 'Freddie, be serious. Exactly how much *do* you earn?'

Being plunged into a barrel of ice couldn't have shocked him more. Feeling his jaw muscles tighten, Freddie said, 'I thought you loved me.'

'Oh Freddie. I like you.' Fenella stroked his face. 'Very much indeed. We've had fun together, haven't we? But it was never meant to be serious.'

Freddie noted her use of the past tense. He also realised that Fenella had done this before, and that while she didn't love Cyril she had absolutely no intention of leaving him.

'I'll be off then.' Feeling crushed, foolish and miserable, Freddie slid out of bed and began hunting for his hurriedly discarded clothes.

Fenella nodded sympathetically. 'Probably best. Sorry, darling.'

Freddie was sorry too. He'd betrayed Giselle, who truly loved him. And now he'd made a complete idiot of himself.

Dressed at last, he turned in the bedroom doorway and said, 'I'll see myself out. Have a nice life.'

'I will.' Nestled against the snowy white pillows, Fenella blew him a kiss and fluttered her fingers goodbye. Belatedly she added, 'You too.'

Freddie sat in his car. It was over. Because he couldn't afford her.

He just wasn't rich enough.

Chapter 31

Cressida sat down on one of the kitchen chairs with a bump. This wasn't supposed to be happening. It was like opening a gloriously gift-wrapped present and discovering it contained a dead rat.

'No, that won't be possible,' Sacha Forbes briskly repeated. 'We're away. One of Robert's district managers is getting married in Kent and we'll be staying down there for the weekend.'

Ringing to check that Sacha and Robert wouldn't mind her taking Jojo with her up to Newcastle had been purely a formality. They'd never said no before, which was why it hadn't occurred to Cressida for one minute that they might this time.

'And Jojo's going with you?' Cressida fought to hide her rising panic. 'It's just that she didn't say anything about a wedding.'

'Well, I'm sure I mentioned it. You know what young girls are like.' Sacha's tone was careless. 'Never pay any attention.'

'Although if it's a work colleague's wedding,' Cressida ventured out of sheer desperation, 'she's not going to know anyone else there, is she? Are you sure you and Robert wouldn't rather leave her with me? Then the two of you can really relax and—'

'No, no, it's too late for all that now. Robert's boss is taking his noisy brats along and we promised him Jojo would look after them. Otherwise they'd cause mayhem.'

The unfairness of this took Cressida's breath away. 'But—'

'Cressida, she's coming with us. We're going to this wedding as a family. Now if you'll excuse me, I do have some important phone calls to make.' Clearly implying that she'd spared Cressida more than enough of her precious time, Sacha said impatiently, 'And maybe you could remind yourself that Jojo's our daughter, not yours.'

The line went dead but the pain inflicted by this last remark cut through Cressida like a Stanley knife, all the more acute because Sacha was right.

Tears filled her eyes as she realised she would have to apologise to Sacha and Robert. Apologise and grovel. It wouldn't do to antagonise them. If they decided they wanted to stop Jojo seeing her, they could.

147

Two strong cups of coffee later, Cressida left another message on Jojo's phone explaining about the wedding.

Then she emailed Tom, telling him they couldn't make it this weekend after all. The fact that she could still make it was irrelevant; he had invited both of them so that Jojo could be a companion for Donny. The whole purpose of the visit was to make it fun for the children and to keep them happy. Turning up on her own would be like promising Donny a trip to Disneyland then dragging him along to B&Q instead.

In fact staying here in Hestacombe this coming weekend was going to feel a lot like one endless trawl through the aisles of B&Q.

What a shame, Tom emailed back from work twenty minutes later. Donny would be so disappointed. Of course, he added (hastily? politely?), he was too. The following weekend Donny was involved in a seven-a-side football tournament, but how about the weekend after that?

Checking the calendar, Cressida discovered that this was the weekend she had volunteered to help out at the local hospital's Autumn Fayre; she was down to run the tombola in the morning and the book stall in the afternoon. So much for good deeds being rewarded.

Cressida could have wept. It was just as well she didn't own a cat; if she had, she would have kicked it.

Fenella gave a little cry of delight and held out her arms to Freddie.

'My darling, just look at you – all silver-haired and distinguished and more handsome than ever! Oh, it's so good to see you again!'

Freddie's head was aching so badly it felt as if his brain were being squeezed in a vice, but if anything was capable of making him forget the pain it was the sight of Fenella in a pink and yellow summer dress and floaty matching scarf. Her dark eyes glowed, she still wore her hair in a gamine Audrey Hepburn crop and her legs were as slender and spectacular as ever. She was sixty-three, Freddie reminded himself. If he hadn't known that, he'd have put her at mid-fifties.

'And it's wonderful to see you.' Bending his head and breathing in the fresh, flowery scent of her perfume, he gave Fenella a kiss on each powdered cheek. 'Thank you so much for coming. Please, let me take care of that,' he added as she unfastened the clasp on her handbag and pulled out a purse. 'It's the least I can do.'

Freddie paid the taxi driver, tipped him a tenner and said, 'If I'd known you were catching the train I'd have met you at the station.'

'Maybe I was worried you might pick me up in that terrible old Austin 7 of yours.' Fenella's gaze, alight with mischief, slid across to the gleaming burgundy Daimler parked on the driveway. 'Is this really yours?

Looks like you've done pretty well for yourself, darling. I'm so happy for you.'

Freddie knew he was behaving like an eight-year-old teased by his peers for not having a bike then getting a brand new one for Christmas and not being able to resist riding up and down the street showing it off. Forty years ago his lack of money had meant Fenella hadn't taken him seriously. Since then he *had* done well for himself but the slight had always rankled like an itch beneath the skin. Seeing her again and showing her what she'd missed out on completed a kind of circle; he was a 64-year-old man careering up and down the street, ringing his bell and crowing, 'Look at me on my shiny new bike.'

They had lunch in the conservatory and caught up with each other's lives. Fenella was full of admiration for the house and Freddie told her how he had built up his property business. In turn he learned that she and Cyril had divorced after twenty-three years of marriage.

'He took early retirement and we moved to Puerto Banus. Being married to someone who's working non-stop at least gives you time on your own,' Fenella confided. 'Once Cyril gave up work there was no escape from him. It drove me mad. *He* drove me mad. He wouldn't even take up golf or serious drinking, for crying out loud! Well, I couldn't stand it. So we broke up and I got involved with Jerry Britton.'

Freddie wondered whether her involvement with Jerry Britton had preceded the break-up of her marriage to Cyril.

'Who played plenty of golf and practically single-handedly kept the bars of Puerto Banus in business,' Fenella continued wryly. 'But he was great fun and he made me feel young and desirable again. After twenty-three years of being married to Cyril that meant a lot, I can tell you.'

'And you married him.' Freddie couldn't resist asking the question. 'Was he wealthy?'

Fenella smiled sadly and said, 'Oh yes. I may have been in my late forties but I still hadn't learned my lesson. Jerry splashed his money about like nobody's business and I loved it when he splashed it out on me. All my life I'd needed the comfort of financial security. I was a silly, shallow woman, I can see that now. Jerry turned out to be a complete and utter bastard of course. I'd never been so miserable. He was sleeping around, he started belittling me in front of all his friends . . . it was just a nightmare.' Putting down her knife and fork, she said sadly, 'And the thing was, I knew deep down that I deserved it. This was my punishment for being so shallow and mercenary all my life. I'd deserved my comeuppance and now here it was in all its glory.'

'Don't be too hard on yourself. At least you were honest about it,' said Freddie.

'Oh darling, and look where it got me.' Fenella shook her head. 'And the really ironic thing is . . . no, nothing, forget it.'

Freddie watched her wave the words away.

'What's the really ironic thing?' he prompted.

Reaching for her glass of Chablis, Fenella said, 'OK, but I warn you it makes me sound completely pathetic.' She paused, took a sip of wine and gazed steadily at him. 'I missed you, Freddie. I loved you. I know I never told you this, but that was because I couldn't. I'd made my bed and I had to lie in it. But I never forgot you. I never stopped comparing other men with you, wishing they could *be* more like you.'

'Like me if I'd been a lot richer.' Freddie's tone was dry.

'No, like *you*,' Fenella insisted. 'Look, it took me a while but I got there in the end. When I divorced Jerry I could have fought for a fabulous settlement, but I didn't. I left without a penny, came back to England and resolved to become a better person. From now on, money wouldn't rule my life. If I met a genuinely nice man who was poor but honest, I'd settle down with him because at last I knew that happiness had nothing to do with the size of someone's bank balance.'

Impressed, Freddie said, 'And did that happen?'

'Only very briefly.' Sadness shadowed Fenella's eyes. 'I did meet a lovely man. His name was Douglas and he worked in a garden centre. He had no money, but it didn't matter. We got on wonderfully well together. I had such high hopes for the future. But two months later he died suddenly of a heart attack.'

'I'm sorry.'

'Thank you. It was a horrible time, just horrible. I felt as if I were being punished for all the bad things I'd done in the past. So much happiness, snatched away. That was eight years ago.' Fenella reached for a handkerchief in her bag and wiped her brimming eyes. 'There hasn't been anyone else since. I'd have liked there to be, but it just hasn't happened. Oh dear, I know this must sound ridiculous but can you understand how excited I was when I opened that letter from your friend Lottie? Discovering that you were looking for me and wanted to see me again? I felt like a teenager! This was my chance to make up for the terrible way I'd treated you before . . . and, less unselfishly, I thought it could be my chance to be happy again with my first love. Because that's what you were, Freddie. I may not have been able to admit it at the time, but it's true. You were my first love.' She stopped and gave a brittle laugh. 'And now I'm here, and it's all gone wrong again. I think I must be jinxed.'

Bemused, Freddie said, 'Why are you jinxed?'

'Because the whole point of coming here today and seeing you again and . . . whatever . . .' another non-specific wave of her left hand, 'was to prove to you that I really have changed! But now I can't, because you aren't poor any more. You have all this!'

Freddie smiled. 'I'm sorry.'

'Not half as sorry as I am, let me tell you.' Fenella sat back in her chair and tucked a stray strand of dark hair behind her ear. 'When you told me your address I assumed Hestacombe House was a block of flats. I expected you to be a normal, not-very-well-off man leading a not-very-well-off life. And I wanted to show you that it didn't matter a bit. When the taxi driver pulled up outside this place I almost fainted. I never imagined you ending up somewhere like this. And it means I can't flirt with you, because if I did you'd think I was only doing it because you're rich.'

'I don't know what to say.' Freddie paused, then decided he may as well come clean. 'OK. If I'm honest, that's one of the reasons I wanted to see you again. To prove to you that I'd made something of myself, against the odds and despite the fact that you broke my heart.'

Fenella's hand flew to her mouth. 'Did I break your heart? Really?'

'Oh yes.'

'I thought you'd just go back to that sweet girl of yours . . . what was her name?'

'Giselle.' Freddie's heart contracted.

'That's it. Pretty little thing. What happened?'

'I messed up. All my own fault. After you and I broke up, I was hard to live with. Giselle hadn't done anything wrong and she couldn't understand why I was so distant. It wasn't an easy time.'

'Oh God, I'm so sorry,' Fenella exclaimed. 'I feel dreadful.'

'These things happen. Call it fate. Anyway, we were struggling on but we were both unhappy,' said Freddie. 'Then I met someone else. And that was it, I finished with Giselle. Started seeing the other girl.'

'Whose name was?'

'Mary. Within six months we were married. She died four years ago.'

'Oh Freddie. And you were happy together? Of course you were,' Fenella exclaimed. 'I can tell by the look in your eyes. That's wonderful. I'm so glad you found the right one in the end.'

Unable to speak for a moment, Freddie nodded.

'Poor darling.' Fenella reached over and took his hand. 'You must miss her terribly. It's the loneliness, isn't it? Not having anyone to share your life with. Oh, it breaks my heart to think of you being so sad.'

'Grief is the price you pay for love,' Freddie said simply, before gathering himself and leaning forward to top up her wine glass. 'Anyway, this isn't very cheerful, is it? You'll be wishing you'd never come to see me.'

'Freddie, it's heavenly to see you. I just can't bear to think of you on your own. You're still a very attractive man, you know.' Breaking into a smile, Fenella said, 'If it wasn't for all this wretched money of yours, who knows what could have happened? The two of us meeting up again might have . . . oh heavens, just ignore me, I'm a silly old woman . . .'

As her voice trailed away Freddie realised he was meant to do the gentlemanly thing and gallantly contradict her. His head was still pounding and he needed his next dose of co-codamol. But first he had to explain to Fenella that any kind of future together simply wasn't on the cards.

'Of course you aren't silly. Or old,' he added hastily. 'But I'm really not looking for a relationship. That isn't why I wanted to see you again.'

Startled, Fenella said, 'Oh.'

'Sorry if I misled you.' Freddie felt guilty, since he clearly had. 'I just thought it would be nice to find out how you were and how life had treated you.'

'Oh well.' Summoning a brave smile, Fenella said, 'And now you know. Is that it? Would you like me to leave now that you're all up to date?'

'No no *no*.' Freddie shook his head vehemently, which did his headache no good at all. 'Fenella, I'm just being honest, letting you know how things are. Any kind of romantic relationship isn't what I'm after. It's only fair that you know that. But I don't want you to leave. We can still have a nice day together, surely?'

'Handsome and persuasive. How can I refuse?' Fenella's gaze softened as she pushed away her plate and leaned closer. 'Now, tell me all about your wonderful wife.'

Chapter 32

There was no torture, Lottie was discovering, like the torture of working for someone you lusted after but couldn't actually get lusty with. Being allowed to look but not touch was starting to get to her in a major way.

Tyler was already there in the office when she arrived at nine o'clock, looking breathtaking as usual in a navy polo shirt and faded jeans and prompting her stomach to do a quick loop-the-loop. He really was causing havoc with her hormones. As ever, the question buzzing around Lottie's brain, bursting to be let out, was *What are you like in bed?*

When he looked up from the computer and broke into a grin – oh crikey, loop-the-loop-*the-loop* – Lottie wondered wildly if she'd accidentally said the words aloud.

'Hi. How are the kids?'

He always asked. It was the only reference Tyler made to their over-before-it-had-begun relationship. He never tried to kiss her or persuade her to change her mind.

Lottie threw her sunglasses and car keys onto the desk and reached for the mail. 'Fine. Getting on well at school.'

'That's good.'

She nodded; it certainly was. It would kill her to think she'd made all that sacrifice for nothing.

'We've got a request for Walnut Lodge.' He tapped the computer screen. 'For the second week in December. They want it for their honeymoon.'

'No problem. Ooh, it's Zach and Jenny!' Leaning forward to read the email on the screen, Lottie exclaimed, 'They came down here last year with a group of friends. They're a lovely couple, but Jenny despaired of ever getting Zach down the aisle because his parents went through the most horrendous divorce when he was young and he'd always vowed never to marry.' A lump sprang into her throat. 'And now they are. Isn't that brilliant? Happy endings still exist.'

'Unless he doesn't know he's getting married and she's arranging it all in secret,' Tyler drawled. 'I always feel sorry for those guys. They go along

153

to what they think is somebody else's wedding then *bam*, find out their bunny-boiler girlfriend's organised the worst kind of surprise.'

'Only a man could think that.' Lottie swiped him on the shoulder with her handful of letters. 'You're so cynical.'

'Trust me, when it happens to you, it's no fun at all.'

Her mouth dropped open. '*Did* it happen to you?'

Tyler winked. 'And you're so gullible.'

'At least I'm not unromantic.' Lottie took another swipe at him with the sheaf of letters. 'All bitter and twisted and—'

'Now you're being unfair.' Deftly catching her wrist Tyler said, 'I can be romantic when I want to be. It all depends on the girl.'

Uh-oh, dangerous. As the adrenaline skipped joyfully through her body, Lottie realised she'd gone too far. Time to pull herself together and back-track fast.

Oh, but she didn't *want* to . . .

Drop the flirting and step away from the man, ordered a stern voice scarily reminiscent of Miss Batson. Step *away* from the *man*.

Lottie stepped away, took a deep breath.

'Right, well, Freddie loves a happy ending. I'm going to tell him about Zach and Jenny. He'll be thrilled. And don't you email them,' she added over her shoulder. 'Just give me five minutes and I'll do it when I get back.'

Lottie let herself in through the kitchen as she did most mornings. As a rule Freddie was ensconced at the table reading the paper and enjoying a leisurely breakfast, but today the kitchen was empty.

Lottie wandered through to the panelled hallway, then saw that the door to the study was ajar. Hearing the faint sound of a drawer being opened she realised that Freddie must be in there.

Afterwards she wondered why she hadn't called out his name as she usually did. Instead, making her way over to the study, she saw the back of a slender dark-haired woman wrapped in an oversized dressing gown, standing in front of Freddie's writing desk.

As Lottie watched through the crack in the door, the woman finished examining the papers in her hand and returned them to the right-hand drawer of the writing desk. Closing it, she then stealthily opened the left-hand drawer and surveyed the contents, pulling out a couple of letters and rapidly scanning them.

Lottie had no intention of interrupting proceedings but the next moment a floorboard creaked beneath her foot and the woman spun round. So this was Fenella Britton.

'I'd ask what you were doing,' Lottie said evenly, 'but that would be a silly question.'

Heavens, Miss Batson would be proud of her. Maybe she should train to become a scary spinster teacher and start wearing tweed skirts and Birkenstocks.

'You almost gave me a heart attack!' Clapping her hand to her chest, Fenella shook her head. 'I'm sorry, I know how this must look. But it's Freddie. I'm just so worried about him.'

Lottie had been worried about Freddie for weeks. With a jolt of fear she wondered if he had been taken ill during the night. 'Why? Where is he? What's happened?'

'Nothing's happened.' Fenella fiddled with the lapels of the olive-green towelling dressing gown. 'But something is wrong with Freddie, isn't it? I saw all the painkillers in the bathroom cabinet, packets and packets of them. Some are prescription only.' Indicating the letter that now lay uppermost on the desk she said, 'And this is from a neurologist. He's talking about the results of the latest scan and the prognosis being poor . . . oh God, I can't bear it! I've just found him again after all these years and now I'm going to lose him. My Freddie's going to die!'

Tears were pouring down Fenella Britton's cheeks. She looked as if she might pass out. Clutching her arms round her thin body she swayed against the desk and pushed the letters back into the drawer.

'You'd better sit down,' said Lottie. 'Where's Freddie?'

'Upstairs. H-having a b-bath. I'm so sorry. Fenella Britton.' Fenella held out a fragile, trembling hand. 'You must be Lottie. Freddie's told me all about you.'

Lottie didn't say that she'd heard all about her too. This was the woman who had discarded Freddie because he hadn't been rich enough to keep him in contention. And here she was, having discovered that he was now very wealthy indeed, snooping through Freddie's private papers. What's more, she'd stayed the night.

'Wouldn't it have been more polite to ask him if there was anything wrong?' Despite the copious tears Lottie couldn't bring herself to warm to Fenella Britton.

'If he'd wanted to tell me, he could have. But he didn't mention it. Typical Freddie,' said Fenella, wiping her eyes. 'He wouldn't want to upset me. He's always been so thoughtful and considerate.'

'Well, you can talk about it when he comes downstairs. Are you leaving this morning?' Lottie checked her watch. 'Because I can give you a lift to the station if—'

'Leaving? How can I leave, now that I know the truth?' Vehemently Fenella shook her head. 'Oh no, I let Freddie down once before. I'm not going to do it again. He's all on his own. He *needs* me.'

'You only met him again yesterday,' said Lottie. Incredulity mingled with suspicion; was Fenella actually planning to move into Hestacombe House?

'I've loved him for forty years,' Fenella said simply. 'Freddie has no family. He can't be on his own at a time like this.'

Lottie wondered if the no family bit was significant in other ways. Was she a truly horrible person for thinking this?

Aloud she said, 'He won't be on his own.'

And then she saw the glint in the older woman's eye and knew she was right.

'You don't want me here, do you? You'd rather deny Freddie the comfort of having someone he cares about take care of him. Why *is* that exactly?' Fenella's voice was as smooth as cream but the underlying challenge was unmistakable.

'I don't know. Were there any bank statements floating around in that desk drawer?'

'No, there weren't.' Fenella tilted her head to one side. 'But that's what you're worried about, isn't it? Freddie doesn't have anyone to leave his money to. And you were hoping to keep it all for yourself.'

'Stop this.' Freddie's voice rang out behind them. 'What's going on here?'

'I caught her snooping in your desk drawer,' said Lottie. 'She was reading the letters from your doctor, and God knows what else.'

'Because I was so worried about you!' Fenella, rushing past Lottie and throwing her arms round Freddie, burst into a fresh torrent of tears. 'And now I know the truth. Oh my poor darling, I can't bear it! How can life be so cruel?'

Freddie actually looked relieved. Lottie watched the tension go out of him as he cupped Fenella's heart-shaped face between his hands. 'It's OK. Sshh, don't cry, I'm sorry.'

Don't *comfort* her, Lottie longed to yell. *Shoot her!*

'Oh Freddie, my Freddie,' Fenella sobbed into the front of his brown and white checked shirt.

Hang on, I'll get the gun!

'Now you know why I said I wasn't looking for another relationship.' Freddie's voice cracked with emotion. 'How could I do that to anyone? It would be too unfair.'

'Oh darling, don't you see? It's already too late,' Fenella whispered. 'You can't control how you feel about other people.'

I certainly can't control how I feel about you, thought Lottie.

'It's already happened,' Fenella went on. 'Whether we want it to or not. And it may not be the easy option and it might not be sensible but we're in this together. You and me, whatever it takes, for as long as it takes.' Lovingly she stroked Freddie's face. 'Because I'm going to look after you. Right to the end.'

There's always the lake, Lottie thought longingly. We could just tie her up and tip her in.

Visibly pulling herself together, Fenella said, 'Darling, OK if I have my bath now?'

'Go ahead.' Freddie smoothed her hair. 'Take as long as you want.'

Fenella's smile was tremulous. 'I will. And you can have a chat with Lottie. Explain to her that I'm not the Wicked Witch of the West.'

Lottie brightened. Witches, now that was an idea. Didn't they used to burn witches at the stake?

Fenella disappeared upstairs to take her bath. In the kitchen Lottie made coffee and listened to Freddie's account of yesterday's events. She especially enjoyed the bit about how Fenella had evidently seen the error of her mercenary ways and had been horrified to discover that he was a multi-millionaire, because the only men she wanted to be associated with nowadays were the kind without two ha'pennies to rub together.

And no, they hadn't slept together last night either. They had simply been laughing and talking together for so long that Fenella had ended up missing the last train home.

After hearing far more than she wanted to hear, Lottie said, 'I know this is none of my business, Freddie, but I still don't trust her. She was going through your private things.'

'But she's explained why.' He looked defensive. 'And I did tell her to make herself at home.'

This wasn't going to be easy. 'She accused me of feeling threatened by her because I want you to leave everything in your will to me. Which *isn't* true, by the way,' Lottie added hastily.

Freddie shrugged. 'So you say.'

'Freddie! I'm not!'

'I know that.' He looked amused. 'But Fenella doesn't, does she? Because she doesn't know you. Just like you don't know her.'

Bursting to retort, *but I know I'm right*, Lottie forced herself not to. She gazed steadily at Freddie.

'Touché. Look, I want you to be happy. It's what you deserve. Just . . . don't do anything hasty, OK?'

'Like rush off to the nearest register office?' One eyebrow went up. 'Or change my will and leave everything to Fenella?'

Exactly. *Exactly.*

Lottie said, 'Something like that.'

'Darling, it's sweet of you to worry about me.' Freddie's tone was consoling. 'I appreciate it. But I'm not some lovestruck teenager. Nor am I senile. I think I can trust myself not to get carried away.'

Lottie, who knew better, said nothing. Of course he couldn't trust himself; he was a man.

'That was a long five minutes,' Tyler observed when Lottie reappeared in the office.

'Sorry. I'll work through lunch.' She sat down and began a to-do list.

'You always work through lunch.'

'You'll just have to sack me then. Oooh, *bloody* pen.' Discovering that her ballpoint wasn't working, Lottie hurled it across the office with such force that the wheels on her chair scooted backwards. The pen bounced off the opposite wall and Lottie clunked the back of her head against the shelf behind her desk. 'Ouch, *bugger.*'

'OK, here's the deal. I won't sack you if you promise not to sue me for injuries sustained in the workplace. It's entirely my fault for allowing a pen to run out of ink.' Manfully attempting to keep a straight face, Tyler said, 'Lottie, what's wrong?'

'You mean apart from the fractured skull?' She rubbed her head. 'I've just met Freddie's lady friend.'

'The old flame from Oxford?' Tyler looked interested. 'He was telling me about her. What's she like?'

'The words gold and digger spring to mind.'

'Oh well, goes with the territory.' With a so-what shrug, Tyler said, 'Does that bother Freddie?'

Lottie stared at him in disbelief. 'What?'

'Well, it clearly bothers you.'

'Because she's a fraud! She's pretending to be in love with Freddie so she can get her hands on his money!'

'According to you.'

'She is!'

'Maybe she likes him anyway,' Tyler said reasonably, 'and the fact that he's wealthy is an added bonus.'

Lottie couldn't believe he wasn't taking her side. This was an outrage. If there'd been another pen on the desk she would have flung it at his head.

'Hey, give them a break, let Freddie have his fun.' Tyler spread his arms. 'If she's really bad news he'll see through her sooner or later. But look on the bright side,' he went on. 'You could be wrong. They might be perfect for each other. They could be deliriously happy together for the next thirty years.'

'No they *couldn't,*' Lottie blurted out. 'That's just it, they—'

'They what?' Tyler raised his eyebrows as she ground to an abrupt halt.

Ashamed of herself for almost having let the cat out of the bag, Lottie shook her head. 'Nothing. They just wouldn't, that's all.'

Chapter 33

The temperature had soared back into the eighties and Lottie was on the beach busy topping up her tan when she felt a shadow fall across her face.

Her stomach instantly tensed. Tyler?

She opened her eyes and saw that it wasn't. Mario was standing over her looking so grim that Lottie knew at once what had happened.

Pushing herself up on her elbows, she shielded her eyes from the sun. 'What's wrong?'

Mario glanced over at Nat and Ruby, who were splashing around in the shallows with a golden retriever belonging to the family currently staying in Beekeeper's Cottage. When he was satisfied they were out of earshot he said, 'Amber's chucked me.'

'Oh no.' Lottie looked suitably shocked. 'I can't believe it! Why?'

'Turns out she's been seeing someone else.' Mario watched as Nat threw a stick into the lake and Ruby and the dog simultaneously plunged in to retrieve it.

'Really?'

Mario nodded and waved back as Ruby, having lost the battle for the stick, waved at him. 'Really. Why are women such liars?'

'How long's it been going on?' Perspiration trickled down Lottie's cleavage as she adjusted her bikini straps.

'And that includes you,' Mario continued evenly. 'Because you're lying now, pretending to be surprised. Amber told me she told you last week.'

Cheers, Amber.

'Oh well.' Lottie wasn't going to feel guilty. 'That's just sisterly solidarity. I was being discreet. Could you move out of my sun?'

Mario sighed and sat down on the beach towel next to her. 'Is that all the sympathy I get?'

'How much do you think you deserve? I'm your ex-wife, remember. You messed around with other girls and we ended up getting divorced because of it. Now Amber's decided she can't stay with you because she can't trust you, so she's found someone she *can* trust instead.' Reaching for her bottle of Soltan and uncapping it, Lottie squeezed a dollop of the

159

cream onto her stomach. 'If I were the type to gloat I'd call it poetic justice.'

Mario's eyes glittered. 'Thanks a lot. Even though I haven't been unfaithful to Amber, not once.'

'Of course you haven't. Not even when Amber was away in France,' Lottie pointedly reminded him. '*Thanks to me.*'

'And that's another thing. It wasn't until she found out you'd spent the whole time acting like a human chastity belt that she realised she couldn't carry on seeing me.' Mario gestured in disbelief. 'If it wasn't for you, we'd still be together.'

'Oh no, don't start trying to shift the blame onto me! Amber was in France with another man while I was being your damn chastity belt!'

'So you're glad this has happened.' Mario's voice rose. 'You think it serves me right!'

'Of course I'm not glad it happened,' Lottie bellowed back. 'I didn't *want* it to happen, that's why I acted like a chastity belt! *Blaaarrrgghh!*' She jerked back as the golden retriever, having bounded out of the lake and raced up to them, shook himself vigorously and showered her with cold water.

Nat, hot on the boisterous animal's heels, said, 'Why are you shouting at Daddy?'

'Because Daddy was shouting at me.'

'Oh. What's a chastity belt?'

'Something you buy in Marks and Spencer to hold your tummy in. Right, we'd better be getting home now.' Lottie checked her watch.

This had the desired effect. '*Nooo,*' Nat protested, charging back down to the water's edge with the dog in tow.

'You know I didn't want you and Amber to break up.' No longer shouting, Lottie reached over and touched Mario's wrist.

He nodded, watching Ruby and Nat as they skimmed stones across the shimmering surface of the lake.

'I know. I just can't believe it's happened. I thought we were so happy.'

Lottie's heart went out to him. He was clearly more upset than he was letting on. Mario had always led something of a charmed life; he was easy-going and cheerful, liked by everyone.

'Oh God, and I'm going to have to tell Ruby and Nat.' His jaw tightened. 'They're not going to like it.'

This was an understatement. Lottie knew they'd be devastated. They loved Amber as much as they hated Tyler, the difference being that this time they couldn't influence the outcome.

'I'm really sorry,' Lottie said quietly.

'Me too.' Mario hesitated, swallowing hard. 'I love her. I didn't know it would hurt this much. I can't stop thinking about her being with someone else.'

Now you know how I felt when you did it to me. The words ran through Lottie's mind but she didn't voice them. Instead she put her arms round him and held him tightly. Mario might no longer be her husband but she still cared for him and right now he was in need of comfort. It hurt to see him like this.

Having spotted them Nat crowed, 'Oooh, *sexxxxy*.' Then his gaze shifted and the smirk faded from his face. Twisting round to see what he was looking at, Lottie saw Tyler making his way along the narrow lane leading to the cottages. Damn, what was he going to think now?

Then again, what did it matter? They were each free to do whatever they liked. She could be having wild sex with Mario if that was what took her fancy.

Well, maybe not on this beach in front of the kids.

Tyler disappeared from view and the dog loped off. Ruby skidded up to them, excitedly clutching a coin in her hand. 'Look, I found fifty pee in the water!'

Mario said, 'That'll be the fifty fish.'

'Daddy! That's gross.'

Nat, who adored toilet humour, snorted with laughter and threw himself down on the sand next to Mario. 'I'm going to find fifty poos! Why was Mummy hugging you? Is it because you're so *sexxxxy*?'

Mario hesitated. Lottie decided to get it over with. 'Dad's fine, he's a bit sad, that's all. He and Amber aren't seeing each other any more.'

Ruby and Nat stared at her, then at Mario.

'Why?'

'These things happen.' Mario shrugged, but his jaw was set.

Ruby's hand crept into his. 'Don't you like her any more?'

'Oh, I do.'

'But she doesn't like you.' Nat's lower lip was beginning to wobble.

'Or us,' Ruby whispered.

'Oh, come on, you know that's not true,' Lottie exclaimed. 'Amber loves both of you!'

'But we're never going to see her again. That's not fair.' Ruby gazed up at Mario. 'What did you do to make her stop liking you?'

'Nothing,' said Mario.

'You must have done *something*.'

'Well I didn't, OK? She just found someone else.'

Nat looked outraged. 'Someone she likes better than you? Where did she find him?'

'It doesn't matter.'

Perplexed, Nat said, '*Is* he better than you?'

'Of course he isn't.' Mario smiled and pulled him onto his lap. 'How can anyone be better than me? Amber just has weird taste in men.'

'Like Mummy,' Ruby chimed in, 'with that horrible Tyler.'

Lottie hoped that that horrible Tyler wasn't currently hiding in the bushes behind them overhearing this. Although it was hardly telling him anything he didn't already know.

'Amber might change her mind,' Nat said hopefully. 'Do you think she'll change her mind and come back?'

'Honestly? No.' Mario shook his head. 'Amber isn't like that. Once she makes a decision, she sticks with it.'

'What's her new boyfriend's name?' said Ruby.

'Quentin,' said Lottie.

'*Quentin?* That's a *dumb* name!'

Nat's eyes sparkled. 'Almost as dumb as Tyler.' Perking up, he said, 'I know, we can make another VD doll of Quentin and stick pins in it. Shall we do that?'

Ruby was scornful. 'Voodoo, durr-brain. Honestly, you're so thick.'

'I'm so hungry.' Lottie, mentally scanning the contents of her fridge, was wondering what she could possibly do that was inventive with half a packet of bacon, a jar of mint sauce and two giant bags of parsnips.

Parsnips, for heaven's sake. Buy One Get One Free had a lot to answer for.

Mario, familiar with that desperate look in her eyes, came to the rescue as they had all hoped he would. 'Come on.' Shifting Nat from his lap he stood up and held out his hand to Lottie. 'Let's take them to Pizza Hut.'

Somewhere downstairs a door creaked and Mario woke up.

He knew where he was without even having to open his eyes. It wasn't as if he'd had tons to drink last night; every memory was crystal clear in his mind.

He opened his eyes anyway and looked around the bedroom at the pink curtains, the chalk-blue walls and the blue and pink rug on the floor. There were most of his clothes thrown over a rattan chair and there was his shirt and leather belt on the floor beneath the window.

Unable to reach his watch, Mario guessed from the light streaming through the curtains that it was around sevenish. He had to get home, shower and change and be at work by eight thirty.

What had caused the door to creak downstairs?

The answer arrived moments later as the bedroom door was nudged open and a black and white cat padded into the room. It stopped when it saw Mario and blinked enigmatically. Then it sprang up onto the bed and began kneading its white paws against the pale pink duvet.

Mario was allergic to cats; they made him sneeze.

He sneezed.

The cat shot him a look of disdain as if to say, you're *allergic*? To *me*? What a wimp!

Next to him, the figure beneath the duvet shifted and stretched. Raising her head meant Mario could at least have his left arm back, which was good as it meant he could see the time by his watch. The bad news was that he now had to speak to the girl with whom he had spent the night.

It was five past seven.

'Hi there,' Gemma murmured sleepily, emerging from beneath the duvet with bird's nest hair and the kind of dopey grin that made Mario's heart sink. Why had he done it? Why, *why?*

Except he knew the answer to that one. He had done it to punish Amber, to make her sorry, to show her that she might not want him any more but plenty of other girls did.

'Hi,' Mario replied, feeling sorry for Gemma and sorrier still for himself. Checking his watch again – still five past seven – he said, 'Oh hell, I'm going to be late for work.'

'You don't have to go yet.' Unaware that the remains of last night's make-up were smudged under her eyes, Gemma probably thought she was pouting prettily. 'Hello, baby, who's a beautiful boy?'

This, thank God, was directed at the cat who was still sitting inches from Mario's face. The cat continued to gaze fixedly at him.

'This is Binky,' said Gemma. 'Isn't he gorgeous? Binky, say hello to Mario.'

Mercifully Binky didn't. That would have been just too weird. Mario said, 'I'm allergic to cats.'

And to you.

'Oh, you can't be! He's my angel! Binky's my best friend,' Gemma protested. 'Aren't you, baby?'

'Well, good. But I really do have to leave. Look, last night was great . . .'

'Oh, it *was*, wasn't it?' Joyfully Gemma exclaimed, 'I'd call it the best night of my life! Honestly, you have no idea . . . I've fancied you for years!'

Mario's heart sank. This was turning into a nightmare. Yesterday evening after his meal with Lottie and the kids in Pizza Hut, he had dropped them at Piper's Cottage and headed back to his own house. He'd even got as far as pulling into the driveway before realising that he couldn't face the emptiness. He needed to be out somewhere, socialising with other people, staving off the cold, lonely sensation of rejection.

He had gone to the Three Feathers in Cheltenham, a popular pub around the corner from the car showroom, and sure enough there had been Jerry and the rest of the crew from work, drinking and laughing laddishly and playing a boisterous game of pool. Mario had been here plenty of times before but he wasn't a regular like Jerry. He vaguely recalled that the barmaid's name was Gemma and, because he had the car with him, ordered a Coke.

Two hours later Jerry nudged him and said, 'You could be in there, you know. She hasn't taken her eyes off you all night.'

That was when it had occurred to Mario that if he wanted to, he could. Why not? There was nothing to stop him now. Just for fun, he had begun experimentally chatting up Gemma across the bar.

It wasn't long before Jerry, possibly jealous, joined them and stage-whispered to Gemma in his laddish way, 'Watch him, love, he's already got a girlfriend.'

'No I haven't,' said Mario.

Jerry sniggered and gave him another all-boys-together nudge.

Looking worried, Gemma said, 'Have you?'

Mario shook his head. 'No.'

At eleven o'clock the landlord called time. Mario wondered what Amber was doing now and drew the obvious conclusion. A mental picture of her in bed with Quentin refused to go away despite the fact that he had no idea what Quentin looked like. In the mental picture he was as scrawny as a skinned rabbit with skin so pale it was almost blue and clumpy leather sandals on his bony – but surprisingly hairy – feet.

To punish Amber, Mario said, 'How are you getting home?' and saw Gemma flush with happiness.

'My flat's only a couple of streets away.'

'Oh, right.' He shrugged, signalling that it didn't matter. 'I was going to offer you a lift.'

Her mascaraed eyes bright, Gemma said breathlessly, 'You still can.'

After that the rest of the evening had followed its predictable course. Jerry and the lads had drunk up and departed, winking and jokily reminding Mario that he had to be at work tomorrow. The pub emptied, Gemma finished clearing up and the two of them left together at eleven forty.

Like Bill Clinton, Mario slept with her because he could. It didn't make him feel any better but by the time he found this out it was too late, the deed was done.

He wasn't proud of himself. And now came the horrible bit.

Propping herself up on one elbow, Gemma said eagerly, 'Tonight's my night off. Do you want to come over here after you've finished work?'

Mario almost wished he had a raging hangover, it would be something else to concentrate on. He also wished the damn cat would stop staring at him.

'The thing is, I don't think I can.'

'Oh. Well, how about tomorrow then? I can pretend I've got flu and—'

'Gemma, I still can't do it. It wouldn't be fair to you. You're a lovely girl, but I just broke up with someone yesterday.'

'So? You've got me now!'

Mario couldn't bear the look of hope in her eyes. Hating himself, he shook his head. 'I'm sorry, but I can't get involved with anyone else. I thought you understood that.'

Gemma's face went all blotchy. 'You mean you don't want to see me again? *Ever?*'

'Well, I'm not saying *ever*.' Attempting to spare her feelings Mario said, 'It's just that this is a bad time for me. Who knows, maybe in a year or two—'

'I don't believe you,' Gemma shouted, causing the cat to turn its head. 'You had sex with me and now you're off!'

'You had sex with me too,' Mario pointed out.

'You bastard! I had sex with you because I wanted to make sure you'd see me again!'

'Sweetheart, I'm really sorry.' He'd got this so wrong. And it was twenty past seven.

'*Aaarrrggh!*' She'd caught him looking at his watch. Gemma threw back her side of the duvet and leapt furiously out of bed. The cat, finding himself abruptly plunged into a world of darkness, let out an ear-splitting yowl and scrabbled frantically to escape. A split second later he emerged at the head of the doubled-over duvet, took one look at Mario and like lightning swiped a paw across his face.

Take *that*, hissed the cat. You scoundrel, you utter cad, how dare you besmirch my mistress's reputation? And while we're about it, get out of my bed.

'Jesus,' Mario gasped as the scratches from the cat's unsheathed claws began to make themselves felt. To add insult to injury he sneezed again. The cat leapt off the bed and shot out of the room like an escaping assassin.

'Good,' yelled Gemma, naked and struggling into her white dressing gown. 'I hope it bloody *hurts*.'

Chapter 34

It was two o'clock in the afternoon and Gemma would surely be delighted that at least one of her wishes had been granted. The three parallel scratches across Mario's right cheekbone weren't deep but they were surprisingly painful. They had also caused untold amusement amongst his staff, who had spent the morning calling him Cap'n Sparrow. It was a relief when they'd disappeared to the café up the road for lunch.

The next moment Mario glanced up from the paperwork on his desk and saw Amber coming into the showroom. His brain went into overdrive. Amber was here, she'd realised her mistake and had changed her mind, and the box she was carrying contained some kind of surprise – maybe a shiny helium balloon emblazoned with the words I'M SORRY, I LOVE YOU – in order to persuade him to take her back.

'Hi.' Amber appeared in his office doorway. 'What happened to your face?'

'Well, I was wrestling with this man-eating tiger.' Mario didn't know if he could cope with this much adrenaline.

Amber smiled. 'What happened really? It looks sore.'

'Got scratched by a cat.'

'You don't know anyone with a cat.'

Wrong, thought Mario, I just wish I didn't know anyone with a cat.

He shrugged. 'It was just a stray, a skinny little thing. I found it at the back of the workshop this morning. I was going to take it to the cat's home but it didn't much like the idea.'

Well, what else could he say?

'Better get a tetanus shot. Anyway,' Amber indicated the box. 'I thought I'd drop your things off.'

Not a helium balloon then. Mario, who had already guessed as much, said, 'What's in there?'

'CDs. DVDs. A few clothes. Your nice purply lambswool sweater – I knew you'd want that one back.'

'You're the one I want back.' The words were out; it might not be cool to beg but he couldn't help himself.

'Mario.' Amber bit her lip. 'Don't. This isn't easy for me either, you know.'

'So change your mind.'

'I can't.'

'You can. I love you.'

For a moment Amber wavered, fiddling with the bangles on her wrist. Then she shook her head. 'Maybe you do, but it still isn't going to happen. Damn, this is why I didn't bring the stuff to your house. I thought it would be easier here.'

Mario took a loose CD out of the box. Gun N' Roses – they'd been looking for it for months.

'Where did you find this?'

'Down the back of the sofa. What did you do last night?'

Shagged the barmaid from the Three Feathers, since you ask. Why, what did you *do?*

Maybe not.

'Took the kids to Pizza Hut,' said Mario. *There, that sounded better.*

'So you told Nat and Ruby. Were they OK?'

'What do you think?'

Amber's eyes glistened. 'I'm sorry.'

'They love you. They're upset. Nat said—'

'Ha ha ha, there he is!'

Mario looked up as the showroom doors swung open, signalling the return of Jerry and the others. From this angle they could see him but not Amber. Jerry, grinning from ear to ear, called over, 'Who's been a naughty boy then? We didn't go to the café for lunch. Popped into the Feathers instead. Miiiaaa*owww*!'

The blood drained from Mario's face. If he slammed the office door shut, Amber would want to know why; she was already giving him an odd look.

'Had a nice chat with Gemma,' Jerry went on, clearly delighted with his scoop. 'Oh boy, is *she* mad with you. Called you a filthy lying cheating bastard *and* a lousy lay. Ha ha, I just wish she'd had a video camera running when her cat shot across the bed and took that swipe at you. Think of the fun we could have had, sending that little clip off to *You've Been Framed.*'

Mario couldn't look at Amber. He felt as if all the air were being sucked out of the room.

In a soft voice Amber said, 'Goodbye, Mario,' then from the doorway added with barely concealed disdain, 'You must be slipping. You never used to be lousy in bed.'

★   ★   ★

167

The web designer's name was Phil Micklewhite.

'Hi,' said Lottie when he answered the phone on the fourth ring, 'I don't know if you remember me, but we spoke—'

'Never forget a voice,' Phil Micklewhite said cheerfully. 'You're the one who rang last week asking about Fenella Britton.'

'That's me. OK, the thing is, you sounded like a really nice person, kind and honest and completely trustworthy—'

'And you haven't been able to stop thinking about me,' said Phil. 'I've haunted your dreams. You want to meet me in person so we can start our mad passionate love affair. I know, I know, this happens to me all the time, but before you turn up on my doorstep I feel it's only fair to warn you that I'm fifty years old, *very* overweight and so ugly I even scare my goldfish.'

Lottie relaxed, liking him even more. 'Actually I wanted to ask you a bit more about Fenella. Is that OK?'

'Fine by me. Not sure I can help you though. I don't know much about her.' He paused. 'Am I allowed to ask why?'

Lottie said, 'Can I trust you to be discreet?'

'Discretion is my middle name.'

Lottie briefly filled him in on the situation. 'So basically I just wondered if you knew anything that might prove me right. Or wrong. Like if you told me Fenella was working as a high-class prostitute,' she said hopefully, 'with men calling round at all hours of the day and night, that would be really helpful.'

'I can see it would.' Phil sounded amused. 'But I'm afraid I've never seen any gentleman callers. We're a pretty quiet bunch here at Hutton Court. There are eight flats and most of the other residents are retired. They're a pleasant enough lot. We say hello and pass the time of day, and the Ramsays in Flat Three come in and feed my goldfish when I'm away, but that's about it. I'm not much of a one for tea parties. Pretty much the only time they knock on my door is when they want to use the internet.'

Lottie knew she was clutching at straws. 'Why do they do that?'

'I'm the only one in the building with a computer. The Ramsays like to send the occasional email to their son in Oregon. The Barkers are cross-word addicts. Eric in Flat One likes buying old cameras. They all pop over every now and again. I don't mind,' Phil went on. 'It earns me brownie points and means they can't moan about the state of my window boxes.'

'Does Fenella use the internet?'

'Hardly at all. Although she did last week.'

'To send emails?'

'Nooo.' Phil sounded amused. 'Fenella wouldn't know how to send an email. She asked me how to go about finding out something. I connected her to Google, showed her what to do and left her to it.'

Not daring to get her hopes up, Lottie said, 'When last week?'

There was a pause, then Phil said slowly, 'Possibly the day after you phoned me.'

Lottie got her hopes up. 'Can you find out what she was looking for?'

'Give me a few seconds.'

She heard the clatter of computer keys as Phil delved expertly into files. He was back on the phone moments later.

'I don't know what she typed into Google but she got through to a website called Hestacombe Holiday Cottages.'

Bingo.

'And it was the day after you rang me,' Phil confirmed.

The day after she'd posted off the letter to Fenella with a first class stamp, a letter telling her that Freddie Masterson would like to see her again. Quickly typing Freddie's name into Google, Lottie saw the many links to Hestacombe Holiday Cottages fill the screen.

She had written the text herself, extolling Freddie's many qualities and charting how he had built up the business over many years. As well as numerous photographs of each of the cottages, there were several of Hestacombe House itself, looking magnificent in all its autumnal glory and not at all like a block of flats.

'Is that helpful?' said Phil.

'It's just what I needed.' Lottie nodded happily; if he'd been there she would have kissed him. 'It's perfect.'

Fenella went very still and looked at Freddie. 'Is this a joke?'

They were outside on the terrace.

'No.' Freddie shook his head. 'If it was, it wouldn't be a very funny one, would it?'

'You want me to leave,' Fenella echoed. 'Because I looked you up on the internet.'

'Because you weren't honest with me,' said Freddie.

She shook her head in disbelief. 'It's that bloody girl, isn't it? Interfering, sticking her nose in where it isn't wanted. And you're just going to let her win! I love you, Freddie. You love me. We can make each other happy!'

Three days ago Fenella had erupted into his life. Two days ago they had driven up to Oxford and returned with three suitcases of her clothes. Yesterday Lottie had taken him aside and relayed to him the details of her conversation with Phil Micklewhite.

And now he was doing what needed to be done.

'You never lied to me before,' said Freddie. 'I thought I could trust you.'

'You *can*,' Fenella pleaded.

'Why would you want to stay with someone who's dying?'

'Because I can't bear the thought of not being with you!'

'Fine, then.' Freddie smiled. 'You can stay.'

Fenella's dark eyes widened with delight. Jumping up from the table she threw her arms round him. As her perfume filled his nostrils she exclaimed, 'Darling! Really? Oh, you won't regret it!'

'I hope you won't.'

'Oh *Freddie* . . .'

'Listen to what I have to say.' Freddie prepared himself. 'You should know that I've spoken to my solicitor. My will has been made and I won't be changing it. Whatever happens, you won't get anything when I'm gone. No property, no money, nothing.' He paused, allowing time for this information to sink in. 'So that's it. I'll understand if you decide to change your mind.'

He knew what Fenella's answer would be before he'd even finished the final sentence. Her shoulders had tensed at the mention of the word *solicitor*. Her breath had caught in her lungs. By the time he'd reached *no property, no money, nothing*, her fingers had slipped from his shoulders, her arms dropping millimetre by millimetre along with, it seemed, the temperature of the air on the terrace.

Freddie gently disentangled himself from her limp grasp.

Finally Fenella spoke. 'So who gets it all? You can't take it with you, you know.'

Take it with him. Freddie considered this. If he could convert the money into high quality diamonds and swallow them, would that count as taking it with him?

Irritated by his lack of response Fenella said, 'Don't tell me you're leaving everything to some miserable animal sanctuary.'

He shook his head. 'It's all been taken care of.'

'Well, I think you're making a mistake. We could have been happy.'

'I don't think we could,' said Freddie. 'Not really.'

Fenella gazed steadily at him. 'When I got that letter I thought you'd come back into my life to rescue me.'

He had no intention of feeling guilty. 'Sorry.'

She took a step away from him, turned to gaze at the wondrous view of Hestacombe Lake, then visibly collected herself. 'I'm sorry too. I'll go and pack my things. Do I at least get a lift to the train station?'

Freddie smiled faintly and nodded. 'Of course.'

Chapter 35

Fundraising for charity was always laudable, of course it was. Being lectured to about the desperate need for further research into such a distressing medical condition was boring but understandably necessary. Everyone in the room had their serious caring faces on and was dutifully paying attention. Lottie, clutching her glass of fizzy water, wondered if they were all battling to control their Oh–God–this–is–*gross* faces as desperately as she was.

Seriously, much more of this and she might actually be sick.

It was the opening night of Jumee, a glamorous new restaurant in the upmarket Montpellier district of Cheltenham. Deeply impressed by the invitation, a silver 3-D hologram printed on Mediterranean-blue perspex, Lottie had been delighted to come along and check out the glamour first-hand on behalf of future visitors to Hestacombe. And the food of course. She had even celebrated by going out and treating herself to a slinky new black and gold dress.

So far so good.

The bad news was, she hadn't counted on having to listen to an earnest grey-haired woman doctor in a fawn, buttoned-to-the-neck cardigan and bristly-looking tweed skirt droning on and on and *on* in stomach-churning Technicolor detail about the horrors of . . .

Eczema.

Half an hour ago Lottie's stomach had been rumbling away in joyful anticipation of the evening ahead. The cooking smells wafting through from the kitchen had been sublime. She deliberately hadn't eaten anything since a KitKat at lunchtime. But now her stomach had undergone an abrupt change of heart; instead of rumbling happily away it had squashed itself into a tight, hard little knot, sullenly daring her – in true teenage fashion – to try and make it accept any food at all.

It clearly wasn't an ideal scenario. Lottie felt sorry for the young couple who had plunged their life savings into this new venture. Having spoken to Robbie and Michelle earlier, she'd learned that it had always been their dream to run their own restaurant. Duly selling their house and emptying their savings accounts, they had been dismayed to discover that they still didn't have enough money to make the business viable. Step forward Michelle's Uncle Bill, a hugely wealthy man, who had generously offered to back them to the tune of eighty thousand pounds. Thus, relieved and grateful, they had accepted the offer and work had duly been completed on Jumee.

When Uncle Bill had suggested using the opportunity of the opening night to raise money for his favourite charity, it would have been churlish to refuse. Even though they already knew his favourite charity was Clearaway UK. Uncle Bill's beloved son Marcus suffered dreadfully from chronic eczema to the extent that he still spent months on end in hospital, his life blighted by the painful disfiguring disease. Uncle Bill had long made it his mission to do as much as humanly possible to eradicate it.

Which was noble and admirable and just went to show what a wonderful compassionate human being he was. But it also had to be said that inviting Dr Elspeth Murray of the Clearaway Research Institute to speak at Jumee's opening night possibly wasn't the smartest idea Uncle Bill had ever had.

'. . . when the skin is cracked and red, when a person's entire body is one mass of swollen weeping wounds, when members of the public turn away in revulsion from the sight of a face so hideously disfigured it is barely recognisable, life becomes *intolerable* for the sufferer,' Dr Murray pronounced. 'And it is our task to do everything in our power to alleviate that suffering.'

Robbie and Michelle, on the platform behind her, looked as though they were suffering intolerably too. Reaching into a large manila folder on the table beside her, Dr Murray withdrew a sheaf of A3-sized photographs and held the first one aloft.

'I would like everyone to pay close attention here. This is what happened to a seventy-three-year-old patient of mine whose eczema overtook his body and sadly became infected. Do *not* look away,' Dr Murray barked as several people at the front flinched, gasped and covered their mouths in horror. 'I want every one of you in this room to look at these photographs and consider how lucky you are not to be similarly afflicted.'

Cowed into obedience, the captive audience gazed in terror at the first full-colour photograph. You could have heard a pin drop. The silence was absolute. Grimly and without speaking, Dr Murray held up a second photograph, this time depicting a close-up of the sufferer's legs and—

'HIIIICCCC.'

It was one of those gulping, barking-in-reverse hiccups, possibly the loudest Lottie had ever heard. Everyone in the room turned to look at the perpetrator who was standing just in front and to the left of her. Tall, male and rangily built, he was wearing a baggy pink shirt, faded jeans and a baseball cap.

Clearly infuriated by the interruption, Dr Murray stared at him.

'HIIICCCCCC.'

The hiccupper made no effort to leave the room. It wouldn't have been easy, surrounded as he was by a solid mass of people who were far too terrified of Dr Murray to move and allow him to escape.

'HIIICCCCCC,' gulped the man, his shoulders jerking in time with the ear-splitting noise. '*HIIIIICCCCCC!*'

Dr Murray was by this time quivering with outrage. Acting on sheer instinct, Lottie squeezed past the fat woman to her left and managed to move up behind the world's loudest hiccupper.

'HIIII – FUCK ME!' The man let out a bellow and leapt into the air as if he'd been electrocuted. Twisting round, fighting to free the back of his shirt, he came face to face with Lottie and burst out laughing. 'I don't believe it. The girl with the perfect arse!'

'HOW DARE YOU?' thundered Dr Murray.

People were starting to whisper and giggle. The man grinned at Lottie, aware that they were now the very centre of attention. Having finally managed to escape the confines of his shirt, the ice cubes Lottie had tipped down the back of his collar dropped out and skittered like kittens across the polished wooden floor.

'HIIICCCCC.'

'GET OUT!' Dr Murray roared across the restaurant, cowing the sniggering audience into silence.

Seb-from-the-supermarket seized Lottie by the hand and dragged her with him. This time, miraculously, the crowds parted like the Red Sea. All eyes were upon them – most of them openly envious – as they made their hasty escape.

Once they were safely outside on the pavement he held her at arm's length and said seriously, 'So, how is it?'

Lottie was still reeling from the surprise of seeing him again. Dazedly she wondered if he meant how was the bottle of Veuve Cliquot he'd presented her with in the supermarket car park before disappearing in a cloud of dust.

'Think I'd better check.' Gently turning her round, Seb nodded appreciatively. 'Oh yes. Still there, still perfect.'

It was probably wildly un-PC but when it came to flattering compliments, being told you had a perfect bum had to be one of the best. So deliriously happy to be out of the restaurant that it was all she could do to stop herself giving a celebratory wiggle, Lottie said, 'Sorry about the ice. I didn't know it was you, I was just trying to stop your hiccups.'

'And you did.' He spread his hands in amazement. 'See? It's a miracle. All gone.'

'What can I say?' Lottie shrugged modestly. 'I'm good at what I do.'

'We must celebrate.' His blue eyes crinkling at the corners, Seb pulled off his baseball cap and ran his fingers through his unruly blond hair. 'You broke my heart last time. I couldn't stop thinking about you. But now fate has brought us together again, given us another chance.'

'Fate could have brought us together again a bit sooner if you'd asked me for my phone number.' Lottie couldn't resist pointing this out.

He laughed. 'You didn't ask me for mine.'

'I didn't get a chance, you just buggered off!'

'But you would have done? Hey, that's great.' Looking pleased, Seb said, 'I like a girl who knows her own mind. So what'll we do now? Are you hungry?'

Eczema. Weeping wounds. Yellow pus oozing through taut cracked skin . . .

'Funnily enough, no.'

'Great. Me neither.' He gave Lottie's perfect bottom a pat. 'Come on, we can discuss our new business venture over a drink.'

'OK, the Dr Murray diet,' Seb announced with relish. 'It'll be bigger than Atkins. All we need is a CD of Dr Murray giving one of her famous talks. Any time a dieter feels peckish they just pop the CD into their Walkman and bingo! Instant nausea. Sound good to you?'

'Brilliant.' Lottie clutched the vodka and cranberry juice he'd ordered for her even though she didn't have cystitis. 'Cheap. Simple. We could call it Now That's What I Call U-sick.'

He grinned. 'And I suppose the charity will want a cut of the profits. Charities are so selfish like that. We'll get some dodgy lawyer to draw up the contract. Two per cent of net royalties to them, ninety-eight per cent for us.'

'The world will be a skinnier place,' Lottie said happily, 'and we'll be super-rich. I've always wanted my own private jet.'

'We're a winning team.' Seb clinked his glass against hers and sat back, surveying her with undisguised pleasure. 'In fact I think the time has come for you to tell me something.'

What was it about him that made him so attractive? Enthralled, Lottie leaned closer. 'Tell you what?'

'Your name for a start. And other pertinent details,' said Seb. 'Like where you live.'

'Lottie Carlyle. Hestacombe.'

'Married?'

'Divorced.'

'Kids?'

'Two. Nine and seven.' Oh God, would that put him off?

'And you are . . . ?'

'Still Lottie Carlyle.'

He smiled. 'How old?'

'Oh, sorry. Sixty-three.'

'Well, you look fantastic for your age.' Seb slid off his bar stool, seized her free hand and kissed it then downed his vodka and cranberry juice in one. 'So, Lottie Carlyle. There's a barman standing over there with nothing to do. How about we help him out by having another drink?'

Chapter 36

'There's something I have to tell you,' Lottie announced as the taxi pulled up outside Piper's Cottage.

'Oh yes, and what's that?'

'You're a bad man.' She nudged Sebastian Gill, next to her on the back seat, and peered at her watch. 'In fact a *bad* bad man. It's one o'clock in the morning and you have spent the last five hours being a very bad influence on an innocent sixty three year old. And if you think you're coming in for a nightcap you're seriously mistaken.'

'You're a cruel cruel woman.' Seb shook his head in mournful fashion, 'but I respect you because you're a virgin. Which I think is extremely decent of me, seeing as this taxi is going to end up costing me near fifty quid. Now, am I allowed out of the car to give you a gentlemanly goodnight kiss, or would that be overstepping the mark? I might be eighty-seven but I'd still like to express my appreciation . . .'

'You may do that.' Fumbling for the door handle, Lottie marvelled that he was still able to enunciate such big words. She'd drunk more tonight than she'd drunk in the last month and her head was spinning like a plate on a stick. With any luck it wouldn't suddenly stop spinning, go all wibbly-wobbly and fall off.

Oh, but what a night it had been. Her sides were aching from laughing so much. She and Seb had had the best time and the more she learned about him the more perfect he became. His full name was Sebastian Aloysius Gill (which was weird, granted, but you couldn't hold someone's middle name against them). He was eighty-seven years old but an administrative error meant that the date of birth on his driving licence put him at thirty-two. He was living in Kingston Ash, midway between Cheltenham and Tetbury, and like herself had been divorced for a couple of years. Best of all, he had an eight-year-old daughter, Maya, which meant he was comfortable around children and less likely to do or say the wrong thing in their company than some people Lottie could mention.

OK, maybe she was getting a bit carried away, envisaging fun-filled

176

afternoons together and idyllic picnics on the beach. She had only known Seb properly for five hours. But it had been a promising start.

'Need a hand, love?' The taxi driver lit a cigarette as Lottie clambered out of the back seat and hesitated at the front gate. 'Sure this is your house?'

Honestly, what kind of a state did he think she was in?

'I'm fine, fine, absolutely fine.' She was fumbling inside her handbag. 'Just looking for my – *oops*.'

'Elephant? Lipstick? Shotgun?' Seb suggested helpfully. 'Jaffa cakes? Come on, give us a clue, how many syllables?'

'Bloody front door key,' Lottie wailed, dropping to her knees and groping blindly around in the darkness.

'God, five syllables. They're always the hardest ones to get.' Seb followed her out of the car and joined her on the ground. 'Where did you drop it?'

'If I knew where I'd dropped it, I'd be able to find it, wouldn't I?' Giggling as his hand brushed her ankle, Lottie said, 'The keyring got caught on something inside my bag so when I tugged it free it flew out of my hand.'

Seb said, 'God, I hate it when that happens.'

'OK, concentrate. This is serious. It could be in the road or on the pavement or in the garden or . . . or . . . *anywhere*.'

'If you ring the front doorbell,' Seb suggested helpfully, 'wouldn't the butler let you in?'

'Sadly it's the butler's night off. A torch would be useful.' Lottie flinched as her searching hands encountered a snail on the pavement. 'I've got a torch in my kitchen . . .'

'Bloody butlers, never around when you need them.' Kneeling up and addressing the taxi driver, Seb said, 'You wouldn't happen to have one with you, I suppose?'

'What, a butler? Nah, mate.' The taxi driver grinned broadly and took a drag of his cigarette. 'More trouble than they're worth.'

Seb clapped his hand to his chest. 'A torch, a torch, my kingdom for a torch.'

'Bleeeurrgh, *slug*.' Lottie uttered a muffled shriek and almost toppled into the gutter.

'Ah, but does it know how to open front doors? Could it maybe *slide* under the door and unlock it from the inside? You look very cute like that, by the way. On your hands and knees.' His teeth gleaming white in the pitch darkness, Seb said cheerfully, 'Like a playful dog.'

'Look, this is all very amusing,' the taxi driver yawned, 'but you're not actually any nearer to finding the damn key, are you?'

'That's because it's the middle of the night,' Lottie regarded him loftily from her playful-dog position at the edge of the kerb, 'and we have no way of finding the damn key because none of us has a torch.'

The taxi driver heaved a sigh and knocked his gearstick into reverse. 'Right, try not to get yourselves run over. I'll back up and shine my headlights onto the pavement.'

'That's an excellent idea.' Lottie nodded with approval. 'Truly wonderful. Now why didn't I think of that?'

'Because you're pissed as parrots, the pair of you.' The taxi driver chucked his cigarette end out of the window. 'Now come on, out the way. And I've still got my meter running,' he added as he executed a neat ninety-degree turn. 'So I just hope you can afford this.'

It was sod's law of course that within seconds of the taxi reversing across the road to light up Lottie's front garden, another car would appear and be unable to get past. Lottie, scurrying around on all fours and praying the key hadn't fallen down the slatted drain cover, heard the second car slow to a halt and their taxi driver yell across, 'Sorry, mate, couple of punters lost their marbles. Give us a minute, will you?'

'Two lots of headlights,' Seb said happily. 'Excellent.'

Then a familiar voice reached Lottie's ears and she looked up too suddenly, causing her head to start spinning again.

'They've lost *what*?'

Lottie froze like a rabbit caught in . . . well, headlights, then said defiantly, 'Our taxi driver thinks he's being funny. All I did was drop my key. The situation . . .' gosh, difficult word to say when you were tired, shichashun '. . . is *completely* under control.'

'Glad to hear it,' Tyler drawled. 'By the way, you've got a snail on your dress.'

Lottie let out a muted scream and gave the snail a swipe, sending it cartwheeling into the bushes. Dazzled by the lights she shielded her eyes and said impatiently, 'You could always help, you know. Seeing as it's all your fault I can't get into my house.'

One eyebrow went up. 'And that would be . . . why?'

'Because I managed perfectly well for years keeping my spare key under the geranium pot next to the front door. Until *you* came along,' Lottie pointed an accusing finger, 'and told me how ridiculous it was to hide a key there, that I was just asking to be burgled by burglars. So I moved it, and now my spare key is sitting in the cutlery drawer in my kitchen, which is what *I* call ridiculous, which is why I think you should be—'

'Found it!' cried Seb.

'Really?' Still on her knees, Lottie swivelled round in relief.

Seb flashed a grin. 'No. Only joking.'

'Oh God!'

'But just for a split second there you felt better, didn't you?'

'And now I feel *worse*,' Lottie wailed, 'and I want to go to bed, but I can't because nobody's helping me to look for my stupid sodding key!'

'Hey, you're beautiful when you're angry.' There was a *thunk* as a car door opened and closed and Seb turned to address Tyler. 'Don't you think she looks beautiful, with her hair falling all over her face and her eyes flashing? Like a stroppy springer spaniel.'

Tyler gave him an odd look. Lottie decided she'd had enough of being told she resembled a dog. Careful not to lose her balance she pushed herself upright and . . . whoops, lost her balance. Just for a moment. OK, lean against the wall and look casual. Better still, look sober. Did she really look like a springer spaniel? And what was Tyler doing out at this time of night anyway? It was *late*.

'Right.' Tyler was standing on the pavement now, hands on hips. 'If you don't know where you dropped the key, which you clearly *don't*,' he added pointedly, 'then you're better off waiting for the morning. Let your friend go home in his taxi. You can stay at my place tonight and we'll find the key tomorrow. How does that sound?'

Lottie stifled a snigger. How did it sound? Like he didn't want Seb hanging around Piper's Cottage a minute longer than necessary.

Seb, who was evidently thinking likewise, surveyed Tyler with amusement. 'Are you her husband?'

'He's my boss.' Lottie wondered if Tyler's suggestion that she should stay the night meant he had more than a working relationship in mind.

'The grumpy one who complains about your work all the time? The one you can't stand?'

'He's joking,' Lottie said hastily. 'I didn't say any of that.'

In the end her bursting bladder made the decision for her. Lottie waved Seb off in the taxi, safe in the knowledge that this time they had each other's numbers keyed into their phones. (With any luck they hadn't had so much to drink that they'd keyed their own numbers into their own phones – wouldn't *that* be hilarious?)

'You're going to have one hell of a hangover tomorrow,' Tyler remarked as he helped her into the passenger seat of his car.

'Thank you for pointing that out. I'd never have thought of it otherwise. We had fun.' Lottie wrestled unsuccessfully with her seatbelt then gave up and allowed him to fasten it for her. It felt like being six years old again. 'I'm allowed to have fun, aren't I?'

'As much as you like. I'm not trying to stop you.'

In the darkness, Lottie smiled. 'Sure about that?'

'Well. You know what I mean. I'd rather you didn't hook up with a

179

complete idiot.' Tyler's tone of voice indicated that this was his opinion of Seb.

'I like him. Don't spoil it for me.' Her head began to spin again as he rounded the sharp bend past the pub. 'Where have you been tonight anyway? Who says you haven't been sneaking off to see some dippy girl?'

'The Anderssons checked out of Walnut Lodge at eight o'clock this evening to fly back to Sweden. At ten o'clock I got a frantic phone call from them at Heathrow,' said Tyler. 'They'd left their passports in the biscuit tin in the kitchen.'

Lottie realised she was glad he hadn't been seeing some dippy girl. Aloud she said, 'So you drove all the way up there. Very noble.'

'Customer relations. They were grateful.' Tyler paused. 'Where are Nat and Ruby tonight?'

'With Mario.' Lottie was bursting for the loo. 'They mustn't find out I stayed with you. They'd give me no end of grief.'

'Luckily we aren't on speaking terms,' Tyler said lightly, 'so they won't be hearing it from me.'

Almost there now. They were travelling along the narrow lakeside track that led to Fox Cottage. Damn, it was bumpy too. Scrunching up her bladder for all she was worth, Lottie said, 'We could sleep together and they wouldn't know. That's ironic, isn't it? But I don't think we should. It wouldn't be right. Not fair on us, not fair on them.'

Heavens, where had that come from? She hadn't even realised those words had been about to come tumbling out. Was it tarty to even think about sleeping with Tyler? Oh, but there was still that tantalising unfinished . . . *thing* between them and it wasn't as if she and Seb were an item; she had only properly met him tonight.

'Well, quite.' Tyler nodded. 'Plus I do try and make it a rule not to sleep with women who have had a lot to drink.'

Defensively Lottie said, 'No? Because they might wake up the next morning and be horrified by what they've done? Are you worried they might sue you?'

'Not at all.' As he pulled up outside Fox Cottage Tyler said equably, 'I'm usually worried they might snore.'

The cheek of it. As if she'd dream of doing anything so unladylike. Bursting for a wee, Lottie launched herself out of the car and hopped from one foot to the other as he struggled to open the front door of the cottage.

'Are you doing that on purpose?'

Tyler paused, surprised. 'Doing what on purpose?'

'Being extra-slow!'

'Oh, that.' He grinned. 'Yes.'

'I hate you.' Snatching the key from him, Lottie jabbed it manically at the lock, finally getting it in on the tenth go. Flinging the door open she raced upstairs to the loo.

Oh the relief, the blessed *blessed* relief . . . Now she could concentrate again on something other than keeping every muscle in her pelvic floor clenched tighter than a clam.

It was two o'clock in the morning and here she was in Tyler's cottage. OK, maybe a teeny bit drunk, but that wasn't her fault. Slightly miffed, Lottie finished washing her hands and studied her face in the mirror above the bathroom sink. Why didn't Tyler want to sleep with her? She was looking fantastic! Surely any red-blooded male would jump at the chance? Even if she had said it wouldn't be a good idea under the circumstances. Now that they were actually here it seemed a shame not to make the most of the opportunity.

Oooh, what was that heavenly smell?

Bacon!

Chapter 37

'I don't snore,' Lottie announced from the kitchen doorway.

Tyler had his back to her. When he turned round she tossed back her hair and dazzled him with her most seductive Lauren Bacall smile.

'Excuse me?'

'I don't snore. Promise. *Youw.*' The seductive moment was spoiled somewhat by the kitchen door swinging shut behind her, trapping her fingers in the door jamb.

'Well, I'm glad to hear that.' Tyler expertly flipped the sizzling rashers of bacon in the frying pan; God, he had forearms to die for.

'And I've changed my mind about tonight.' Unobtrusively sucking her pinched fingers – God, that had hurt a *lot* – Lottie said, 'This could be our only chance. I think we should go for it.'

'You do?'

'Well, it seems a shame not to. We both know we want to, don't we?'

'Er, hang on . . .'

'Oh please! Don't pretend you don't.' Lottie spread her arms and shrugged. 'So why shouldn't we?'

Tyler considered this. Finally he said, 'Because you're drunk and I'd prefer it if you were sober?'

'Excuse me,' Lottie was indignant, 'that is *so* hurtful! Are you suggesting I'm no good at it when I'm drunk? Because I'll have you know I'm every bit as fantastic in bed when I've had a few drinks as when I'm stone cold sober!'

'But—'

'It's true,' she exclaimed, sensing that she hadn't yet won him over. 'You can ask Mario! Well not now, obviously. Tomorrow you can. I like mine really crispy, by the way.'

That caught his attention. Pausing with the spatula in mid-air, Tyler said, '*What?*'

'My bacon.' Lottie nodded at the pan, crammed with five rashers. 'I like it crispy. Is that two rashers for you and three for me?'

'It's five rashers for me,' Tyler said slowly. 'You went to review a restaurant tonight, remember?'

'But we didn't eat. We . . . kind of left in a hurry. That's where I met Seb again.' Lottie beamed. 'You see, he had these *massive* hiccups and I tried to stop them, and then we invented this brilliant diet that's going to make us *millions* – oh well, it's a long story.' Despite her enthusiasm Tyler was looking less than riveted; she hoped he wasn't going to be selfish and try to fob her off with a measly two slices of bacon. 'So you see, that's why I'm so hungry. Ravenous, in fact.' Slinking across the kitchen and sliding her arms sexily round Tyler's waist she murmured, 'And we need to keep our energy levels up, don't we? Hmm? Don't want to be too weak and racked with hunger pangs to—'

'Lottie.' Tyler turned round as she pressed kisses against his shoulder blades. Disentangling himself from her grasp he gazed deep into her eyes. 'I can't cook if you're going to keep distracting me like this. You're absolutely right, we both need to eat a proper meal. So why don't you go through to the living room and make yourself at home, and as soon as the food's ready I'll bring it through. Does that sound like a good idea?'

'It sounds like a great idea.' Lottie grinned, because he was right, it was the perfect solution. 'Can we have fried bread and mushrooms and tomatoes too?'

'All that,' Tyler promised, and the way his mouth curved up at the corners proved too much for Lottie to resist. Teetering up on tiptoe, she kissed him. Entirely his fault for having such a delectable mouth.

'You're gorgeous.' Lottie stroked his lightly stubbled jaw. 'We're going to have such a great time. We'll never forget tonight.'

'We certainly won't,' Tyler agreed, still smiling as he shooed her away. 'Now off you go. The sooner you stop molesting me the sooner I'll have this meal cooked.'

And the sooner I can ravish your glorious body, Lottie thought happily as she managed to locate the kitchen door and simultaneously wiggle her pinched fingers in a flirtatious fashion at Tyler. He grinned and wiggled his own unpinched fingers back at her.

OK, living room.

Sofa.

Seductive music, oh yes indeed. Must have seductive music. Investigating the CD collection, Lottie found an Alicia Keys album and put it on. Then she turned the CD over and put it on again so it would play.

Oh yes. Perfect.

Now, back to the sofa. Slipping out of her shoes, she arranged herself alluringly against the velvet cushions and made sure her skirt wasn't rucked up. Well, not *too* rucked up, a discreet amount of rucking was allowed.

There, now when Tyler opened the living room door he would see her looking elegant, relaxed and completely irresistible . . .

'Lottie.'

'BandAid.'

'Lottie, wake up.'

Someone was shaking her. Possibly the same person who'd glued her eyes shut. As the shaking intensified, Lottie rolled over onto her side, wincing as something heavy rolled in tandem and went clunk inside her head. Yuk, her brain.

Slowly she peeled open her eyelids. Oof, sunlight.

And Tyler. Looking highly amused.

'So you wouldn't call yourself a morning person then.'

Oh God. The events of last night came crashing back, unwanted. Lottie would have given anything to hide her head under the blanket if only she had one. But she hadn't. He'd left her there all night on the sofa without so much as a tea towel to keep her warm.

'What time is it?'

'Eight o'clock. Time to get up.'

He clearly wasn't planning on being remotely sympathetic. Well, she could hardly blame him for that. Lottie pictured him slaving over a hot stove before finally, triumphantly, bursting into the living room with two plates piled high with bacon, sausages, fried bread and mushrooms, only to find her asleep on the sofa. Out for the count, basically, after all his hard work.

Not to mention the other promise she'd made him.

Hmm, definitely best not to mention that one. No wonder he was a bit short on sympathy this bright morning.

And crikey, it *was* bright.

'I've got a bit of a . . . a headache.' Shielding her eyes, Lottie peered hopefully up at him. 'Would you have any aspirin going spare?'

'Sorry, I don't.' He didn't *sound* sorry. 'You can pick some up from the pharmacy later. What's with the BandAid anyway?'

'Excuse me?'

'You were asleep. I called your name and you said BandAid.'

'Oh.' She remembered now. 'I was having a dream. I'd unzipped a banana that wasn't supposed to be unzipped, so I was trying to close it back up again. But then I ran out of Sellotape, so . . .'

'Hmm.' Tyler raised an expressive eyebrow.

Blushing furiously, Lottie said, 'OK, I'm getting up. And I'm really sorry I fell asleep while you were cooking my food. If you didn't throw it away, I'll eat it now.'

'Are you serious?' His dark grey eyes glittered, registering disbelief.

'Of course I am! I'm starving!' It was perverse but true; no matter how hideous the hangover, Lottie's appetite invariably remained as boisterous as a Labrador puppy on a beach.

'I meant do you seriously believe I cooked you a meal last night?'

'Oh. Didn't you?'

'When I knew for a fact you'd be snoring like a buffalo within thirty seconds of hitting that sofa?' Evidently enjoying the look on her face, Tyler drawled, 'I made myself a bacon sandwich. It was great. Five rashers of bacon all to myself. And guess what? They were really crispy.'

'So you weren't upset that I fell asleep before . . .' Lottie couldn't quite bring herself to utter the rest.

'Upset? Are you kidding, the state you were in? Let me tell you, I was counting on it.'

'Oh.'

'One-night stands aren't my style,' said Tyler.

'Right.' Lottie felt very small and very cheap. Last night she'd pretty much announced that she was going to shag him senseless, having taken it completely for granted that it was what he wanted too.

'Especially when we have to work together.'

'Of course. Sorry.' Now she knew how it felt to be regarded as – what was the American expression? – trailer trash. In fact she was worse than trailer trash. She didn't even have a trailer.

'No need to apologise,' said Tyler. 'We'll forget it happened, shall we?'

Oh yes, that was *so* likely.

'OK, I'll make you a quick cup of tea.' He made a move towards the door. 'Feel free to use the bathroom. And there's a spare toothbrush on the shelf next to the basin.'

The spare toothbrush that was kept expressly for overnight guests who were too drunk to go home. Hauling herself off the sofa, Lottie said, 'Did I really snore like a buffalo?'

Tyler regarded her gravely for several seconds. Finally he said, 'That's something only me and my bacon sandwich will ever know.'

If Tyler had been a short, skinny weedy type she could conceivably have borrowed a shirt and a pair of jeans from him. But he wasn't, and he probably wouldn't have lent her anything anyway.

'Tell me again where you were when you dropped it,' he ordered now.

Lottie sighed. 'I didn't drop it. The keyring got hooked on the zip of my make-up bag and when I pulled out my make-up bag the keyring just flew off the end. Kind of like a catapult.'

'OK.' Tyler managed to make it sound like: typical-stupid-bloody-woman. 'I guess we just keep looking until we find it.'

Feeling utterly ridiculous in her glitzy black and gold dress and black satin stilettos, Lottie did her best to ignore her raging hangover and get on with the task in hand. She couldn't change her clothes until she could get into the cottage. What's more, when they did finally find her keyring, they then had to drive into Cheltenham and retrieve her car which was currently parked in the pay and display car park in Montpellier without a pay and display ticket. That is, if it hadn't already been clamped and towed away.

Last night she and Seb had been scrabbling around on this very pavement searching in the darkness for her keys when Tyler had come along and complicated matters.

This time it was even worse.

A car slowed and a voice called out, 'Don't let the ants get away from you. Offer them enough money and maybe they'll stay and be your friends.'

Oh perfect. Lottie bit back a retort, swept her hair out of her face and sat back on her black satin high heels.

'Mummy! What are you doing?' Nat popped his head out of the passenger window, agog. 'Are you really chasing ants?'

'You're so stupid.' Ruby, in the back seat, was scornful. 'Of course she isn't. Mummy, why are you still wearing the dress you had on last night?'

Mario grinned. 'Good question. I was wondering that myself.'

It was eight thirty and the children, smart in their blue and grey uniforms, were on their way to school.

'I just dropped my keys, that's all,' said Lottie. 'I'll see you two later, OK? You don't want to be late for school.'

'I do,' Nat said eagerly.

But Ruby's eyes had already narrowed in Tyler's direction. 'What's *he* doing here? And where's your car?' Like a mini Mother Superior she demanded icily, 'Where did you sleep last night?'

Oh heavens. Flustered, Lottie blurted out, 'Here, of course!'

'So why are you still wearing that dress?'

'Because . . . well, because I like it! And so many people last night said how nice it was, I thought I'd wear it again today.'

Ruby's mouth was pursed like a cat's bottom. 'And your car?'

She'd make a terrifying barrister one day.

'Um . . . um . . .' Lottie was floundering badly, too hungover to keep track of what she was saying. 'Well . . .'

'Lottie, we don't have all day,' Tyler broke in. Turning to address Nat and Ruby he said, 'Your mother had a few drinks last night and left her car in Cheltenham. She rang me this morning and asked me for a lift to go and pick it up. So I turned up here ten minutes ago and as she was

186

coming through the front gate she managed to drop her keys. Which means we're all going to be late for work.'

Nat and Ruby didn't look at Tyler while he was telling them this; they acted as though he didn't exist. In fact they were so intent on refusing to acknowledge his existence that their eyes were roaming everywhere but in his direction.

'So there you go,' Lottie exhaled with relief when he'd finished. 'Happy now?'

'I don't know.' From the back of the car Ruby muttered darkly, 'Is it the truth or just another big fat *lie*?'

'Ruby—'

'Is that them over there?' Nat was leaning precariously out of the passenger window, pointing at a rose bush adjacent to the front wall.

Lottie followed the direction of his finger and saw that he was right. There, glinting in the sunlight and jauntily swinging from one of the lower branches, were her keys.

And to think she'd never won anything on a hoop-la stall in her life.

'Thank God for that.' Hastening over to the rose bush, Lottie retrieved the dangling keyring.

Nat said hopefully, 'Do I get a reward?'

'Maybe later. Off you go to school now. I need to pick up my car.' Hurriedly she gave each of them a kiss then tapped her watch and said to Mario, 'Miss Batson'll have your guts for garters if they're late for registration.'

'Miss Batson loves me.' Mario was cheerful bordering on smug. 'She thinks I'm great. Anyway, I'll just tell her we would have been on time but you were so hungover you couldn't find your car keys.'

'You're all heart. In fact if you do that, you'll end up with sole custody,' said Lottie. 'And it'll jolly well serve you right.'

Chapter 38

Still laughing, Mario drove Nat and Ruby off to school. Lottie let herself into Piper's Cottage, changed out of her stupid glittery dress into white trousers and a plain grey top and helped herself to a bottle of iced water from the fridge.

'Can you remember where you left your car?' said Tyler as they drove into Cheltenham.

'Of course I can remember!' Lottie was offended. She might not be able to recall *exactly* where she'd left her car but she knew which car park it was in.

'Fine. Just checking. There's a garage up ahead,' Tyler nodded, 'if you want to pick up some painkillers.'

Lottie, who had already swilled down three paracetamols and a pint of water at home, said heroically, 'No thanks. I'm OK.'

Which was, frankly, ridiculous. She'd announced her intention to give her boss the night of his life, been politely turned down *without even realising it* and to cap it all had fallen asleep in a sozzled heap on his sofa.

I mean let's face it, what could be less OK than that?

'Your phone,' Tyler prompted as a muffled sound emanated from the handbag at Lottie's feet.

'Morning, gorgeous!' It was Seb, sounding disgustingly chirpy.

'Morning.' Lottie smiled, not feeling overly gorgeous but delighted to hear from him anyway.

'Did you spend the night with that scary boss of yours?'

'I didn't have a lot of choice.'

'I hope he behaved himself. Didn't attempt to take advantage of the situation, force his attentions upon you . . .'

'No, no, nothing like that.' Lottie hastily pressed the phone hard against her ear to stop his words spilling out.

'But does he have designs on you? After all, he is your boss,' said Seb. 'And you do have the most perfect bottom. It can't be easy for him, having to work with—'

'Actually he's here,' Lottie blurted out. 'Right next to me.'

Seb laughed. 'Lucky him. Anyhow, the reason I'm calling. I want to see you tonight.'

Tonight! Crikey. Flattered but not at all sure she could persuade Mario to take Nat and Ruby for a second night, Lottie grimaced and said, 'The thing is, I'd need to find a babysitter.'

'Or you could bring the kids along with you.' Seb was unfazed. 'There's a fair on Ambleside Common. Would they be up for that, d'you think?'

Would they be up for a trip to the fairground? Was he serious?

'They'd love it. If you're sure you wouldn't mind.' Flustered, Lottie realised that Tyler had stopped at a junction and was waiting for directions. 'Sorry. Left, then second right by that blue van. Um, look, I'll ring you back in a bit. We're just picking up the car.'

Seb paused. 'This boss of yours. Have you slept with him?'

'No!'

'Did he hear that?'

'Yes,' Tyler replied. 'He did.'

'Speak to you later.' Lottie hurriedly ended the call before Seb could cause any more mischief. 'Turn left again after the flower shop. Nearly there now.'

'Sounds like you've got yourself a date for tonight.' Tyler's tone was expressionless.

Did he care? Really care? A wave of regret swept through her, because if she had the choice she wouldn't choose Seb. But it wasn't a viable dilemma anyway, was it? She was a mother whose children had taken that decision for her. A squiggle of excitement mingled with fear in Lottie's stomach at the prospect of introducing Seb to Nat and Ruby. What if they hated him as much as they hated Tyler? Aloud she said casually, 'Sounds like I have.'

'No. No way. I can't do it,' Seb declared flatly. 'Anything but that.'

'You have to.' Giggling helplessly, Ruby dragged him past the hoop-la stall. 'I'm going to make you go on it.'

Seb dug his heels in like a dog. '*Won't* do it.'

'Why not?'

'You want to know why not? OK, I'll tell you.' Counting off on his fingers, Seb recited, 'Number one reason: because I'll scream like a girl. Number two reason: I'll cry like a girl. And number three reason: I'll be sick.'

Nat was busy tugging on his other arm. 'You won't. You have to come on it with us. Mum, tell him.'

'You have to,' Lottie told Seb, 'because someone has to sit here and look

189

after the soft toys, and looking after soft toys really isn't a job for a grown man.'

Seb allowed himself to be hauled off to the Ghost Train and Lottie settled down on the grass to wait for them. As the lights and colours of the fairground flashed and swirled around her she breathed in the evocative smells of hot dogs, frying onions, toffee apples and diesel. It was hard to believe that in less than two hours Seb had won over both her children so effortlessly and completely. Although in truth he had achieved it within two minutes. Somehow there had been that magical spark when she had first introduced him to Ruby and Nat. Being a father himself undoubtedly helped. He was comfortable with them, relaxed and funny and interested in what they had to say. He clearly enjoyed their company but wasn't making the mistake of trying too hard to impress.

And it had worked, beyond Lottie's wildest dreams. The last couple of hours had been a revelation. She hadn't realised it was possible for her children to have this much genuine uncomplicated fun with a man who wasn't their dad.

A lurid lime-green stuffed dinosaur toppled against her knee. Lottie sat it firmly back upright next to the fluorescent orange fluffy spider and the giant purple pig they'd won at the shooting gallery. How Nat and Ruby's eyes had lit up when Seb had pulled out his wallet and handed each of them a tenner. When she had tried to protest he had insisted, explaining, 'Otherwise it wouldn't be fair. Because I'm not stopping until I've won that purple pig.'

Nor had he. As far as Seb was concerned, failure wasn't an option. Even if the cheap, cross-eyed pig had ended up costing him close to fifty pounds. When the stallholder had finally handed it over, Nat had said, 'What are you going to call it?' and Seb had replied, 'Well, I've got this sister called Tiffany . . .'

'Oh God, never again,' Seb groaned, reappearing with Nat and Ruby in tow. 'That was scary. There were real ghosts in there.'

'He was frightened.' Nat was proud. 'I wasn't.'

'OK, back to the rides. That one.' Seb pointed to the contraption Lottie had been most dreading, the warp-speed upside-down spinny thing.

'I'd love to,' she patted the stuffed toys, 'but these need looking after. You lot go. I'll stay here and watch.'

He pulled a face at Ruby and Nat. 'Your mum's scared.'

'Honestly,' said Lottie, 'I'm not. I *love* upside-down spinny things, I just—'

'I was scared of the Ghost Train,' Seb said patiently, 'and look at me. I overcame my fears.'

'But I—'

'It's the children I feel sorry for.' Shaking his head, he turned to Ruby and Nat. 'Children, I feel sorry for you. What must it be like to have a mother who's a wimp?'

'I *told* you,' Lottie protested, 'someone has to look after everything we've won.'

'Exactly. *Someone* does.' Seb gathered up the fluffy spider, the lurid dinosaur and the purple pig. Marching over to the warp-speed upside-down spinny thing he flashed a disarming smile at a couple of young teenage girls, exchanged a few words with them and handed over the toys. Returning, he said, 'But it doesn't have to be you.'

After the upside-down spinny thing came the Waltzers, the Octopus and the Dodgems. By ten o'clock they'd been on every ride at the fair, won many more stuffed toys and eaten far too many toffee apples, sticks of candyfloss and chips with curry sauce.

'That was brilliant.' Ruby heaved an ecstatic sigh as they made their way back across the field to where they'd left the car. 'Thanks, Seb.'

'Thank *you*,' Seb replied gravely, 'for looking after me on the Ghost Train.'

'Can we go out again soon?' Nat gazed eagerly up at him.

Lottie winced in the darkness; seven-year-olds could be alarmingly direct. Even if it was a question she was interested in hearing the answer to herself.

'The thing is, I don't know if your mother would like that,' said Seb.

'Why not? She would!'

'She might have decided she doesn't like me.'

Nat was incredulous. 'She wouldn't! She does like you, don't you, Mum?'

'*See?*' demanded Seb when Lottie hesitated, floundering around for a reply. 'She's trying to be polite because she doesn't want to hurt my feelings, but I think she's secretly in love with another man.'

'*Who?*' Ruby's eyes were like saucers.

Seb lowered his voice to a stage whisper. 'Tyson, is that his name? Her boss.'

'Noooo!' Nat let out a howl of disdain. 'She doesn't like him. We won't let her.'

'His name's Tyler,' Ruby chimed in with relish. 'And we hate him.'

'Ruby,' Lottie protested.

'Well we *do*.'

'Your mum might not like me,' said Seb. 'We don't know yet, do we? I mean, has she said anything to you?'

Ruby, her eyes bright, replied helpfully, 'When we asked her what you were like she said very nice.'

'Well, that's a start.'

'And good looking.'

Oh great, thought Lottie.

'I'm flattered.' Seb ruffled Ruby's hair. 'But she still might secretly hate me.'

'She doesn't. Mum,' Nat ordered, 'tell Seb you love him.'

'Nat, *no!*' Thank goodness it was dark.

'Why not?'

For heaven's sake. 'Because . . . because it just isn't the kind of thing grown-ups *do*.'

'But we can all go out with Seb again. We can, can't we?'

Lottie's skin was prickling with mortification. And Seb was laughing at her, the bastard.

'If it's OK with him, it's OK with me.'

'Result,' Seb crowed, clenching his fists and punching the air.

'Give me a piggyback!' Nat leapt up and Seb expertly caught him on his back, racing off across the field while Nat clung on and let out whoops of delight.

'He's fun,' said Ruby, watching them turn in a wide circle before cantering back. 'I really like him.'

'Mm, I can tell.' Lottie's nod was non-committal but inside she was experiencing a warm Ready Brek glow.

'My turn,' Ruby shrieked as Nat was tipped to the ground. Seb expertly scooped her up and carted her off.

'I like Seb,' Nat confided, sliding a warm grubby hand into Lottie's. 'He's nice. Almost as good as Dad.'

'Yes.' A lump sprang into Lottie's throat. Maybe this time they'd all found the man of their dreams.

Chapter 39

The following evening Nat did something that caused Lottie's heart to contract in alarm. He and Ruby were stretched out on their stomachs on the living room floor playing a fiercely contested game of Uno when Nat, pausing to study his cards, absently scratched behind his left ear.

Lottie stiffened, realising belatedly that it wasn't the first time she'd seen him do it this evening but until now the awful significance hadn't registered.

'Ow, Mum, geddoff.' Nat tried to wriggle free as she dropped to the floor and grabbed his head between her hands. 'I'm winning.'

Lottie ignored his protests. Her mouth dry, she began frantically parting his dark hair, hoping against hope that the scratching didn't mean what she thought it . . .

Shit.

'Mum!' Delighted, Nat said 'You said the sh- word!'

'Sorry, sorry, I thought I'd only said it in my head.' Still kneeling, Lottie leaned back on her heels and let out a wail of dismay. 'Oh Nat. You've got nits.'

Nat shrugged, concentrating on his hand of Uno cards. 'Thought so.'

Lottie paled. 'You *thought* so? Why didn't you *say* so!'

Another shrug. 'Forgot. Some of the people in my class have got nits. We had a letter about it from school last week.'

'Last week! You didn't give me any letter!'

Nat was indignant. 'I found that squashed beetle in the playground, remember? I had to use the letter to wrap it up and bury it.'

'Have I got nits?' Eager not to be left out, Ruby crawled across the carpet and thrust her head into Lottie's lap. This time it took less than five seconds to confirm the worst.

'Yes.' Lottie wondered if bursting into tears would help.

'Great! Does that mean we don't have to go to school?'

'No it does not. It just means hours and hours of combing.'

Helpfully Nat said, 'Mummy, you might have nits too.'

Oh *God*.

Leaping to her feet, Lottie rushed upstairs. The old metal nit comb was in the back of the bathroom cabinet. Ten minutes of heart-in-the-mouth combing finally reassured her that her own hair was free of uninvited guests. But it wasn't that reassuring, because she still had to face up to the possibility that Seb might be another unwitting host.

Actually it was less of a possibility and more of a likelihood. Lottie briefly closed her eyes, picturing him with Nat and Ruby last night at the fair. When they had been crammed together into the seats on the various rides. When Seb had been crouching beside Nat, showing him how to take aim and fire at the targets in the shooting gallery. When he had given Ruby a piggyback and Ruby, screaming with delight, had clung on to his neck, her long curly hair falling over his forehead.

Lottie flinched. She had to tell Seb. Oh hell, how was he going to react to this? He was a man, and a glamorous one at that. He would recoil in horror, be utterly repulsed, assume she and her nit-ridden children were dirty. He might never want to see her again. And frankly, who could blame him?

Two hours, three baths and a family-sized bottle of conditioner later, Lottie had combed everyone's hair so exhaustively that her arms were ready to drop off. But for tonight, at least, they were bug-free. Despite Nat having begged to be allowed to keep the captured headlice in a matchbox.

Now, with the children safely in bed with clean sheets and pillowcases, came the part she had really been dreading. The necessary evil, thought Lottie, feeling slightly sick but determined to go through with it. Tightening the belt of her white dressing gown and curling up on the sofa, she called Seb's mobile.

OK, here we go.

'Hello?'

The line was crackly and not particularly clear but the voice definitely belonged to a female. For a split second Lottie wondered if Seb had been lying to her and was married. Then as the female chirruped distractedly, 'Hello, hello, who is this?' she realised who had answered the phone.

'Oh hi, could I speak to Seb please?'

'Actually he's a bit busy right now. Is that Lottie?'

'It is.' Lottie felt ridiculously flattered that Seb's sister knew her name.

'Hi, Lottie! This is Tiffany! Is it urgent?'

'Well, yes, it is quite. Um . . .'

'The thing is, we're on our way down the M5 and Seb's driving. I won't let him speak on the phone while he's in charge of the car, you understand. Otherwise we'd be killed. So you just tell me what it is, Lottie, and I'll pass the message on.'

Tiffany sounded like a younger, more fastidious version of Margot Leadbetter. Lottie blanched at the prospect.

'It's OK, don't worry, nothing that won't keep.' She managed to inject a note of sangfroid into her voice. 'Tell Seb I'll give him a call later, OK? Bye.'

With the connection broken, Lottie buried her hot face in her hands. How typical that something like this had to happen to her. After three long arid years of singledom she'd finally met a man she liked who not only appeared to like her in return but also, miraculously, got on brilliantly with Ruby and Nat. Last night they had all shared a memorable evening together at the fair and Seb had lavished them with money and affection.

And what had they given him in return?

Nits.

The phone was ringing.

'Oh ya, hi, me again. Seb says you can't keep him in suspense like this. You know how impatient he is. He says he needs to know what's so important *right now.*'

For the life of her Lottie couldn't think of a convincing lie, a substitute reason for phoning him so urgently. Oh well, maybe it was easier telling him via a go-between, a kind of 'my mate really fancies you, he wants to know if you'd go out with him' scenario.

'Hello? Hello? Are you still there?' warbled Tiffany.

'Yes, still here.' Lottie took a deep breath and plunged in. 'The thing is, I'm really sorry but my children have nits. Which means Seb may have them too, so he'll need to get himself . . . um, checked out.'

'Sorry? Hang on, just gone under a bridge. Say again?'

'NITS,' said Lottie.

'What's that? I don't know what that is.' Tiffany sounded baffled, she had evidently never heard the term before. Too posh, undoubtedly. Far too well brought up ever to have encountered such an undesirable accessory.

'Headlice,' Lottie reluctantly explained. Lice sounded so much worse than nits. Bigger and crawlier and—

'What? Are you SERIOUS? OH MY GOD THAT IS DISGUSTING!' bellowed Tiffany, accompanied by a bashing sound as if she were shaking the phone in case hordes of headlice were at this very moment crawling out of the mouthpiece. 'UGH, HOW COULD YOU DO THIS? IF SEB'S CAUGHT THEM FROM YOU, DOES THAT MEAN I'VE CAUGHT THEM FROM HIM?'

In the background Lottie could hear Seb, mystified, saying, 'What? *What?*'

'Please . . . let me speak to Seb.'

'No you *can't* speak to Seb,' Tiffany yelled back. 'I told you, he's driving the damn car! Oh God, I'm going to be sick, I feel so *dirty*, I can't bear it—'

'Lottie?' It was Seb's voice. 'Bloody hell, what's going on here? Tiff's practically climbing out of the car. What in God's name have you just told her?'

'UGH, UGH, *UGH*,' Tiffany wailed in the background.

'Tiff,' Seb said sharply, 'give it a rest.'

Lottie quavered. Was this how it felt when you had to tell a new boyfriend you'd accidentally given him syphilis? Or genital herpes? Or Aids? 'Look,' she blurted out, 'I already said I'm sorry. Ruby and Nat have nits, which means you might have them too.'

'Nits?' said Seb.

'Not nits!' Tiffany bellowed. *'Headlice!'*

Oh God, that hideous word again. Feeling terrible, Lottie said hurriedly, 'Really, it's not that bad, you just need to—'

'Headlice?' Seb echoed in disbelief. 'Oh for fuck's sake.'

That was it then. Lottie, her palms slippery with humiliation, stammered, 'I only found out tonight, otherwise I'd never have let them near you.'

'I don't believe it. You mean to tell me all this fuss is over a few nits? Tiff, you have to get a grip here. It's not what's generally considered a calamity.'

Lottie, holding her breath, heard the irritation in Seb's voice and Tiffany in the background whimpering, 'But I feel so *dirty*.'

'Lottie?' He was back. 'I do apologise on behalf of my sister. Now, what time do you go to bed?'

Seb arrived at eleven thirty, having dropped Tiffany off first. Lottie opened the front door and there he was, wearing a sea-green linen shirt and jeans, all twinkly-eyed and grinning at her.

'Hey, gorgeous, I just happened to be passing and I wondered if you had a nit comb I could borrow.'

Lottie could have kissed him. 'I'm so sorry.'

'Don't be daft. These things happen.' As he made his way through to the living room Seb said, 'I have had nits before, you know. So has Tiffany, for that matter. She was so traumatised by it, she's wiped it from her memory.'

'Why was she traumatised?' Lottie sat him down on the chair in the middle of the room and slung a white towel round his shoulders.

'Because I took the mickey out of her for about a year. And told all her friends.'

'That was mean.' Lottie carefully parted his surfer's blond hair into sections and began combing each section through.

'I was ten. Besides, she was so easy to wind up. That's what being a brother's all about.'

196

She smiled. 'I thought you'd never want to see me again.'

'Hey.' Seb slid a playful hand round her waist. 'Takes more than a few creepy crawlies to get rid of me. Found any yet?'

'All clear so far.'

'You know, I'm quite enjoying this. It's like you're grooming me.'

Lottie, who was enjoying it too, took a step back and said, 'It's like you're groping me.'

'Probably why I'm enjoying it so much.' Seb shifted his grip and drew her back to him, pulling her down onto his lap. 'Do you realise I haven't even kissed you yet?'

Lottie experienced a delicious twizzle of anticipation; funnily enough, this small detail hadn't escaped her notice either.

Aloud she said, 'That's because you've got nits. *Yuk.*'

'Have I?'

'Actually I haven't found any.' Lottie waggled the nit comb. 'But you still need to buy one of these to be on the safe side. You have to—'

'Keep combing. I know.' Shaking his head, Seb said, 'First you chuck ice cubes down my back. Then your children give me headlice. And still no kiss. I have to tell you, this isn't the most conventional relationship I've ever had.'

'And is that such a bad thing?' Lottie was unable to take her eyes off his mouth; he really did have the most mesmerising smile.

'I'm enjoying it actually. Nobody could ever call you run-of-the-mill. But there is something I'd like to do . . .'

He kissed as expertly as Lottie had imagined he would. Winding her arms round his neck, still clutching the nit comb, she kissed him back. Oh yes, this was more like it. Maybe there wasn't quite the glorious adrenaline rush she'd experienced with Tyler but you couldn't expect that to happen every time, could you? And at least they were alone together, completely unobserved, not like the other week when she and Tyler had been kissing outside Fox Cottage, blissfully unaware that they were being spied on by the two small Jenkins boys lurking in a nearby tree . . .

And look at the kerfuffle that had caused.

'You're beautiful.' As Seb murmured the words, his left hand began to wander. Lottie retrieved it just before it disappeared up inside the front of her lime-green sweatshirt.

'No?' He gave her a quizzical look.

'Not now.'

'Why not?'

Lottie wondered if she'd just lost him. Was he annoyed? Had he assumed he was here for the duration, that she was up for a night of torrid passion? Oh well, too bad.

Aloud she said, 'Nat or Ruby might wake up.'

Seb did the Roger Moore thing with one of his eyebrows. 'Is that a genuine excuse or are you too polite to tell me you find me about as attractive as a bucket of sick?'

Smiling, Lottie smoothed his streaky blond hair back from his forehead and kissed him again. 'My kids aren't used to finding strange men in my bed. I don't want to . . . alarm them. And I wouldn't be able to relax.'

'So no sex. Just nits.' Seb mournfully shook his head. 'I bet Mick Jagger never has this happen to him.'

'Sorry.' Lottie hoped he wouldn't try to change her mind.

'Hey, not a problem.' He broke into a smile. 'We'll take it slowly, let the kids get used to the idea of me being around.'

As she stood on the front doorstep waving him off, those words danced through Lottie's mind. Taking things slowly and letting the kids get used to the idea of Sebastian Gill being around.

That sounded as if he meant business.

Chapter 40

It was a warm sunny Friday afternoon in late September but as far as Cressida was concerned it felt like Christmas morning. Her stomach was jumping with excitement. This time nothing was going to go wrong. Robert and Sacha had been only too delighted to let Jojo come away with her for a weekend. In an hour Jojo would be back from school and they'd be rattling up the M5 together. She had even checked the air pressure in her tyres and bought a special sachet of windscreen wash by way of celebration. If the sight of her came as something of a disappointment to Tom, he could at least be impressed by her sparklingly clean windscreen.

Just picturing seeing Tom again was enough to set off the pleasurable palpitations in Cressida's chest. With rising anticipation she consulted her watch for the fifteenth time in ten minutes, checked her reflection in the dressing table mirror and fiddled with the lacy sleeves of her white shirt. Favourite shirt, new creamy-pink lipstick, new pink velvet waistcoat. It was naughty but she hadn't been able to help herself. And who knew, maybe at this very moment up in Newcastle Tom was tearing around the shops frantically searching for a new sweater with which to impress her, or a smart new pair of shoes.

Did men do that?

Anyway, concentrate. Things to do. Zipping up her weekend case and lugging it downstairs, Cressida parked it in the narrow hallway and consulted her trusty list. She still had to parcel up a consignment of cards and take them to the post office. The houseplants needed watering. And she and Jojo would need a selection of CDs to play on the journey, as well as a couple of packets of fruit gums to keep them going.

But first the concentrated windscreen wash had to be mixed with water and poured into the reservoir under the bonnet. In the kitchen, Cressida filled a plastic jug from the tap and carefully snipped the corner off the sachet. Even more carefully she poured the bright turquoise liquid into the jug of water and stirred it in with a spoon. This was the kind of thing that had driven Robert crazy when they were married – if he were here now he'd be rolling his eyes in disbelief at the thought that anyone could be so stupid as to change into their best clothes *before* tackling a potentially messy task.

But he wasn't here now – ha! – so it didn't matter a bit. Feeling smug, Cressida picked up the jug with both hands and made her way over to the door.

The noise was as sudden as gunshot and almost as loud. Something hit the kitchen window with an almighty thud and Cressida let out a reflexive shriek of alarm. Her arms jerked and her brain leapt into action, yelling, 'Not on the clothes, *not on the clothes*' so forcefully that the jug instantly toppled away from her body.

Turquoise water sloshed out of the somersaulting jug and cascaded over the kitchen table. Throwing out her hands in a desperate attempt to somehow catch it, Cressida screamed, '*Noooo,*' and saw it all happen in nightmarish slow motion in front of her. The white box containing the cards took the full force of the onslaught. The lid of the box was off because she hadn't yet printed out the invoice to be sent with the order. The order that had – absolutely *had* – to go out *this afternoon without fail*.

The implications were so horrible that Cressida couldn't fully take them in. Gazing down at herself in a state of deep shock, she saw that not a single drop of turquoise water had landed on her clothes.

But the cards . . . oh, *the cards* . . . were ruined. Every last one of them. Her hands now trembling violently, Cressida pushed up her sleeves and picked out the first neatly stacked pile. Each one bore the words Emily-Jane is here! in silver script. Pale pink marabou feathers, silver beads, iridescent sequins and glitter-strewn netting had been painstakingly glued into place. She had drawn a baby in a cot on the front of each card and every edge was bordered with pink velvet ribbon.

Needless to say, they were the most intricate cards she had ever been commissioned to make. Each one had taken thirty minutes to complete and there were eighty of them.

But it didn't end there. It wasn't only the most lucrative single order Cressida had ever taken, oh no. This order had been placed by the owner of a chain of upmarket card shops in the UK, a man who didn't take kindly to being let down in any shape or form. His wife, at the age of forty-two and after many heartbreaking attempts at IVF, had just given birth to their first baby and Cressida had been both flattered and delighted when they had chosen her to make the cards announcing Emily-Jane's safe arrival into the world.

Which made pleasing them rather crucial, since she had no doubt whatsoever that failing to fulfil her part of the deal would result in him refusing to stock any of her cards forthwith.

This would result in an instant and dramatic loss of earnings and possibly kneecaps.

Still in a daze, knowing what this meant but still not able to face up to it, Cressida left the water drip-drip-dripping off the table and headed outside into the back garden to see what had caused the almighty crash that had prompted her to spill the water in the first place.

A starling lay on the stone path, quite dead. Its eyes were open, its head bent back at a horrible angle. Flying along happily, it had crashed into the kitchen window and been killed in an instant. One minute your neck wasn't broken, the next minute it was. Boom, gone.

Cressida bent down and picked up the limp, still warm body. It had caused so much trouble she should resent it. On the other hand, if the bird were still capable of thought it would undoubtedly resent her for having killed it. She had, after all, spent an hour at lunchtime cleaning her windows for the first time in a year. The starling, fooled by the lack of surface dirt, simply hadn't realised the glass was there.

She was a bird murderer and there was a lesson to be learned from this. Cleaning windows – on either houses or cars – was asking for trouble.

Hot tears squeezed out of Cressida's eyes as she cradled the soft little body in her hands.

Bang went her weekend.

Again.

Tom said at once, 'Well how about if we come to you instead?'

'There's no point. It's going to take me all weekend to re-do the cards. I'll be working non-stop.' Shaking her head, Cressida said, 'I had to ring the man who placed the order and tell him he wouldn't be getting them before Tuesday and he wasn't thrilled, let me tell you.'

'If we came down to Hestacombe couldn't we help you make the cards?' Tom sounded hopeful. 'Then you'd be finished in less than half the time.'

Oh God, it was so nice of him to make the offer, but Cressida knew she couldn't say yes. People assumed it was so easy to glue a few bits and pieces onto a card. No skill required. Yet producing an end product that was of consistently professional quality and didn't look as if it had been made on *Blue Peter* was far more difficult than everyone imagined. Whenever Jojo offered to help her with an order, Cressida had to feign delight with the end results then quietly file them in the waste paper bin after she'd left. But Tom wasn't twelve and he wouldn't be so easy to fool.

'Tom, that's kind of you, but it wouldn't work. We're just going to have to forget it. I'm really sorry.'

'Don't worry.' Over the phone Tom sounded distant and cool, but that was probably because she'd called him at work. 'No problem. Maybe some other time.'

'We were looking forward to seeing you.' Cressida hoped he knew she meant it.

'Yes, well.' He cleared his throat and said, 'We were too.'

There was that offhand tone again. Was he cross with her for spoiling his plans? Feeling more miserable than ever, Cressida realised that for all her foolish fantasies, she didn't actually know Tom Turner well enough to be able to tell.

'Aunt Cress? It's me. Sorry to interrupt when you're busy.'

Cressida sat back and eased her aching spine. It was nine thirty on Friday evening and so far she had completed eight cards. Only seventy-two to go.

'That's all right, darling. Where are you?'

'Up in my bedroom. Mum and Dad have got friends round for dinner. Well, not real friends,' Jojo amended. 'People from work. You know the kind.'

Poor Jojo, relegated to her room while the grown-ups sat downstairs earnestly discussing sales targets. Robert had sounded distinctly put out when Cressida had rung to let him know that she and Jojo wouldn't after all be away for the weekend.

'Have you eaten?' She knew it was ridiculous to worry about such a thing, but Robert and Sacha could be thoughtless sometimes.

'There wasn't enough dinner party food, so I had a pizza up here. Much better than what they had,' Jojo said cheerfully. 'Anyway, I wanted to tell you that Tom was a bit worried in case you'd made up the story about the cards being ruined, but it's OK now because he knows it really happened.'

Cressida was stunned. *'What?'*

'He thought you might be making an excuse, like, sorry I can't see you tonight, I'm washing my hair, that kind of thing. Because you couldn't be bothered to drive up to Newcastle or you'd had a better offer or something. Men can be funny like that, can't they?'

'Hang on,' Cressida blurted out. 'How do you know all this?'

'It says so in my new copy of *Phew!* There's a piece in it about how boys get nervous about—'

'No, no. I meant how do you know that's what Tom was thinking?'

'Oh, Donny told me.'

Bemused, Cressida said, 'He called you?'

'Texted me. In his own grumpy way.' Jojo sounded amused, like a mother accustomed to indulging a truculent teenage son. 'Said it was no skin off his nose but was it true about the cards being wrecked. So I texted back and said of course it was true, was he calling you a liar, and he said no, it was just that his dad was gutted and wondering what was really going on. So I said you were pretty fed up too and when I came over to your place after school you'd been crying—'

'Oh Jojo, you didn't!' Every muscle in Cressida's body contracted in horror like a slug doused in lemon juice.

'Why not? It's the truth, isn't it? You *had* been crying.'

Didn't it say anywhere in Jojo's wretched magazine that it wasn't the done thing to let members of the opposite sex know you'd wept over them? Sobbed helplessly at the thought of not seeing them?

'I was crying because the starling was dead,' Cressida floundered.

'Aunt Cress, you know that's not true. And you don't have to worry, because Donny's dad was really pleased when Donny told him. So that's all straightened out,' Jojo said briskly, 'and we talked about fixing another date. Donny's got a boring school trip to Belgium next weekend but the weekend after that should be OK.'

'Er . . . fine,' Cressida said faintly.

'Well, I'll leave you to get on with your cards. Oh, by the way,' Jojo remembered as an afterthought, 'we thought maybe they should come down to us this time. Might be easier. I said you had plenty of room to put them up.'

Chapter 41

It was the beginning of October. Autumn had arrived. The air was distinctly cooler now, there was a blustery breeze and conkers, falling from the chestnut trees, were scattered like boules across the broad terrace.

Freddie, standing at the drawing room window of Hestacombe House, gazed out at the garden where Nat and Ruby were racing up and down the leaf-strewn lawn competing to collect the most conkers. He smiled at their endless enthusiasm, tangled hair and rosy cheeks.

'What are you thinking?' Lottie came into the drawing room behind him carrying a tea tray.

'Me? How lucky I am.' Freddie turned and made his way over to the leather sofa. 'I've just seen my last summer. You know, I'd hate to have just dropped dead without any warning. I like knowing I'm seeing things for the last time. Gives me the chance to appreciate them.'

They had shared enough conversations by now for Lottie to have overcome her squeamishness on the subject of his future. Or lack of it.

'It might not be your last time. Tumours can stop growing.'

'Maybe, but mine hasn't. I had another scan yesterday.' Taking the cup of tea she'd poured for him, Freddie said, 'My doctor told me I must start to expect things to go wrong. In fact he said I was bloody lucky to have got this far without more signs and symptoms. Which I'd already pretty much worked out for myself. Particularly after sitting in that waiting room yesterday, waiting for my scan.'

Lottie looked at him. 'I don't want to hear it, but you're going to tell me anyway.'

'There was another man in with his wife. His name's Tim and he has a tumour like mine,' said Freddie. 'He's in a wheelchair because he's lost the use of the right side of his body. His speech is badly affected too. And he's incontinent.' He paused. 'He's also thirty-one years old and has two children aged two and four. Which is why I'd call myself lucky.'

'Oh Freddie. Life isn't fair.' Shaking her head, Lottie blurted out frustratedly, 'Why didn't you tell me you had another scan? I could have come with you.'

'I'd still have a tumour though, wouldn't I?' Freddie's voice softened. 'You couldn't go Abracadabra and make it disappear. Anyway, you can't keep taking time off work. And there's something else I want you to do for me.'

'Anything,' Lottie replied at once, her back very straight. Freddie sensed that if he were to ask her to swim the Channel or climb Everest she'd give it her best shot.

'Have another go at finding Giselle.' As he said it, a lump sprang into Freddie's throat. Time was running out; yesterday had brought that forcibly home to him. But the longing for closure was still there.

'Right, we will. But I think we should contact a professional agency. They'll know how to track her down, they have all kinds of clever methods—'

'Maybe, maybe. But give it one more try.' Freddie knew he was being irrational but some superstitious urge wanted Lottie to be the one to find Giselle. 'Now listen, I've had a word with Tyler and he's said I can borrow you tomorrow. Will you go up to Oxford and see if you can pick up any clues?'

'Of course I will.' Jumping up as Nat rat-tatted on the glass, Lottie hauled open the sash window and helped first him then Ruby over the window ledge and into the drawing room.

'You have the best conkers,' Nat excitedly told Freddie. 'We've got hundreds!' Rummaging in his bulging carrier bag he pulled out a good-sized sample. 'Here, you can have this one if you like.'

'Why thank you. Most generous.' Freddie took the glossy conker, weighed it in his palm. 'Is this the best one?'

'No,' said Nat. 'The best ones are in my pockets.'

'Sensible boy.' Tickled by his honesty Freddie said, 'I keep the best ones in my pockets too,' and slipped each of them a pound coin.

'Freddie,' Lottie scolded. 'They're spoiled enough.'

'No we're not,' whispered Nat.

'Grab a pen,' Freddie instructed Lottie. 'I'm going to give you as much information about Giselle as I can remember.'

Endlessly curious, Ruby said, 'Who's Giselle?'

'When I was young, she was my girlfriend.'

'Did you love her?'

'Yes, I did.'

'Kiss her?' Ruby was interested.

'Often.'

'That's romantic. Where does she live?'

Freddie shrugged. 'I don't know. We're hoping to find her.'

'Like my football.' Nat nodded sagely. 'I kicked it over the fence and never saw it again. I think somebody stole it.'

'Freddie didn't kick his girlfriend over the fence, *duh*. And nobody stole her.' Looking thoughtful, Ruby turned back to Freddie. 'Are you looking for her because you want her to be your girlfriend again?'

Freddie and Lottie exchanged glances. 'No, nothing like that.' Freddie did his best not to smile. 'I'd just like to see her again, find out how she is.'

'Now who's a *duh*.' Nat turned back triumphantly to Ruby. 'For one thing he's too old to have a girlfriend. And for another, she'd have found someone else by now.'

It was windy, it was raining and it was as if Giselle Johnston and her family had been beamed up by aliens and carried off to another planet. That was the difference between towns and villages, Lottie was discovering as she trudged the streets of Oxford battling to stop her umbrella being blown inside out. If someone were to come to Hestacombe enquiring about her in forty years' time, people would be able to tell them where she was living now and exactly what she'd been up to. They would just *know*.

But it was different here. Giselle had lived with her parents in an ordinary Victorian terraced house in Cardigan Street to the north of the city. In recent years it had clearly been designated an up and coming area and the homes had been tarted up out of all recognition by yuppies and developers. Lottie, who had spent the last two hours knocking on glossy front doors, had spoken to many upwardly mobile mothers with young children and even more nannies and au pairs employed to look after the young children while the upwardly mobile mothers went out to work. None of these near neighbours knew each other, let alone a family who had lived in the street forty years ago.

Having first peered through the front window of number 274 Cardigan Street, Lottie knocked at the front door and waited without expectation for a reply. Whoever lived here was out and she sensed that anyone who decorated their living room in charcoal and silver and was so evidently a devotee of urban chic wasn't likely to have known the Johnstons.

She turned away and braced herself for another onslaught of rain, which was pelting down at such an angle now, it was coming under her umbrella. A small round figure clad in an electric-blue Pacamac and carrying a black bin bag was trotting briskly down the road towards her. Lottie, fully expecting her to trot past the front gate, was astounded when the figure paused, clicked the gate open and hurried up the front path of number 274.

'Afternoon,' said the woman pleasantly. 'Can I help you?'

She had to be around seventy. Springy grey hair, orange lipstick and an interested look in her eyes.

'Do you live here?' As she said it, Lottie was eyeing the front door key in her hand.

'Good grief, I hope you're joking! Have you had a look through that window?' The woman's eyes shot up into her hairline. 'It's like a flaming spaceship in there. Do I look the type who'd want to live in a spaceship?'

'Well, no . . .'

'Go on, take a peek!'

'I already have,' Lottie admitted.

'So what're you doing here? Selling something?'

'Looking for someone.'

'Sorry, love. Mr Carter's out at work.'

'Not Mr Carter. I'm trying to trace someone who lived here in this road forty years ago. Her name was Giselle Johnston.'

The woman fitted the key into the front door and opened it. 'Giselle? Oh yes, I remember her. You look like a drowned puppy, love. Want to come in for a cuppa?'

The woman's name was Phyllis and she lived three streets away. Had lived three streets away her whole life. Now a grandmother, she worked two days a week cleaning other people's houses.

'Are you sure Mr Carter won't mind?' Lottie was aware that she was dripping puddles of rain onto the spotless white kitchen floor.

'What the eye doesn't see, the heart won't grieve over. Here, love, give me your coat. Heavens, you're wet all over. Soaked through!'

Phyllis wasn't wrong there. Furthermore, she'd removed her bright blue Pacamac and her lemon-yellow acrylic twinset was bone dry.

This was when you knew you were knocking on, thought Lottie. When you began to realise that a Pacamac was in fact a Very Useful Thing, if not Downright Desirable.

'He works for an advertising agency,' Phyllis went on. 'Leaves this house at seven thirty every morning, never back before six. I just come in when it suits me for a couple of hours, have a clean around and let myself out. Lovely little job. Cash in hand. Me and my hubby went on a cruise round the Med last year.'

'And you do his washing for him,' said Lottie as Phyllis began loading the contents of the black bin bag into Mr Carter's tumble drier.

'Nooo, love. I just borrow this to dry my own clothes. He's a nice chap, he wouldn't mind.' Phyllis froze and said cautiously, 'You're not from the Tax Office, are you?'

'Now I really hope *you're* joking.' Lottie was genuinely appalled. 'Do I look like I work for the Tax Office?'

'Sit yourself down then. I'll make us that cup of tea.' Having switched on the tumble drier, Phyllis began to fill the streamlined black kettle. 'So what's all this about you looking for Giselle?'

At last.

'A friend of mine knew Giselle when she was much younger. He'd like to see her again. Freddie Masterson,' said Lottie, suddenly realising that Phyllis could be about to slap her thigh and exclaim, 'Freddie Masterson? Well I never! How *is* dear old Freddie these days?'

But no thighs were slapped. Instead Phyllis pursed her orange mouth and said, 'Oh. *Him.* Well, no wonder he sent you to do his dirty work.'

Yikes. 'Why?'

'Because he wouldn't get a warm welcome if he did find her, mark my words. I remember Freddie. Broke that girl's heart, he did. Poor thing, she'd done *nothing* to deserve it. How many sugars?'

'Two.' Lottie excitedly blinked rain from her eyelashes. 'And he's really sorry he hurt her. So does she still live round here?' Crikey, this was fantastic; maybe she could meet Giselle this afternoon, persuade her to come back to Hesta—

'No, love. Went to America. Milk?'

America. Bugger. Lottie nodded. 'Are you still in touch with her?'

Phyllis shook her head. 'I'm talking almost forty years ago, pet. We knew each other and all but you wouldn't say we were best friends. She met an American lad with a funny name and got engaged to him. They went off to the States to get married. That was the last I heard of Giselle. And then her parents moved away too – but they'd be dead now.'

Oh well, anything was better than nothing. Taking a notebook and pen out of her sodden handbag Lottie said, 'What was the funny name of the American lad?'

'Tuh, don't ask much, do you? Polish, it was. Started with a K. Ended with offski. All manner of twiddly syllables in between. Kiddlyiddlyoffski, something along those lines. That any good to you?'

Sometimes, it appeared, anything wasn't better than nothing after all. So as not to hurt Phyllis's feelings, Lottie wrote Kiddlyiddlyoffski in her note-book.

'Can you remember his first name?'

'Not a clue, love. Tom, Ted, Dan, something like that. Never met him myself. Here, get that tea down you. How about a biscuit to go with it?'

'Oh, thanks.' Lottie helped herself to a chocolate digestive. 'Any idea whereabouts in America they might have gone?'

Phyllis frowned, as if trying hard to squeeze an answer out of her brain. 'Could it have been . . . Toronto?'

It seemed her brain was constipated.

'Is there anyone else around here who might know?' Lottie wondered if it was too late to hope for a miracle.

'Sorry, love, can't think of a soul. It's all change around here, you know. Nobody left from the old days. Ooh, it's time for my programme.' Having glanced up at the futuristic clock on the wall, Phyllis picked a remote out of the stainless steel fruit bowl and switched on the portable TV.

'Well, thanks anyway. You've been really . . . um, helpful.' Lottie finished her cup of tea and swallowed the last mouthful of biscuit. She put away her notebook and shrugged her arms back into the sleeves of her soggy jacket. So much for miracles. If this had been a film, Phyllis would have said at the last minute, 'Oh, how silly of me not to have thought of it before, of course I know how to find out where she is!'

But it wasn't and Phyllis the cleaner, munching her third chocolate digestive, was already engrossed in an episode of *Quincy*.

'I'll be off then,' said Lottie.

'Right you are, love. Nice to meet you anyway. When you see Freddie Masterson you can tell him from me he's an old bastard. And if he doesn't manage to find Giselle Johnston it jolly well serves him right.'

Chapter 42

'You're an old bastard and it jolly well serves you right.'

Freddie chuckled, although there was sadness in his eyes. 'Suppose it does. Good old Phyllis, always one to speak her mind.'

He was sitting at the polished oak desk in his office surrounded by paperwork. Producing a printed-out sheet of A4, Lottie said, 'We're still going to find Giselle. I've done my best but it's time to call in the professionals. Here's a list of companies that trace missing persons. Pick one of them and they'll track her down in no time. Just think, Giselle might have been waiting forty years to throw a drink in your face.'

'Run me over with a steamroller, more like. Disappointed that you couldn't find her yourself?' said Freddie, sitting back in the swivel chair.

'You know I am. We both wanted me to be able to do it.'

'Never mind. I've got one more for you to try. Should be a bit easier this time.' His mouth twitched with amusement as Lottie reached eagerly for her trusty notebook. 'Her name's Amy Painter.'

'Not another old girlfriend. Honestly, who d'you think you are?' Lottie was busy scribbling down the name. 'Jack Nicholson?'

'She's about your age.'

'Freddie! You *do* think you're Jack Nicholson!'

'Amy isn't an old girlfriend.' As Lottie's eyes widened he added hastily, 'She isn't my daughter either.'

'Oh.' Lottie fanned herself energetically. 'Thank goodness for that. You had me going there for a minute.'

'You'll like Amy. Everyone does. In fact you may even recognise her,' said Freddie. 'I'm pretty sure the two of you have met before.'

As Lottie was leaving the house ten minutes later, Freddie said, 'I haven't even asked. How's it going with this new chap of yours?'

'It's going great.' Lottie blushed slightly, because last night, for the first time, Seb had stayed at Piper's Cottage. They had spent the night together and made love twice. 'We really have fun. Nat and Ruby love him.'

'I'll have to meet him myself, give him the once over. See if he deserves you.'

'Oh, he does. I'm just not sure I deserve him.' Touched by the genuine concern in his eyes, Lottie could hardly bear to think that Freddie might not be with them for much longer. 'He's away for three weeks from tomorrow, organising a polo tournament in Dubai. But as soon as he's back I'll bring him over here, I promise.'

'So if we go to Blenheim Palace, will we be able to meet the Duke and Duchess of . . . Blenheim?'

Lottie carefully didn't meet Tyler's eye – he was sitting across from her in the office. The Mahoneys, over from Minnesota, were visiting England for the first time and had their hearts set on being introduced to anyone with a title. They'd already visited Windsor Castle and been sorely disappointed not to have been greeted personally at the front gate by Queen Elizabeth and Prince Philip. Now, clearly, they were prepared to lower their standards.

'I think they're pretty busy.' Lottie did her best to let them down tactfully. 'But it's still a fantastic place to visit. You can—'

'Highgrove Castle?' Maura Mahoney was riffling through her tourist's guidebook. 'Would Charlie be there?'

'Highgrove House isn't actually open to the public.' Lottie was aware of Tyler raising his eyebrows at her. If her legs had been twenty feet longer she would have kicked him. Hard.

'Highgrove *House*? He's the Prince of England and he doesn't even live in a *castle*? You guys should take more care of your royal family,' Maura chided. 'OK then, how about Gatcombe Palace? If we just dropped by to say hi, d'you reckon Princess Anne would at least give us her autograph?'

More like a V sign, thought Lottie, casting wildly around for a satisfactory solution. 'The thing is, the royals don't really go in for . . . for . . .' Her voice faltered as the door swung open and Seb breezed into the office. 'For, um, autographs.'

'Who wants my autograph?' Seb flashed a wicked grin, raised a hand in casual greeting at Tyler then said to Lottie, 'Got a couple of minutes? I'm on my way to the airport.'

Lottie's hand flew to her chest; with his floppy, upper-class blond hair and super-fit body, the sight of Seb when she wasn't expecting to see him still had the ability to send her heart into overdrive. 'I'm busy at the moment. Can you hang on a bit?'

Maura Mahoney was avidly taking in every detail of Seb's spectacular six-foot-two-inch body. Her gaze fastened upon the blue and white polo shirt bearing the Beaufort Polo Club logo. 'Excuse me for asking, but do you play polo?'

'Why yes, I do.' In return surveying Maura's squat body, bulging curves

211

and size twenty-something Burberry trousers, Seb said gravely, 'Do you play as well?'

'Are you crazy? I'm way too old for that kind of thing!' Maura blushed and fluttered her mousy lashes. 'But you sure look the part! You don't play with the princes, I suppose?'

Seb nodded. 'Regularly. We're great mates. Why?'

'Oh my Gaad! I don't believe this.' Fanning herself energetically with her tourist's guide, Maura gabbled, 'You've made my holiday! And you talk just like them too! Would you do me the world's biggest favour and let me take your photograph? Or better still . . .' Almost garrotting herself as she attempted to unloop the Canon from around her neck, Maura thrust it into Lottie's hands. 'Here, sweetie, would you take a few pictures of the two of us together?'

Lottie ushered them out of the office and solemnly took a ream of photos of Maura, bursting with pride, standing next to Seb. When Maura and her hot flush had been duly despatched, Seb swung Lottie into his arms and said, 'Jesus, are all Americans that gullible?'

'Sshhh.' Lottie jerked her head meaningfully at the office door, which was after all only about six feet away.

'What? Oh.' Amused, Seb strolled over and stuck his head round the door. 'Sorry.'

Tyler, sounding as if his teeth might be gritted, said politely, 'Don't mention it.'

'It's like buses. You don't see a Yank for ages then two come along at once.' Seb looked thoughtful for a moment. 'Not that I've ever caught a bus.'

Hurriedly Lottie said, 'I didn't know you played polo with the princes.'

'God yes, have done for years.' Seb's eyes danced. 'Gavin Prince and Steve Prince.'

More disappointed than she cared to admit, Lottie said, 'I won't tell Maura that.'

'Oh dear. Is that a let-down? I do know the other princes too, but only to say hello to.' Sliding his arms back round her, he pulled her towards him. 'Does this mean you won't miss me while I'm gone? How about a quickie, just to remind you what you'll be missing?'

OK, this was getting the teensiest bit awkward now. Tyler was inside the office overhearing every word, whether he wanted to or not. Attempting to draw Seb away from the door and meeting with some resistance, Lottie realised he was doing it on purpose.

'I'll miss you.' She tried to murmur it into Seb's ear but he was having none of that.

'Show me how much you'll miss me,' he teased.

'No. I have work to do and you have a plane to catch.'

'You mean you want to show me but you're embarrassed because we're not alone. Your boss is listening. I tell you what, forget the quickie. I'll just kiss you really quietly and you try and be quiet too. No sloppy noises, no heavy breathing and positively *no* groaning in ecstasy. Think you can manage that?'

Two minutes later the muddy green Golf roared off and Lottie returned to the office.

'He was only joking, you know. It was just a bit of fun.' This was absolutely true, but she knew she sounded defensive.

'No business of mine.' Tyler, working away on the computer, didn't even look up. 'So long as you do your job.'

'He only said it to embarrass me in front of you. We weren't even kissing, I—'

'Lottie, you don't have to explain. You're an adult, old enough to choose who you see.' From Tyler's tone of voice it was abundantly clear what he thought of her choice. 'Now, could we get back to work?'

He was definitely pissed off. Seb had too obviously enjoyed winding him up. It was fair to say that they would never be bosom pals.

'Still, he made Maura's day.' Lottie couldn't help herself; any veiled criticism of Seb felt like a criticism of her own ability to choose a boyfriend.

'Sure.' Tyler nodded curtly as the phone began to ring. 'Are you going to get that or shall I?'

Four days later, back from settling a family of new arrivals into Beekeeper's Cottage, Lottie found Tyler in the office being interviewed by a journalist for a travel magazine. The female journalist, who was middle-aged and certainly old enough to know better, was flirting outrageously with Tyler. The lanky photographer, waiting his turn, was perched on Lottie's desk eating an apple and reading his horoscope in yesterday's paper.

'Well, I think that's probably everything.' Dimpling coquettishly at Tyler, the journalist uncrossed her legs and leaned over to switch off her tape recorder. 'That's great, thanks *so* much. Davey, over to you.'

Davey yawned, put down his apple and picked up his camera. He couldn't dimple coquettishly if he tried.

'At this point we usually ask people if they'd like to take a quick peek in the mirror, check they're looking their best,' the journalist twittered on, 'but I can assure you, that's not necessary in your case.'

'This is Lottie, by the way. My assistant,' said Tyler.

'Lovely. Now, where shall we have you? So to speak! Shall we start off in here then move on down to the cottages?'

Tyler said, 'How about Lottie? Would you like her to be in the photos too?'

Lottie preened inwardly; maybe it wasn't modest to admit it but she did love having her picture taken. When Freddie had owned the business he had always included her in any photographic spreads.

'I don't think so.' The journalist didn't even give the photographer time to open his mouth. 'I'd rather just concentrate on you.'

Witch. Ugly witch with unshaven hairs poking through her American Tan tights. Lottie fantasised about asking the woman if she wanted to borrow a lawnmower.

'OK.' Tyler shrugged, unconcerned either way and blithely unaware that this was the wrong reply.

Lottie couldn't believe it. Didn't he realise she'd just been snubbed? How could he be so *blind*? She glared at him across the office.

'What?' said Tyler, mystified.

Nettled, Lottie mimicked his blithe shrug. 'Nothing.'

'Good.' He turned to the photographer. 'Now, how do you want me?'

'Ooh,' simpered the journalist, 'don't ask questions like that!'

Utterly pathetic, plug-ugly hairy-legged witch. This time really unable to help herself, Lottie said in a brittle voice, 'Sounds like you've made a conquest. Well, I'll leave you to it . . .'

'Oh, by the way,' Tyler called after her, 'your boyfriend rang earlier. He says he'll give you another call later and he hopes you're behaving yourself.'

This was another of Seb's jokes. If he'd wanted to, he could perfectly easily have phoned her on her mobile. But being Seb, he preferred to leave the message with Tyler.

'Doesn't he trust her then?' As she left the office, Lottie heard Hairy Legs confide cosily, 'I must say, I'm not surprised. She looks a bit of a handful to me.'

214

Chapter 43

'Mum? Phone!'

Lottie, lying in the bath listening to the storm raging outside, heard Nat galloping up the stairs. The bathroom door burst open and he charged in clutching her mobile.

'Euww, Mum, I can see your big bosoms.'

'Sshh. Give me that.' Nat hadn't yet grasped that even when he wasn't speaking into the receiver he could still be overheard. Reaching for the phone, Lottie could just imagine Seb's ribald response. 'Hi, sorry . . . oh, hang on a sec, I've got shampoo in my ear . . . right, all sorted now.'

'It's me.' Tyler's voice caused her to juggle and almost drop the phone in the bath. 'Sorry to bother you when you're busy. But I've got a bit of a problem and I wondered if you could help me out.'

Hmm, having trouble getting rid of Ms Hairy Legs perhaps? Was she at this very moment wrapping them determinedly round his waist and begging to have his babies?

Cautiously Lottie said, 'Doing what?'

'I'm down at Harper's Barn. I need your help.'

There was an edge to his voice that Lottie hadn't heard before. She sensed immediately that whatever came next would entail climbing out of her delicious cocoon of hot water. Bathus interruptus. There was something almost painful about having to get out of a bath before you'd been planning to.

'Did you murder someone and need a hand shifting the body?' If it was Hairy Legs she'd do it.

'Dora cleaned the barn this afternoon after the Averys left,' said Tyler. 'Remember Trish Avery's perfume?'

'God, don't remind me.' Remember it? Lottie could still practically taste it on her tongue. It was the most overpowering perfume known to man, with top notes that made your eyes water and undertones of wild skunk.

'Well, she must have spilled the bottle in the master bedroom. Dora told me it was horrific when she went in there. What she forgot to tell me was that she'd left all the windows wide open to try and get rid of the smell.'

215

'All the windows? Including the dormer ones upstairs?' Lottie's heart sank like a stone.

'You got it. And the Thompsetts are due to arrive at ten.'

'I'm in the bath, you know.'

Tyler said, 'I'd gathered that. Well?'

'OK, OK. I'll be there. Oh *God*.' Lottie winced as Nat danced back into the bathroom having stripped off his school shirt.

'What's wrong now?' said Tyler.

'Taa-daa!' Strutting around like Mick Jagger, Nat cried ecstatically, 'Look at me, Mum. I'm wearing your bra!'

Every light was blazing in Harper's Barn. As Lottie climbed out of the car she was almost knocked sideways by the howling gale sweeping across the lake and the torrential rain slamming into her body. It was like getting out of the bath all over again. Taking a deep breath and seizing the bags of clean laundry in both arms she raced up the muddy path and through the front door Tyler was holding open for her.

'Thanks for doing this.' Closing the door, he took the heavy polythene bags from her grasp.

'Don't mention it. All part of the service. Although I shall be expecting a pay rise.' Gasping for breath and wiping rain out of her eyes, Lottie bent and tugged off her pink and white spotted wellingtons. Her short grey skirt was clinging to her thighs but it would dry quickly enough. The same with her pink fleece. She really was going to have to invest in a Pacamac. At least the central heating was on and the house was warm.

'We need to change the beds, mop up the wooden floors and do our best to get the carpets dry. I've cleaned up the ensuite bathroom,' said Tyler as she followed him up the stairs. 'And I did try to get hold of Dora but she wasn't at home.' Baffled, he went on, 'According to her husband it's . . . dingo night?'

'Bingo.' Unless Dora had invented some marvellous new game involving Australian wild dogs.

'Excuse me, but I don't think you're in any position to smirk. Who's the one around here whose son wears a bra?'

'Fine. Let's just get on with it.' Lottie took one of the laundry packs and began ripping off the cellophane wrapping. The windows were closed but they were going to have their work cut out mopping the sodden areas of carpet.

'I feel like a chambermaid,' Tyler drawled as they remade their third bed.

'Bet you're glad you bought this business now.' Though she wouldn't admit it for the world, there was actually something incredibly sexy about a man making a bed. Distracting herself from the sight of his hands expertly folding and smoothing the dark blue king-sized Egyptian cotton sheets, Lottie said playfully, 'So when are you going out to dinner with that journalist?'

'Don't.' Tyler looked amused. 'She dropped enough hints. Not my type.'

'No? Her legs would keep you warm on a cold night.'

'Miaow.'

'She started it.' Lottie began stuffing a pillow into one of the pillowcases. 'She wouldn't let me be in any of the photos.'

'Did you want to be? You should have said.'

'That's not the point. And she called me a handful.'

Tyler picked up another pillow. 'You are a handful.'

Indignantly Lottie said, 'I am not!'

'Sometimes you are. It's not necessarily a bad thing.'

'Cheek!' She took a swipe at him across the bed with the pillow. As she did so, making contact with his shoulder, everything went black.

Oh fuck.

Tyler's disembodied voice said, 'Did you do that?'

'Only if you're a fuse box.' Putting down the pillow, Lottie inched her way gingerly over to the window. This bedroom overlooked the lake and the other properties dotted around it. More unrelenting blackness greeted her gaze. 'Bugger, that's all we need.'

'So that means power's out all over the village.' Tyler's voice, now unexpectedly close behind her, made her jump. 'Any idea how long it's likely to last?'

'You can never tell. Sometimes it's just a few minutes. Or it can stay out for hours.' Turning back, unsure exactly where he was standing, Lottie waited for her eyes to adjust enough to be able to make out shapes. 'Oops, sorry.' Her outstretched hand brushed against warm flesh.

'Don't apologise.' Tyler's voice was oddly comforting. She felt his breath on her neck and experienced a twinge of . . . crikey, something she shouldn't really be experiencing. 'Will the kids be OK?'

'Fine. They're over at Mario's. I didn't leave them home alone, if that's what you were wondering.'

'Right. Good.' He paused. 'And they like this new guy, I take it? This . . . Sebastian?'

'They think he's great.' As she said this, she heard him exhale.

'Takes all sorts.'

'Do you just not like him full stop, or are you jealous?' If the lights had been on, Lottie knew she wouldn't have had the nerve to ask the question. For several seconds there was silence apart from the raging storm outside, the wind whistling through the trees and the rain being flung like handfuls of gravel against the creaking windows.

217

'I don't think he's good enough for you,' Tyler said finally.

'And?'

'And I don't know why you think he's so fantastic.'

'And?'

'And . . . I probably am a bit jealous, yes. Since you ask.'

Oooh, there was that delicious feeling again. Quivering with pleasure, Lottie took a step towards him and held her breath. It was naughty and she shouldn't even be thinking it, but if Tyler were to kiss her now she knew she wouldn't be able to stop herself kissing him back. That is, if they could manage to find each other's mouths in this pitch-blackness.

'But then I'm pretty sure you already knew that,' Tyler drawled.

Zingy shivers darted down Lottie's spine. Oh heavens, this wasn't supposed to be happening to her – she and Seb were a proper couple now. How many times had she lectured Mario on the evils of cheating? And now here she was, turning into him. She was nothing but a tarty trollop who should be thoroughly ashamed of herself. The trouble was, her conscience appeared to have taken a leaf out of Mario's book and gone AWOL. Seb was great but there was no escaping the fact that her feelings for Tyler were stronger, and at this moment all she could think about was how it would feel to be—

Ding-de-diddle-de-dooo, chirruped Lottie's phone, shattering the moment. Dazed, she fumbled in the pocket of her fleece and took it out.

'Mum? We've got a power cut!' It was Nat, sounding excited.

'I know, sweetheart. We have too.'

'All the lights have gone out! And the television! Even the PlayStation doesn't work!'

Lottie smiled. 'That's why it's called a power cut.'

'And the toaster doesn't work either! But Dad says we can cook plain bread on a fork on the fire and that'll make it into toast, so we're going to do that in a minute. Isn't that so *cool*?'

'Cool.' Lottie nodded in agreement as Tyler moved away from her. From the tiny amount of light emitted by her phone screen she was just able to make out the remote expression on his face. She was speaking to her son and Tyler was distancing himself both mentally and physically.

Nat chose this moment to say beadily, 'What are you doing, if it's dark at Harper's Barn?'

Good question. Preparing to hurl myself sluttishly into the arms of your least favourite person on the planet, thought Lottie. 'Well, we've got an awful lot of water to mop up. I suppose we'll have to find some candles and carry on working— oh.'

The lights flickered and came back on. Power was restored. The bedroom seemed blindingly bright.

'Oh no!' Nat was distraught. 'The electricity's come back. Now we won't be able to make toast on the fire – I was really looking forward to doing that!'

'Right,' Lottie said when she'd hung up the phone. 'Well, at least the power's on.' For a split second she experienced a wild, Nat-like urge to turn it off again, plunging them back into darkness. But it was no good, the moment had passed. Reality had intruded and brought them to their senses, the lights in the master bedroom acting like a bucket of icy water. Slightly ashamed of herself, Lottie realised that she hadn't quite been panting like a dog, but not too far off.

Tyler, who had been watching her intently, reached down and picked up one end of the duvet. 'Just as well. We'd better get on with the job.'

Chapter 44

Lottie bumped into Cressida outside the village shop. Glancing into Cressida's shopping basket, she raised an eyebrow.

'Always had you down as more of a *Good Housekeeping* girl myself. Care to explain the offside rule to me?'

Cressida blushed. 'Tom and Donny are coming down this weekend.'

'And you're going to challenge them to a game of football?'

'Don't make fun of me. They're staying in the spare bedroom,' Cressida explained. 'I've just put fresh sheets on the bed and made the room as welcoming as I can, but there wasn't much for Donny. If he wakes up early he might want something to read. And he likes football.'

'He's thirteen,' said Lottie. 'He'd probably prefer *Playboy*.'

'Oh yes, I'd really do that, march into Ted's shop and buy a copy of *Playboy*.' Cressida pulled a face. 'Anyway, Donny's only a young thirteen. He isn't like that.'

Lottie didn't have the heart to shatter her illusions. 'Only teasing. You'll have a great time. Are they coming down on Friday evening?'

'They are.' Barely able to contain her excitement, Cressida said, 'I can't wait. Nothing's allowed to go wrong this time. I know it's silly, but I can hardly believe I'm going to see Tom again. I haven't felt so excited for years! It's like being back at school and getting into a tizzy over the Christmas disco.'

'Except this time try not to get drunk on cider and end up covered in lovebites.'

Cressida was shocked. 'Is that what you did? Surely they didn't serve alcohol at your school discos!'

Lottie loved it that Cressida was so law-abiding. 'Of course they didn't serve it. We brought our own and drank it secretly in the cloakrooms. Otherwise how else could we bring ourselves to hold snogging competitions with the boys?'

'Speaking of snogging competitions,' Cressida said playfully, her gaze following the progress of an approaching car. 'How are things at work?'

Lottie turned her head as Tyler drove past, raising a hand briefly in greeting. He was on his way into Cheltenham for a Business Awards lunch and had even dug out his dark blue suit in honour of the occasion. Damn, he looked good in it too. Distracted, Lottie said, 'Sorry, what?'

'That answers my question.' Cressida nodded with satisfaction. 'Mind you, I expect I'd find it hard to concentrate with someone like that around all day. It must be like having to work in a Thorntons truffle shop when you're on a diet.'

Lottie nodded sadly. 'It is a bit.'

'You must be so tempted to have a nibble.' Her imagination working overtime, Cressida said daringly, 'Or just grab him sometimes and tear his wrapper off!'

'Now you're getting carried away. Besides, I have Seb.' Lottie felt it was only fair to point this out.

'And? Am I allowed to ask how it's going?'

'Everything's fine.'

Playfully Cressida said, 'Everything?'

She was implying sex. Which was fine, of course it was, it was just that if Lottie were honest, sleeping with Seb wasn't quite the thrilling, heart-stopping experience she'd been hoping for. It was nice rather than spec-tacular, adequate rather than dazzling. Oh well, maybe they just needed more practice. Anyway, she couldn't tell Cressida this; it wouldn't be fair on Seb. Lottie smiled and said firmly, 'It's all great.'

'So,' Cressida went on, 'which one do you prefer?'

'Honestly? Marks out of ten? Seven for Seb, nine for Tyler.' Lottie paused, wondering if Tyler was actually a ten. 'But it doesn't matter which one I prefer. Nat and Ruby adore Seb. They can't stand the sight of Tyler.' She shrugged and said, 'So they've made that decision for me. It's not as if I have the choice.'

'And you're happy with that?' Cressida looked concerned.

'Hey, it's not as if they're making me go out with Bernard Manning. You haven't met Seb yet. Just wait until you see him,' said Lottie. 'He's gorgeous.'

Lottie was downloading the addresses of potential clients who had requested brochures via the website when the door opened and Kate Moss walked into the office.

Not really Kate Moss, but similar enough to bring the name instantly to mind. This girl had long, wavy, light-brown hair, a delicate heart-shaped face and incredible cheekbones. She was wearing a slithery olive-green dress, high-heeled boots and a billowing cream wool coat with a burnt-orange silk lining.

Lottie, wondering whether a film crew, a stylist and a make-up artist were about to burst in behind her, said, 'Hi there, can I help you?'

'I sure hope so. I'm looking for Tyler?' The girl was hesitant, American; she had the face of Kate Moss and the voice of Jennifer Aniston. Now how could that be fair?

'He's not here. He's gone to an awards lunch in Cheltenham.' Lottie scooted sideways away from the computer and picked up a pen. 'Can I take a message? Or maybe I can help you?'

The girl shook her head prettily. 'No, that's OK. Do you have any idea when Tyler might be back?'

'Sometime this afternoon. I couldn't give you an exact time. Give me your name,' Lottie said efficiently, 'and I'll tell him you were here.'

OK, not efficiently. Nosily.

But to her frustration the girl was shaking her head again. She smiled and reached for one of the colour brochures Lottie had been preparing to send off.

'Don't worry, I wouldn't want to put you to any trouble. I'll catch up with him later. All right if I take one of these?'

She had perfect teeth like little pearls and an Audrey Hepburn smile. Feeling more and more like Hagrid, Lottie said, 'Feel free.'

'Thanks. Bye.' The girl flashed another smile and gracefully retreated from the office. Moments later Lottie heard a car start up and pull away. Launching herself across the desk she seized the phone and punched out Tyler's number.

It was turned off. Understandably, seeing as he was at an awards ceremony. Hmm, to leave a message or not to leave a message? Hi Tyler, this is Hagrid. Now listen, I don't know if you're interested but there's been this absolutely stunning looking American girl here asking for you. Sorry? Prettier than me? Crikey, *loads* prettier than me!

Lottie pulled a face at her reflection in the PC monitor. Maybe not.

Was that immature of her? Oh well, he'd be back soon enough anyway, and then she'd have a chance to find out who the girl really was.

Two hours later Ginny Thompsett from Harper's Barn came into the office to return the bottle of Superglue she'd borrowed earlier to fix the snapped heel on her shoe.

'All mended. Thanks for that. They're my favourites,' said Ginny. 'And of course Michael's thrilled because it saves him from having to dig out his credit card and pay for a new pair.'

'You could tell him you need a new dress to go with them,' Lottie suggested. 'To celebrate saving so much money on new shoes.'

Ginny laughed. 'Absolutely a girl after my own heart. Listen, we're having a bit of a party tonight to celebrate Michael's fortieth. His family are all coming over from Dursley, they're great fun. If you're not doing anything else, would you fancy joining us?'

Lottie had taken an instant liking to the Thompsetts, helped along by the fact that when they'd arrived last week they hadn't whinged about the still-damp carpets in the bedrooms of Harper's Barn and had taken the lingering traces of Trish Avery's nostril-curling perfume in good part.

'I'd love to.' Even better, Mario was taking Nat and Ruby off to the cinema this evening to see some awful sci-fi film. Delighted to be invited to a party instead, Lottie said, 'I'll bring a bottle. What time d'you want me?'

'Around eightish. We thought we'd invite Tyler along too,' Ginny added cheerfully.

'That's . . . fine!' It was, Lottie told herself. Nat and Ruby tolerated her working with Tyler because they had to, but they wouldn't like it if they knew she was socialising with him after hours. Which was why it was extra-handy that they'd be out with Mario at the cinema.

'So can I ask if there's a little something or other going on between you and Tyler?' Ginny had her head tilted to one side and an enquiring twinkle in her eye.

'We just work together.' The harder Lottie tried not to blush, the hotter her cheeks grew.

'Call me a nosy witch, but I think there could be more to it than that.'

Damn, was it that obvious? Attempting to sound like a Jane Austen heroine, Lottie said primly, 'I have a boyfriend.'

'Oh I'm sorry, I didn't realise. Well, bring him along with you.'

'He's in Dubai.'

'OK then, don't.' Mischievously, Ginny said, 'Do you want me to ask Tyler, or will you?'

So much for primness.

'It's your party, you can invite him.' Lottie gave up; first Cressida, now Ginny Thompsett. Honestly, was Hestacombe awash with meddling women?

'I'll pop a note through his letterbox.' Ginny paused. 'By the way, any idea who that girl is, outside his house?'

Outside Tyler's house? Lottie's heart sank. 'Is she pretty?'

'*Very*. And wearing the most gorgeous cream coat.' Ginny gestured with enthusiasm. 'I just came past Fox Cottage on the way up here and there she was in her car by the front gate. Just sitting there in the driver's seat. But I know Tyler isn't seeing anyone at the moment because I asked him the other day. That was when I decided you two would be perfect for each other, by the way.'

Touched, Lottie smiled and said drily, 'She came in here earlier asking where Tyler was.'

'Well, I've got to nip up to the shop for cigarettes. But if you like,' Ginny offered, 'I can ask her what she's up to on my way back.'

'Thanks, but it's OK.' As she said this Lottie sensed that it wasn't going to be OK at all, not from her point of view at least. 'I'll go down there now and check her out.'

Chapter 45

Last week's wild storms had passed and the Hestacombe valley was once more looking as a Cotswold valley should look in the depths of autumn. The trees were a riot of colour and the sun had turned the fallen leaves to crisps. Crunching her way along the narrow leaf-strewn lane, Lottie had to dodge chestnuts as they dropped, gleaming and waxy, from their prickly casings. A fox darted in front of her, its russet tail brushing the ground as it searched for the scent of easy prey amongst the undergrowth. In the distance a rook cawed, its plaintive cry echoing across the glassy surface of the lake. Lottie, her hands stuffed into the pockets of her red jacket, realised she was holding her breath as she rounded the bend in the lane that would reveal Fox Cottage ahead. The best thing would be if Kate Moss had got tired of waiting for him and gone. The very best thing would be if she'd got tired of waiting and gone back to America.

But no. The very best things had a habit of not happening when you wanted them to. The car, a nondescript grey Audi, was still there. The girl, about as far from nondescript as it was physically possible to be, was sitting in the driver's seat.

She pressed a button to lower the window as Lottie approached the car. Smiled.

'OK, I know what you're probably thinking but you don't have to worry, I promise. I'm not a mad stalker.'

This was just what Lottie was afraid of. Mad stalkers were easily despatched; they could be carted off by the police and charged with mad stalking. You couldn't ask them to arrest a completely normal girl because she was too beautiful.

'My name's Liana.' A slender hand was held out for Lottie to shake, the fingers delicate and Barbie-like. 'I'm a good friend of Tyler's.'

That was the other thing Lottie had been afraid of. She wasn't proud of it but she couldn't help herself. Next to Liana even Halle Berry might feel a bit dumpy and plain.

Dumpily Lottie said, 'Is he expecting you?'

'No, I wanted it to be a surprise. Although he has invited me over lots of times,' Liana hastened to explain, 'so hopefully it'll be a nice one!'

The brochure lay on the passenger seat next to her, open to the page showing a map of the grounds. This was how she had located Fox Cottage, Lottie realised. Under the circumstances she could hardly order the girl off the property, tempting though it—

'Hey, that could be him now.' Liana's eyes lit up at the sound of an approaching car. 'Oh wow, I'm so excited! Is it him? Is it? Oh my God, it *is*!'

Lottie found herself almost splattered cartoon-style against the side of the car as Liana flung open the driver's door and leapt out. Metaphorically picking herself up, Lottie watched as she raced over to Tyler. His response was all-important here; if he looked appalled and tried to lock himself back in his car, that would indicate that she wasn't in fact as welcome as she imagined. Whereas if he—

'You're here! Hey, I don't believe it! This is *incredible*.' Tyler, his arms outstretched, enveloped Liana in a hug and swung her round. 'It's so good to see you again. Why didn't you tell me you were coming? My God, let me look at you. More beautiful than ever.'

'Sshh, you're making me blush.' Liana laughingly pressed a perfect Barbie-type finger to his lips. 'And we're not alone. You mustn't embarrass other people.'

'Trust me, nothing embarrasses Lottie.'

Feeling foolish because Tyler had never even so much as mentioned Liana when he clearly should have done, Lottie said, 'Well, I'll leave you to it. Um . . . Ginny Thompsett's invited you to a party tonight at Harper's Barn.'

Tyler said, 'I don't think so. Not now that Lee's here.' He gazed down at Liana. 'How long are you staying?'

'As long as you like. I'm easy.' Liana gave his hand a squeeze. 'My cases are in the trunk of the car.'

Lottie knew when she was beaten. Whoever Liana was, she was here now. Maybe it was just as well she hadn't got herself involved with Tyler, if girlfriends of this calibre were likely to pop up out of the woodwork. Turning to leave, she said, 'I'll tell Ginny you can't make it.'

'Thanks.' Clearly distracted, Tyler said, 'Have you been invited?'

'Me? Yes.' Lottie watched as Liana opened the boot of her car to reveal four enormous powder-blue suitcases.

'Have fun then,' Tyler said easily.

'Oh, I will.'

'You have a great time at the party,' Liana chimed in, cheerily waving Lottie goodbye. 'It's been real nice to meet you. See you around!'

★   ★   ★

'I don't know how to tell you this.'

'Tell me what?' As always the sound of Tom's voice on the telephone caused Cressida's heart to miss a beat. She smiled, convinced that he was teasing her. It was Friday morning and she was in the kitchen making a shepherd's pie for when Tom and Donny arrived tonight.

'My mother's had a fall and broken her hip,' said Tom.

This time Cressida's heart skipped a couple of beats, and not in a happy way. 'Is this a joke?'

'I wish it was. She's been taken to hospital and they're going to operate tomorrow. But she's got herself into a state,' Tom went on wearily. 'She wants me there with her. How can I refuse?'

'She's your mother. Of course you have to be there.' Tears of disappointment and frustration slid down Cressida's cheeks. Appalled by her utter selfishness she dashed them away. 'Poor thing, she must be so upset. Don't worry about us, you go to your mum. I'll make her a special Get Well Soon card.'

'I'm sorry,' said Tom.

Poor man, he sounded wretched. 'So am I. But it doesn't matter a bit.' Consolingly Cressida said, 'By the time we're in our nineties we're bound to meet up.'

When she came off the phone she vented her rage on the bag of Maris Pipers on the table, hurling potato after potato at the kitchen wall.

'Why me?' Cressida bellowed, ducking as a potato ricocheted off the ceiling and missed her face by inches. 'Why meee?' It was like going berserk at a coconut shy with no chance of winning a coconut. The next potato hit her favourite coffee mug and sent it flying into the sink. That did it. Now her favourite mug was broken. Grabbing every potato in the bag, she began flinging them in every direction like a demented cricketer. 'Aaarrrgh, why meee, why meee, why ... bloody ... bollocking ... fucking ... meeeeee?'

Oh Jesus, how long had the doorbell been ringing?

Panting like a cornered animal, Cressida froze. The doorbell shrilled again. Whoever it was must have heard her. She couldn't pretend not to be in. Hastily she wiped her face, combed her fingers through her agitated hair and forced herself to take deep breaths.

Right, just act normally. Maybe she hadn't been as loud as she thought and they hadn't heard anything at all.

Ted from the village shop was standing on her doorstep.

'Are you having a nervous breakdown?' Ted approached the subject with his habitual tact and finesse.

'No, Ted, I'm fine.'

'Didn't sound fine to me, wailing like a banshee.'

227

Cressida did her best to look haughty. 'Sorry, I was just a bit . . . upset about something. I'm OK now. How can I help you?'

Ted mopped his forehead with a big hanky. 'You were in earlier asking for a walnut cake and I told you the delivery van hadn't arrived yet. Well, now it has. So if you want a cake, you can come over and get one.'

Why was he looking behind her like that? Turning, Cressida saw that there were potatoes scattered along the hall carpet.

'That's really kind of you, Ted. But I was expecting guests and now they're not coming, so I won't be needing a walnut cake after all.'

What must he think of her? Cressida didn't have to wait long to find out.

'Fine.'

'Sorry you've had a wasted journey.' If you could call ambling up the High Street a journey.

'I wouldn't call it wasted. I'm very glad I came.' Ted paused, shook his head and said heavily, 'You're not a bad looking woman, you know. I've had my eye on you for some time.'

Eek! 'Oh . . . er . . .'

'You're on your own, I'm on my own,' he went on. 'To be honest, I thought we might make a go of things, you and me. I was going to ask you if you'd like to come out for a drink with me one night.' Ted waited again, breathing noisily through his nose. 'But now I've heard the kind of language you use, I'm afraid you've blown your chances. I won't be inviting you out after all.'

'OK.' Looking suitably chastened, Cressida closed the front door. She headed back into the kitchen, collected up a few loose potatoes and said, 'Thank fuck for that.'

Chapter 46

Lottie had been at her desk for almost two hours when Tyler arrived in the office the next morning. She glanced at the clock on the wall – ten to eleven – and heroically resisted the urge to say good afternoon.

Because that would be childish.

'Everything OK?' Tyler took off his jacket.

I don't know. Is it? Did you spend last night having sex with Liana?

Lottie didn't say this either. Instead she said easily, 'Everything's fine. That was a nice surprise for you yesterday, Liana turning up like that.'

The look Tyler gave her told Lottie that she wasn't fooling anyone.

'It's kind of a tricky situation. Liana's a friend.'

'Quite a good friend by the look of things.'

Tyler came and sat on the edge of her desk. He looked thoughtful.

'Remember I told you why I came here? Why I quit my job in New York?'

'Your friend died.' Lottie was super-aware of his proximity, his denim-clad thigh.

'Curtis.' Tyler nodded in agreement. 'My best friend since we were kids.' Another pause. 'He and Liana were engaged.'

Engaged. Relief rolled over Lottie like a wave on a beach. Liana had been Curtis's fiancée, nothing more than that. So she and Tyler really were just good friends.

Except . . . that wasn't quite right, was it? There *was* more to it than just that.

'So if things had worked out between you and me,' Lottie said slowly, 'would she still have turned up?'

'No.' Shaking his head, Tyler picked up a pencil and began tapping it against the desk. 'This is why I have to explain what's going on. We've kept in touch since I came over here. Liana asked me if I was seeing anyone and I said no. Because I wasn't.'

'Right.' Lottie nodded. Thanks to Nat and Ruby, it was true.

'Liana's a fantastic girl. She met Curtis at a party two years ago. It was love at first sight for both of them and when he introduced her to

229

me I could see why. They were perfect for each other.'

'Were you jealous?' said Lottie. 'Did you wish you'd found her first?'

'No, nothing like that.' Tyler shook his head firmly. 'I was just glad Curtis had found himself a girl I got on well with. I didn't secretly lust after her. She was Curtis's girlfriend . . . I wouldn't even consider her in that way. And Liana didn't either,' he went on before Lottie could ask another bad-taste question. 'We liked each other, enjoyed each other's company. Nothing more than that. When Curtis told me they were getting married I couldn't have been happier. He asked me to be his best man. If they'd had children, I'd have been a godparent.' There was a pause.

'But that never happened,' said Lottie.

'No,' Tyler agreed, 'because Curtis died fifty years before he was supposed to die. You can imagine the effect that had on Liana.'

'On you too.'

'It was worse for her. Curtis was her whole life. She was in a desperate state.' The pencil between Tyler's fingers was tapping faster now. 'We spent a lot of time together. I did what I could to help her through those first months. She could talk about Curtis, knowing I'd understand. But we were just friends, nothing more. It was purely platonic.'

Lottie looked at his left foot jiggling away. 'Until . . .'

'Until one night four months after Curtis had died. Out of the blue, Liana asked me if I thought she'd ever meet anyone and be happy again. I told her of course she would, she was a beautiful girl with everything going for her. Then she started crying and I wiped her eyes,' said Tyler. 'That was when she started kissing me.'

It was horrible, hearing something you had absolutely no right to object to but feeling sick with jealousy anyway. 'And you kissed her back,' said Lottie.

'It was one of those weird situations I'd never expected to happen.' Tyler was gazing out of the window. 'We got a bit carried away. I honestly hadn't thought of Liana like that before, because in my mind she belonged to Curtis.'

Lottie knew she shouldn't ask but keeping quiet had never been her forte. 'You slept with her.'

Tyler nodded, his jaw taut. 'I did. We didn't stop to ask whether or not it was a good idea. Of course, by the next morning I'd realised it wasn't. Liana was still grieving for Curtis. The last thing she needed was to jump into a new relationship. We were friends and we didn't want to risk spoiling that for the sake of some crazy rebound relationship that would only end in tears. It was too soon for anything serious.'

The pencil flicking between his fingers abruptly flew across the desk, hitting Lottie just below her left nipple. *Ouch.*

Tyler smiled briefly and said, 'Sorry. Anyway, we talked it through and Liana agreed with me. Neither of us wanted to spoil what we already had. So that was it, we put it behind us and carried on as if that one night had never happened. And we did the right thing.' He shrugged. 'Because it worked. We're still friends.'

And she still looks like Kate Moss, Lottie wanted to shout at him. It was no good, this was all way too romantic for her liking. Liana had arrived for an indefinite period and was sharing Fox Cottage with Tyler which, let's face it, had only one bedroom.

Moreover, eight months on from the loss of her fiancé, Liana wasn't looking exactly prostrate with grief.

Jojo was down by the lake taking photographs of the swans when she heard footsteps behind her.

'Don't mind me,' said Freddie as she turned round. 'Snap away.'

Jojo liked Freddie. 'It's for my school geography project. I've got to map their path of migration from the Russian Arctic tundra to here. Dad lent me his digital camera. It's great, you can take as many pictures as you want and you never run out of film.'

Her bag of bread crusts lay on the ground next to her feet. The swans, eyeing the bag greedily, swam back and forth like celebs impatient to be snapped by the paparazzi.

'Why don't I take a photo of you feeding them?' said Freddie.

Jojo reached for the camera when he'd finished. 'OK, my turn now. You sit on that rock and I'll get a picture of you with the lake in the background. No, sit on the rock,' she repeated as Freddie took a couple of steps in the wrong direction and gazed blankly past her. 'OK, if you'd rather stay standing I'll— oh!'

Without uttering a sound Freddie had slumped to the ground. Jojo let out a whimper of fear and raced over to him. His eyes were half open, his lips were grey and his breathing laboured. Terrified he was about to die, Jojo dropped to her knees and shouted, 'Help!' before grabbing handfuls of tweed jacket and hauling Freddie onto his side into the recovery position.

There was no one else around and she didn't have her phone on her. 'Mr Masterson,' Jojo croaked, cradling his head and praying she wouldn't have to try mouth to mouth resuscitation. 'Can you hear me? Oh no . . . please, somebody *help* . . .'

A dribble of saliva slid from the corner of Freddie's mouth. He was making robotic chewing movements now. Her heart pounding, Jojo shooed away the swans who had waddled out of the water and were clamouring for attention, peering down at Freddie and wondering when the hell they were going to get fed. Oh God, should she stay with him or run and get help? What if he died while she was gone? What if he died because she hadn't?

Never had the sound of running footsteps been more welcome. From being gripped with panic, Jojo felt weak with relief when she saw that a grown-up had come to take charge of the situation. Tyler Klein, wearing jeans and with his blue shirt flapping open to reveal his chest, skidded to a halt at her side and said, 'I heard you shouting for help. What happened here?'

'He just . . . went a bit funny,' stammered Jojo. 'Then he fell over. I put him on his side and he was making funny noises with his mouth. And his breathing was kind of shallow . . .'

'Good girl, well done.' Tyler was taking Freddie's pulse, checking that his airway was clear. 'Looks like he's starting to come round now.'

Oh thank God. 'Shall I go and phone for an ambulance?'

'Hang on, I've got my mobile in my pocket.'

'Don't call the ambulance,' Freddie mumbled, rolling onto his back and opening his eyes. Focusing with difficulty on Tyler, he said weakly, 'It's OK, it's happened before. No need to go to hospital. I'll be fine now.'

'Well, we're not going to leave you here,' Tyler retorted. 'You can't just crash out and expect us to carry on as if nothing's happened.'

'Help me up then. I suppose I'd better come clean.' Ruefully Freddie said, 'It was bound to happen sooner or later.' Then he turned to Jojo. 'Sorry about that, sweetheart. I must have frightened the life out of you. Is your camera OK?'

'It's fine.' Jojo smiled and realised she'd been trembling. 'I'm so glad you're all right. I thought you were going to die.'

Freddie patted her arm, then turned back to Tyler. 'You could give me a hand if you like, help me back to the house.'

Lottie was in the office on Monday morning opening the post when Tyler came in.

Without preamble he said, 'I know about Freddie's illness.'

'Oh yes?' Lottie carried on slitting open envelopes in order of interest, dealing with the most boring ones first. If Tyler was bluffing, she wasn't going to be the one to give the game away.

Game. If only it was that.

'He collapsed down by the lake yesterday afternoon. I took him back to the house afterwards. He told me about the brain tumour.'

'Oh.' Lottie looked up, a lump forming in her throat. Somehow the fact that Freddie had told someone else made it all the more real.

'And how long the doctors are giving him.' Tyler shook his head. 'He should be having treatment. I know why he's chosen not to, and I can kind of understand his way of thinking, but it's hard to accept that this is really what he wants to do.'

'I know. But Freddie's made up his mind and you have to respect that. What kind of a collapse?' Lottie said worriedly.

'Some kind of minor epileptic attack. It was the third one apparently. He's going to take some tablets prescribed by his doctor to try and stop it happening again.' After a pause Tyler went on, 'So now I know why he told me I could buy Hestacombe House after Christmas. You can imagine how that made me feel.'

'Out with the old, in with the new.' Lottie shrugged and opened the next letter. 'If Liana's still around I'm sure she'll be pleased. At least then the two of you won't be so cramped.'

'Thanks for that.' The look Tyler gave her indicated that he wasn't fooled by her flippancy for a second. 'But I'm worried about Freddie being on his own. What if he has more blackouts? How's he going to manage if anything else goes wrong?'

'We're sorting that out. Freddie knows what he wants to happen. It's under control,' said Lottie, her gaze skimming over the address at the top of the letter she'd just unfolded. 'In fact . . .'

'What is it?' Tyler looked concerned as she scanned the contents of the letter. 'What's wrong?'

Upset on Freddie's behalf, Lottie clumsily pushed back the swivel chair and rose to her feet.

'Sorry, looks like everything isn't under control after all. If it's OK with you I'll go over and see Freddie now. There's something he needs to know.'

Chapter 47

Freddie couldn't fault any of the nurses who had cared for his beloved wife Mary during her time in the hospital. They had all been cheerful and efficient. But Amy Painter had been special, she was the one he and Mary had most looked forward to seeing.

When she came on shift Amy's dazzling smile lit up the ward. She was always ready with a sympathetic ear or a naughty joke, whichever was appropriate at the time. Her bleached blonde hair was cropped short, her blue eyes were by turns sparkling and compassionate and she never failed to brighten Freddie's day. If he and Mary had been blessed with a daughter, they would have wanted one like Amy. She was the most perfect, funny, generous and caring 23-year-old you could wish for.

Freddie still had the letter she'd written to him after Mary's death. She had attended the funeral too, and wept until her eyes were swollen and red. And four months later she had sent him a postcard from Lanzarote, just a few cheery lines telling him that she had left Cheltenham and was enjoying a holiday in the sun before starting work at a hospital in London. The message concluded: 'Dearest Freddie, still thinking of you. When I grow up I want to be as happily married as you and Mary. Love and hugs, Amy xxx'.

He'd kept this postcard too; it had meant a lot to him. And when he had received the news of his own condition from Dr Willis and it had been necessary to consider his future, such as it was, Freddie had known at once who he wanted to take care of him in his last days.

He wasn't completely selfish; he was aware that Amy had her own life to lead and that such a degree of disruption was asking a lot of her. But that was the great thing about having money. She could name her price and he would happily pay it.

Now, looking at the expression on Lottie's face, Freddie sensed that all wasn't going according to plan.

'I spoke to someone at the hospice who used to work with Amy,' Lottie said. 'Officially they're not supposed to pass on personal details, but I explained about you wanting to see her again and she gave me Amy's mother's address. Her name's Barbara and she lives in London. So I wrote to her.' Pausing, Lottie held out the letter she'd opened in the office. 'And now she's written back.' Reluctantly she said, 'I'm so sorry, Freddie. Amy's dead.'

Dead? How could someone like Amy be *dead*? Feeling winded, Freddie reached across the kitchen table for the letter.

Dear Lottie,

Thanks ever so for your nice letter about my daughter. I'm very sorry to have to tell you that Amy was killed in a car accident three years ago. She had volunteered to work in a children's hospital in Uganda and was loving her time there. Sadly a jeep overturned and Amy was thrown out. I'm told her death was instantaneous, which has been a comfort to me – although I'm sure you can understand that the last three years have been hard to bear. Amy was my whole world and I still find it hard to believe she's really gone.

I hope this news won't upset your friend too much. You say his name is Freddie Masterson and his wife's name was Mary. Well, I remember Amy telling me about them. She was so very fond of them both and envied them their long and happy marriage. My beautiful girl always got fed up with her boyfriends after a couple of months and dumped them, so it was always her big aim in life to find someone who didn't get on her nerves or bore her rigid!

Anyway, I'm waffling on. Sorry to have been the bearer of bad news. Thanks again for your letter – it's lovely to know that Amy hasn't been forgotten and is fondly remembered. That means so much.

Yours,

Barbara Painter

The flat was on the tenth floor of a modern council block in Hounslow. Now that he was no longer allowed to drive, Freddie had hired a car and driver for the day. Climbing out of the car, he told the driver to return in two hours.

Then he entered the building and rode up to the tenth floor in the graffiti-strewn lift.

'This is so strange,' said Barbara Painter, 'but so nice at the same time. I can't believe you're here. I feel as if I know you.'

'Me too.' Freddie smiled and watched her fill their tea cups. The flat, not much to write home about from the exterior, was warm, tidy and welcoming on the inside. The living room was bright with cushions and paintings, and there were framed photographs of Amy on every surface and at every stage of her life.

Barbara saw him looking at them. 'A couple of people have told me I'm turning the place into a shrine but they've always been there. I didn't suddenly put them out after she died. Her father took off before Amy was born so it was only ever just the two of us. Why shouldn't I have photographs out of the person I loved most in the world?'

'Exactly.' Freddie didn't know how Barbara Painter could bear to carry on. The unfairness of it all was beyond him. When there were muggers and rapists and mass murderers in the world, why did a girl like Amy have to die?

Barbara, reading his mind, said, 'You just take it one day at a time. Force yourself to get out of bed every morning. Try to have something to look forward to, however small and insignificant it might be. Oh God, listen to me, I'm starting to sound like a counsellor.'

'Did you go and see one?'

She pulled a face. 'I did. Not for long. I swept all the papers from her desk and told her to fuck off.'

'So long as it made you feel better,' said Freddie with a grin. Barbara was a plump, motherly woman in her fifties with dark blonde hair, bright eyes and a subversive sense of humour. Since his arrival over an hour ago they had exchanged reminiscences about Mary and Amy, talked about his brain tumour and struck up quite a rapport.

'And then she got down on her hands and knees and picked up every last paper herself,' Barbara went on. 'Told me it didn't matter a bit! My God, I couldn't believe it – I was like the Princess and the Pea! I could have scribbled all over her face with a felt-tip and she'd have let me do it. Wouldn't that have been a laugh? I could get away with *anything*. Oh look, you've finished your tea. Can you manage another cup?'

'Thanks.' Checking his watch, Freddie saw that it was time for his afternoon dose of medication. Taking the bottle out of his inside pocket he struggled for a few moments with the childproof cap before shaking a carbemazepine tablet into the palm of his hand. Then, because his head was pounding, he added a couple of painkillers.

'That was a bit tactless of me,' said Barbara, 'talking about having things to look forward to. How long did the doctors say you probably had?'

'A year. Ish.' Freddie appreciated the straightforward approach. 'Well, that was back in the summer, so more like eight or nine months now.'

'Amy would have been so flattered to think you'd wanted her to take care of you. So what will you do now?'

Freddie shrugged and swallowed the pills, one after the other. 'Advertise, I suppose. Hold auditions, try and find someone I can bear to have around. Something tells me I'm not going to be the most patient of patients.'

'You mean you're a stroppy bugger. I've dealt with plenty of those in my time, let me tell you.' Barbara looked amused. 'When Amy was looking after your wife, did she ever happen to mention what I did for a living?'

'Not that I can recall.' Shaking his head, Freddie said, 'Why? What were you, a nightclub bouncer?'

'The cheek of you. Take a look at that photo over there on the board.'

Freddie obediently rose from his seat and went over to the cork board, where several unframed photos were randomly pinned amidst the cab company cards, scribbled reminders and phone numbers. One of the photographs was of Barbara and Amy laughing together, listening to each other's chests through stethoscopes and wearing matching uniforms.

'You're a nurse?'

'I am.' Barbara nodded.

'Where are you working?'

'Nowhere. I retired in March.' She paused then said, 'And been going mad with boredom ever since.'

Freddie was almost afraid to ask the question. 'Would you consider taking care of a stroppy bugger for a few months until he kicks the bucket?'

'If you shout at me, would I be allowed to shout back?'

'I'd be offended if you didn't,' said Freddie.

'In that case, let's give it a whirl. You wanted Amy but she couldn't do it, so you're getting me instead.' Barbara Painter's eyes glistened as she smiled proudly at the snap on the cork board of Amy and herself. 'You know what? I think she'd be tickled pink about that.'

Chapter 48

Lottie's mobile phone rang and five hundred pairs of eyes bored into her. Mouthing sorry, sorry, to all and sundry she leapt up from her chair and made a bolt for the exit.

It was Seb.

'Hey, gorgeous girl, how are you?'

'Mortified. I forgot to switch my phone off and now I'm the centre of attention.'

'Good God, don't tell me you're in church.'

'Worse than that,' Lottie said gloomily. 'Chess tournament.'

'What?' Seb evidently found this hilarious. 'Are you serious? I didn't even know you played chess.'

'I don't. It's Nat, he joined a chess club at school. Then his teacher entered all the kids into this Monster Chess Challenge and by some mad fluke Nat managed to get through to the second stage of the world's third largest chess tournament. That's why I'm here at Etloe Park School at ten o'clock on a Sunday morning,' said Lottie, 'about to die of boredom. Except I'm not allowed to die of boredom because I have to be here pretending to be a supportive parent for the next six hours.' As she said this one of the organisers of the event abruptly rounded a corner and whisked past, his big bristly beard quivering with disapproval.

'Well that's not what I wanted to hear,' Seb drawled. 'What's the point of me flying back a day early because I miss you so much, then finding out you've made other plans for the day?'

Lottie's stomach gave a bunny-like skip of excitement. 'You haven't!'

'Bloody have. I'm on my way down the M4 right now. I was going to arrive on your doorstep and ravish you.'

'I'm sorry. If you want to go ahead and arrive on my doorstep anyway, you can ravish Mario if you like. He's redecorating Ruby's bedroom.' Oh no, *another* of the tournament organisers had just swept by and overheard her. Why did they have to be so nosy?

And why did they all have such extraordinary beards?

'I'll save myself, thanks. How about tonight then?'

'Tonight,' Lottie agreed, realising that the next six hours were going to be even more interminable now. Out of all the Sundays in all the year, the bearded men had had to choose to hold their stupid tournament on this one.

Having firmly switched off her phone, Lottie sidled back into the hall and pretended not to notice the glares of disapproval, like pointy arrows, being aimed in her direction. She sat back down, opened her bag and took out a packet of fruit gums. More evil looks. Honestly, you'd think it was a ghetto blaster. Quelling the urge to stick out her tongue at the glarers, Lottie gave up trying to unwrap a fruit gum and put her bag under the chair.

Time always went more slowly when there was an enormous clock on the wall. Lottie gazed at it until her eyes started to cross. The tick-tock, tick-tock sound it made was almost hypnotic. Oh no, mustn't fall asleep.

They were eleven minutes into the second game of the day. The huge vaulted school hall was silent apart from the mouse-like clicking of chess pieces being moved and stopwatches being reset. Rows and rows of numbered tables had been set up across the width of the hall and the children faced each other over their boards, engrossed in battle. Most of the parents, including Lottie, sat around the perimeter of the hall at a safe distance from the action but a fair number of competitive dads, unable to stay seated, were prowling around the tables checking the moves made by their genius offspring and attempting to silently psyche out the opposition. Much smirking, chin-stroking and smug nodding was going on. From where she was situated Lottie could see Nat moving a chess piece then hastily returning it to its original position. The father of Nat's opponent rocked back on his heels and exchanged a grin of satisfaction with his swotty son. If she'd had a catapult in her bag she would have shot the father with a fruit gum and sod the noise. Lottie silently willed Nat on.

Tick tock, tick tock.

At last the second game was over. Nat shook hands with his smirking opponent, pushed back his chair and came over to where Lottie was hovering by the exit. She knew by the set of his mouth that he was struggling to maintain his composure.

'I didn't win.' Nat's tone was studiedly nonchalant and her heart went out to him. He'd lost the first game too. Giving him a hug Lottie whispered, 'Oh sweetheart, never mind. Don't forget, lots of these children have been playing since they were babies. You only learned how to play chess a few weeks ago.'

Nat surreptitiously wiped away a lone tear. 'I hope I win the next game.'

Lottie hoped so too, but the signs weren't encouraging. Taking out her packet of fruit gums she gave a red one to Nat and said, 'It's only a silly game.'

'But I hate losing. It makes me look *stupid*.'

'You don't look stupid.' She gave him another hug and a kiss. 'I know, why don't we leave? We don't have to stay here with all these nerdy swotty types. We can go home and have a lovely day doing whatever *we* want to do!'

One of the organisers went past, clutching a clipboard and shooting her a filthy look.

'No way.' Firmly, heartbreakingly, Nat shook his head. 'I'm staying. There's six more games to play, so I'm bound to win some of them.'

'Come on, let's go to the cafeteria.' Lottie checked her watch; they had twenty minutes before the start of the next game and all around them competitive fathers armed with magnetic mini chess sets were earnestly explaining to their sons where they'd gone wrong during the last match. 'We'll have a doughnut and a Coke.'

By lunchtime Nat had played four games and lost four. A vast chart pinned on the wall out in the school corridor monitored the progress of each of the competitors with a series of gold stars and black crosses. Several of the competitive dads were videoing the chart while their offspring pointed with pride to the four gold stars alongside their names.

'Nobody else has got four crosses,' said Nat in a small voice. 'Only me.'

Lottie could barely speak; there was a lump the size of a table tennis ball in her throat.

'But you did so well just to get here,' she managed at last. 'This is the Monster Final! Think of all the thousands of children who weren't good enough. You did better than all of them, which is *fantastic*.'

Nat slid his hand into hers. 'I don't want all crosses at the end. I'd just like to win one game.'

Cheating was utterly reprehensible and Lottie deplored it. She had never cheated at anything in her life. But if there was any way of finding out in advance who Nat was playing next, she would corner them and happily offer them vast amounts of money to throw the match.

Except there was no way. Desperate to help, Lottie said nobly, 'Do you want me to stand by your table and watch?'

'No, Mum, I think you'd only put me off. And it's not as if you're any good at chess.' Nat was stoical. 'We both know you're rubbish.'

The bell rang, calling everyone back into the hall for the fifth game of the tournament. Lottie gave Nat an encouraging hug and watched him make his way over to the table with his number on it. In his oversized sweatshirt and baggy combats he looked heartbreakingly small and defenceless. And, oh God, he was playing against a cocky looking boy with Harry Potter glasses who had his father with him. Nat and Lottie had seen them in the cafeteria, poring over a chess textbook, and Lottie had heard the father saying things like, 'Now that's where you should have moved *en passant*, Timothy. Remember Polonowski versus Kasparov.'

The invigilator announced that the fifth game of the day was about to start. Lottie sat on her chair and sent invisible hate rays in the direction of Timothy's father, who was already strolling in a deliberately intimidating fashion around the table. All Nat needed was to win one measly game. Was that too much to ask? Damn, Timothy had already taken a pawn.

Tick tock, tick tock.

Thirteen minutes into the game the double doors opened and closed at the back of the hall. By this stage thoroughly trained in the art of not making a sound or moving a muscle, Lottie didn't look round. But Nat, glancing up from his game, broke into a broad grin and surreptitiously waggled his fingers in greeting before gesturing to Lottie to see who was behind her.

It was Seb, just inside the doorway, beaming at Nat and in turn being glared at by one of the organisers guarding the door. Letting out a delighted bat-squeak of disbelief, Lottie beckoned him over. Seb grimaced and in turn beckoned to her. Attracting yet more waves of disapproval, Lottie rose from her seat and threaded her way between parents over to the doors.

Once they were both safely outside in the corridor Seb said, 'You were right about it being boring in there. Bloody hell, it's like a morgue.'

'I can't believe you're here!' Lottie was overjoyed to see him.

'Couldn't wait to see you.' His blue eyes sparkled as he eased her up against the wall and kissed her. 'Mm, that's better. Well, it's a start. Tell you what, why don't we slip away for a while? I could show you just how much I've missed—'

'Stop it,' breathed Lottie as Seb's warm hands wandered down over the curve of her bottom.

'Spoilsport. Just checking it's still perfect.'

'Trust me, it is.' She unclamped his left hand. 'And we can't slip away because Nat's game will be over soon. He's lost every match so far.'

'Something to be grateful for,' Seb observed drily. 'If he gets keen he might want to become a chess tournament organiser. And Nat would look ridiculous in a beard.'

The game ended and children and parents poured out of the hall. Bracing herself and scarcely able to look, Lottie waited in the doorway for Nat.

He hurtled into her arms like a bullet. 'Mum! Guess what? I won!'

'No!' Lottie was so shocked she almost dropped him. 'Seriously?'

'I did! I really won! I was losing and then Seb came and all of a sudden I started to win!' Letting out a whoop of delight, Nat exchanged high fives with Seb. Tears of joy swam in Lottie's eyes as Timothy and his father passed them, the father with a face like a hatchet. Nat, flinging himself at Seb, squealed excitedly, 'I can't believe I did it!'

Seb swung him up into the air. 'You're a star.'

'So are you! We've *missed* you,' Nat exclaimed. 'Come on, let's go and see them putting up the gold stars. And Mum, don't come into the hall for the next game, OK? Because every time you sat there I lost, but as soon as you went out I won.' He looked seriously at Lottie. 'So it's better if you stay outside because it was probably you putting me off in the first place.'

'Can't give me the same excuse this time,' Seb murmured as, inside the hall, the organiser signalled the start of the next match. 'We have at least twenty minutes of quality time together without interruption.'

'You are outrageous.' Lottie stifled a smile as several other parents banned from the hall drifted past them up the corridor. 'Haven't I made enough of a spectacle of myself already? This is a respectable school.'

'Sshh, don't be such a grown-up. Besides, I need some help with my map-reading.' Taking her by the hand, Seb pulled her down the corridor and turned left at the end, then left again. Pausing at a door on the right he pressed Lottie up against it and kissed her before springing the door handle and ushering her inside.

They were in a deserted classroom with maps covering the walls and the blinds drawn at the windows. With a mischievous gleam in his eye, Seb steered her to the teacher's desk at the front of the room. 'Ever done it in a swivel chair?'

Lottie said, 'Something tells me you've been here before.'

'I'll have you know I seduced my geography teacher in this very room.' Seb grinned as he began to slide his warm hands playfully beneath her pink shirt.

'This was your school? You didn't tell me that on the phone.' It didn't come as a huge surprise; Etloe Park was the most exclusive private school in the area.

'Thought I'd give you a surprise when you said where you were. I couldn't resist it. Hey, relax, no one knows we're in here.'

Delighted though she was to see him, Lottie couldn't relax; some people – OK, Seb – evidently found the idea of illicit sex in a school classroom a turn-on, but it wasn't working for her. His fingers were exploring the zip on her jeans now. She removed his hands, placed them round her waist and kissed him on the nose. 'You didn't really seduce your geography teacher.'

'I did. Her name was Miss Wallis. I was sixteen, she was twenty-eight.'

'That's outrageous,' said Lottie. 'She should have been sacked.'

'Be fair. I was pretty irresistible.' Seb lifted her onto the desk and pulled her closer. 'Every Wednesday she'd give me a detention and I'd have to stay behind. It was every schoolboy's fantasy. And we never got caught. Sure you don't want to give it a try?'

'Not here. Not now.' Lottie wound her arms round his neck and smiled, gazing into Seb's eyes. 'Maybe later.'

'So you're glad to see me, then?'

Lottie thought of Tyler and Liana and drew him towards her, wiggling forward on the edge of the desk so that Seb's hard denim-clad thighs were either side of hers. 'Oh yes, I'm definitely glad—'

The door crashed open and one of the tournament organisers burst into the classroom. Lottie jumped and tried to push Seb away but her legs remained clamped between his. Guiltily she attempted to smooth her ruffled-up hair, refasten her shirt – God, how had *that* happened? – and wipe smudged lipstick from her mouth.

'What do you think you're doing?' the organiser demanded icily.

'I'm sorry . . . we . . .'

'I was just showing Lottie my favourite classroom,' Seb drawled. 'We were admiring the . . . er . . .'

'I think we can all guess what you were admiring. Out you go. Come on, *shoo.*' Making sweeping gestures, the organiser indicated that they should vacate the room like the shameless animals they were.

'Shoo?' Seb raised an eyebrow in amusement. 'Can't say I've ever been asked to shoo before.'

'First time for everything. I've been asked to escort you off the premises.'

Escort them off the premises? Horrified, Lottie blurted out, 'I can't leave! My son's in the chess tournament.'

The look on the organiser's face told her that he was already aware of this fact.

'Then maybe you should return to the hall with the other parents.' Turning to Seb he added coolly, 'And you can leave.'

'Fine by me.' Seb gave Lottie a kiss, eased himself away from her and said, 'I'll see you later. How about if you come over to my place around eight?'

'OK.' Struggling to keep a straight face, Lottie realised that he had just deftly, single-handedly unfastened her bra.

'One thing.' Seb addressed the disapproving organiser on his way to the door. 'How did you know we were in here?'

The man nodded up at the corner of the room. 'CCTV.'

'God, can't get up to anything these days.' Shaking his head in wonderment Seb said, 'Just as well they didn't have hidden cameras here when I was sixteen.' Then he paused, thought about it and chuckled to himself. 'Or maybe they did.'

Chapter 49

'Mum, I'm trying really hard to be nice to Ruby but she won't stop *singing*,' Nat complained, 'and it's getting on my *nerves*.'

'I know, sweetheart. She's just excited.' Lottie gave him a cuddle as the kitchen door flew open and Ruby came dancing in.

'I'm ten, I'm ten, I'm ten ten ten.'

Nat rolled his eyes in disgust. '*See?*'

It was Thursday. Far more important, it was Ruby's tenth birthday and nobody was being allowed to forget it. Since the party to which all her schoolfriends were invited was being held on Saturday, this evening Mario was coming round straight from work and the four of them were going out to Pizza Hut.

In fact – phew, relief – wasn't that his car pulling up outside now?

'Sounds like Dad's here,' said Lottie, prompting both Nat and Ruby to let out whoops of joy and cannon off each other as they raced down the hallway to the front door. Lottie checked her watch; it was twenty to six. Mario must have left work early and—

'Yaaaaay!' A scream of delight echoed down the hallway, prompting Lottie to follow Nat and Ruby out of the kitchen. Kneeling there with a child clamped to each hip and a slew of wrapped presents on the floor was Amber.

'You're here,' Ruby cried ecstatically. 'I thought we weren't ever going to see you again, but you didn't forget.'

'Oh Monster Munch, how could I forget your birthday?' Kissing each of them in turn, Amber said, 'And I told you I'd be here, didn't I? When I phoned.'

Ruby instantly looked sheepish and glanced over her shoulder to see if Lottie had overheard.

Lottie, who had, said, 'Is this something I don't know about?'

'God, sorry.' Amber pulled a face. 'I rang on Tuesday night and Ruby told me you were in the bath. I just wanted to know if it would be OK for me to pop over this evening and she said it was. I thought she'd pass on the message.'

Ruby said quickly, 'I forgot.'

Lottie knew at once that she hadn't. 'It's fine by me.' She looked at Amber. 'It's just that Mario's coming over. We're going into Cheltenham for dinner.'

'Well, I can't stay long. I'll probably be gone before he gets here.' As Amber said it, Lottie realised that she had been banking on Mario having to work his habitual Thursday evening late shift.

'Or you could come with us to Pizza Hut.' Ruby turned hopefully to Lottie. 'She could, Mum, couldn't she? That'd be great.'

Lottie and Amber exchanged glances, both acknowledging that this had been Ruby's Big Plan.

'Sweetie, I can't. It's really kind of you to think of it,' Amber said carefully, 'but my friend's waiting outside for me. My car broke down yesterday so he gave me a lift here in his.'

Ruby's face fell. 'What kind of a friend?'

'Well . . . I suppose he's my boyfriend.'

Lottie said, 'Does he want to come in?'

'He's fine.' Amber shook her head. 'Really. He has his laptop with him and plenty of work to keep him busy.'

'Is he nice?' said Nat.

'Oh yes, very nice.'

'Dad doesn't have a girlfriend.'

'Doesn't he? I'm sure he'll find one soon.'

Nat stuck out his bottom lip. 'He said he's waiting for Keira Knightley.'

'Lucky old her. *Anyway,*' Amber went on brightly, 'it's somebody's birthday and I'm here for the next hour, so are we going to make the most of it and have fun?'

'Yay.' Ruby rested her head on Amber's shoulder. 'Will you do my hair in a French plait?'

'Of course I will. Can your mum still not do them properly?'

'No, she's rubbish.'

'Thanks very much,' said Lottie, picking up the scattered birthday presents. 'I think I'll open these myself.'

When Mario arrived at Piper's Cottage he had to park behind a very clean imperial blue Ford Focus. As he climbed out of his car he saw a man sitting in the driver's seat. Briefly glancing up, the man acknowledged Mario with a polite nod before returning his attention to the laptop he was using.

Through the two-inch gap in the window Mario said, 'Are you OK? Not lost?'

The man looked up again and smiled pleasantly. 'I'm fine thanks. Just waiting for someone.'

Guests from the holiday cottages, Mario guessed. Or maybe Lottie had given one of the other children from Ruby's class a lift home from school.

'Daddy, you're here! Guess who's in the living room?' Nat dragged Mario down the hallway.

'Keira Knightley I hope.'

'*Loads* better than that!'

Ruby was sitting cross-legged on a chair in the middle of the room, beaming all over her face and having her dark hair expertly fashioned into a French plait by Amber. Mario, his mouth dry, realised at once who the owner of the Ford Focus was. Bloody hell, what was Amber doing with someone who looked like a geography teacher?

'Daddy! It's my birthday!' Keeping her head still, Ruby beamed and waved both hands at him. 'And look what Amber bought me! Isn't it brilliant?'

It took some effort for Mario to nod and admire the green sparkly top Ruby was wearing, and act as if Amber wasn't in the room. How many weeks had it been now since he'd last seen her? She was looking fantastic in an apricot angora cropped cardigan, pinstriped orange and cream jeans and cream, rhinestone-studded cowboy boots. Her earrings were huge gold hoops. He had always loved her idiosyncratic style of dressing. Oh God, he had missed her *so much*.

'And she bought me an electric spider,' Nat chimed in, 'to make up for it not being my birthday.'

'I've shown her my room.' Ruby was intensely proud of her redecorated bedroom. 'She wishes she had pink glittery wallpaper like mine.'

'Just say the word,' Mario attempted humour, 'and I'll be round with my pasting table.'

Amber smiled, fastened the ends of Ruby's plait with a pink hairband and said, 'There, all done. You look like a princess.'

How do *I* look? Mario longed to ask. As bloody awful as I feel? I haven't slept with anyone else, you know. I just don't want to. My new nickname at work is Cliff Richard, I'm so celibate.

'Oh, I forgot to tell you, I won a certificate!' exclaimed Nat. 'For playing chess! I'll get it and show you.'

Nat disappeared upstairs to peel his precious certificate off his bedroom wall to show Amber. Amber, in turn widening her eyes at Lottie, said, 'Chess? Good grief, it'll be quantum physics next!'

'It was a nightmare. A whole Sunday at Etloe Park School, hundreds of little boys doing the Monster Chess Challenge.' Lottie shuddered at the memory.

'Etloe Park? Oh, I know about that! One of Quentin's friends helped to organise it.'

Mario kept a straight face; Lottie had regaled him with details of the men-in-beards.

'Did you hear about what happened?' Amber was gazing at Lottie expectantly. 'You know, all the shenanigans?'

'No.' Lottie was busy on her hands and knees collecting discarded lengths of silver ribbon and sheets of crumpled turquoise wrapping paper. 'What shenanigans?'

They still had Ruby with them, which hampered Amber somewhat. Tilting her head to one side she said in a tone of voice that was simultaneously vague and meaningful, 'Quentin's friend caught this couple in one of the classrooms. Seems like there was a bit of you-know-what going on. At a chess challenge of all places!'

Lottie's face was hidden by her hair but she was still busy picking up shreds of paper. Smaller and smaller pieces, Mario noted, and more and more slowly.

'I didn't hear about that.' Lottie sounded distracted.

'Well, they probably didn't want to broadcast it! But can you imagine something like that happening? And getting caught out?' Turning to Mario, Amber said cheerfully, 'Actually, it's just the kind of thing *you'd* get up to.'

'Actually, it isn't.' Since his ill-fated encounter with Gemma the barmaid with the bad-tempered cat, Mario hadn't got up to anything with anyone at all, but since Amber wouldn't believe him he didn't bother saying it. Besides, he was far more interested in why Lottie was still crawling around on the floor picking up flecks of wrapping paper so minuscule she might soon be reduced to splitting the atom.

'Here's my certificate!' Nat charged back into the room and showed it proudly to Amber, who hugged him and told him he was a genius.

'I won a match and got a gold star.' Nat inveigled himself onto her lap. 'And Seb came to cheer me on, except there wasn't any cheering allowed because everyone had to be really quiet. But it was like magic – as soon as Seb turned up, I started to win!'

'That's great, sweetie.' Amber was stroking his tangled hair. 'I've heard all about him but I haven't met him yet. So you like Seb?'

'He's the best. He's really funny and nice.'

Ruby, joining in, said, 'He's the best boyfriend Mum's ever had.'

'Well, that's good news.' Amber turned to Lottie. 'Such a relief for you, after the last one.'

Lottie was happy with Seb. Amber was happy with Quentin. Mario almost couldn't bear it; the last weeks had been the most wretched of his life.

Amber, checking her watch, pulled a face. 'I didn't realise I'd been here so long. Poor Quentin, he'll be wondering if I'm ever going to leave.'

Quentin. How could she bring herself to sleep with someone with a name like that? Mario glanced out of the living room window and said, 'He's gone. Must have got fed up with waiting and driven off.'

Annoyingly Amber didn't jump up and peer out of the window to check he was still there. Instead, gathering together her things, she replied easily, 'Quentin wouldn't do that. He's not the type.'

Her tone might have been easy but she gave him a certain look as she said it. What was that look supposed to mean? Filled with indignation Mario said, 'Neither am I. I'd never drive off and leave you.'

'No, I don't suppose you would.' Amber smiled briefly at him. 'But the chances are you'd spend your time out there chatting up any pretty girl who happened to walk past.'

'I would not.' The accusation was like a slap in the face. Mario was defensive. 'I *wouldn't.*'

Ruby, her expression pitying, said, 'Daddy, you probably would.'

Chapter 50

'This is worse than the ghost train.' Seb stood back to survey his handiwork. 'I'm scared to look at any of you.'

'Raaaarrrggh,' roared Nat, barely recognisable beneath the green and red face paint.

'My teeth are making me dribble.' Giggling uncontrollably, Ruby slurped up saliva and pushed her vampire fangs more securely into place.

'Daddy, you have to dress up too,' Maya ordered, her own face a startling shade of purple with heavy black shadows beneath her eyes. 'You and Lottie have to be scary as well.'

'Mum can wear the teeth that are all brown and rotten,' Ruby chimed in. 'And Seb can be a ghost.'

'Oh no, poor Lottie, you can't make her wear the horrible teeth. My dad can have them. Come on, let's get them ready.'

Lottie sat back as together Ruby and Maya worked on her face. Next to her on the sofa, Seb was having his done by Nat. Smiling at the expressions of earnest concentration on their faces, Lottie realised that she was experiencing a moment of undiluted happiness, the kind of memory you captured in a box and treasured forever.

It was Halloween and they were going out trick or treating, all five of them together because Maya was down from London for the weekend visiting Seb. Mildly apprehensive that Nat and Ruby might not hit it off with Seb's eight-year-old daughter, Lottie's fears had been allayed within minutes of them meeting each other for the first time. Sparky, blonde and bursting with confidence, Maya hadn't been remotely intimidated by the prospect of being introduced to Ruby and Nat. In no time at all they had bonded, become a trio. Sunday lunch had been at the house in Kingston Ash that Seb shared with his sister Tiffany now that their parents were living in the south of France. The afternoon had been spent watching the new Harry Potter video, playing a raucous game of Name That Song and planning what to dress up as in order to terrify innocent householders on their own doorsteps.

'There, done,' Ruby pronounced with pride, stepping back at last and allowing Maya to hold up the mirror. Lottie surveyed her reflection. She had black lips, fluorescent orange eyeshadow, green mascara and big brown moles all over her face. She looked at Seb, wearing a mad professor wig, warty false nose, charcoal-grey face and the stomach-churning rotten teeth.

'Why, Mith Carlyle, you're tho beautiful.' Struggling with the teeth, Seb solemnly took her hand and with a ghastly slobbering noise attempted to kiss it.

'Mr Gill.' Lottie fluttered green lashes back at him. 'At last I've met the man of my dreams.'

'Ugly,' Maya pronounced, 'but not *quite* ugly enough.' Gleefully she seized the dark red make-up stick. 'Keep still, Daddy, I'm just going to give you some more spots.'

Last Halloween it had rained, everyone's make-up had run and Ruby's witch's hat had disintegrated. Tonight the weather couldn't have been more perfect. The air was thick with swirling fog through which lights gleamed eerily and sounds seemed muffled or distorted. It was eight o'clock and they had been back in Hestacombe for an hour, trick or treating friends and rival groups of ghouls. Having finished with the High Street, they were now making their way towards the holiday cottages, the children zigzagging excitedly ahead of them down the lane. In the darkness Seb took out his teeth and kissed Lottie.

'We'll have to leave at nine,' he murmured between kisses. 'I'm driving Maya back to London tonight.'

'It's been fun.' Lottie hoped his dark red spots weren't imprinting themselves on her chin; she had enough moles as it was.

'It'll be even more fun when we trick or treat your boss.'

'Oh no, we're not doing that.'

'Why not? He lives down here, doesn't he?' Without the gruesome false teeth, Seb's own gleamed white in the darkness. 'We can't miss him out.'

'Nat and Ruby won't want to do it,' Lottie protested.

'Hey, the guy's a Yank. They're big on Halloween, right? Besides, the kids can play a trick on him. They'll love that.'

Encouraged by Seb, they probably would. Lottie breathed a sigh of relief when they finally reached Fox Cottage and saw that all the lights were off.

'They're out.'

'Or scared. Quaking in the darkness. Or in bed,' said Seb with a wink. 'Go and try the doorbell, kids.'

'I'm not,' said Ruby.

'I'm not,' said Nat.

'I will.' Maya raced up the path and rang the bell with all her might. Twenty seconds later she shrugged, disappointed. 'No, no one there.'

Phew, thought Lottie.

Maya said longingly, 'Shall I put a plastic spider through their letterbox?'

'*Yes.*' Nat spoke with relish. 'Put *loads* of spiders through their letterbox.'

'Sshh.' Ruby raised a hand. 'What's that?'

Maya said innocently, 'Your hand.'

'No, that noise. Someone's coming down the lane.'

They listened, heard the fog-muffled sound of voices.

'I bet it's Ben and Harry Jenkins.' Nat's eyes gleamed at the thought of meeting their greatest rivals. 'They said they'd be out tonight. We can scare them!'

'OK, everyone hide,' Seb instructed.

Everyone hid, melting into the darkness behind trees and bushes. Lottie and Ruby tucked themselves out of sight behind the wall bordering the garden of Fox Cottage. Above them, pale clouds drifted across an almost full moon. At ground level the fog was swirling like dry ice, so dense and impenetrable that Lottie couldn't even see her own feet.

They heard a burst of laughter and approaching footsteps. Lottie whispered, 'Doesn't sound like the Jenkins boys.'

'Mum, *ssshhhh.*'

Lottie did as she was told. Seconds later she heard a voice that definitely didn't belong to either Ben or Harry Jenkins, partly because it was a couple of octaves lower than anything they could hope to produce but chiefly because she knew who it did belong to.

'RaaaAAARRGGHHH!' roared Seb, Maya, Ruby and Nat, leaping in unison from their hiding places and waving their arms in scary monster fashion.

'Jesus Christ!' wailed Liana, leaping back in fright and cannoning into Tyler.

'Trick or treat!'

'You scared the life out of me.' Clutching her front, Liana said testily, 'I don't have anything *on* me.'

'Trick then!' Maya gleefully took aim and fired her water pistol.

Liana let out a high-pitched shriek as something dark sprayed the front of her cream coat. 'My God, are you completely mad? You can't *do* that!'

'It's *okaaay.*' Maya rolled her eyes at the over-reaction. 'It's disappearing ink. In two minutes it'll be gone.'

Behind the garden wall, Lottie cringed and let out a low groan. She hadn't even known that Maya was carrying a pistol of disappearing ink. And Seb, who undoubtedly had, was only a man so wouldn't understand that while the blue colouring might disappear in a matter of minutes, there was a good chance that a still-discernible mark like a grease stain would remain on the coat *forever*.

251

'This coat cost thousands of dollars.' Liana was still shaking her head in horrified disbelief.

'Hey, it's Halloween,' Seb protested. 'We're just having a bit of fun.'

Peering over the top of the wall, Lottie saw Tyler looking less than amused. Belatedly realising who it was beneath the make-up, he surveyed Nat and Ruby in silence before addressing Seb. 'Does Lottie *know* what you've got her children doing?'

Ruby and Nat were eyeing Tyler with dislike. Seb, placing a protective arm round each of their shoulders, said, 'I don't know, why don't we ask her?' Raising his voice he turned towards the wall and mimicked, 'Lottie? Do you *know* what I've got your children doing?'

Oh God, this was awful. Slowly Lottie rose to her feet, hideously aware of her black lips, drawn-on wrinkles and the big witchy moles all over her face.

'OK, now look.' Tyler sounded resigned. 'I'm not trying to be a killjoy here, but this is beyond a joke. You could give someone a heart attack jumping out of the fog like that. You could kill one of our guests.'

'They're a bunch of kids.' His eyebrows raised, Seb indicated Maya, Ruby and Nat. 'At the risk of repeating myself, it's Halloween. And we heard your voice,' he added casually, 'so we knew who was coming down the lane.'

So he *had* known. Lottie didn't know whether to laugh or cry.

Liana, clearly upset, demanded, 'And if my coat's ruined?'

'Then we'll pay for a new one, of course. Come along, kids.' Seb ushered them protectively past Tyler and Liana. 'Have to start saving your pocket money. Thanks to *some* people having no sense of humour you could find yourselves landed with a hefty bill.'

Monday morning. Lottie was a bundle of defiance and guilt. Ordinarily always the first to apologise, she was finding it impossible to do so now. Last night Tyler and Liana had demonstrated their contempt for her and her children. This morning Liana had taken her super-expensive coat into Cheltenham to see if having it dry-cleaned would get the marks out. They clearly regarded Nat and Ruby as no better than out-of-control savages, and her as an irresponsible mother. But if she tried to point out that Maya had been the one with the water pistol, she would sound as if she were distancing herself from Seb and his daughter. And under the circumstances that was something she quite simply couldn't bring herself to do.

Oh please God, let the dry-cleaners get the stains out.

'Look, it was an idiotic trick to play,' Tyler repeated. 'You have to admit that.'

It *had* been an idiotic trick to play, but Lottie was damned if she'd admit it. Instead she said heatedly, 'Maybe when you have children of your own, you'll lighten up a bit and stop being so . . . so petty and uptight. The kids were having fun. They've been looking forward to Halloween for weeks.'

'That's all well and good.' Tyler raised his hands. 'I'm glad for them. But they shouldn't—'

'Enjoy themselves? Be a bit mischievous? You know what, we went all round the village last night and everyone else we met was really nice. They all got into the spirit of the occasion. Not one other person threatened to see us in court.'

'Don't give me that bullshit. We didn't say that. I'm just pointing out that an apology might be in order. Maybe you should have a word with your . . . younger contingent and make them understand that they need to say sorry. Not to me,' Tyler went on coolly, 'but to Liana.'

'Maya lives in London. Nat and Ruby didn't even know she had a water pistol, let alone one with ink in it.' This was a lie; it had transpired that Maya had shared this information with them in advance, but Lottie felt this was irrelevant. 'Neither of them pulled the trigger. I don't see why they should have to apologise.'

Tyler said, 'In that case, maybe your boyfriend could do the honours.'

Oh yes, that was highly likely to happen. Struggling to regain control over her breathing, Lottie heard a car pull up outside. 'Fine, I'll tell him. In fact we'll both apologise. Would on bended knee be good enough, do you think, or would prostrate on the ground be required?'

'Lottie—'

'As I said, one of these days you might have kids of your own. I just hope for their sakes that you learn to be a little less pissy and a bit more tolerant.'

They glared at each other across the office. The door opened. Any paying guest walking in would instantly have been aware of the hostile atmosphere.

Luckily it wasn't a paying guest, it was only Liana.

'Oh no, you two haven't been arguing, have you? I feel terrible! Lottie, I'm *so* sorry about last night. Can you forgive me for being such a grump?'

Terrific, what was she supposed to do now? Feeling her face redden, Lottie summed up her apologetic voice and said, 'You weren't. We're the ones who are sorry. We shouldn't have . . . messed up your coat.'

Why did Tyler have to be here, listening to every word and with – she suspected – something dangerously close to a smirk twitching at the corners of his mouth?

'No, no, you mustn't apologise, it was all my fault for being so miserable. I can't bear to think I might have upset your children.' Liana, enchanting in baby-pink cashmere and Earl jeans, went on, 'The next time I see them, I'll make it up to them, I promise. But here, I got them some candy. Call it a belated Halloween treat. Will you give it to them and say Liana's sorry?'

Worse and worse. Miserably, Lottie took the expensive bags of sweets Liana had picked up in Thorntons. 'Thanks. Of course I will. You didn't need to do that.'

'Oh, but I *did*. And the lady in the dry-cleaners has promised me my coat will be fine. She's dealt with disappearing ink stains before.'

'Good. Well, I'd like to pay the dry-clean—'

'Don't say that, I wouldn't *hear* of it!' Liana waved her pretty hands in protest then glanced at her watch. 'Right, I must shoot, my aromatherapist awaits.' Blowing a kiss at Tyler she said, 'See you later, honey. I've booked that table for dinner at Le Petit Blanc.'

Lottie watched her leave and wondered what it must be like to have an aromatherapist waiting to . . . aromatherapise you. She wondered what it might be like to blow kisses at Tyler and call him honey. If that was Liana's pet name for him, they definitely had to be sleeping together.

'One thing.' Tyler broke into her muddled thoughts.

'What?'

'The business with the ink last night. You can argue with me until you're blue in the face, but as soon as it happened you knew it was wrong.'

Lottie looked at him. Evenly she said, 'Did I?'

Tyler smiled his I-win smile and pinged a rubber band across the office at her. 'Everyone else had jumped out at us. Remember? But you stayed hidden behind the wall.'

Chapter 51

'Aunt Cress? It's me.'

Only Jojo called her that, otherwise Cressida wouldn't have recognised the voice on the other end of the phone. The words sounded as if they were being scraped across coarse-grade sandpaper.

'Jojo? Sweetheart, what's wrong?' Oh no, please don't say what I think you're going to say.

'I'm not very well,' Jojo croaked, 'but you mustn't worry, OK? My teacher's just rung Dad and he's on his way to pick me up and take me home. I think it's flu.'

Cressida blinked. Of course it was flu. What else could come along to so comprehensively decimate their plans for the weekend? It was the afternoon of Friday, 5 November, and she had splashed out on two return easyJet flights from Bristol to Newcastle. Tom, in turn, had bought four tickets for the biggest firework extravaganza Newcastle had to offer. How could they not have guessed that something like this would happen? It would be a miracle if it didn't.

'Oh, sweetheart. Poor you.' *Poor me*, thought Cressida, appalled by her own selfishness.

'I know. I've been feeling worse and worse all morning. But the thing is, you can still go to Newcastle without me.'

Could she? Heavens, could she really? Her spirits lifting, Cressida said automatically, 'Sweetheart, it wouldn't be the same. Really, you mustn't worry about—'

'Aunt Cress, I have to go. My dad's here.' Jojo coughed and spluttered for a few seconds then rasped, 'I still don't think you should cancel. I know it wouldn't be the same without me, but it might still be good.'

Feeling terrible and shameless and as guiltily excited as a teenager, Cressida phoned Tom at work and explained about Jojo being ill. Then she paused.

Tom sounded gratifyingly disappointed. 'We must have done something really bad in a previous life to have this much bad luck.'

Was she doing something really bad now? Taking a deep breath, Cressida said, 'Or I could come up on my own.'

This offer was greeted by a nerve-wracking silence.

Then Tom said, 'Would you?' and there was an unmistakable note of delight in his voice.

Like the brazen hussy she evidently was, Cressida said breathlessly, 'Of course I would. I mean, we can still go to the firework thing, can't we? It won't be so much fun for Donny, but—'

'Don't worry about Donny, he'll be fine. So I'll meet you at the airport as planned? Minus your chaperone.'

'Minus my chaperone.' Cressida clapped a hand over her wildly beating heart and felt naughtier than ever. It was confirmed now, she was officially a selfish and self-centred person. Oh, but this could turn into the kind of weekend she hadn't even dared dream about.

Sounding happy and relieved, Tom said, 'Can't wait.'

According to a piece in last week's *Phew!* magazine, shaving your legs was, like, *sooo* last century. The only way to get your legs silky smooth these days, evidently, was with Veet. Jojo, yet to enter the traumatic world of surplus hair removal but passionately interested in the subject nonetheless, had frowned and said, 'Aunt Cress, which do you think's best?'

Cressida had then realised that in all her years she had never once tried any method of leg depilation other than with her trusty razor. Was that some kind of world record? She had always shaved. Waxing hurt, surely. And plucking was downright ridiculous – just one leg had to be the equivalent of five hundred eyebrows' worth of pain. As for dissolving the hair away with cream, someone had brought a tube of Immac into school once when she was fourteen and they had all had a go at rubbing the stuff onto their forearms, wrinkling their noses at the peculiar smell and declaring that it made them feel sick.

But that had been over twenty-five years ago and Immac wasn't Immac any more, it was Veet. The chances were that it no longer smelled funny. Looking forward to the weekend ahead and deciding that the time had come to climb out of her rut and be adventurous, Cressida had treated herself to an aerosol can of Veet mousse. It even described itself on the packaging as pleasantly fragranced. And guess what? It actually was.

She was sitting on the edge of the bath with her legs covered in white foam like Santa's beard, when the doorbell went.

Honestly, were there hidden cameras in this house? Did people do it on purpose? If it was Ted from the shop calling to offer her a second chance with him she might have to attack his beard with pleasantly fragranced Veet.

But since she was mentally incapable of leaving the door unanswered, Cressida clambered out of the bath and gingerly wrapped herself in her

256

full-length dressing gown so as not to scare whoever might be on the doorstep and send them screaming off down the street.

'Cressida.' If her ex-husband was taken aback by the sight of her in her dressing gown at three o'clock in the afternoon he didn't show it. Looking her straight in the eye, Robert said, 'Favour.'

It was a tone of voice Cressida knew well: announcing, rather than asking, that the favour be granted.

'Robert, I'm—'

'Sacha and I have an important meeting in Paris. And I do mean important. Can you take care of Jojo?'

Cressida gripped the lapels of her towelling dressing gown. 'Robert, I'm sorry, I can't. You see—'

'No, *you* have to see.' Firmly, Robert shook his head. 'You *asked* us if you could have Jojo for the weekend. We generously said you could. And now we've made other arrangements. Just because Jojo's ill doesn't give you the right to change your mind and decide you don't want her any more. We have people flying in to Paris to meet us at the Georges Cinq. Can you comprehend how vital this is?'

'But—'

'Cressida, believe me. It's not the kind of appointment you can cancel.'

Anger welled up in her throat. For years Robert and Sacha had treated Jojo like an inconvenient pet. Well, this time they'd gone too far.

'No, I'm sorry, I can't do it,' Cressida said bravely. 'Jojo's your daughter. She's sick and she needs *you*. Besides, I've made other . . . other . . .' Her voice trailed away as she detected movement on the back seat of Robert's car, glimpsed a chalk-white face and dishevelled hair. 'Who's that?'

'Who do you think?' Robert looked at her as if she were a moron. 'Jojo, of course.'

'What's she doing in the car if she's ill?' Cressida knew the answer to this before the words were even out of her mouth. It was Robert's version of a fait accompli.

'I brought her over here. What was I supposed to do, make her walk?'

'How ill is she?' Cressida looked at Jojo in the back of the car, hollow-eyed and miserable.

'The doctor says it's flu. She's pretty rough.' Blithely unaware of the irony, Robert said, 'All she needs is some TLC.'

Oh, the temptation to slap his horrid self-important face. But Jojo was watching them and Robert clearly had no intention of backing down. Imagine having to witness two adults arguing because neither of them wanted you. Overwhelmed with shame and remorse, Cressida said, 'Bring her in then. You can't leave her out there.'

'I'm so sorry,' Jojo whispered when Robert had carried her into the

257

house wrapped in a blue and white flowered duvet. He went back out to fetch her overnight case from the boot.

'Don't be silly. You can't help being ill.' Kneeling down next to the sofa, Cressida stroked Jojo's sweat-soaked fringe away from her forehead.

'But I've spoiled everything now. You could have gone up to Newcastle and had a nice time with Tom and Donny.' Jojo began to cough helplessly again, her thin shoulders heaving and arms trembling with the effort. 'It's such a waste of plane tickets.'

Robert reappeared in the living room, dumping Jojo's case by the door. He stared at Cressida. 'Good grief, what's happened to your legs?'

Cressida had forgotten all about the Veet. White foam was trickling down to her ankles and puddling on the floor.

'It's hair remover,' Jojo croaked, peering over the edge of the sofa.

Robert snorted. 'You always used to shave your legs when you were married to me. I remember the stubble.'

'I remember yours,' Cressida retorted, stung.

When Robert had left, Jojo said weakly, 'I really am sorry, Aunt Cress.'

'Oh, just ignore him. I do. Men can't help saying rude things.'

'Not that. I meant about the trip to Newcastle.' Hot and shivering beneath her duvet, Jojo rested her head on Cressida's arm. 'And it's the firework thing. Tom bought the tickets for it, remember? I couldn't have picked a worse time to be ill.'

'Don't say that. I wouldn't have gone without you.' Stroking Jojo's burning forehead, Cressida realised that she would have to sneak upstairs and phone Tom without being overheard. 'Who wants to go to a silly fireworks party anyway?'

Chapter 52

Freddie was sitting in front of the fire when Lottie burst into the drawing room of Hestacombe House and greeted him with a kiss on the cheek.

It was like being nuzzled by a big, boisterous dog.

'You're cold,' Freddie protested.

'That's because it's freezing out there!' Her nose pink and her eyes bright, Lottie peeled off her gloves and unwound the blue glittery knitted scarf from around her neck. 'There's ice on the puddles. We're all going to be slipping and sliding down to the beach tonight. Are you sure you won't come?'

'You make it sound irresistible.' Freddie gave her a dry look. 'Bloody hell, two broken legs. That's all I need.'

'We could wheel you down, dipstick.'

'No thanks.' Now that his balance was iffy and his left leg increasingly weak, Freddie had acquired a wheelchair for outings, but tonight he was more than happy to leave the intrepid ones to it. 'We'll stay in the warm and watch it from here.'

The bonfire and fireworks party down by the lake was an annual event in the village. Freddie and Mary had begun the tradition twenty years ago. There had been so many happy times . . .

'What are you thinking?' Lottie's gaze searched his face.

'Just wondering about this time next year. Whether Tyler will carry it on.'

'He will. I'll tell him he has to.'

Freddie smiled; he didn't doubt it for a second. 'You never know, you might not be here by then either. Seb might have whisked you and the kids away from Hestacombe. You could be living in Dubai.'

From the look Lottie gave him, he gathered the prospect didn't appeal. 'I don't know about that. I can't imagine not living here.' Then she relaxed. 'But I'm glad you like Seb.'

'Of course I like him.' Lottie had brought Seb over one evening last week. He'd seemed a nice enough chap, possibly a bit feckless but with buckets of charm. And Lottie was clearly keen. Freddie wouldn't put money on it being a happy-ever-after scenario, but then who could ever make that kind of prediction with any confidence? He'd had a pretty rackety past himself, hadn't he? Talk about a lousy track record when it came to relationships. Let's face it, nobody who'd known him forty years ago would have bet tuppence on his marriage to Mary lasting the course.

It just went to show, you never could tell. Love was a lucky dip. Maybe he was wrong now and Lottie would end up being deliriously happy with Sebastian Gill. Just as Tyler might be equally happy with Liana. OK, so things hadn't turned out as he'd secretly hoped they might for Lottie and Tyler, but—

'Lottie love, could you pull that table over a bit?' Barbara came in from the kitchen carrying a tray of whisky and hot buttered teacakes. 'Brrr, you're going to be cold down by that lake tonight.'

Freddie watched as Lottie jumped up to help. Just as she had needed his approval of Seb, so he had desperately wanted her to get along with Barbara when she had arrived at the house to take care of him. And to his relief she had. Lottie and Barbara had liked each other at once. There had been no eye-narrowing this time, none of the mistrust that had existed between Lottie and Fenella.

'You'll have a great view of the fireworks from up here,' said Lottie. 'They'll light up the whole lake. If our feet freeze to the ground you may have to chip us free in the morning.'

'Have a quick Scotch before you go,' Barbara urged, 'to warm you through. It's only some cheap muck of Freddie's.'

Freddie loved her irreverence; it was actually a Glenfarclas, a thirty-year-old Speyside malt.

'Oh well, in that case. Just a quick one.' The grandfather clock out in the hall chimed seven, reminding Lottie that she had to be on her way. 'The main reason I popped in was to say I got through to that guy at the tracing agency. He hasn't had any luck yet.'

Freddie was disappointed but not surprised. If the man had been able to locate Giselle, he would have been on the phone to them at once.

'How about if you try another agency?' Barbara was eager to help. 'Maybe they'd have more luck.'

'This chap's doing everything he can,' said Lottie. 'It's just that these things, well . . .'

'Take time.' Freddie supplied the missing words. 'It's OK, you can say it.'

'I told him to do his best. He knows we want a result as soon as possible.' Knocking back the Scotch in one gulp, Lottie gasped and clutched her throat. 'Yeesh, it's like swallowing petrol.'

260

'My darling girl.' Freddie shook his head fondly. 'You are such an oik.'

Down by the lake the bonfire burned merrily and the party was well underway. Having opened the sash windows just enough to hear the shrieks of the children and the oohs and aahs that accompanied each fresh explosion of fireworks, Freddie and Barbara sat together in the drawing room and watched the display light up the star-spangled sky.

'Could be the last fireworks I see.' Freddie was feeling pleasantly relaxed, thanks to more whisky than was good for him. If he'd been planning on seeing ninety, he wouldn't have drunk this much. As it was, what the hell. He could drink the whole damn bottle if he liked.

'Aren't fireworks beautiful?' Barbara had her feet up and was keeping him company with a glass of Tia Maria. 'You know, I heard about a man who asked to be cremated when he died. Then he arranged for his ashes to be packed into a giant firework and set off in his favourite place.'

'Could be tricky,' said Freddie, 'if your favourite place happened to be Marks and Spencer.'

'I thought it sounded wonderful. I'd love to be packed into a firework and exploded over Regent's Park. Just like that.' Barbara made a sweeping gesture with her free hand as a series of pink and purple chrysanthemum bursts filled the sky. 'Wouldn't that be magnificent? Great fun!'

Freddie took another pleasurable sip of Glenfarclas. 'I'll just have mine scattered over the lake, thanks.'

'You're the boss.' Tilting her head, Barbara smiled at him. 'Ready for your next lot of pills?'

'Bloody things. I suppose so.' Knowing that they were helping him didn't mean Freddie enjoyed taking them. 'D'you know, when I was first diagnosed and my doctor told me I had maybe a year left if I was lucky, I thought I'd kill myself. Not then, not right at that minute,' he added, needing Barbara to understand. 'But when . . . you know, the time came. I found out what I had to look forward to and I made up my mind that I'd rather die before I reached that state. It seemed like a sensible decision. Do many people think that?'

Barbara considered the question. Finally she said, 'I think they probably do.'

'I think so too.' Freddie nodded. 'But the thing is, when the time does come, do many of them do it? Do they actually go ahead and commit suicide?'

Shaking her head, Barbara said gently, 'No, I'd say most of them don't.'

'I guessed that. I wanted to do it but now I can't. And I don't think it's a matter of being brave or cowardly, I just can't contemplate doing it now.' Looking resigned, Freddie put down his tumbler and rested his head against the back of the chair. 'It's fucking annoying, I can tell you. Why does that have to happen?'

'I suppose it's the will to live.' Barbara was sympathetic. 'Self-preservation kicks in.'

'But I didn't want it to! I thought I could skip the last few months, because who in their right mind would want to go through them anyway? Except now it seems I'm stuck with them after all. I want to wake up tomorrow morning and the next morning and the morning after that, for as long as I physically can. I want that useless fucking investigator to find Giselle. I want to enjoy Christmas, I want to be able to show you the garden next spring, I want . . . oh, fuck it.'

'Here.' Barbara pressed a tissue into his hand.

'Sorry. Sorry.'

'Oh Freddie. It's allowed.'

Wiping away the tears, Freddie cleared his throat and gazed blindly out of the windows. All of a sudden he was consumed with grief and rage because he didn't want to die and there was nothing he could do to stop it happening. What if he'd given up too easily, when the diagnosis had first been made? If he hadn't refused treatment, might he have been on the road to recovery by now? Would his doctor be shaking his head in baffled wonderment, declaring, 'I have to say, this is a far better result than we could have hoped for, Freddie. The tumour's practically disappeared!'

What if? Well, he'd never know now. Life had seemed so bleak then, he had been ready for it to be over.

But that was before he'd met Barbara. Enjoying her company during the last few weeks had given him a reason to want to carry on. Here, Freddie knew, was a woman he could have fallen in love with. If he'd met her six months ago . . .

And if his brain could have remained tumour-free . . .

Then again, if he hadn't had the tumour he would never have met Barbara in the first place.

There was a lesson in there somewhere, thought Freddie. But he was buggered if he knew what it was.

'OK?' Barbara gave his hand an encouraging squeeze.

'Yes thanks.' Freddie nodded and smiled briefly, the anger behind him now.

Bang, bang, bang – BANG went the fireworks, waterfalls of crimson and electric-blue light streaming out of the sky and meeting their reflections in the silvery-black waters of the lake.

'Actually, forget Regent's Park. When Amy was sixteen we went to Paris for a long weekend. Have you ever been there?'

'Oh yes. With Mary.' Freddie had magical memories of their time together in Paris.

As a spectacular barrage of vibrant purple and emerald-green chrysanthemums crackled and spread across the sky, Barbara said comfortably, 'I think I'd rather be fired off the Eiffel Tower instead.'

Chapter 53

'Oh hi, I thought Tyler would be here?'

Lottie clicked off the game of patience she'd been surreptitiously playing on the computer and glanced up at Liana in the doorway of the office. As well as looking adorable and sounding like an angel, she even smelled like one too. How did *that* happen?

'He's working down at Pelham House.' Curiosity overcame Lottie. 'What's that scent you're wearing?'

Liana's eyes lit up. 'Oh, this? It hasn't really got a name! I went to a perfumier in Knightsbridge and he blended it for me . . . you know, to kind of complement my pheromones kind of thing?'

Of course. Silly question. The most glorious scent in the world had been created expressly for the most glorious creature in the world. Lottie really wished she hadn't asked. If she were to visit a perfumier he'd probably chuck a few toads and stinging nettles into a blender and add a dollop of ketchup.

'It's so sweet of you to notice,' Liana exclaimed. 'Now, do you think Tyler will be long? What's he doing down there?'

'Fixing the four-poster bed. The Carringtons managed to bring down the canopy and break two of the horizontal poles.'

'You're kidding! What were they doing to cause that much damage?'

'God only knows.' Lottie grimaced, because the Carringtons were in their late sixties and didn't look at all like the kind of people who would ever have anything so revolting as sex. They seemed more likely to wear their matching tan anoraks in bed than to athletically swing from it. Unless – yeuch – they did both . . .

'I can tell what you're thinking,' Liana said playfully.

'I don't *want* to think about it.' Lottie took a slurp of Evian and managed to dribble some down her chin. She hurriedly wiped it away. God, couldn't she even drink water without showing herself up? 'The Carringtons have left, by the way. If you want to see Tyler you can go on down there.'

'If I do that, I might be tempted to push him onto the bed and ravish

264

him.' Liana's eyes sparkled. 'Don't worry, I'll catch up with him later. It was just something about our plans for Thanksgiving.'

So that was it; they were definitely sleeping together.

And Thanksgiving? That was still weeks away. How much longer was Liana going to be here?

'You know, I was just saying to Tyler this morning that we really must get together,' Liana went on.

'Oh?' What did *that* mean?

'You and Seb must come over for dinner one evening.'

Good grief, was she mad? Busy twanging an elastic band that was wrapped round her fingers, Lottie said bluntly, 'I don't think Tyler would enjoy that very much.'

'Hey, I know he isn't wild about your boyfriend. But all the more reason to give them a chance to get to know each other properly! I mean, wouldn't it be so much nicer if we could all be friends?'

Nicer? *Nicer?* Was Liana's middle name Pollyanna by any chance? Lottie made non-committal noises and willed her to go away.

Not that it happened. By this time perched on the edge of Lottie's desk, Liana went on chattily, 'You know, you wouldn't believe the difference being here has made to me. You should have seen the state I was in after Curtis died. And it's all thanks to Tyler. He's changed my world.'

'Mm.' Lottie nodded, feeling slightly sick.

'I never thought I'd fall in love again,' Liana went on. 'Never imagined having a sex life again, for that matter! But when you're with someone like Tyler . . . well, he's just so . . .'

Stop. Too much information.

'Anyway, I don't know what I'd do without him now.' Tilting her head to one side, Liana said, 'Isn't it strange how these things turn out? You think your life is on track, then all of a sudden everything's different. You just never know, do you, what's going to happen next?'

Freddie took a turn for the worse. His doctor was called and made grim predictions about his illness. He didn't have long to go now; had the time perhaps come for him to move into a hospice?

'No.' Propped up in bed, Freddie shook his head wearily. 'I'm not going to change my mind. I want to stay here.'

'Very well.' The doctor accepted his decision. 'I'll speak to Barbara about the pain management.' Nodding approvingly he added, 'You chose a good one there.'

'Hands off. You've already got a wife at home,' said Freddie.

The doctor smiled and scribbled out a couple of prescriptions. 'Just take things easy. Get plenty of rest.'

Ha. 'Give up the rugby, you mean? All I do is lie here and rest.'

'And admire the best view in England.' Turning, the doctor indicated the lake, the hills rising up beyond it and the sun hovering just above the treeline turning the clouds pomegranate pink. 'I can think of worse things to do.'

'God, I'm so *tired.*' As he yawned, Freddie realised that his words had begun to slur again. And it had been a week since his last drink.

'I'll leave you to it,' murmured the doctor.

Freddie was asleep before he'd even closed the bedroom door behind him.

The phone was ringing as Lottie let herself into the kitchen of Hestacombe House. Barbara, watering the pots of basil and coriander on the window ledge, picked it up and said, 'Yes?'

Lottie waited for Barbara to finish dealing with the call.

'The thing is, Freddie's not able to come to the phone just now. Why don't I take your name and pass on a message, then he can get back to you later.' Miming to Lottie that Freddie was sleeping, Barbara grabbed a pen from the fruit bowl on the dresser. Lottie helpfully supplied her with the back of an envelope. Having listened carefully for a minute, Barbara scribbled down a name then paused, looked over at Lottie and said, 'Mr Barrowcliffe, can I ask you to hold on for just a few seconds? I need to speak to someone else.'

'Barrowcliffe. Jeff Barrowcliffe?' Lottie's eyebrows went up, betraying her surprise.

Nodding, Barbara covered the receiver. 'That's the one. Freddie told me about him. He's ringing to invite Freddie to a party in December.'

A lump swam into Lottie's throat. Reaching for the phone she said, 'I'll do it.'

Freddie had taken to delegating the task of informing others of his illness to Lottie and Barbara. Introducing herself to Jeff Barrowcliffe, Lottie explained to him that Freddie was unwell and wouldn't be able to attend the party.

Jeff sounded distinctly put out. 'But it isn't for another five weeks. He might be better by then.'

Gently Lottie said, 'I'm sorry, but he won't be. Freddie's very ill.'

There was a pause.

'What's wrong with him?'

'He has a brain tumour.' Lottie hated having to say it.

'Oh God. That's awful.' Jeff was clearly shocked. 'He seemed so well when he came down to Exmouth.'

'Actually, he was diagnosed just before that. Being told he didn't have long to live was what prompted him to get in touch with you.'

'He didn't tell me that.' Lottie heard the distress in Jeff Barrowcliffe's voice. 'I had no idea.'

'He preferred it that way. But it's not something we can hide now. Look, I'll tell him you rang,' said Lottie. 'If he's feeling up to it he might call you back tomorrow, but I have to warn you that his voice is a bit slurred now. He's not always easy to understand on the phone.'

'OK, OK . . . yes, just tell him I called,' Jeff went on hurriedly. 'And send him our best wishes. It was good to see him back in the summer.' He paused again, cleared his throat. 'Is he . . . *very* ill?'

Nodding slowly, Lottie said, 'Yes. Yes he is,' and felt Barbara's hand, warm and comforting, on her shoulder.

'Tell him I'm sorry,' said Jeff.

The next morning Freddie watched as Barbara bustled around his bedroom, rearranging a glass bowl of scented white winter roses on the window ledge and dusting the silver photo frames.

'Do you know, I'm feeling better today.' Freddie carefully tilted his head from side to side to see how bad the pain was. It was definitely less severe.

'Could be something to do with your morphine dosage being increased.'

'Oh. Right.' He was probably high as a kite without even realising it. 'Am I slurring?'

She smiled. 'A bit.'

'Join me in a glass of champagne?' Freddie looked hopeful.

'It's eleven o'clock in the morning. I'll make you a cup of tea, how does that sound?'

'Like a desperately poor substitute. Who's that?' They both heard the sound of a car pulling up outside.

Barbara peered out of the bedroom window. 'No idea. New guests arriving, I imagine. Lottie's dealing with them. Now how about a chicken sandwich?'

'I'm not hungry.'

'You should have something.'

'I've got a nagging nurse, isn't that enough?' Indicating the chair beside his bed, Freddie said, 'Stop faffing around, woman, and help me with the damn crossword. I used to be able to finish it in ten minutes flat.'

'Let me just sort out your pillows. You've gone all crooked.' Barbara helped him forwards and with her free hand expertly plumped up the goosedown pillows. 'There, isn't that better? Now where did you put the pen?'

'Dropped it,' said Freddie.

The door burst open while Barbara was on her hands and knees searching under the bed for the pen. Lottie, looking fifty per cent shocked and fifty per cent as if she'd just seen Father Christmas, said in an odd voice, 'Freddie? You have a visitor.'

Typical. Just as he and Barbara were about to tackle the crossword. Freddie frowned, deciding he wasn't much in the mood for visitors. 'Who is it?'

Lottie was breathing rapidly. She waited for Barbara to retrieve the pen and crawl out from under the bed. Finally she said, 'It's Giselle.'

Chapter 54

It seemed to Freddie that the clock in the room had stopped ticking. How could Giselle be here, when the tracing agency hadn't even been in touch to say they'd tracked her down? Unless they had, and this was Lottie's idea of a surprise. Although she wasn't acting like someone in on the secret, that was for sure.

Bemused, Freddie said, 'They found her?'

Lottie, shaking her head, replied, 'No, they didn't.'

For a moment he wondered if the increased dose of medication was causing him to hallucinate. Or maybe he was asleep and dreaming this whole situation. But it certainly felt real enough.

And now Lottie was coming towards him, smoothing his hair and fussing with the collar of his pyjama jacket. She reached for his Penhaligon's cologne and splashed some on his cheeks, then straightened the bedcovers and stepped back. 'There, you'll do.'

Freddie supposed he should be grateful she hadn't licked the corner of her hanky and wiped his mouth with it. He felt like a messy five-year-old. Aware now that his speech was clumsy he said, 'Is she going to be shocked when she sees me?'

And that was when a floorboard creaked and a figure appeared in the doorway.

'No, Freddie.' Giselle stepped into the bedroom. 'I won't be shocked.'

If this was a dream, Freddie wasn't complaining. Lottie discreetly closed the door behind herself and Barbara, leaving them to it.

'It's really you.' It was a ridiculous thing to say but he couldn't help himself. Giselle's wavy hair was the same warm brown shade he remembered, framing her sweetly rounded face. Her eyes were unchanged, her smile hesitant. She was wearing smart cream trousers and a light brown angora sweater over an ivory shirt. One side of her shirt collar was sticking up slightly, which made Freddie think that this wasn't a dream, because it wasn't the kind of detail it would ever have occurred to his brain to make up.

'Oh Freddie, it's so good to see you again.' He read the conflicting

269

emotions on her face – genuine pleasure mixed with pity for his plight. Carefully, Giselle rested her arms on his shoulders and kissed him on each cheek. She smelled of gardenias. Freddie gestured towards the chair. He wanted to look at her, to apologise to her properly and discover how her life had turned out.

'I don't understand how you're here,' he said carefully as Giselle sat down. 'We've been looking for you.'

'So I hear. Well, I mean I did kind of know.' She clasped his hand. 'But Lottie's just told me she went to Oxford and spoke to Phyllis Mason.'

'Great help she was,' Freddie grunted. 'Couldn't even remember the name of the chap you married.'

Giselle smiled. 'Well, to be fair, it was a long time ago. And it wasn't the easiest of names. Kasprzykowski.'

'Bloody hell, it must have been love!' Bursting with questions he needed to ask her, Freddie said, 'Tell me how you're here today. I still don't understand.'

'You mean that for once in my life I have the upper hand?' Her eyes bright, Giselle said teasingly, 'I think I should make the most of it, don't you?'

'I suppose I deserve that much.' Freddie was just happy to have her here. 'Can I say sorry? I know how much I hurt you, and you didn't deserve it. I behaved appallingly. I've always felt bad about that.'

'Clearly.' Stroking the back of his hand, Giselle said, 'Otherwise you wouldn't have tried so hard to find me.'

'Guilty conscience.' Freddie shook his head. 'It's a terrible thing.'

'Don't be so hard on yourself. You fell out of love with me and in love with somebody else. We broke up. It happens all the time. At least you and Mary stayed together.' Her eyes sparkled. 'And if it helps, I ended up making the right choice too.'

That was a tremendous weight off Freddie's mind. Hearing it, he felt almost physically lighter. 'So you're still Mrs Kasprzy . . . whatever.'

'Yes.' Giselle nodded. 'Oh yes, I'm still Mrs Kasprzykowski.' She paused. 'Officially, at least.'

'What does that mean?'

'Peter took me back with him to America. We got married. His parents hated me because I wasn't Polish. Or Catholic. We shared a house with them in Wisconsin.' Giselle shook her head matter-of-factly. 'I can't tell you how much I regretted leaving home. Peter was a mummy's boy, far too bone idle to last longer than a month in any job. I stuck it out for two years working in a hardware store and saving up a few dollars every week. Finally I had enough money for my boat fare back to England. Peter had warned me that if I ever tried to leave him I'd live to regret it.

So I ran away one night, came home and never contacted him again.'

'All my fault.' Freddie couldn't begin to imagine how unhappy she must have been.

'What doesn't kill us makes us stronger. At least Peter and I hadn't had children. Anyway,' said Giselle, re-crossing her legs and leaning forwards, 'I took a job as a nanny for a family in Berkshire. Then one day on my weekend off I decided to visit an old schoolfriend in Oxford. I caught the train up. Got off at the station. And that was when I saw him, just standing there on the platform waiting for *his* train to come in. I couldn't believe it. He spotted me and came over. We started talking and that was it. I never did go and visit my old schoolfriend.'

'Who was it?'

'The man who's made me happy for the last thirty-six years,' Giselle said simply. 'The father of my children. The man I'll love until the day I die, even if he does have his faults.'

Freddie was picturing the scene on the station platform, two complete strangers gazing at each other, knowing instinctively that This Was It. Just like it had been for Mary and himself.

'Love at first sight.' He gave Giselle's hand a squeeze. 'What's his name?'

'Hardly love at first sight,' Giselle retorted with amusement. 'And his name's Jeff Barrowcliffe.'

Downstairs in the kitchen Jeff was stirring his tea, trying to explain his reasons for hiding the truth from Freddie.

'I was jealous, pure and simple. Freddie was supposed to be my friend and he took my girl away from me. That's not to say I didn't deserve it, what with the way I was back then, but I'd lost Giselle to him once before and I wasn't about to let him do it again.'

'I can understand that,' said Lottie.

Barbara nodded. 'Me too.'

'We hadn't seen Freddie for forty years,' Jeff continued defensively. 'Then all of a sudden I get the email from you. I was curious to see him again but I didn't know what he wanted. I didn't trust him. So I took down the family photographs and sent Giselle off to spend the day with our eldest daughter. When Freddie arrived he told me he was looking for Giselle, but he didn't say why. All I saw was an old rival, good-looking and well dressed, still with all the old charm. He didn't tell me he was ill.'

Lottie was puzzling something out. 'But yesterday you rang to invite Freddie to a party.'

'I know.' Looking shamefaced, Jeff said, 'It took a while, but Giselle finally made me see sense. The thing is, meeting Freddie again was . . . great. Catching up on old times, hearing about the life he'd led. It got us thinking, after he'd left. We decided to track down a few old friends of our own and throw a big reunion party before Christmas. And Giselle told me I had to invite Freddie. She promised not to run off with him. And of course I knew she was right. We couldn't have a party without Freddie.' He paused, took a sip of tea and carefully placed the cup back in the saucer. 'Although now it looks as though we'll have to. I felt terrible after I spoke to you yesterday. As soon as I told Giselle she said we must come up and see him.'

'So she isn't your wife,' said Lottie. 'She's still Mrs Kiddly-Iddly-Offski.'

'Her husband would never have given her a divorce back then. The family were devout Catholics. We've just lived together for the last thirty-six years. In sin,' Jeff added. 'Although everyone calls her Mrs Barrowcliffe.'

'That's why the private detective couldn't find her.'

Jeff chuckled. 'Private detective? Blimey, you meant business. She'll be made up when she hears she's had a private detective on her tail in the mean streets of Exmouth.'

'Except she hasn't,' said Lottie. 'He hasn't managed to tail her anywhere. Between you and me, I think he's a bit crap.'

Wiping her eyes, Giselle came into the kitchen and said, 'He's getting tired now. Jeff, he wants to see you before he goes to sleep.'

Jeff was on his feet in a flash. 'How's he looking?'

'Just like himself. Only dreadfully ill.' Giselle fumbled in her pocket for a fresh tissue. 'Oh dear, I wish we could have seen him sooner.'

'Never mind,' said Lottie as Barbara went to refill the kettle. 'You're here now.'

So that was that. He'd found Giselle at last. Well, he hadn't, but one way or another they had managed to find each other. A bit like losing your reading glasses and turning the whole house upside down, then finding they'd been in your jacket pocket the whole time.

Freddie opened his eyes. It was dark outside now, which meant he'd been asleep for some time. The inky-dark sky was bright with stars and an almost full moon was out, reflected in the still, glassy surface of the lake. Had the doctor called in again earlier? Freddie had a vague memory of him murmuring to Barbara while he had been dozing. His head wasn't hurting, but he suspected that if he tried to move it, it would. Never mind, he was fine right here, comfortable enough. Under the circumstances, who could ask for more?

'Freddie? Are you awake?' It was Barbara's voice, low and gentle; he wasn't alone after all. She was sitting in the chair pulled up next to the bed. Now her warm hand was resting on his arm. 'Is there anything you need? Anything I can get you?'

Sensing that if he attempted to speak it would come out all wrong, Freddie imperceptibly moved his head from side to side. There was nothing he needed. Giselle and Jeff had forgiven him. He was sleepy again now. Sleeping was so much easier than trying to stay awake. And when he slept he was able to dream about Mary. While he waited to doze off, Freddie returned to one of his favourite memories – the one that made him shudder to think it could so easily not have happened. But that was fate, wasn't it? That was serendipity. The tiniest decisions were capable of changing your whole life . . .

It had been a gloriously sunny June morning and Freddie was on his way to a meeting with his bank manager. Early for his appointment and finding himself with thirty minutes to spare, he debated whether to stop off at the coffee bar or to wander down to the car showroom at the other end of Britton Road to harmlessly ogle the cars he couldn't afford.

Harmless ogling won the day and Freddie turned right instead of left. Moments later he encountered a girl standing on the pavement rattling a collecting tin. Feeling in his trouser pocket, he found only a couple of coppers. Aware of the girl's eyes upon him, Freddie approached her and did his best to disguise the fact that he was sliding such a paltry sum into her tin.

Sadly his sleight of hand wasn't up to Magic Circle standards. The girl looked him straight in the eye and said bluntly, 'Is that all?'

Freddie was nettled. He'd bothered to contribute, hadn't he? Other people simply walked on by. Torn between apology – for he wasn't normally mean – and irritation, he said, 'It's all the change I have.'

And that was when it happened. The girl's mouth curved up at the corners and what felt like a hand in a velvet glove simultaneously closed round Freddie's heart. Her tone playful, she said, 'I'm sure you could do much better if you tried.'

Feeling oddly breathless, Freddie turned out both trouser pockets to show her how empty they were. Then he turned and made his way down Britton Street, tinglingly aware of her presence behind him.

The cars in the showroom weren't able to hold his attention. He went into the newsagent opposite and bought a box of matches.

'That's an improvement.' The girl's dimples flashed as he dropped a series of silver coins into her collecting tin. She had bright blue eyes and long straight hair the colour of corn, and was wearing an above-the-knee purple shift dress that showed off a glorious pair of legs.

'Good,' said Freddie. This time he walked past her in the opposite direction for almost a hundred yards before turning back and sliding another handful of two-shilling pieces into her tin.

273

'Now you're getting the idea,' said the girl.

Freddie looked at her. 'Tell me your name.'

She smiled playfully and jangled her tin at him. This time he took a pound note from his wallet, rolled it up and fed it into the slot.

'Mary.'

'Mary. You're costing me a fortune.'

'Ah, but it's in a good cause.'

If he'd gone to the coffee bar in the first place, their paths wouldn't have crossed. Freddie double-checked that she wasn't wearing a wedding ring. 'I've got to go and see my bank manager now. Will you still be here when I come out?'

Mary raised one eyebrow. 'Might be, might not.'

Another pound note into the tin. 'Will you?'

Her eyes danced. 'Oh, all right then.'

'And when I get back, can I take you for a coffee?'

'Sorry, no.'

Freddie panicked. 'Why not?'

'There's a problem.'

'What is it?'

'I don't drink coffee. I only like tea.'

His skin prickled with relief. 'Can I take you for a cup of tea then?'

Mary, breaking into a huge smile, said, 'I thought you'd never ask.'

Freddie's eyes were closed again now. Every moment of that summer's morning was engraved on his heart. He and Mary had met for tea – it was a wonder he'd been able to afford it after dropping so much money into her blasted collecting tin – and that had been it. From then on there was no going back. They had both known they were meant to be together for the rest of their lives.

And they had been, for the next thirty-four years. The last four and a half years without Mary had been an ordeal but she seemed so close now. Freddie felt as if all he had to do was to allow his thoughts to drift away and there she'd be, waiting for him . . . and yes, here she was, smiling that dear familiar smile and reaching out towards him . . .

Filled with indescribable joy, Freddie relaxed and went to her.

Chapter 55

Pulling into the driveway of Hestacombe House the next morning Lottie saw Tyler outside the office waiting for her, and she knew.

'Freddie's gone. He died in the night,' Tyler said gently when she climbed out of the car.

It was expected. It was inevitable. But it still wasn't the news you wanted to hear. Lottie covered her mouth.

'Barbara says it was very peaceful. He just slipped away.'

Freddie hadn't been in pain. He'd made his peace with Giselle and he had stayed *compos mentis* until the end. As deaths went, who could ask for more?

'Oh Freddie.' It came out as a whisper.

'Come here.' Tyler put his arms round her and Lottie realised tears were sliding down her cheeks. Taking shameful comfort from the feel of his hands on her shoulders and her wet face against the soft, much-washed cotton of his denim shirt, she mumbled, 'I'm being selfish. I'm just going to miss him so much.'

'Sshh, it's OK.' Tyler's voice, soothing and in control, broke through Lottie's defences. Silent tears gave way to noisy, uncontrolled, chest-heaving sobs.

Finally, when she was feeling like a wrung-out floorcloth and doubt-less looking like one too, Lottie's outburst subsided.

'Sorry.'

'Don't be.'

Of course he was used to comforting bereft women, he'd had months of practice with Liana. Except Liana wouldn't end up in a mess like this, Lottie thought, with her eyes all froggy and her whole face streaked with mascara.

'Barbara's with him,' said Tyler, 'and the doctor's on his way over.'

'Poor Barbara. She'll be upset too.'

'She says you can go on up and see him if you want to.' Tyler indicated Freddie's bedroom window, glinting in the morning sunlight.

Lottie wiped her face with a shredded tissue and hoped Freddie wouldn't mind her looking a fright.

Nodding, she took a deep breath. 'I'd like that.'

★   ★   ★

'How are you doing? Need a hand with anything?'

Flustered and emotional, Lottie saw that Tyler was in the kitchen doorway looking concerned.

'Um, well, the drinks are waiting to be poured and someone has to fill the ice buckets and I'm worried we won't have enough glasses—'

'Whoa! OK, don't panic, let me handle it. And you only answered one half of my question.' Tyler began uncorking bottles of wine. 'I asked how you were doing.'

'The best I can. Not very well,' Lottie admitted. 'I thought organising outside caterers would take the pressure off, but two of the waitresses haven't turned up and the ones that have are rubbish, so I'm just panicking instead, and it feels as if I'm letting Freddie down.'

'Well don't, because you haven't.' Tyler shoved a glass of icy white wine into her hand. 'Now shut up and drink this. *Slowly*,' he added before Lottie could down the lot in one go.

Lottie nodded and obediently took a sip. She felt as if she'd run a marathon. The service at Cheltenham Crematorium had been emotionally draining and now Hestacombe House was crammed with mourners she didn't feel equipped to deal with. It was like trying to host a huge party when you were going down with flu. Practically everyone from the village was here, ready to give Freddie the kind of memorable send-off he deserved, and all she wanted to do was go to bed.

'Seb not turned up?' said Tyler. 'I thought he might have been here.'

'No. He only met Freddie once.'

'All the same, he could have come along to support you. Wouldn't you have preferred to have him here?'

Lottie took another sip of wine. Yes, she would have preferred it, but Seb had told her he was busy today meeting potential sponsors for the next polo tournament, and when she'd tried ringing him earlier his phone had been switched off.

But she wasn't going to tell Tyler that.

'I don't need my hand holding. I'm old enough to come to a funeral on my own. Anyway, I'm not on my own, am I?' Indicating the rest of the house, Lottie said, 'I know practically everyone here. Half the people out there have known me since I was born.'

'OK, don't get defensive. I only asked where your boyfriend was.'

'He has an important meeting. And those wine glasses need filling up.' Lottie leapt to her feet. 'Oh God, and the bruschettas need to go into the oven.'

'Give me thirty seconds,' said Tyler. 'I'll be back.'

He was, with a dozen or so assorted villagers in tow, Cressida among them.

'You daft thing, getting into a flap and trying to do it all yourself.' Cressida whisked the tea towel out of Lottie's hands and gave her a hug. 'We're here, aren't we? Between us we'll have everyone fed and watered in no time.'

'Not that many of us are planning on drinking water,' Merry Watkins put in with a grimace. 'Freddie would have something to say about that if we did.'

Tyler steered Lottie out of the kitchen. 'Come on, I think you can leave them to it.'

Relieved, Lottie murmured, 'Thanks.'

'Don't mention it.'

'Oh, look at you with your hair all falling down!' Liana, rushing up to her, exclaimed, 'And your eye shadow's gone all creased at the corners . . . You look *exhausted*.'

She meant *awful*. Which was undoubtedly true, but not what Lottie needed to be told. Presumably when Curtis had died, Liana had remained gorgeous throughout the funeral without so much as an eyelash out of place.

'Sorry, that was tactless of me.' Liana was instantly contrite. 'I was a complete wreck after Curtis's funeral. If I hadn't had Tyler there to look after me, I don't know how I'd have got through it.' Glancing around, she said, 'Is Seb not with you?'

Were they in league with each other? Was this some kind of have-a-dig-at-Seb conspiracy? Lottie jumped as a voice behind her said, 'No he isn't, but I'm here. And I'm great at cheering girls up.'

Turning and flashing Mario a smile of gratitude, Lottie gave his arm a squeeze.

'Eeurrgh! Worse than I thought!' Catching sight of her creased eye shadow and red-rimmed eyes, Mario recoiled in mock horror.

'OK, I get the message.' Lottie altered the friendly squeeze to a painful pinch. 'I'll go and do my face.'

Upstairs in the enormous blue and white bathroom she washed away the old make-up and applied a fresh layer. Downstairs the party was starting to buzz, getting into its post-funeral stride. Lottie took out her phone and tried Seb's number again but failed to get through. Oh well, that was business meetings for you. Since there was no point in leaving a message she dropped the phone back into her bag, gave her neck a squizz of Jo Malone's Vetyver, and readied herself to head back downstairs and rejoin the throng.

'Oh!'

'Sorry, didn't mean to startle you.' Fenella, who had evidently been waiting for her to emerge from the bathroom, took in the reapplied make-up and refastened hair combs and gave a nod of approval. 'That's better. You looked a bit of a fright before.'

'So everyone keeps telling me.' Startled because she'd had no idea Fenella was even here, Lottie took in the familiar chic haircut, lustrous eyes and immaculately tailored black suit. 'How did you know Freddie had . . . ?'

Except it was pretty obvious.

'I saw the announcement in the *Telegraph*.' Fenella paused, gently cleared her throat. 'Well, I'd kind of been looking out for it. Hoping *not* to see it, obviously, but knowing that sooner or later it would appear.'

Lottie nodded, feeling awkward. Did that mean she was now duty bound to shake Fenella's hand and politely thank her for coming? More to the point, why *was* Fenella here? Was she perhaps still hankering after a mention in Freddie's will?

'No,' Fenella read her mind with ease. 'I'm not expecting him to have left me anything. I just wanted to pay my respects. Freddie may not have been the love of my life, but I was still very fond of him.'

'We all were.'

'So who gets his money?' Fenella's eyes were bright. 'You?'

'No.' Lottie shook her head. 'Not me.'

'Bad luck. Anyway, I just wanted to say hello before I left. It's never easy going to a funeral when the only person you know is the one in the box.' Pausing, Fenella added, 'Unless you think it might be worth my while to hang around for a bit longer. If there are any eligible men you think I might like to meet, please don't hesitate to point me in their direction.'

Ted, from the village shop? Envisaging the two of them together, Lottie said, 'No one springs to mind.'

'Not even that handsome American? Tyler?'

'I think you'd have to be thirty years younger.'

'I imagine so.' Fenella acknowledged the dig with amusement. 'But you wouldn't. Who's the very pretty girl with him?'

She was doing it deliberately. Witch. 'A friend,' said Lottie.

'Disappointing for you.'

'Not at all. I'm seeing someone far nicer.' Feeling like a fifteen-year-old, Lottie boasted, 'He organises polo tournaments. He's gorgeous looking *and* loads of fun.'

Luckily it seemed she wasn't the only one capable of juvenility. Fenella, arching her pencil-slim eyebrows, said, 'Really? What's he doing with you, then?'

They looked at each other for a long moment. Lottie smiled first. 'Thanks. You've actually made me feel better.'

'My pleasure.' Fenella returned the smile, then glanced out of the landing window at the sound of an approaching car. 'Ah, here's my taxi.'

'Come on, we'll walk down together.' Lottie held out an arm. 'Freddie was glad he'd seen you again, by the way. He didn't regret doing it.'

Side by side they descended the staircase. Fenella said, 'Did he ever manage to track down Giselle?'

'Yes.' As she said it, Lottie belatedly realised that Fenella and Giselle had once met.

'Really?' Fenella's gaze darted with interest over the thronged guests in the hall below. 'I say, how fascinating. Is she here now?'

Lottie hesitated fractionally. 'No.'

Laughing, Fenella said, 'That means she is. Maybe I should find her and say hello.'

'And maybe you shouldn't.' Lottie steered her swiftly down the last couple of stairs and in the direction of the front door. 'Your taxi's waiting outside, remember. Thank you for coming. Bye.'

Fenella laughed, her expression softening as she leaned forward and kissed Lottie on each cheek. 'Darling, I may be a gold digger but I'm not that much of a bitch.'

The taxi roared off up the drive in a Technicolor swirl of leaves and Lottie made her way back into the house. The noise level had cranked up another couple of notches by now as people reminisced happily about Freddie and relaxed into their second and third drinks.

She found Giselle and Jeff in the drawing room, chatting away to Barbara. Jeff's dark suit had the air of one that has been pulled, blinking in astonishment, from the back of the wardrobe where it has languished for the last twenty years.

'Here she is.' Giselle looked up as Lottie approached and handed her a photograph from the selection she'd been showing Barbara. 'Jeff and I were going through the old albums last night. Have a look at this one. That's Freddie on the left there next to Jeff.'

Smiling, Lottie gazed at the snap of Freddie and Jeff with more hair than they'd possessed for years, larking about outside someone's house. They were spraying each other with shaken-up bottles of beer while a gaggle of girls looked on and giggled, arms raised to protect their hair.

'That's you!' Lottie pointed to a sweet-faced brunette in a bright orange mini-dress and white PVC boots.

'I had a twenty-two-inch waist back then.' Nodding, Giselle said, 'They were happy days.' Then she tapped Jeff and added, 'Except *you* were drinking like a fish.'

'And look what happened when I stopped.' Jeff in turn tapped his head. 'I went bald.'

'Oh, I meant to ask.' Giselle gazed up at Lottie. 'Who was that woman we saw you saying goodbye to just now? The one who left in a taxi? Only I know it sounds daft but I'm sure I've seen her somewhere before.'

Forty years ago, Lottie thought but didn't say. You and Freddie went along to a party thrown by that woman and her husband. Freddie had a torrid affair with her behind your back, but he wasn't rich enough for her so she dumped him and he came back to you.

Lottie shook her head. 'God, I'm terrible with names. I can't even remember now. I think she's just an old friend of the family.'

'I'm just being silly then.' Giselle shrugged, but she was still frowning.

'Or maybe she's been on the TV and that's why you think you recognise her,' Barbara joined in reassuringly. 'I was shopping in Camden Market once and I said hello to a girl I could have sworn I knew. Turned out it was Kate Winslet.'

'Do you know, you could be right.' Nodding, Giselle said, 'She looked just like that opera singer we were watching on TV the other night.'

Phew.

'Only older,' said Jeff.

Lottie kept a straight face. If Fenella were here now she'd rip his head off.

Just as well she was gone.

Later, as Lottie mingled and chatted with those who had known and loved Freddie, she overheard Merry Watkins saying bracingly to Tyler, 'Now you know what the antidote to a funeral is, don't you? A lovely romantic wedding! How about you and that pretty girlfriend of yours making an announcement, hmm? That'd cheer us all up!'

Chapter 56

Two weeks after the funeral, Lottie and Barbara took the small rowing boat out into the middle of the lake. Gazing at the frost-covered hills rising up all around them, the swans floating serenely on the water and the rooftops of Hestacombe amongst the trees, Barbara said, 'I suppose there are worse places to end up. Although I still fancy the Eiffel Tower myself.'

'If we don't get a move on, Freddie's going to end up in a swan's stomach.' Having eased the airtight lid off the pot with a soft *pfhut*, Lottie saw that the swans had metaphorically pricked up their ears and abruptly altered course. Greedily imagining that it was feeding time they were now heading in a stately convoy towards the boat.

'Did I ever tell you I was scared of swans?' said Barbara.

'You big Jessy. They won't hurt you.'

'I once had my arm broken by a swan.'

Lottie's stomach contracted in alarm. '*Did* you?'

'Well, no, but I know it's technically possible. Remind me again why I'm out here?'

'Because this is where Freddie wanted his ashes to be scattered.'

Barbara pulled a face. 'Couldn't we have just done it from the edge of the lake?'

'In the middle's better. Then they can spread out in all directions. Right, shall we do this?' Carefully lifting the pot and tilting it with the reverence it was due, Lottie allowed the first ashes to spill out. Oh . . . *phh, tppph* . . .

'Stop!' cried Barbara. 'They're going in your hair!'

'They're going in my *mouth*.' Spluttering and coughing, Lottie almost dropped the pot into her lap. A gust of wind had sent grey dusty ash flying into her eyes, up her nose and down her throat.

'Oh God, the swans are coming . . . GO AWAY,' Barbara shrieked, leaping to her feet and causing the boat to rock wildly from side to side. One of the male swans, startled by her dance technique, rose up and began beating his wings. Barbara panicked and stumbled against an oarlock, knocking the oar free.

'Don't let it slip, *don't let it slip.*' Still tasting ashes and blindly rubbing her eyes, Lottie felt the pot wobble in her lap and made a grab for it.

'The bloody swans are eating Freddie's ashes!' wailed Barbara. 'Oh my God, make them go away, now they're trying to climb into the boat . . . *aarrgh . . .*'

The boat overturned as neatly as a toy, tipping Barbara and Lottie, equally neatly, into the lake. The all-over blast of iciness took Lottie's breath away and caused every muscle in her body to contract in horror.

It took a few seconds to reorientate herself. The water wasn't what you'd call tropical. Relieved, at least, to have had the ashes washed out of her hair and eyes, Lottie bobbed up to the surface and came face to face with Barbara. Barbara might be terrified of swans but at least she could swim. And the swans had taken off; disgusted by the flurry of activity and lack of palatable food, they had retreated to the far end of the lake in high dudgeon.

Treading water, Barbara blinked and said, 'Are you sure this is a heated pool?'

'I think they forgot to put fifty pence in the meter.'

'Sorry. I panicked. Poor Freddie, it wasn't supposed to happen like that.'

'He wanted the lake. He g-got the lake.' Lottie's teeth were chattering. 'C-come on, race you to the beach.'

Tyler was standing there waiting for them, shaking his head. 'I saw the boat tip over. I *was* going to dive in and rescue you.' Leaning forward, he reached out a warm hand and helped first Lottie then Barbara out of the water, 'But basically the water was just too damn cold.'

'Wimp,' Barbara said cheerfully.

'Maybe. But you're wet and I'm dry.' His dark eyes glittered with amusement. 'Oh, and here's another tip. Always best to check the direction of the wind before you start scattering ashes.'

'It's done now.' Maybe not in quite the way they'd planned, but done nevertheless. The pot containing Freddie's ashes lay at the bottom of the lake and the contents had been well and truly scattered. Lottie, shivering and dripping, said, 'You know, a gentleman would give up his sweater.'

'You're joking, it's cashmere. Come on,' Tyler said good-naturedly as Lottie shook her head, attempting to shower him with water, 'let's get you two up to the house.'

Hestacombe House, not Fox Cottage. Lottie was still getting used to the idea that it was Tyler's home now. So much had changed in the space of a fortnight. A week after the funeral when he had announced that he would be moving into Hestacombe House the following day, she had retorted indignantly, 'Shouldn't you wait until it's actually yours?'

That was when Tyler had explained that it was in fact already his, that he had bought the house from Freddie three months ago.

Showered and changed into an oversized white towelling robe of Tyler's, Lottie made her way back downstairs. Tyler was in the kitchen making mugs of tea and eating a toasted cheese sandwich.

'Barbara's train leaves at two thirty. That means we have to leave here in,' he checked his watch, 'five minutes. If you go home and change now, you might not make it back in time to say goodbye.'

'I know.' Lottie seized her mug of steaming tea and glugged it down. 'I'll wait here until you've gone. If that's all right.'

'Of course it's all right.' Tyler offered her the other half of his toasted cheese sandwich. 'You don't want to miss waving her off.'

Barbara was leaving, going back to London. Lottie shook her head, knowing she would miss her terribly. When the contents of Freddie's will had been relayed to them, nobody had been more touched and amazed than Barbara to learn that Freddie had bequeathed almost half his fortune to the children's hospital in Uganda where her daughter Amy had been working when she died. Barbara was now planning to travel to Uganda to visit the hospital and advise how the money might best be spent in Amy's memory.

The other half of Freddie's fortune had gone to the hospice on the outskirts of Cheltenham where Amy had helped to nurse Mary through her last months of life.

The remainder of the estate had comprised an assortment of personal bequests that had brought a lump to Lottie's throat.

For Jeff Barrowcliffe, ten thousand pounds to be spent on the motor-bike of his choice, to make up for the Norton 350 Freddie had written off all those years ago.

For Giselle, ten thousand pounds to make up for everything else.

For the villagers of Hestacombe, five thousand pounds to be splurged on a rip-roaring party in the Flying Pheasant.

And for Lottie Carlyle five thousand pounds to be spent on an even more rip-roaring family holiday in Disneyland, Paris.

Lottie's eyes filled with tears now at the thought of her conversation with Freddie way back in the summer, when he had asked her where she would go if she could travel anywhere in the world. That had been on the day he'd told her about his brain tumour, yet still he had remembered.

'Here.' Tyler handed her a tissue, something he'd grown accustomed to doing over the last couple of weeks.

'Sorry. Being daft.' Wiping her eyes and noisily blowing her nose, Lottie forced herself to stop. 'It's thinking about Disneyland, gets me every time.'

'Hey, you'll have a great time. Will Seb be going with you?'

'Maybe. I haven't even thought about dates yet.' In truth Lottie was torn. Seb would be brilliant, would love every minute, and Ruby and Nat would adore having him there. But a part of her, ridiculously, sensed that this hadn't been Freddie's intention. Nothing had ever been said, but in a weird way she felt he would be disappointed if she went with Seb.

'Don't move. You've got something in your hair.'

Lottie stayed still while Tyler teased apart the wet ringlets in order to reach whatever she hadn't managed to wash out of her hair in the shower.

'What is it?' It was certainly taking him long enough.

'Nothing.'

'Dead leaf?'

Tyler gazed down into her eyes. 'Dead beetle actually.'

'Really?'

He held up the offending creature, a glossy dark brown corpse missing a couple of legs.

'Oh well, could have been worse.' Lottie patted her hair. 'Could have been a dead rat.'

Then her stomach lurched into washing-machine mode because Tyler wasn't smiling at her feeble attempt at humour, he was looking as if he wanted to kiss her.

A lot.

Oo-er. Lottie gazed helplessly back, heart racing, all sensible thought wiped from her mind. Was he going to do it? Was he waiting for *her* to do it? Should she—

'Hel*loooo*? Tyler, could you be an angel and give me a hand getting these cases downstairs?' It was Barbara's voice, echoing from the landing. 'Then I'm all set to go. Don't want to miss my train!'

That was it, they'd said their goodbyes and Barbara was gone. Waving until the car had disappeared from view, Lottie closed the heavy front door and made her way through to the drawing room. She needed to get home and change into dry clothes, but not just yet.

The sage-green velvet sofa was piled with cushions and facing the window. Curling up on one end of it, Lottie bent her head and sniffed the towelling lapel of Tyler's dressing gown to see if it smelled of him. Yes, it did, faintly . . . oh God, had he really been about to kiss her just now or had she imagined it? Had it been a case of wishful thinking on her part? Was she turning into a sad old bag, fantasising that men fancied her when they didn't? And what about Seb, who definitely *did* fancy her and surely deserved better than this?

Dammit, why did life have to be so *complicated*?

'Now what is it that this reminds me of?'

Jerking awake with a start, Lottie saw who had spoken.

284

'Oh yes, that's it.' Liana clicked her fingers. 'Goldilocks and the Three Bears.'

Lottie prayed she hadn't been dribbling in her sleep. It was bad enough that the front of the towelling dressing gown had worked loose and was gaping saucily, making it apparent that she wasn't wearing anything underneath.

'Feel free, just make yourself at home.' Liana was smiling her usual angelic smile but there was a faint edge to her voice. Tilting her head enquiringly to one side she said, 'And excuse me if this is impertinent, but am I allowed to ask what you're doing here, all alone in the house, wearing Tyler's robe?'

Liana had been to the hairdresser's; her rippling hair was newly and artfully highlighted in expensive shades of amber, nutmeg and honey. She was wearing a dove-grey polo-neck sweater, size eight – if that – grey wool trousers and a chunky silver belt draped round her teeny tiny hips. God only knew what she must be thinking. And frankly, who could blame her? As Tyler's girlfriend she had a right to be miffed. Tugging the hem of the robe over her bare legs and feeling horribly ashamed – not to mention *big* – Lottie levered herself into a sitting position.

'Sorry, I didn't mean to fall asleep. Barbara's gone. Tyler's taken her to the station to catch her train.'

Liana frowned, still puzzled. 'And you're waiting for him to come back?'

'No, *no*, nothing like that! Barbara and I went out in the boat to scatter Freddie's ashes.' Lottie heard herself gabbling. 'But the swans started to chase us and Barbara panicked and, well, you can guess the rest. The boat went over and we fell in. Tyler insisted we came back here . . . well, obviously Barbara had to, because she's been living here . . . and we needed to shower and change into something dry. All my wet clothes are in a black bin bag in the kitchen. I'm taking them home now.' Rising hastily to her feet – her *big, bare* feet – Lottie discovered that her wet hair had left a huge damp patch on the green silk cushion she'd been resting against. 'I really didn't mean to fall asleep, it's just that so much has happened in the last couple of weeks. I think everything just all of a sudden caught up with me.'

'Oh, you poor thing.' Liana's expression had changed to one of sympathy. 'I'm so sorry, I knew I shouldn't have doubted you. Of course you couldn't help it. I know how it feels – I was exactly the same after Curtis died. You spend days not being able to sleep a wink then all of a sudden it comes over you without warning and you can't help yourself, you're just completely out for the count.'

Lottie nodded, hideously aware that in the moments before she'd dozed off, she'd been fantasising about being kissed by—

'Tyler,' said Liana. 'He was the one who got me through it. He made me realise my life wasn't over.' She smiled warmly at Lottie. 'And you've got Seb to help you. We're so lucky, aren't we? Look, if you want to go upstairs and sleep a bit longer, that's fine by me. I'll tell Tyler when he gets back. He'll understand.'

'No, I'm fine, I'll just shoot home and change then get back to work. After all, that's what I'm being paid for.' Lottie, hastening towards the door in Tyler's dressing gown, felt more ashamed of herself than ever. Was there anyone on the planet more forgiving and beautiful, more generous and guilt-inducing than Liana?

Chapter 57

Cressida was busy putting the finishing touches to an order for wedding invitations when – talk about a coincidence! – she happened to glance out of the window and saw her ex-husband's car pulling up outside the house.

Unusual, seeing as it was ten o'clock on a Wednesday morning. Even more unusually, Robert had Sacha with him. Sensing that something was up – oh, how marvellous if they'd booked a skiing holiday and had come to ask her if she'd have Jojo for a week before Christmas – Cressida put down her hot glue gun and hurried to the front door.

Five minutes later and the happy squiggle of anticipation in her stomach had been replaced by the dull weight of dread.

'You mean . . . you're actually moving to *Singapore*?' Cressida wondered if she had somehow misunderstood them. 'You're *all* moving to Singapore?'

'It's the most marvellous opportunity! This is what all the urgent meetings have been about, flying off to Paris at short notice, having to keep everything hush-hush!' Sacha, her eyes bright with triumph, said, 'Honestly, it was like being a secret agent! Being head-hunted is such a cloak and dagger business, you have no *idea*. Well, of course you don't have any idea, because I don't suppose much head-hunting goes on in the world of hand-made greetings cards! You've got glitter down the front of your jumper, by the way.' Fanatically neat and tidy herself, she indicated the incriminating area on the yellow sweater so Cressida could brush it off.

Cressida, her heart going like a punchbag in her chest, said, 'But . . . what about Jojo?'

'She's coming with us, of course. Oh, she'll settle down in no time. Singapore's a wonderful place to live, it's got everything a child could possibly want.'

But what about me? What about what *I* want? Unable to speak, Cressida listened to the buzzing in her ears and wondered if she was about to faint. How could Sacha and Robert whisk Jojo away from her? How could they *know* that she'd settle down in a strange country? Jojo was pale and freckly . . . her skin would burn . . . oh please, this couldn't be happening.

'Well, we just thought we'd drop by and let you know the news.' Robert beamed, pleased with himself. 'It's all jolly exciting stuff, isn't it? And the amount of money they'll be paying us . . . well, you wouldn't believe the package we've negotiated.' He gave Sacha a nudge as they both rose to leave. 'Enough to make her eyes water, eh, love?'

Sacha smoothed back her hair and said smugly to Cressida, 'Just goes to show how much they wanted us.'

Cressida wept unashamedly after they'd gone. Her heart felt as if it had been wrenched from her chest and stamped on. She was going to lose Jojo and it hurt so much she didn't know how she was going to bear it. Jojo was her surrogate child. This was like losing her own baby all over again.

The doorbell rang at four o'clock. Thinking it might be Jojo, Cressida took a deep breath and checked her face in the mirror before answering it.

Jojo wasn't on the doorstep. It was Robert and Sacha back again. The sense of anticlimax caused Cressida's shoulders to sag. What did they want now?

'Right, we'll come straight to the point,' Robert announced. 'One question. If Jojo wanted to stay in this country instead of coming with us to Singapore, would you be willing to become her legal guardian?'

What? *What?* 'I . . . er . . . I . . .' stammered Cressida.

'Yes or no,' Sacha said bluntly. 'That's all we need to hear. And no pressure either. It's entirely up to you.'

Yes or no? They were actually giving her the choice? Hastily, before they could change their minds and withdraw the offer, Cressida blurted out, 'Yes . . . yes . . . definitely YES!'

Sacha smiled and gave a brisk nod of satisfaction. 'Sure?'

'Yes . . . my *God* . . .' Beginning to tremble, Cressida was so overwhelmed she could have hugged them. OK, maybe not. 'I still can't believe it. Thank you *so much* . . .'

'That's excellent then. All sorted.' Robert rubbed his hands, just as he always did when concluding a successful deal. 'Now as you can imagine, we're pretty much rushed off our feet right now, lots to get organised. It would help us out if you could have Jojo for the next few days while we make a start on the arrangements.'

'Where is she?' Cressida couldn't wait. 'At home? Go and get her now!'

Robert and Sacha left. Less than twenty minutes later Sacha returned with Jojo in the car.

'Aunt Cress!' Jojo scrambled out of the passenger seat as Cressida rushed down the front path in her slippers. 'You said yes!'

Cressida, her heart bursting with love, threw her arms round Jojo. 'Oh sweetheart, of course I said yes! I'm so happy I don't know what to do with myself.'

'Right, well, I'll leave you to it.' Sacha's tone indicated that while some people might have nothing more important to do than dance around outside in their slippers, others had vital business to be getting on with.

'Bye, Mum. Thanks again.'

'Bye, darling. And good luck with the school concert.' Sacha was already busily revving the engine. 'What time does it start?'

It started at seven thirty; Cressida had had it written up on her kitchen calendar for weeks. Startled by Sacha's show of interest, she said, 'Will your mum be coming along to the concert?'

Both arms clasped lovingly round Cressida's waist, Jojo rolled her eyes. 'What do you think? In eight years she's never been to a single one of my school concerts. I can't honestly see her starting now, can you?'

Back inside the house Cressida discovered that, unbelievably, Sacha and Robert had broken the news of their move to Singapore to Jojo last night.

'I went berserk.' Jojo related what had happened. 'Well, not berserk – I'm not really the berserk type, am I? – but I told them I didn't want to go. I mean, can you really see me in Singapore? While Mum and Dad are working all hours heading up this new company? I mean, I don't mind flying out to see them during the school holidays, but I love living in England. All my friends are here. You're here. Everything's brilliant at school. I begged them to ask if I could stay with you, but they weren't sure you'd say yes. I wanted to phone you last night but they wouldn't let me. Mum said you were great as a childminder but actually having to take full responsibility for me might be too much to ask.'

From this, Cressida deduced that this morning's visit from Sacha and Robert had been designed to deliberately upset her, giving her the rest of the day in which to realise how much she would miss Jojo when she was gone. That way, when they turned up again in the evening and made their take-it-or-leave-it offer, she would be that much more likely to say yes.

Except they hadn't needed to do that because she would have agreed anyway. Cressida wondered if it was possible to feel happier than this. Stroking Jojo's thin face, she said joyfully, 'Oh sweetheart, I'm glad you went berserk.'

Jojo disappeared upstairs to shower off the mud from hockey earlier, and to text all her friends to let them know her big news. Cressida, congratulating herself on having caught up with her backlog of work, efficiently finished the last of the wedding invitations and parcelled them up ready for posting. In the kitchen, having checked the contents of the vegetable basket, she then set about making Jojo's favourite, cottage pie.

Jojo came flying downstairs as she was peeling and slicing the carrots.

'What are you doing?'

'Juggling while riding a unicycle.' Cressida threw a carrot from one hand to the other, then curtsied. 'What does it look like? I'm making a cottage pie.'

'Put the carrot down. We're not eating here. I've decided,' Jojo pronounced with an air of importance and a flourish, 'to take you out to dinner to celebrate you becoming my legal guardian. My treat. Although I don't actually have my purse with me so you'll have to lend me the money and I'll pay you back.' She shrugged. 'Sorry about that, but it's the thought that counts.'

'Absolutely.' Cressida was touched by the thought. 'That sounds wonderful. Where shall we go to celebrate?'

'Burger King.'

Ah.

'Lovely.' Cressida said it with good grace. As long as she and Jojo were together, what did it matter where they ate? She'd certainly rather share a plate of fries with Jojo in Burger King any day than a table at Le Manoir aux Quat' Saisons with Robert and Sacha.

'Go and get changed then. No point hanging around.' Bossily Jojo whisked the carrot from her grasp. 'I'm starving, aren't you?'

Cressida did as she was told and headed upstairs to change into her ballgown and tiara. OK, a clean blue fleece and jeans. She ran a brush through her hair, dabbed on some eye shadow and lipstick and belatedly remembered to reapply her deodorant by manoeuvring the roll-on stick up under her white T-shirt.

'Ready?' Jojo called up the stairs. 'Come on, let's go.'

Cressida looked at her watch. It was ten past five and they were heading out to dinner. At this rate they'd be home again by six.

'No, not this turning,' Jojo instructed as they headed into Cheltenham and Cressida indicated left. 'There's a new Burger King just opened. Carry straight on.'

'A new one?' Cressida obediently cancelled the indicator and stayed on the main road.

'This is my surprise. It's bigger,' Jojo proudly announced, 'and better. Everyone says it's brilliant.'

Cressida smiled at her enthusiasm. 'Can't wait.'

Several miles further on, Cressida said, 'We're coming up to the big roundabout. Which way now?'

'Hang on, wait till we get closer.' Jojo squinted through the windscreen as the enormous road sign loomed up at them out of the darkness. 'You have to turn right.'

'Sweetheart, that's for the motorway. Do you mean straight on?'

'No, definitely right. We just get on the motorway and off again at the next exit. Sorry.' Jojo was apologetic. 'Didn't I mention that? But it'll be worth it, I promise. My friends all say it's the best Burger King *ever*.'

Just as well there was petrol in the car. Taking a deep breath as she was overtaken by a huge articulated lorry, Cressida braced herself and turned onto the sliproad of the M5. She usually had to mentally gear herself up beforehand for motorway driving.

Once they were installed on the motorway and doing a steady (if wimpish) sixty miles an hour, Jojo took a tube of fruit gums out of her bag and offered one to Cressida. 'By the way, I lied about turning off at the next junction.'

'What?'

'The next junction,' Jojo repeated patiently, 'we won't be turning off there.'

Cressida was bewildered. 'We're not going to Burger King?'

'Oh yes. The thing is, we're going to the one in Chesterfield.'

'*What?* But that's—'

'Halfway between Newcastle and here,' Jojo said cheerfully. 'Exactly halfway, in fact. That's where we're meeting Tom and Donny.'

Chapter 58

By some miracle Cressida didn't jam her foot on the brake. Dazedly she said, 'No we aren't.'

Jojo beamed. 'Oh yes we are, as they say in all the best pantomimes. It's all arranged.'

Cressida really wished Jojo hadn't chosen to break this news to her as they were driving along the M5. 'But it *can't* be arranged. You've got school tomorrow. You can't miss school!'

'Oh, Aunt Cress, of course I can. It's called skiving off. Pulling a sickie. All you have to do is phone in tomorrow morning and tell them I've gone down with flu again. It's Thursday. I'll miss the concert tomorrow night – well, hooray, who cares about a stupid concert anyway? And then on Friday we break up for Christmas so nobody will be doing any work anyway. And after that it's the holidays, so really it couldn't work out better.'

Feeling winded and utterly stunned by this glib explanation, Cressida said, 'When did you decide this?'

'Ooh, about an hour ago. As soon as Mum and Dad left your place. It's a surprise,' Jojo said eagerly, 'to celebrate everything that's happened today. I thought you'd love it, after all the times we've made plans to meet Tom and Donny and it's all fallen through. It's like in my *Phew!* magazine, they said we have to take control of our lives and make things happen. So that's what I decided to do. Now are you going to have a fruit gum or not?'

'I don't know.' Faintly Cressida said, 'Does *Phew!* say I should have one?'

'*Phew!* says you should definitely have one.' Jojo smiled and passed her a red fruit gum.

'Does Tom know about this?'

'Of course he knows! Otherwise we'd get to Chesterfield and there wouldn't be anyone there to meet us, would there?'

Cressida's heart broke into a gallop at the prospect of actually . . . finally . . . *unbelievably* seeing Tom again. In Chesterfield, wherever that might be. 'But how . . . how did you . . . ?'

'I rang Donny. We text and email each other all the time. I told him the plan and we decided to go for it,' Jojo said easily. 'He told his dad that we were already on our way, so he had to set off straight away to meet up with us. Donny's going to have tonsillitis tomorrow, we decided. I don't know what Tom's going to have. Maybe food poisoning.'

This was too much to take in. 'They're taking the day off as well?'

'Duh, they kind of have to. But it doesn't matter, because we're making things happen and sometimes it's actually a *good* thing to just be spontaneous and take a couple of days off work.'

Was that something else *Phew!* recommended?

'So where are we staying?' said Cressida.

'Oh, we'll find a hotel in Chesterfield for tonight. Then tomorrow we'll go up to Newcastle.' Jojo was confident. 'I thought we could stay for a week.'

She was also thirteen.

'I have no clothes.' As she pointed this out, Cressida experienced the first stirrings of panic. 'No spare underwear, no toothbrush, *nothing*. And nor do you.'

'That's why it's going to be an adventure!'

'And I have a business to run . . .'

'You're up to date with your orders. Anyway, you deserve a rest.'

Oh Lord. 'But I haven't even sent off the invites I finished this afternoon. I was going to take them to the post office first thing tomorrow.'

'Lottie's got a spare key. Ask her to do it for you.' Jojo paused. 'Or we can go home now if that's what you want. I thought you'd be pleased that I'd done this, but if you don't want to see Tom and Donny again—'

'Oh sweetheart, it's not that!' Realising she was hurting Jojo's feelings – tonight of all nights – Cressida cried, 'I *am* pleased! If I'm honest, I'm panicking because I *do* want to see them again.' Another lorry overtook them as she reached for Jojo's hand and gave it a grateful squeeze. 'I'm just making silly excuses because I'm nervous. And I bet if we stop at the next service station they'll sell toothbrushes and . . . stuff.'

'Spare knickers,' Jojo said helpfully as her mobile phone beeped to let her know she had a text. 'It's from Donny, asking where we are.'

A sign whizzed past. 'Coming up to junction nine. The Tewkesbury turn-off.'

'They're at junction fifty-nine on the M1. Darlington.' Jojo looked up in amusement. 'And he says his dad's dead nervous about seeing you again.'

'What are you sending?' demanded Cressida as Jojo began texting in return. Beaming, Jojo held up the phone.

On the illuminated screen she'd put: 'Ah, aren't old people sweet? Mine 2!'

★   ★   ★

It was almost nine o'clock at night. After three and a half hours of driving and one short break at a service station they had arrived in Chesterfield. Jojo had the road atlas open across her knees and was on the phone now to Donny as they negotiated their separate ways towards the Taplow Road branch of Burger King. So far Cressida had had to stop the car three times to ask directions.

And now, finally, they had found it. There was the familiar logo as the brightly lit restaurant loomed ahead of them out of the darkness. Breathlessly turning into the busy car park, Cressida felt gloriously intrepid, like Indiana Jones finally discovering the Holy Grail. If only she had an Indiana Jones hat to cover her frazzled hair.

Oh Lord. A fresh wave of butterflies broke free in her chest. Why couldn't she be wearing something remotely flattering? Was the stray lipstick she'd found in the bottom of her bag too bright? She wasn't even wearing any foundation, for heaven's sake. At this rate the moment Tom clapped eyes on her he was going to run screaming out of the car park.

'Don't fuss,' said Jojo when Cressida had nervously parked between a filthy green van and a gleaming Audi. 'You're fine.'

'I'm not, I look a sight!' Peering frantically in the rear-view mirror, Cressida attempted to rearrange her fringe into some kind of order. Her fingers shook as she ruthlessly pinched colour – *ooch* – into her pale cheeks.

'OK, now listen to me. Donny and I have been texting each other for weeks. And if anyone knows, he does. Aunt Cress, Donny's dad wants to see you again every bit as much as you want to see him. He doesn't care whether or not you're wearing posh shoes and make-up. He'd be just as happy if you were wearing a gnome suit.'

Cressida wasn't so sure about that. She definitely wouldn't be overjoyed if Tom were to turn up wearing a gnome suit.

Beep-beep, went Jojo's mobile. Having read the text, she opened the passenger door. 'Right, me and Donny are going in for a burger. You two can join us when you're ready.'

Numbly Cressida nodded; it was nine o'clock on a hitherto normal Wednesday evening and she was here in *Chesterfield*. 'Thanks.'

Jojo paused halfway out of the car. 'Is that a sarcastic thanks?'

'No, sweetheart.' Oh, how she loved Jojo. 'It's a real thanks. You arranged a fantastic surprise.'

'Well, Donny helped too. We did it between us.'

Cressida was struck by a thought. 'Are you and Donny . . . ?'

'Urrgh, no way!' Jojo's eyes widened in disbelief. 'I wouldn't fancy Donny in a million *years*. He's a friend, that's all. Like in *Phew!* it's always saying how important it is to have boys who are friends because then you can chat to them and find out how the opposite sex ticks. Well, that's how it is with Donny and me. We're just mates who chat to each other.'

'That's great.' Smiling at Jojo, Cressida thought that sometimes *Phew!* did actually make sense.

Jojo headed into the restaurant to meet up with Donny. Cressida watched her run inside, then took a deep breath and climbed out of the car herself. Brrr, it was cold. On top of everything else she was going to be greeting Tom with watering eyes and a pink nose, which would really knock his socks—

'Hi, Cress.'

Turning, Cressida saw him standing twenty feet away, a green wool scarf wrapped twice round his neck and the collar of his overcoat pulled up around his ears. His hands were stuffed into his coat pockets and his breath hung in white clouds of condensation before him.

Cressida said, 'Fancy meeting you here.'

'Damn.' Tom moved towards her. 'I was going to ask you if you came here often.'

'Sorry.'

'Don't be. You're here.' Taking his hands out of his pockets he greeted her with a kiss on each cheek and Cressida felt how cold he was. It was so wonderful to see him again. She'd forgotten quite how much she loved the little lines fanning out from the corners of his eyes.

'What have our kids done to us, eh?' He shook his head.

'I know. I suppose it was the last thing you needed to hear this afternoon.'

'The last thing?' Tom's laughter lines deepened. 'It was the *best* thing I could have heard. I've already rung my boss and told him I'm taking a few days off work. The only problem is . . .'

'What?' Cressida's imagination instantly careered into overdrive: he had a girlfriend, he was gay, he'd booked a one-way trip to Mexico. Fearfully she said, 'Tell me.'

'OK. Well, Donny kind of sprang this on me.' Rubbing the back of his head, clearly embarrassed, Tom said, 'Tomorrow you're coming back to stay at our house. So the thing is, I have to warn you that it's not going to be what you'd call tidy. In fact it's a bit of a mess.'

Cressida blinked. 'That's the problem?'

'It's quite embarrassing, you know,' said Tom. 'You're going to think I'm a complete slob. When we get home you'll see last night's dishes still waiting to be washed up.'

'I have dishes in my sink,' said Cressida.

'And the living room carpet needs vacuuming.'

'Mine does too.'

'My ironing pile is spilling out of its basket.'

295

'Snap.'

'Come here.' Visibly relieved, Tom drew her towards him until their misty breath mingled and melted together. 'I suppose we ought to join Jojo and Donny. But before we do, can I just say how much I'm looking forward to the next week?'

He kissed her. Cressida stopped worrying about her messy hair and lack of make-up. As customers left the restaurant and headed past them back to their cars, she kissed him back and whispered joyfully, 'Me too.'

Chapter 59

Mario wasn't looking forward to next week. Or the one after that. He'd quietly planned to carry on at work without drawing attention to it but Jerry had put the kibosh on that. Fat, stubbly-chinned Jerry was now impossibly smug as a result of having found himself a skinny, smooth-chinned girlfriend. Studying the office holiday planner up on the wall yesterday, he'd said over his shoulder, 'Blimey, you've still got twelve days to use up before the end of the year. Better get on and take them, mate. They won't let you carry them over.'

Mario, studying his computer screen, had said casually, 'I'm not going to bother. Jerry, have you seen last month's sales figures for—'

'Whoa! Hold your horses just one cotton-pickin' minute there, boy.' Jerry's new girlfriend was a huge line-dancing fan and had been dragging him along to classes.

'Jerry, I'm really not bothered about taking time off work.'

'Now *that* is the saddest thing I ever heard.' Jerry was incredulous. 'You and Amber broke up months ago. I can't believe you haven't got over it yet and found yourself a replacement. I mean, look at me and Pam! She's changed my life!'

She'd certainly made him an annoyingly cheerful person. Mario wondered if that was a good enough reason to sack someone.

'You need to get yourself a new bird,' Jerry went on confidently. Bird, *ugh*. 'That'll sort you out. And what kind of loser comes into work when he doesn't even have to?'

'So I stay at home and do what exactly? Make model aeroplanes?' Mario gestured out of the window at the grey sky and bundled-up passers-by hurrying past in hats and scarves. 'Because it's too bloody cold to go out and fly them.'

'You're depressed, that's what you are. You ain't even thinking straight, pardner.' Pointing a chunky index finger at Mario, Jerry said, 'Get a grip, man. You don't have to stay at home! You can buy a plane ticket and fly off to some place where it isn't cold enough to freeze the whatsits off a brass monkey. Get yourself off to somewhere with a bit of life to it and cast your eye over a few babes in bikinis. Treat yourself to a fortnight of mindless sex, man. Tenerife, that'll do the trick.'

'No thanks.' Mario suddenly felt incredibly tired. He didn't want a holiday and a fortnight of mindless sex. He just wanted Amber.

Amber was wearing a calf-length dark blue velvet dress, neat shoes and discreet pearl studs in her ears. She looked as if she might be on her way to church.

She was also looking pretty startled.

'Sorry,' said Mario. 'Maybe I should have rung first, but I needed to see you. Can I come in?'

It was seven o'clock in the evening and Jerry's suggestion had been dancing through his brain all afternoon. Finally he had made up his mind and driven over to Tetbury.

From the expression on Amber's face he guessed she'd have preferred it if he hadn't.

'Mario. Actually, I'm on my way out.'

'Just five minutes. It's important.' God, she had no idea how important.

'Quentin's going to be here in five minutes.'

'Where's he taking you? To the Tory Party conference?' As soon as he said it Mario knew he'd made a huge mistake.

Amber's eyes flashed. 'To meet his parents if you must know. They're quite elderly. I wanted to make a good impression.'

Mario hated it that making a good impression on Quentin's parents was important to her. 'You don't need to. Listen, you know how I feel about you. I *love* you. Come away with me.' Reaching for Amber's hand he said, 'I've got two weeks' holiday to use up, starting from now. Let me take you somewhere amazing. We'll have the best time ever, I promise.'

Amber said, 'Mario, are you mad? I'm not coming on holiday with you.'

'Please.'

'I mean, apart from anything else, it's *December*.' She emphasised the month as if it might have escaped his notice. 'And I have a busy salon to run.'

'The other girls can cover for you. I'll pay them to do it.' He'd already thought this through. 'I'll pay double.'

Ignoring the offer, Amber raised an eyebrow. 'And what would I tell Quentin?'

Recklessly Mario said, 'Oh, I don't know, how about telling him you're going on holiday with your friend Mandy. That's what you usually do, isn't it?'

Bong. If the jibe about her outfit had been wrong, this was worse. Tumbleweed rolled past. Amber's jaw tightened and in that moment he knew he'd lost her.

298

'You shouldn't have come, Mario. Quentin will be here any minute now. He's taking me to meet his parents and—'

'That's why you're dressed as Margaret Thatcher?'

'What I choose to wear is none of your business,' Amber retorted.

'You don't even look like you.' He indicated the understated make-up, the neatly tied-back hair. 'Did you ever see *The Stepford Wives*?'

'I'm not going to argue. You live your life the way you want to live it,' said Amber, 'and I'll stick to mine, OK? Now please go.'

'Wait. I'm sorry.' Mario began to panic. 'I'm only saying it because I love you.'

'You love everyone. That's your trouble.' Amber was closing the door on him. 'Never mind, I'm sure you'll find someone else to take on holiday. Have a nice time now. Bye.'

Mario woke up the next morning and groaned. He'd well and truly done it this time. In fact, where the hell *was* he? Blinking and rolling over in the double bed he blearily took in pink and cream flowered wallpaper, matching ruffled curtains and a raspberry-pink satin eiderdown that had slid to the ground. Not whilst he and whoever had been doing something sexually athletic, he sincerely hoped.

Someone was moving around in the kitchen; he could hear a kettle being boiled, the clinking of tea being made. Shit, he couldn't believe he'd got himself into this situation again. How could he have been so—

'Jesus!' Mario exclaimed as the bedroom door swung open to reveal a horrible sight.

Jerry, resplendent in rumpled Bart Simpson boxers and carrying a mug of tea, retorted, 'Not looking so hot yourself, sonny Jim.'

Mario did a lightning rethink. His last memory of yesterday evening was of ringing Jerry and arranging to meet up with him and Cowgirl Pam after their line-dancing class. He ran a bemused hand through his hair.

'Where am I?'

'Spare room.'

'What? *Your* spare room?' The last time Mario had slept here the walls had been bare and the only items of furniture had been a never-used exercise bike and an old ironing board.

Jerry looked abashed. 'It was a bit of a mess before. Pam persuaded me to redecorate. She chose all the wallpaper and stuff.'

The spare bedroom now resembled a giant pair of old ladies' frilly bloomers. The next time Jerry told him he was a sad bastard, he'd be able to retaliate. Holding out a hand for his tea, Mario said, 'Did I have a lot to drink?'

'Put it this way. The bottle of Scotch I bought my dad for Christmas is now an empty bottle of Scotch. And I had to confiscate your phone.'

Hmm, that rang a distant bell. Mario dimly remembered fighting a losing battle to keep it. 'Go on then. Tell me why.'

'You kept ringing Amber. Well, trying to ring her. She had it switched off after the first time.' Jerry grinned and scratched his sizeable stomach. 'But you left a couple of messages for her, something about how you hoped she was enjoying the Tory Party conference.'

'Oh God.'

'That was only the start of it. You had a few things to say about Quentin as well. And his parents. Oh yes, and you told Amber you hadn't had sex with anyone for months, and you loved her, and she was making the biggest mistake of her life staying with a boring old fart who—'

'Stop it, stop it! Don't tell me any more!'

Jerry looked pleased with himself. 'That's why we wrestled your phone away from you.'

'Oh fuck.' Mario had his head in his hands. 'Fuck, *fuck*.'

Modestly, Jerry said, 'You can say thank you if you like.'

'Right then! Lovely! And when do you want to go?'

The travel agent was wearing an acid-yellow blouse and an oh-so-perky smile. She spoke in exclamation marks, which was a bit much at nine thirty in the morning when you had a headache the size of Cheltenham Town Hall.

'Today,' said Mario.

'Today!! Ooh, how *exciting*! So, whereabouts in Tenerife? Somewhere quite lively, I'm guessing!'

'How about we just see what's available and then I'll decide.' Mario nodded at the computer screen on her desk.

'Of course! Let's do that! Now, how many of you are going?'

Mario made an unwise attempt at humour. 'How many of me? Just the one. I'm the only me I know.'

'You mean . . . oh, I'm sorry.' The travel agent looked momentarily surprised. 'You're actually going away on holiday *on your own*?'

'Yes. That's what I'm doing.'

Hastily she recovered herself. 'Well, that's great!'

'Not really. My girlfriend and I broke up.' Now why had he even said that?

'Oh, poor *you*.' Eyeing him flirtatiously the travel agent said, 'Actually, I'm single too. So if you ever feel like meeting up when you get back from Tenerife, you know where to find me!'

Mario had no intention of meeting up with her when he got back, but he forced himself to smile. 'Thanks for the offer. Now could we—'

'My name's Trina, by the way!'

'OK. To be honest, Trina, I'm in a bit of a rush here. Could we just get on and find me somewhere to go?'

'So that's it,' Mario concluded as Lottie juggled baked potatoes out of the oven and onto a row of plates. 'I'm flying out tonight. Everything's booked. I should have asked you if that's OK. Sorry, I didn't think. Seeing Amber again last night just kind of knocked me for six. Am I messing up any plans?'

'Stop making out you're indispensable. We're fine.' Slicing the baked potatoes in half, Lottie scalded her fingers yet again. 'And the kids'll understand. You need this break. Who knows,' she added brightly, 'you might meet the girl of your dreams!'

Mario's answering smile was bleak, like a hospital patient attempting to be polite when he hears it's lamb stew for lunch. Taking a folded sheet of paper out of his jacket pocket along with his phone, he said, 'Right, I've written down all the details of where I'm staying. If you need to get hold of me, this is the number of the—'

'Can't I just ring you?'

'I'm leaving my phone here.' Mario pushed it across the kitchen table towards her. 'You can look after it for me. That way it won't be so easy to make a dick of myself if I have a few drinks and decide to phone Amber again.' Wryly he added, 'Well, not more of a dick of myself than I already have.'

'OK.' Lottie nodded as she piled tuna and sweetcorn into one bowl and chilli with sour cream into another. Then she put down the chilli pan, made her way round the kitchen table and gave Mario a hug, because she hated seeing him so down.

'Is dinner ready? Urrgh, they're hugging. Don't do that, it's sexy,' ordered Nat.

'I've just realised,' Mario said during dinner, 'I'm going to miss your Christmas concerts.'

'I'm not bothered.' Nat shrugged. 'I'm only a sheep. I get to look in the manger and say, "Look, it's the Baby Jesus, *baaaa*."'

'You'll miss my show too.' Past the age of Nativity plays, Ruby's Christmas concerts were rather jollier affairs. 'I'm singing and dancing and everything.'

'Oh Rubes, I'm sorry.' Stricken, Mario reached for her hand.

'But we'll be there cheering you on,' Lottie jumped in quickly. 'Me and Nat. And we'll take loads of photos, won't we?'

Her dark eyes huge, Ruby said, 'Will Seb come too? I'd like it if he was there.'

'We'll ask him.' Lottie experienced a warm glow in her stomach because in her children's eyes Seb could do no wrong; since his return from Dubai their relationship had gone from strength to strength. 'If he doesn't have to work I'm sure he'll want to come and see you.'

Ruby gave Mario's hand a consoling squeeze. 'That's all right then. Don't worry, Daddy, we'll have Seb instead. Do they have donkeys in Tenerife?'

Relieved, Mario said, 'I'm sure they do.'

'So you'll be able to ride them on the beach like me and Nat did when we went to Weston.'

'You might find a girlfriend,' Nat added helpfully. 'Then you won't be all on your own.'

Ruby spoke through a mouthful of tuna and baked potato. 'Oh Daddy, you might be lonely. If we didn't have school we could have come with you to keep you company.'

'And I would've lent you my GameBoy.' Nat, ever practical, shook his head regretfully at Mario. 'But not for two whole weeks.'

Chapter 60

Mario had got away in the nick of time. Overnight, temperatures plummeted and the first snow of winter fell, sending Nat and Ruby into paroxysms of delight.

Particularly when Seb arrived on Saturday lunchtime in his new 4x4 with two toboggans in the boot. Ruby, lovingly stroking the sleek red toboggan, said, 'All we've ever had before was tea trays.'

'Poor deprived children. Come on, get your coats on,' ordered Seb. 'We're going to test these babies out on Beggarbush Hill.'

Now, screaming like banshees, Nat and Ruby were racing down the hill on their toboggans along with a cluster of other children bundled up against the cold. Beggarbush Hill was *the* place to come for anyone who enjoyed travelling over snow at warp speed.

'They won't have any teeth left,' Lottie marvelled as Nat, using his wellington-booted feet as brakes, threw himself off the toboggan seconds before it collided with a bigger boy already lying spreadeagled in the snow.

'Kids are tough. They bounce. Now, are you going to be a lily-livered woolly-wimp or will you be giving it a go yourself?' Seb was wearing an idiotic red and yellow jester's hat and a fluorescent orange ski jacket already dusted with snow.

Beggarbush Hill was notoriously steep and Nat and Ruby had shot down it like lightning. Hesitating for a fraction of a second, Lottie said, 'I've never been on a toboggan like this before. They're quite . . . aerodynamic, aren't they?'

'Chicken.' Seb seized on the hesitation with glee. 'Feeble female. Wimp.'

Lottie hated being called a wimp. She prided herself on giving anything a try. 'I didn't say I *wouldn't* do it. I'm just pointing out that I haven't *ridden* on a—'

'You're probably too old anyway,' said Seb. 'Too weak and feeble and downright past it. Maybe you should stick to knitting.'

'Mum, these toboggans are *wicked*.' Ruby had arrived, pink-cheeked and panting, back at the top of the hill. 'Did you see how *fast* we went?'

'Uh-uh.' Seb wagged a finger. 'Don't mention the f-word. Your mother doesn't do fast. Between you and me, I think bowls might be more her thing.'

'Oh, give me that.' Having been goaded enough, Lottie seized the toboggan from Ruby. How hard could it be anyway?

'Yay!' Ruby clapped her mittened hands. 'Mum's having a go!'

'But she's only a weak and wussy female,' Seb pointed out, 'so don't expect her to do more than two miles an hour.'

Right, that was it. Lottie threw down the toboggan with a flourish and positioned herself on it, feet either side of the runners. Fearlessly she beckoned Seb over and said, 'Give me a push.'

Ruby, unfastening her cycle helmet, said, 'Mum, do you want to borrow—'

'No!' Ha, safety helmets were for cissies. 'Come on, big push, as hard as you can . . . *wheeeeeeeeeee*! . . .'

It was nothing like sitting on an old-fashioned wooden toboggan. This one was made of sleek moulded plastic with go-faster stainless steel runners. And it *was* going faster, Lottie discovered. Yikes, her eyes were streaming, the icy air was whistling in her ears and her hair was whipping across her face. Clinging onto the steering rope for grim life, she juddered over a patch of bumpy ground and whipped past a Labrador having a pee against a tree. This was like being on a scary fairground ride without the safety bar across your lap. She was zipping past people so fast, they were little more than a blur . . . OK, it was only Beggarbush Hill, any second now she'd reach the bit where the ground began to level out and you gradually reduced speed before coasting to a halt at the bot—

THUNNKKK, the toboggan hit a rock sticking out of the snow. Lottie, catapulted into the air, discovered how it felt to be fired from a cannon. Arms and legs flailing wildly, she let out a scream that echoed all the way across the valley before coming to an abrupt halt as she landed and all the air was knocked – *whooosh* – from her lungs.

But only the scream came to an abrupt halt; Lottie continued to tumble over and over, the world cartwheeling dizzily past her eyes until with a final *flummpp* she landed – and stayed – face down in the snow.

'Oh, pphuck.' Lottie let out a groan, spitting snow and blood from her mouth and feeling sick with the pain. Everything hurt so much she didn't know where to start.

'Mummy! Are you all right?' Nat was the first to reach her. Kneeling at her side he said, 'Are you hurt?'

'Just a tiny bit.' The pain in Lottie's lower back was excruciating. Turning her head to smile weakly at Nat, she said, 'Is Seb on his way down?'

'Yes, he's coming now with Ruby.' Nat reached out and stroked a strand of wet hair away from Lottie's eye, a gesture that brought a lump to her throat. 'Poor Mummy, you should have worn a crash helmet.'

Lottie nodded. Ironically the one part of her body that wasn't screaming in agony was her head.

'Mummy!' This time it was Ruby, skidding to a halt with her hand in Seb's. 'You were *flying*!'

'I know.' Lottie winced. 'I was there.'

'Talk about attention-seeking.' Crouching beside her, Seb said cheerfully, 'I think your mum's hoping someone's caught it on video so she can sell it to one of those TV programmes.' He gave Lottie a hearty pat on the back. 'OK now? Need a hand getting up?'

Getting *up*?

'I hate to sound like a feeble female,' said Lottie, 'but I think you're going to have to call an ambulance.'

By the time Lottie was finally settled in her hospital bed and the doctor had left to write up his notes, it was six in the evening. Seb and the children, allowed back onto the ward at last, clumped in in their snow clothes and wellies. Nat and Ruby, eyeing the intravenous drip and the plaster cast, treated Lottie with new respect.

The pain radiating from Lottie's back was still intense, but hospital-strength painkillers were doing their bit to take the edge off it. She kissed Ruby and Nat then looked at Seb. 'The doctor's just told me I'm probably going to be in here for a week. The tests showed a haematoma on one of my kidneys. It's a kind of bruise or bleed or something. Anyway, I have to stay in bed until it clears up.'

Seb looked surprised. 'A week. Bloody hell.'

Bloody hell indeed. One short toboggan ride and here she was, parked up in Cheltenham General with a broken left foot, a badly sprained right wrist, several bruised ribs and one damaged kidney.

And a partridge in a pear tree.

'The problem is, the kids.' Lottie had been unable to think of anything else since discovering she was being admitted. 'Mario's in Tenerife. Cressida's up in Newcastle so she isn't able to look after them. If you could go back to the cottage and find the phone number Mario left, I can call and tell him to come home, but I don't know *what's* going to happen tonight.'

'Hey, don't panic.' Seb sat on the edge of the bed. 'There must be someone else you can ask. How about the other mothers from school?'

'I had a few phone numbers in a notebook I kept in my bag.' Lottie cursed herself for not being more organised. 'But then my bag was stolen last year and I never got round to collecting the numbers all over again. I didn't expect this to happen . . . oh God, what a time for Mario to be away.'

'OK. No problem,' said Seb. 'I'll take them.'

'What?' Lottie's heart leapt – Seb had already told her he had an important business dinner tonight, which was why she hadn't dared ask him
before. 'But what about . . . ?'

'I'll just have to cancel it, won't I? These two can come and stay with
me.' He ruffled Nat's hair and broke into a grin. 'How about it then, kids?
Fancy that? Or would you rather spend the night in some old bus shelter?'

'We'll stay with you,' Nat said happily. 'Can we play Monopoly?'

'Maybe. Ruby, how about you?'

Ruby looked hopeful. 'Scrabble?'

Oh, the relief. Feeling the weight of responsibility fall away, Lottie smiled
up at Seb and whispered, 'Thank you.' Then, turning her attention to Nat
and Ruby she added, 'And you two have to promise to behave yourselves.'

Nat was offended. 'We always do.'

'OK. Now you'll need the key to the cottage.' She indicated the bedside
locker where her bag was stowed. 'And could you drop by Hestacombe
House and let Tyler know what's happened? And Mario's phone number
is on a piece of paper in the kitchen somewhere. I think it's on the dresser.'

'I'll give him a call,' said Seb. 'You get some rest now. We'll be in to see
you in the morning.'

'What would I do without you?' Lottie tried not to flinch as he leaned
over to kiss her, his hand brushing her badly bruised shoulder.

Seb winked. 'I know. I'm a saint.'

This was above and beyond the call of duty. As he drove back to Kingston
Ash, Seb mulled over the problem; basically, the timing couldn't have been
worse. Lottie was great and he was extremely fond of her kids, but to have
this happen today of all days was just a complete pain. Karina – heavenly
Karina – had flown in from Dubai for the weekend and he'd already made
his excuses to Lottie, explaining that he had a meeting tonight to secure
sponsorship for the next polo tournament.

And now he'd told her he'd cancel the meeting in order to look after
Nat and Ruby instead. Well, what else could he have done under the
circumstances? Called social services and asked them to take the kids for
the weekend?

Plus, what with being the one who'd brought along the toboggans and
persuaded Lottie to have a go, he couldn't help feeling slightly responsible.

At that moment a plan began to unfold in his mind. Seb tapped his
fingers against the steering wheel and smiled to himself; the night might
not turn out to be a complete wash-out after all.

'Seb?' Next to him in the car Nat said excitedly, 'This is like an adventure, isn't it? Wouldn't it be brilliant if Maya could come and stay too?'

'It would be brilliant, but she's in London with her mum. Maybe next time,' said Seb as he pulled into the snowy driveway. 'OK, here we are. Don't forget your bags, kids.'

'Seb?' Nat exchanged a hopeful look with Ruby. 'Do we have to brush our teeth at your house?'

Seb grinned, because Maya was just the same. 'Are you serious? Of course you don't have to brush your teeth.'

Nat and Ruby were in the living room setting up the Monopoly board and painstakingly sorting out the money. Making sure the kitchen door was shut, Seb rang Karina's number. She answered on the third ring.

'Change of plan,' Seb announced before briefly explaining what had happened.

'Oh, for God's *sake*!' Karina wailed. 'I don't believe it! I've come *all* this way—'

'Hey, hey,' Seb's tone was soothing. 'Let's not get our knickers in a twist.'

'Easy for you to say, you bastard. I'm not wearing any. I'm in the sodding bath, getting ready for *you*.'

'Listen.' He shook his head. 'What other choice did I have? There wasn't anyone else to look after them.'

'Isn't that what social services are for?'

'They're terrific kids. We're just about to play a game of Monopoly.'

'Whoop-dee-doo.'

'And then I'll be putting them to bed.' Seb paused then added meaningfully, 'Up in the spare bedroom, right at the top of the house. They'll be going to bed at . . . ooh, around nine o'clock, at a guess.'

Karina perked up in an instant. 'And then you'll come over to the hotel?'

Seb shook his head in amusement. 'Bloody hell, darling, you can tell you don't have kids. Abandon them like that and you tend to get arrested. But like I said, they'll be fast asleep by nine thirty. And there's nothing to stop you hopping in a taxi and coming over here.'

Karina sounded as if she was smiling. 'You drive a hard bargain, babe.'

'It'll be worth it.'

'Got any stuff?'

Seb grinned; he'd paid a visit to his dealer only yesterday. 'What did I just tell you, sweetie? I said it'd be worth it.'

Chapter 61

Ruby couldn't sleep. Playing Monopoly with Nat and Seb had been brilliant, especially beating Seb, but as soon as nine o'clock had come around he had put them to bed in the attic bedroom and now she was feeling a bit funny. It was sheets and blankets for a start, not a duvet like she was used to. And Seb had said he was going to bed, but he wasn't; earlier a car had pulled up outside and now she could hear noises and voices downstairs that didn't sound like the television.

It was ten fifteen. In the twin bed next to hers Nat was fast asleep. Propelled partly by thirst and partly by curiosity, Ruby slipped out of bed and silently opened the bedroom door. On the way downstairs it occurred to her that maybe the visitor was Maya, that Seb had arranged for her to join them for the weekend as a surprise.

The hall floor was cold beneath her bare feet. The living room door was firmly shut but there was definitely someone else in there with Seb. Tiptoeing over to the door in her blue pyjamas, Ruby crouched down and peeped through the keyhole.

Oh no, no, that couldn't be right. Jerking away in horror, then needing to double-check to prove to herself that she hadn't imagined it, Ruby looked again. Seb was on the sofa with a woman, and the woman was wearing her underwear and Seb, who didn't have his shirt on, was leaning forward over the coffee table with something that looked like a straw up his nose.

This was drugs, Ruby was almost sure. She'd seen people doing that sniffing thing on television. Then she froze in horror as she stepped back and one of the floorboards creaked.

Inside the room, the woman said, 'What was that noise?'

Ruby, her heart thumping, melted into the dark space beneath the stairs. Moments later she heard the living room door open. Finally Seb said, 'It's OK, there's no one out here.'

The woman giggled. 'If it's those kids, just lock them in the cellar.'

'Don't worry. They're asleep. Unlike me . . .' Seb purred before closing the door again.

From where she was hiding, Ruby saw Seb's mobile phone on the spindly-legged table diagonally across the hall from her. Darting out, she grabbed it and raced up the staircase.

'Mummy . . . Mummy . . .' Back in the safety of the attic bedroom, rocking on her knees, Ruby managed to find Lottie's name on the list of favourites and rang her mother's number. 'Answer the phone, oh *please* answer the phone . . .'

But the message service kicked in and Ruby felt her eyes fill with hot tears. Clutching the mobile tightly she waited for the Beep then whispered, 'Mummy? Are you there? I wanted to . . . it's just . . .' She broke off, wiped her wet cheeks with the back of her hand and said in a wobbly voice, 'I want to go home.'

Lottie couldn't work out if she was dozing off or actually dreaming when she heard a female voice saying, 'He won't go away until he's seen you.'

Lottie opened her eyes and saw the nurse beside her bed. 'Excuse me?'

'Your boss. Tyler, is that his name? I told him visiting hours were over but he's quite insistent. I said he could pop in for five minutes if it's all right with you.'

The nurse had a furtive look on her face, indicating that she was bending the rules.

'Do I look terrible?' said Lottie.

'Honestly? Yes.'

'Oh well. Fine, send him in.'

When Tyler made his way up the ward, Lottie guessed how he'd been able to persuade the staff nurse to bend the rules. He was wearing a dinner jacket and a dazzling white dress shirt, and a bow tie was dangling from his jacket pocket.

'Hey, you look awful,' Tyler announced.

The silver-tongued charmer.

'Thanks. You too. Still working as a nightclub bouncer, I see.'

'We only got home thirty minutes ago.' Keeping his voice low so as not to disturb the other sleeping patients, he pulled up a chair. 'Found the note pushed through the letterbox, but all it said was that you'd had an accident and were in hospital, and that you'd be off work for a few weeks. I was going frantic, not knowing which hospital you were in or what was wrong with you.' He paused. 'What *is* wrong with you?'

Lottie told him, moved by his concern and the efforts he'd made to track her down. It was a comfort to see him. Well, considerably more than a comfort but some things were better left unsaid.

'So where are Ruby and Nat?' Tyler asked when she'd finished.

'Staying at Seb's place in Kingston Ash. He's been brilliant. In fact he may have left a message for me, letting me know if he managed to get through to Mario.' Pointing with her drip-free hand, Lottie said, 'My phone's in the locker but we're not allowed to have them switched on in here. Could you take it outside and see if there's any word from Seb or Mario?'

More relieved than he'd been letting on that Lottie was OK, Tyler left the ward. Outside in the freezing night air, Tyler saw that there was one message from Seb.

Except it wasn't.

He listened in silence to Ruby's stumbling, tear-choked words. And knew that there was no way in the world he could pass this message on to Lottie.

Without hesitation he rang Seb's mobile. On the fifth ring it was answered. Evidently having seen whose phone the call was coming from, Ruby whispered with a heartbreaking tremor in her voice: 'Mummy?'

'Hey, Ruby, your mom's not allowed to make calls from the ward. This is Tyler.' He said it as gently as he could, as if she wouldn't already have guessed the moment he opened his mouth. 'Now are you OK? You sounded pretty upset when you left your message. Because if there's any kind of problem I can come straight over and pick you and Nat up.'

The silence hung between them. He was the Enemy. He knew that only too well and Ruby knew it too. Finally she said in a stiff little voice, 'No, it's all right,' and hung up.

Tyler stayed where he was under the outside light, trying to figure out what he should do now. Not tell Lottie, that was for sure; she'd go out of her mind with worry. But Ruby's voice had betrayed more than just simple homesickness. And why wasn't Seb answering his own phone? Should he be calling the police or—

The phone rang again. His heart in his mouth, Tyler answered it.

'Yes,' whispered Ruby, her voice quavering.

A few flakes of snow drifted down. Tyler said, 'You want me to come and fetch you?'

'Yes. Will you be here soon?'

Tyler exhaled with relief. 'Don't you worry, sweetheart, I'm on my way. Now listen, I know you're in Kingston Ash but I don't know which house. Are you on the main road through the village?'

'Yes, we're up in the attic bedroom. I can see the road from the window.'

'That's great. OK, give me ten minutes then as soon as you see a car, start switching the bedroom light off and on so I'll know where you are. Got that?'

'Yes.'

'Good girl. Is Nat with you?'

'Yes.'

'And Seb? Is he there in the house?'

'Yes.' Ruby's voice was wobbling again. 'He's downstairs with . . . someone else.'

Tyler's jaw tightened. 'OK, now you two just hang on in there. I'm on my way. Don't worry about a thing.'

''Kay. Bye.'

Back on the ward he found Lottie dozing again, her dark hair spread out over the pillow, her cut lip swollen, the bruises on her bare arms already spectacular. The temporary plaster cast on her left leg was sticking out from under the bedclothes and her right arm, swathed in bandages, rested across her stomach. As ever, the sight of her caused something inside him to quicken.

'No messages,' Tyler said quietly, causing her eyes to flicker open. 'Mario'll probably call in the morning. Right, I'm off. I may as well take your phone with me.'

'Fine.' Sleepily Lottie smiled at him. 'Thanks for coming over. Sorry about work.'

He'd never wanted to kiss anyone so badly in his life, and was ashamed of himself for even letting the thought cross his mind. Right now he had a more important task on his hands.

'Don't worry about work. You take care of yourself. Everything's going to be fine,' said Tyler.

He hoped.

It was starting to snow again properly now as he approached the village of Kingston Ash. Carefully he manoeuvred the car along the slippery road, keeping an eye out all the time for an upstairs light being switched on and off.

Moments later he rounded the bend past the church gates and saw what he was looking for. The house, one of the biggest in the village, had a gleaming 4x4 parked on the driveway. More importantly, the light in one of the attic bedrooms was switching on and off, illuminating two small figures framed in the window.

Tyler made his way to the front door and rang the bell.

Nothing.

He rang it again.

Finally he heard footsteps and the rattle of keys. The door opened a couple of inches and there was Seb, barefoot and tousle-haired, wearing nothing but a pair of jeans.

'Hi. Lottie asked me to come and pick up the kids.'

Seb laughed. '*What?*'

'You don't need to keep them any more.' Tyler could tell at once that Seb was sky-high on something. 'I'm here to take them off your hands.'

'They're asleep. And . . . how can I put this? . . . they hate your guts. Goodbye.' Seb, still laughing wildly, attempted to slam the door shut but Tyler already had his foot in the way and it ricocheted back on him. Caught off guard, Seb staggered sideways. The doors to the kitchen and dining room were open. Pushing past him, Tyler made for the only one that was closed.

'Jesus Christ, who are you?' shrieked a blonde girl, naked but for the man's shirt she was clutching in front of her. 'Get the fuck out of here, I'm calling the police!'

'Excellent.' Taking in at a glance the white powder scattered across the glass-topped coffee table and the matching white rings around her nostrils, Tyler said pleasantly, 'Tell them to bring the sniffer dogs – they'll think it's Christmas.' Closing the door, leaving the girl gaping in shock, he turned and saw Ruby and Nat huddled together at the top of the stairs. Gesturing for them to join him he said, 'OK, you two, let's get out of here.'

'You bastard,' hissed Seb, 'coming over here and fucking up my life. I know why you've done this, it's because you're—'

'Don't try it,' Tyler warned.

Ignoring the warning, Seb launched himself with fists flying. Catching first one wrist then the other and twisting them up behind his back until he was yelping like a dog, Tyler bundled Seb out through the front door and into the garden. One clean punch to the jaw sent him flying into a snow-covered flowerbed where he lay groaning while Tyler ushered Nat and Ruby past him and into the car.

Then Tyler went back and stood over Seb, still boiling with fury but willing himself not to beat him to a bloody pulp.

'You're not going to see Lottie again. Don't even try to phone her. And if she ever claps eyes on you,' said Tyler, 'I'd advise you to run for your life. She *trusted* you to look after her children.'

'OK, OK. Jesus, it's fucking cold down here.' Still lying bare-chested and flat on his back in the snow, Seb said blearily, 'You've got what you wanted. I hope that makes you happy.' He held out an arm. 'Just give me a hand up, will you? Before I freeze to death?'

Tyler viewed him with distaste. 'I don't think so. Get yourself up. Or better still, freeze to death.'

Chapter 62

When Kingston Ash was behind them, Tyler stopped the car and turned round to look at Nat and Ruby on the back seat. It was at this moment he realised that if he'd been expecting an iota of gratitude he was going to be disappointed.

Luckily he hadn't.

'OK, I'm going to take you back to my place. Hestacombe House,' Tyler added, in case they thought he meant Fox Cottage.

'I want to see Mum,' said Ruby.

'I know, I know you do, but she's asleep now. And they wouldn't let you onto the ward. So we can't—'

'I'm not staying at your house.' Nat, his tone final, was gazing fixedly out of the window.

Breathe deeply. Patience. 'It won't just be me. Liana's there too.'

Nat folded his arms. 'Still not doing it.'

'Well, you don't have a lot of choice,' Tyler pointed out. 'What with being seven. Ruby, tell him.'

Ruby's dark eyes were expressionless. 'I don't want to stay at your house either. Just leave us at the hospital and we'll sit in the waiting room till Mum wakes up.'

Oh, for crying out loud.

'Now listen to me. I didn't just *kidnap* you,' said Tyler. 'You were the one who phoned me, remember? You asked me to come and fetch you.'

'I didn't,' Nat retorted. 'I didn't want anyone to come and get me. I was asleep until *she* woke me up.'

'Don't *poke* me.' Ruby gave Nat a shove in return.

'So what do you want me to do? Turn the car around and take you back?'

Silence.

'Tell me,' Tyler persisted. 'I'm interested. Is that really what you want?'

Finally, in a low voice, Ruby muttered, 'No.'

'But we don't want to go back to your house either,' Nat repeated stubbornly.

'OK, but I have to warn you, your options are pretty limited. Your dad's in Tenerife. And Lottie tells me her friend Cressida's not around. So do you want me to ask Ben and Harry Jenkins' mother if you can share their bunk beds? Or, let me see, would you rather stay with Ted from the shop? Or, hang on, what's the name of that teacher your mom's so scared of? Miss Bat-something,' said Tyler. 'Would she take you in, d'you think?'

More silence.

Nat said, 'We'll stay at the hospital.'

'You won't, because someone would call the police and you'd both be arrested.' Tyler sighed as the snow began to fall more heavily, clogging up the windscreen. 'Right, this is my final offer. Tomorrow we'll sort out a better solution but just for tonight you stay at my place.'

Ruby, fiddling in the pocket of her trousers, produced a key. Triumphantly she said, 'We'll stay at *our* house.'

'Not on your own you don't.'

'You wouldn't call the police.'

'I bet I would.' With a glimmer of a smile Tyler said, 'And they'd throw you in jail for a week.'

Unamused, Ruby glared at him for several seconds. Finally she shrugged. 'Well, you're not having my mum's bed. You can sleep downstairs on the settee.'

Honestly, talk about surreal. Lottie was beginning to wonder if she'd landed on her head after all. One minute there she was thinking she felt better, the next minute she knew she must be hallucinating because Nat and Ruby were heading up the ward towards her with – ooh, *weird* – Tyler following in their wake.

Except, even weirder, he appeared to be real.

'What's going on?' Lottie craned her neck to see past them. 'Where's Seb?'

'Hello, Mummy. We're fine.' Having planted a kiss on each cheek, Nat and Ruby moved away from the bed.

'They'll be back in ten minutes,' said Tyler as they ran out of the ward. 'And you can see they're OK. I just need to—'

'What happened?' Lottie instantly conjured up mental pictures of an accident, Seb losing control of the car in the snow, the ambulance crew managing to get Nat and Ruby out unscathed but unable to reach Seb before being flung back by a violent explosion. Sick with fear she blurted out, 'Oh God, tell me he's all right!'

Ten minutes later Tyler had told her everything. Rigid with horror and disbelief, Lottie listened in silence. By the time he reached the end she was ready to rip the intravenous drip from her arm and launch herself like Frankenstein's monster out of bed – except she couldn't even *walk*.

'I'm sorry. Here.' It wasn't until Tyler passed her a handful of tissues that she realised tears were rolling down her face. 'Hey, don't cry. I know it's a shock, but you can do better than him.'

Lottie clumsily wiped her eyes with her unbandaged left hand. 'Do you seriously think that's why I'm upset? Because that dirtbag was cheating on me? My God, what kind of a person do you think I am!'

Tyler paused. 'But you're crying.'

'Because I'm so relieved my kids are OK!' Incandescent with rage – *how* could he be so dense? – Lottie hurled a sodden tissue at him. 'Because I can't believe I was so *stupid*.' She hurled another. 'Because I trusted another person to look after my children and I *shouldn't have!* Because I got it wrong and I'm a lousy judge of character and . . . oh God, *anything* could have happened to them.'

'But it didn't. They're fine.' Tyler's tone was soothing. 'Besides, how could you have known?'

'I just should have done.' Noisily Lottie blew her nose. He must be bursting to say 'I told you so'. Because he never had liked Seb.

'Did you know he used cocaine?'

'No!' Although now, of course, everything made more sense. Seb's over-enthusiasm, his episodes of almost over-the-top hyperactivity, the way he sometimes laughed a bit too much at something that wasn't *that* funny. His over-the-topness was one of the reasons Nat and Ruby had enjoyed being with him. Feeling stupider than ever, Lottie said, 'Did you?'

'It crossed my mind. Hey,' Tyler handed her a clean tissue, 'I worked on Wall Street, remember? There was a bit more of that kind of thing going on in New York than you're used to in Hestacombe.'

This didn't make Lottie feel any better at all. She still wanted to tear Sebastian Gill apart with her bare hands. While he'd been high on coke and cavorting in his living room with some tart, Ruby had been upstairs so desperate to escape that she had been forced to accept help from, of all people, *Tyler*.

'I'm sorry I threw those tissues at you.'

'That's OK.' He sounded amused. 'I'm a man. I can handle soggy tissues.'

'And thanks for rescuing Nat and Ruby.' There was still so much she had to say. 'So does this mean they don't hate you any more?'

'Wouldn't that be nice?' Tyler gave her an ironic look. 'Sadly, there's no danger of that happening. Your children still hate me every bit as much as before.'

'Oh.' Disappointed, Lottie said, 'Is Mario on his way home yet?'

'We haven't been able to contact him.'

'Bloody hell.' She shook her head in exasperation. 'What's he playing at?'

'No, we can't find the piece of paper with his details on. We've turned the kitchen upside down, looked everywhere.' Tyler shrugged. 'It's gone. Can you remember the name of the hotel?'

Lottie looked blank. 'No.'

'We're back,' Nat announced.

'Oh, sweetheart.' Ready to burst into tears all over again, Lottie held out her good arm. 'Come here.'

Nat, dodging smartly out of the way, said, 'Yuk, get off, not if you're going to cry.'

'Poor Mummy, be nice to her.' Ruby stroked Lottie's shoulder.

Making an effort to retain control, Lottie whispered, 'I'm so sorry about last night, sweetheart. Are you sure you're all right?'

Ruby nodded before jerking her head in Tyler's direction. 'Except for having *him* looking after us.'

Lottie was mortified. 'Oh Ruby, don't say that. Look what he *did* for you . . .'

'I still don't like him.' Ruby spoke matter-of-factly. 'Anyway, Dad'll be home soon.'

'He won't be if we can't contact him. Now think,' Lottie cajoled. 'The hotel and phone number were written on a sheet of yellow paper. It was on the dresser on Friday. It can't have just disappeared.' As she said this, she saw Nat's dark lashes flicker. 'Nat? Any ideas at all?'

'No!' He sounded outraged.

'Because if there was some kind of an accident, then that's fine,' Tyler joined in casually. 'But if it *is* still there, we'll just have to keep on looking until we find it.'

Nat glanced furtively around the ward before saying hurriedly, 'I spilled Ribena on it and the ink went all blurred. So I threw it away.'

'You *plonker*.' Ruby let out a wail of disbelief.

'Well, that's not a problem.' Tyler looked relieved. 'All we have to do is go through the kitchen bin.'

It was a measure of how desperate he was to get Nat and Ruby off his hands, Lottie felt, that he was willing to trawl through a disgusting smelly mess of empty baked bean tins, potato peelings and old chicken bones.

'I didn't want anyone to find out what I'd done,' Nat mumbled. 'So I threw it down the toilet and pulled the flush.'

Lottie and Tyler looked at each other. Nat said in a defensive voice, 'It was an *accident*.'

Ruby rolled her eyes. 'And it's practically the first time in your whole life you've ever pulled the flush.'

This was too true to be funny. And now they had no way of contacting

316

Mario. Beckoning over a passing nurse, Lottie said hopefully, 'If I promise to stay in bed, could I go home?'

The nurse rolled her eyes exactly as Ruby had just done. '*No.*'

Oh.

'I've got an idea,' Ruby said suddenly. 'Amber!'

'Yay, Amber! She could look after us.' Nat's face lit up as he clutched Lottie's arm. 'She can, can't she, Mum? We *like* Amber.'

'Give her a ring,' Lottie told Tyler. 'Her number's on my phone. Fingers crossed she can do it.'

Tyler was gone from the ward for a good fifteen minutes. When he returned he wasn't looking giddy with relief.

'She can't.'

'Oh no.' Lottie had been pinning all her hopes on Amber riding to the rescue.

'That's not fair! Why not?' wailed Nat.

'She's too busy, rushed off her feet at work. Everyone wants their hair done before Christmas,' said Tyler. 'And she's doing house visits in the evenings as well.'

'Could we just stay with her today?' Ruby pleaded. 'It's Sunday. Amber never works on a Sunday.'

'She can't do that either.' Raking his fingers through his hair Tyler said bluntly, 'Quentin's taking her to meet his aunt in Oxford.'

So that was that. Amber had been their last hope.

'It's no use glaring at me,' Tyler told Nat. 'I didn't want this either. But it looks like we're stuck with each other for the next few days. So we may as well make the best of it.'

'There isn't any best. We don't *want* you looking after us,' said Nat.

'And this is my worst nightmare,' Tyler retorted. 'So that makes us even.'

'All this bickering isn't doing me any good, you know,' said Lottie.

Tyler raised an eyebrow. 'Stop doing it then.'

Oh God. The three of them were as bad as each other. Now she knew how the teachers at Oaklea felt when they were called upon to settle a playground spat.

One of the nurses came bustling over. 'Lottie, the porters are here to wheel you down for your pyelogram.'

Tyler said, 'We'll leave you to it.'

Ruby shot him a suspicious look. 'What're you going to do with us?'

'Lock you in the garage.'

When they'd left the ward, the nurse said with an indulgent smile, 'Mum goes into hospital and Dad doesn't know what's hit him. Most of them don't have the first idea when it comes to taking care of their kids, do they?'

317

'He's not their dad,' said Lottie. 'He's my boss.'

'Really? Heavens, lucky old you!' The nurse softened. 'And how lovely of him to be looking after your children!'

The porters had arrived to wheel her bed out of the ward. Bracing herself for knocks and judders, Lottie said wearily, 'Believe me, he didn't have a lot of choice.'

Chapter 63

'What's in here? It weighs a ton.' Ask a silly question. Tyler picked up Nat's school bag, unzipped it and found it packed with − what else? − stones.

'It's *stones*. Aren't I allowed to collect stones?' Nat was ostentatiously picking crispy shards of black from the surface of his Marks and Spencer lasagne.

'Absolutely. Am I allowed to ask why?'

'It's what soldiers do in the army. To make them strong. This is really burned.'

Tyler rose above this slur on his culinary skills. 'I call it char-grilled.'

'I call it burned.'

'That's how soldiers eat it.' Burrowing amongst the muddy stones, Tyler pulled out a mangled, muddy sheet of turquoise paper. 'What's this?'

Nat mumbled, 'Letter from school.'

'How long has it been in here?'

'I don't know. This is *so* burned.'

Tyler began to read the photocopied letter, issued to all pupils by the school headmistress and so jollily worded that at first he found himself lulled into a false sense of security.

It took a few seconds to realise what it was actually instructing him to do.

'It's half past eight on Monday night,' Tyler said slowly, 'and it says here that all children must bring cakes into school on Tuesday morning for the cake stall.' He looked first at Ruby, then at Nat. 'But we don't have any in the house and all the shops are shut.'

'You aren't allowed to buy them from the shop,' said Nat. 'You have to make them.'

Oh great. 'Ruby? Do you have one of these letters too?'

'No.'

Tyler exhaled. 'Well, that's something at least.'

'I think I lost mine,' Ruby said helpfully.

'So what happens if you go to school tomorrow without homemade cakes?'

319

They looked scandalised. 'We have to. Or we'll get in trouble.'

Tyler carried on reading. Everyone, the letter chirpily announced, was expected to attend the Christmas Tree and Cakes Fair on Tuesday evening and enjoy the carols being sung by Year 5 pupils in their festive Victorian attire.

He turned to Ruby. 'What year are you in?'

She gave him a *duh* look. 'Five.'

This was a learning curve and no mistake. 'You're singing carols tomorrow night?'

'It doesn't matter. I'll tell them I can't go.'

'And the festive Victorian attire? Where does that come from?'

'You have to ask your mum and she makes it. But she's in hospital,' said Ruby, 'so we won't be going to the Tree and Cakes Fair anyway. So don't worry about it.'

Tyler looked at her. This was a *vertical* learning curve.

'Don't try and make any cakes either,' Nat added. 'Because if you did they'd only end up burned.'

'You made *what* last night?'

'Twenty-four fairy cakes.'

'But why . . . ? Oh my God! The Tree and Cakes Fair, I forgot all about it!' Lottie couldn't believe it had slipped her mind. 'And Ruby's supposed to be . . . oh well, they'll manage without her.'

'No, it's OK, we're going. I know about the festive Victorian attire,' Tyler said drily. 'And I've tracked down a shop in Cheltenham that hires out fancy dress.'

'You don't have to do that,' Lottie protested.

'But it has to be *right.*'

'This is Oaklea Junior School, not the London Palladium. She can go as a street urchin,' Lottie explained. 'Old pair of trousers cut off below the knee to look raggedy. Some shirt buttoned up all wrong, hair messed up, streaks of dirt on her face.'

Relieved, Tyler said, 'OK.'

'Don't forget to take a camera.'

'Right.'

'Oh, and I volunteered to help with selling the Christmas trees.'

'I'll do that then.'

'You'll need gardener's gloves.'

'Why, to stop Nat biting me?'

'They don't still hate you, do they?'

'More than ever. But that's OK, I can handle it.'

'What about Liana?'

'She doesn't hate me.'

'She must be getting a bit fed up.' Lottie did her best to sound concerned.

'Can't be helped.' Abruptly changing the subject, Tyler pulled the crumpled school letter from his jacket pocket. 'Now, it's Nat's Christmas play tomorrow night.'

'The Nativity play. He's playing one of the sheep. That's easy too,' said Lottie. 'Just wrap the sheepskin rug round him and tie it on with a couple of belts.'

'He's been upgraded. Charlie Johnson's off with flu so Nat's been promoted to chief shepherd. I already checked with one of the other mothers this morning when I dropped them off at school.' Tyler was looking pleased with himself. 'Tea towel on head. Big shirt, bare feet, walking stick. No problem.'

Lottie's eyes prickled with tears. She was going to miss the Nativity play.

'Don't worry, the head's videoing it,' said Tyler. 'I'm not allowed to go either.'

'You won't be there?' Lottie couldn't bear it.

'I've been banned by Nat. I have to wait outside the school hall.' Tyler waited. 'Of course I'm going to be there. He just won't know about it, that's all.'

When they arrived back at Piper's Cottage the post had been delivered. Ruby, scooping the postcard up off the mat, said, 'We did a project at school on Australia. This is Sydney Harbour Bridge.'

Tyler looked over her shoulder. 'It isn't.'

'Yes it is.'

'No it's not.'

'Yes it *is*.'

'Turn it over then. See what it says.'

Ruby turned the card over.

'See?' Tyler pointed to the printed lettering at the bottom. 'The Tyne Bridge, Newcastle-upon-Tyne.'

Annoyed, Ruby said, 'How did you *know*?'

'Because I'm very clever.' He smiled. 'Yours was a pretty good guess though. They're very similar.'

'It's not fair.' Ruby heaved an irritated sigh. 'I wish I knew everything. I can't wait to be a grown-up and always get everything right.'

Tyler thought of Lottie and Liana and the events of the past few months. 'Trust me,' he told Ruby with feeling, 'being a grown-up doesn't mean you get everything right.'

'Do you make mistakes?' Nat looked delighted.

Was he kidding? 'Oh yes, I've made some big mistakes. Like the time I thought you'd stolen your mom's clothes while she was swimming in the lake.'

'It wasn't us,' said Nat.

'Of course it wasn't you. I know that now. But at the time it was an honest mistake.'

'And when you threw away my noonoo.'

'That too.' Tyler nodded in agreement. 'And I said I was sorry.'

'Noonoos are for babies anyway.' Nat was proud, these days, of his noonoo-less state.

'You killed Bernard,' Ruby chimed in before it could sound as if they might be on the verge of forgiving him. Bluntly she added, 'That was murder.'

'I know. But I really didn't mean to kill him. It was an accident.' Tyler shook his head. 'I told you, grown-ups still make mistakes.'

'Anyway.' Firmly changing the subject, Ruby held up the postcard. 'This is for Mum, from Cressida. Should I read it?'

'You shouldn't really read other people's mail,' Tyler pointed out.

'It's only a postcard. Everyone reads *them*.'

This was true. 'Go on then.'

Ruby cleared her throat importantly and read aloud, '"Newcastle is perfect. So is Tom. I've never been happier in my life. The view from up here on Cloud 9 is spectacular – may not want to come down again! Love Cress. Pssss, hope all's well with you and Seb." Ha, wait until she hears about *him*.'

'So this man Tom is going to be Cress's new boyfriend. They'll be all lovey-dovey.' Nat rolled his eyes.

Lucky them, thought Tyler.

'If Cress hadn't gone up to see him,' Nat continued, 'she'd be looking after us now, instead of you.'

With difficulty Tyler managed to keep a straight face. 'I guess she's just had a lucky escape. Now, anyone want to give me a hand with dinner?'

Nat looked appalled. 'My favourite programme's about to start.'

'The more help I get, the less likely it is to be burned.'

It was Ruby's turn to heave a sigh. 'I suppose I'll have to help you then. But only for a bit.'

'Thank you.' It was a minor victory but it felt . . . God, it felt *great*. When Nat had raced off to watch TV, Tyler nodded at the postcard in Ruby's hand and said easily, 'By the way, that bit at the end. It's P.S., not Pssss.'

Ruby bristled. 'I knew that.'

'Hey, of course you did.' She looked so much like Lottie when she was defending herself. 'In fact I prefer *Psss*,' said Tyler. 'It sounds like a secret you're whispering to someone. Much better than boring old P.S.'

Ruby almost, *almost* smiled. She nodded confidently. 'Me too.'

Having skipped down the steps and raced across the playground to where the Christmas trees were being sold, Ruby hovered to one side for a few seconds before blurting out, 'Did you see me?'

Her breath hung in misty clouds in the freezing night air and she was wearing her street urchin outfit.

'I saw you. And heard you. We all did.' Tyler indicated the other helpers before untying the blue sweater from round his waist. 'You did great. Now why don't you put this on before you catch pneumonia?'

'It's *yours*.' Ruby eyed the sweater with alarm, as if he'd offered her one decorated with live cockroaches.

'But you left your coat at home, remember? And now you're cold. No, don't want it? OK, just put it over there on the wall.'

Three minutes later Ruby said, 'Did you hear me doing my solo verse in O Come All Ye Faithful?'

'Are you kidding? Of course I heard it. I was the one clapping and whistling the loudest.' Tyler paused. 'Actually, better not tell Lottie I was doing that. She might think sticking your fingers in your mouth and whistling is the kind of crass thing only a dumb American would do.'

Ruby looked envious. 'I've never been able to whistle like that. With my fingers.'

'Oh well, I can teach you how to do that. Learned all about whistling when I worked on a cattle ranch in Wyoming.' Someone came up at that point to choose one of the Christmas trees. By the time Tyler had finished dealing with them Ruby had wandered over to chat to her friends around the hot chocolate stand, but she was wearing his sweater.

A small concession, but maybe . . . *maybe* . . . a start.

'I can't get my stupid tea towel on straight! It keeps going sideways and falling over my eye!'

'OK, OK, don't panic, I'll sort it out.'

'I'm going to be *late*.' Nat's voice rose. 'It's starting *now*.'

'Better keep still then.' Crouching in front of him in the car park, Tyler whipped off the tea towel and headband and started all over again while Nat hopped impatiently from foot to foot. Having visited Lottie in the hospital and left plenty of time for the journey to school, they hadn't allowed for a lorry jack-knifing across the A46, causing a twenty-minute delay and so much agitation on Nat's part it was a wonder he hadn't exploded through the roof of the car.

'Quick, quick!'

'There, all done. You look terrific.' Tyler patted him on the shoulder. 'Go on in, it's showtime.'

Nat gazed up at him. 'Where will you be?'

'Don't worry, I'll wait in the car.'

After a moment's hesitation Nat said, 'Is it true that you worked on a cattle ranch, like a real cowboy?'

'Of course it's true.' So Ruby had told him about that. 'I even learned how to use a lasso.'

'And whistle really loudly with your fingers in your mouth.' Nat paused, blinked. 'You can come in and watch if you want.'

Tyler was careful not to react. But inside he was marvelling that being invited to watch a Nativity play could feel like winning the lottery. Aloud he said, 'Really? You're sure you don't mind?'

Clearly itching to get inside, Nat shrugged. 'You can if you like.'

'Thanks.' As Nat turned to leave, Tyler called after him, 'If it's a good show, am I allowed to whistle at the end?'

It was too dark to be able to tell for sure, but he was fairly certain Nat was smiling as he yelled back, 'You can if you like.'

Lottie almost had a relapse there and then when her visitors made their way onto the ward on Friday afternoon and she saw that Nat was holding Tyler's hand.

When Nat grinned and waved at her she nearly had another one. 'Oh my God, I didn't even know your tooth was loose!'

'It wathn't. I fell over in the playground during morning break and my tooth broke in half.' Intensely proud of his gap, Nat wiggled the end of his tongue through it. 'And it hurt like anything tho Mith Batson phoned your mobile and Tyler anthwered and came and picked me up and took me to the dentitht. And the dentitht gave me a huge injection and that *really* hurt but I wath brave and then he pulled out the tooth and there wath loadth of blood *everywhere*.'

'Oh Nat!' Lottie hugged him before anxiously searching his face for signs of emotional trauma. 'And I wasn't there!'

'Mum, you're choking me. My mouth wath all numb and flubbery afterwardth. It wath cool! And then I went back to thcool even though there wath blood on my shirt.' This had evidently been a badge of honour. 'And Tyler gave me a pound for being brave at the dentitht. *And* he'th taking uth ithe-thkating tomorrow, to an ithe-thkating rink in Brithtol.'

'Good grief.' Lottie was busy kissing Ruby and stroking her hair.

'And I heard Miss Batson talking to Tyler when we went to pick up

324

Nat this afternoon,' Ruby chimed in. 'She was laughing and telling him what a good job he was doing, looking after us.'

Good *grief*.

Nat grinned at Tyler. 'I thaw that too. She looked ath if she wanted to kith you.'

Lottie blinked; this was truly mind-boggling stuff.

'If Miss Batson even tried to come *near* me,' Tyler warned, 'I'd stick my fingers in my mouth and whistle so hard her eardrums would burst.'

'That'th what I'm going to do when the girlth try to kith me,' said Nat.

'Tell Mum the other thing,' Ruby prompted Tyler.

'What other thing?' Lottie was beginning to feel quite light-headed.

Tyler's dark eyes glittered with amusement. 'OK, Miss Batson told me how nice it was to see your kids so happy now, because you'd got your-self involved with a man not so long ago who'd caused all kinds of prob-lems.' Modestly he added, 'She said thank goodness you'd come to your senses and that I was clearly a much better choice. With which sentiment I naturally agreed.'

'And that'th when I told her,' Nat lisped exultantly. 'I thaid Tyler wath the one we'd hated because he'd been tho horrible to uth!'

For the first time Lottie was glad she was confined to her hospital bed. Picturing Miss Batson's formidable face she murmured faintly, 'Then what?'

Tyler said, 'Miss Batson leaned over and whispered in my ear, "Do you know, if I weren't a teacher I'd suggest boiling them in oil."'

The world was becoming more surreal by the minute. It was mad enough that Nat and Ruby were on speaking terms with Tyler, but getting to grips with the idea that Miss Batson might actually be human . . .

'Oh yeah, and Dad phoned latht night.' Nat belatedly produced the other snippet of information they had to pass on – far less important than his bashed-out front tooth.

'He did? At *last*.' Lottie heaved a sigh of relief. 'Is he flying straight back?'

Ruby shook her head. 'He offered. We said there was no need. We're OK without him now, aren't we?'

OK without Mario. OK with Tyler. Lottie silently digested this. A few months ago it would have been more than she could have hoped for, a turnaround on Nat and Ruby's part beyond her wildest dreams.

But that was before Liana had arrived on the scene and installed herself back in Tyler's life.

'Sweetheart, I'll be discharged from here soon. The hospital are lending me a wheelchair but I'm going to be pretty useless at home. I'll need help with everything.'

'But we've told Dad he doethn't have to come home.' Nat, chomping his way through her grapes as efficiently as a plague of locusts, said, 'Anyway, we've broken up now. We can help you.'

'Thanks, darling. I know you will.' Lottie stroked his tangled curls and wondered how she was really going to manage in a wheelchair. Piper's Cottage had narrow doorways and the bathroom was so small it—

'You *pig*,' wailed Ruby, shoving the brown paper bag at Nat's chest. 'There's only stalks left. You've eaten all the grapes!'

'Don't throw it at *me*. I'm allowed to eat them becauthe I've been to the *dentitht*.'

Separating them with an outstretched arm, Tyler said calmly, 'Ice skating. Yes or no?'

Nat and Ruby looked at each other and subsided onto the bed.

'You know, I'm starting to get the hang of this,' said Tyler.

He looked so pleased with himself. Touched, Lottie said, 'Handled like a pro.'

Nat, giving Ruby a nudge, said, 'But he thtill burnth everything he cookth.'

Chapter 64

'Here she is,' sang the nurse. 'Lottie, you've got another visitor.'

It was Friday evening and Lottie was engrossed in an article in a magazine about a woman giving birth to twins in her bathroom when she hadn't even realised she was pregnant.

Looking up and seeing Liana standing there at the foot of the bed gave her much the same feeling.

'You look awful.' Liana was taking in the yellow bruises, the hair in need of a wash, the bandaged wrist and the plastered foot. 'How are you feeling?'

'Oh, um . . . better thanks.' Lottie put down the magazine.

'And smug, I should think.' Liana was smiling but in a way that didn't quite reach her eyes.

'Sorry?'

'Oh yes, that too. Sorry, but not sorry enough to put a stop to it.'

'Put a stop to what?' But Lottie had already guessed what this was about; it was pretty self-evident that Liana was fed up with the fact that for the last six days she'd hardly seen Tyler.

And in all honesty, who could blame her?

'You *know* what,' said Liana.

'OK, but there wasn't much else I could do, was there?' Lottie did her best to sound reasonable. 'I'm stuck in bed here and somebody had to look after Ruby and Nat.'

'And guess who that someone turned out to be? *My* boyfriend.'

Yikes. 'Well, I'm sorry. But the doctors think I might be able to go home on Monday, so then we'll be out of your hair.'

'And where will you be staying? In that poky little cottage of yours?' Liana was a lady so she didn't snort – *would* never snort – but it was a close-run thing.

The cheek of it! Lottie, who loved her home with a passion, retorted, 'Plenty of people manage to live in poky cottages and—'

'So Tyler hasn't told you then? That he wants to move you into Hestacombe House?'

'*What?* No!'

Liana's knuckles were white as she gripped the metal rail at the foot of the bed. 'We had the most massive row about it last night. He was most insistent, going on about the doorways being wide enough for your wheel-chair and how he could turn the drawing room into a bedroom – any excuse he could think of, basically. So long as he's got you under his roof. Anyhow, I told him I'd had enough. I said if you moved in, I'd be gone. And guess what? I'm gone.'

Lottie was numb, too shocked to move or speak. Luckily Liana was on a mission to offload everything that was on her mind.

'So that's it. Looks like you won.' Tilting her head to one side she said, 'I bet you can't believe your luck, huh? Because I'm telling you now, I sure as hell can't figure it out. I'm the one who deserves him, you see. I'm beau-tiful, everyone says so. I'm a perfect size six. I'm intelligent and I'm always real nice to people. Everyone likes me. And my fiancé died, which means I've suffered enough. God knows, if anyone deserves to be happy, it's me.'

Her words sounded brittle, like dry twigs being snapped. Liana couldn't comprehend the reality of rejection, let alone the possibility that she may have lost out to someone who weighed three stone more than she did.

Unless – the unedifying thought crossed Lottie's mind – maybe she hadn't. Maybe Tyler, eager to get rid of Liana, was simply using her as a handy excuse.

Lottie shuddered. God, how awful if *that* hadn't occurred to her before she'd hurled herself into his arms.

'I mean, look at you.' As if to illustrate the point Liana indicated Lottie in her red dressing gown, sporting the glitter-strewn Get Well badge Ruby had presented her with last night. 'Your hair's a mess. You eat carbs like they're going out of fashion.'

Lottie was unable to resist it. 'I thought carbs *were* out of fashion.'

But Liana's sense of humour had never been her strong point. She shook her head and said bluntly, 'I don't mean to be rude here, it's just that I truly don't get it. I take care of myself, it's as simple as that. I spend a fortune keeping my body in peak – I mean absolutely *peak* – condition. And you don't.'

'No, I don't,' Lottie agreed.

'May I ask you a personal question? Have you ever had a professional pedicure in your life?'

Lottie looked at her toes, the Day-Glo pink nails varnished yesterday by Ruby with a lot of love and care but maybe not that much accuracy.

'No, I haven't.'

'And as for your wardrobe. You wear the most extraordinary outfits sometimes. You *never* co-ordinate your accessories . . .'

'I'm sorry.' Lottie kept a straight face.

'But nobody seems to mind! That's what gets me! You're a single parent with two young children . . . I mean, that should be a major turn-off in anybody's book. *And* your last boyfriend was a drug addict, which doesn't say much for your powers of judgement.'

Stung, Lottie said, 'Now hang on a minute, that's not fair. I didn't *know* about—'

'Hey, no offence.' Liana held up her hands. 'Don't you see? There's no need for you to defend yourself because it doesn't seem to matter what you get wrong. Everyone forgives you anyway.' She paused. 'Whereas *I* never do anything wrong *and* I take care of myself and I spend more money on one pair of shoes than you spend on clothes in a *year*, but when it comes right down to it, for some reason they still prefer you.'

It was fantastic to see Amber again, and even more fantastic to discover she'd brought along her hairdressing scissors. Since coming out of hospital three days ago, Lottie had been getting used to manoeuvring her wheel-chair around the ground floor of Hestacombe House. Now, showing off, she swung a bit too cavalierly into the sunny drawing room and scraped the knuckles of her left hand against the door frame.

'You need L-plates. I can't believe so much has happened in the last ten days.' Once the brakes had been applied, Amber fastened the towel round Lottie's shoulders and took out her comb and scissors. 'You in hospital, Nat and Ruby being looked after by Tyler. Do you know, when they met me at the bottom of the drive they were speaking with just a *smidgen* of an American accent.' Smiling as she began Lottie's long-overdue cut, she went on, 'Imitation's the sincerest form of flattery. If they're doing that, he's definitely won them over.'

'He has. And Liana's gone back to America.' Lottie gazed at the Christmas tree and listened to the comforting snip-snip of the scissors. The other reason she was so pleased to see Amber was because she was desperate for a girlfriend to confide in.

'So it's all systems go, you and Tyler together at last! About six inches or a bit more?'

Lottie was taken aback. Crikey, talk about coming straight to the point. 'Um, I haven't had—'

'I mean six inches when it's curly. If you straightened it out it'd be longer than that.' Amber reached over and held up a length of Lottie's hair. 'See? Boiiinngg, like a spring! It's grown so fast I think you could do with at least that much off.'

'Fine, go ahead.' Lottie pulled an *eeek* face. 'Sorry, you don't want to know what I thought you were talking about.'

329

'I know exactly what you thought, you trollop. And now you've happened to mention it, why don't I make that my next question?'

'You can ask, but I can't tell you.'

'Rotten spoilsport!' Amber grabbed a handful of hair. 'Hang on, let me just hack off this huge chunk of—'

'I'm not being a spoilsport,' Lottie said hastily. 'Tyler and I aren't together like that.'

'Oh. Sorry. Doctor's orders, I suppose. If you've just come out of hospital you can't start—'

'I mean Tyler and I aren't together in *any* way. He's my boss. I'm his employee.' Lottie blinked as a snipped bit of hair landed on her eyelashes. 'And that's as far as it goes.'

Amber stopped cutting and moved round to look at her. 'Seriously?'

'Seriously.'

Amber's face was a picture. 'But . . . why?'

'I don't know!'

'Has he said anything?'

'No!' wailed Lottie.

'Have you asked him?'

'Nooo!'

'Do you want me to ask him for you?'

'Nooooo!'

'OK, OK, don't burst my eardrums.' Amber was frowning. 'But I thought he was crazy about you.'

'So did I!'

'And the only thing stopping you being together was Nat and Ruby hating him, except they don't hate him any more. And Liana and Seb are out of the picture now, so everything should be . . . well, all systems go.'

'Exactly.'

'So why isn't it?'

'Truthfully?' Lottie hated having to say the words. 'I think he's changed his mind.'

'Why?'

'Because Tyler doesn't hang around. If he was going to say anything he would have said it by now. He's had a million opportunities, but he just hasn't done it. The way he's treating me, it's like we're brother and sister. He's helping me out by letting us stay here, but it doesn't *mean* anything.' Lottie fiddled with the heavy strapping on her wrist. 'Basically, I think he was crazy about me, but that was months ago and now those feelings have worn off. Like buying the best pair of trousers in the world and loving them so much you never want to take them off.' She paused. 'Then a few weeks later you realise they aren't that flattering after all.'

330

Amber said robustly, 'Well, I can't believe you haven't tackled him about it.'

Lottie couldn't either. It wasn't like her at all. But there was so much at stake she was terrified to make any kind of move in case it all went horribly wrong. 'I just can't. Anyway, look at me.' She indicated the cast on her foot, the still spectacularly bruised wrist and the wheelchair. 'It's not as if I can pounce on him, is it? Wrestle him to the ground and force him to change his mind? And at least if I don't say anything I'll still have some pride left.'

'So how long will you stay on here?' Amber resumed cutting.

'Only a few more days. As soon as the wrist's better I'll be able to get around on crutches. Then we can go home.' Keen to change the subject, Lottie waved her hand. 'Anyway, enough about me. How's it going with you and Quentin?'

'Oh, fine! As good as gold! I've been rushed off my feet at work but he never complains.' Amber said fondly, 'I got home at ten o'clock last night and he'd cooked the most amazing roast dinner, can you believe it?'

'Mario would never have done that,' said Lottie.

'I *know*. That's the difference between them.' Amber's turquoise and silver earrings swung from side to side as she shook her head. 'Quentin's so thoughtful. And trustworthy. He's so . . . caring, do you know what I mean? All he wants to do is make me happy.'

Lottie said, 'Yes, but does he make you laugh?'

'If you start on me,' Amber pointed the business end of the scissors at her, 'I shall run down to the office and ask Tyler why he hasn't made a pass at you. I'll tell him you *luuuurve* him and that you want to—'

'I'm not starting!' Lottie hurriedly raised both hands in surrender.

'Promise?'

'Promise.'

'Good.'

'There's just one tiny thing I want to mention, if that's allowed.'

Already suspicious, Amber narrowed her eyes. 'What?'

'Mario rang me yesterday. He hasn't slept with anyone while he's been on holiday. Not one single solitary girl. He just hasn't wanted to,' said Lottie.

'That's what he says.'

'But it's the truth, because he doesn't need to lie to me, does he? In fact,' Lottie pointed out, 'I'd have been a lot happier if he had been sleeping with girls, as many as he liked, because I'm starting to worry about him. Mario's *never* been celibate before. You know, I really think you—'

'Don't say it!' Amber tapped her on the head, quite painfully, with her metal comb. 'I don't care what you think. I've got Quentin and he makes me happy, thank you very much.'

331

'Do you mind? I'm an invalid.' Rubbing her head, Lottie belatedly remembered the golden rule: never annoy your hairdresser halfway through your own haircut.

Maybe Amber didn't mind that Quentin didn't make her laugh.

Chapter 65

As each new delay had been announced, every other passenger had become increasingly bad-tempered. Now that they were home at last their collective mood improved. The plane had landed nine hours late but they were finally back in Bristol and thank God for that.

The exception was Mario, who basically wasn't bothered either way. As far as he was concerned the airport was as good a place as any to pass a bit of time. Apart from seeing Nat and Ruby again, what else did he have to look forward to?

Nothing at all.

Oh well. Hauling his case off the luggage carousel, he wheeled it through the milling crowds and made his way towards Customs. Even hiding bottles of spirits in your luggage and sneaking them through the Nothing to Declare channel was no fun any more now that you were allowed to bring back as much as you wanted.

Bloody EU.

The glass doors slid open and Mario found himself in the arrivals hall, decorated for Christmas and still busy despite the fact that it was gone midnight. A couple of nuns were sitting at a café table drinking tea from a flask, groups of returning travellers were being greeted with cries of delight by friends and relatives and there was a girl sleeping on a bench with a woolly hat on. At first glance Mario experienced a cattle-prod jolt of recognition because beneath the woolly hat she had blonde hair like Amber's, but he was becoming accustomed to these jolts now. Several times a day on holiday he'd glimpse someone in the distance and think for a heart-stopping moment that it was Amber.

This one was wearing Amber-type clothes, which was what had captured his attention: a short ruffled purple skirt, pink glittery sweater and rainbow coloured hat and scarf. She was wearing pink cowboy boots, Mario observed, knowing perfectly well as he moved towards the bench that it wouldn't be her but needing to prove it to himself nevertheless.

It was her.

Oh God, it *was* her.

Mario forgot to breathe. He gazed down at Amber, peacefully asleep with her head resting on one arm and her sequinned handbag clutched to her chest.

What was she doing here? If she was waiting for bloody Quentin, he'd ... well, he'd ... oh Jesus, was this really happening or was *he* still asleep in the departure lounge in Palma?

Reaching out, Mario touched her shoulder and gave it a tentative shake. When Amber's eyes opened he snatched his hand back as if she were a growling pitbull.

Terrific, very manly. And what was he supposed to say, now that he'd gone and woken her up?

'Off on holiday?' Mario couldn't believe he'd just said that. Pathetic or what?

Amber looked at him. 'No.'

'Oh.'

'What's the time?'

He checked his watch. 'Half past midnight.'

'Of all the planes in all the world,' said Amber, 'you had to be on that one.'

Mario didn't allow himself to hope. 'It was delayed. We were supposed to be here nine hours ago. There was a fault with one of the engines, then they thought they'd fixed it but it turned out they hadn't, then it *was* finally fixed but we missed our next slot for take-off.'

'That's typical of you,' said Amber.

Still not daring to hope but compelled to ask the question, Mario said, 'Have you been waiting here since three o'clock this afternoon?'

'No I have *not*.' Amber pulled herself into a sitting position and took off her hat. She waited a couple of seconds then added, 'I've been waiting here since *six* o'clock this morning.'

'Why?' Mario braced himself for bad news.

'Why? Because Lottie didn't know what time you were flying back, did she, so I had to make sure I got here early enough to meet every plane.' Exasperated, Amber said, 'Except I didn't, did I? I fell asleep instead, on a stupid metal *bench*. You could have walked straight past me without even realising I was here. I'd have spent all that time waiting for nothing!'

Mario exhaled slowly. 'I don't think I could ever walk straight past you without realising you were there. It just wouldn't happen. And you do have to tell me what's going on, by the way. Because at the moment I'm at a bit of a loss for ...'

'Sausage rolls?' Amber raised her eyebrows as he gestured helplessly. 'Premium Bonds? Furniture polish?'

'That's it! Furniture polish.'

'You know exactly what's going on. I'll also have you know, it's all your interfering ex-wife's fault.' Amber paused. 'So, how was your holiday?'

'Terrible.'

She smiled. 'In that case I'm glad I didn't go with you.'

'If you'd gone with me it wouldn't have been terrible.' Reaching out, Mario pulled her to her feet. 'Where's Quentin?'

'That's all over. I told Quentin yesterday.'

'I bet he took it well,' said Mario. 'Like the thoroughly decent chap he is.'

'He did.' Amber nodded. 'And he *is* a thoroughly decent chap.'

'But?'

'He wasn't enough. Dammit, he wasn't *you*.'

Those were the words he wanted to hear. His heart expanding, Mario said, 'Does that mean I'm indecent?'

'Don't gloat. Oh God,' Amber groaned, 'I can't help wondering if I'm going to regret this.'

He loved her so much. 'You won't. And that's a promise.'

She fixed him with a warning look. 'You'd better keep that promise. Because I'm telling you now, if you *ever* cheat on me, I swear I'll—'

'I never have,' Mario forestalled her, because the nightmare one-night stand with Gemma didn't count, surely – that had happened after Amber had dumped him. 'And I never will. And excuse me for mentioning it, but you were the one who played away, sneaking off on holiday with another man. Road-testing him before you decided whether or not to choose him over me. And to cap it all, his name was *Quentin*.'

'You're right. And I'm sorry, I was wrong to do that.' Amber shook her head. 'I swear on my life I'll never do anything like that again.'

Mario touched her face, momentarily unable to speak. If he was honest she'd been right to do it. Discovering the hard way how it felt to be cheated on and dumped had been the wake-up call of his life. If you wanted to be really icky about it, you could even say the experience had changed him for the better.

But he wasn't going to tell Amber that. He wasn't completely stupid. 'Come on, let's go home. I just need to find the parking ticket machine.'

'You've got your car?' Amber looked dismayed. 'I didn't realise you'd driven down here. I've got my car too.'

Mario took her in his arms and kissed her properly. 'Sshh. You don't know how much I've missed you.'

'Actually, I think I can guess.' Pink and out of breath, Amber said, 'Will you behave yourself? There's nuns over there.'

Mario hadn't fancied the fifty-mile drive from Bristol back to Hestacombe anyway. 'In that case I think we'd better find a hotel. Get a room.'

Chapter 66

'Ow, bugger, *fuck*,' yelped Lottie as she lost her balance, toppled over sideways and at a stroke destroyed the festive tableau she'd spent the last twenty minutes painstakingly arranging.

The door opened and Tyler appeared. 'Are you all right?'

'Oh wonderful! Really, couldn't be better.' Lottie gestured from the floor, surrounded by holly branches, swathes of variegated ivy and pine cones. 'I had the fireplace looking gorgeous, like something out of a *magazine*, and now it's all wrecked!'

'Here.' Reaching down, he helped her to her feet – OK, *foot* – and plonked – plonked! – her back into her wheelchair. Feeling like a stroppy toddler, Lottie pointed to the berries scattered over the carpet. 'And this holly's rubbish. All the berries just bounced off! How can I decorate a fireplace with naked holly? It's just going to look *stupid*.' Oh dear, now she was starting to sound like a stroppy toddler. Was it any wonder Tyler was treating her like one?

'Do you want me to go out and cut some more?'

'You won't know which trees to avoid. I don't want any more of this useless stuff.'

'Fine.' Tyler abruptly left the room. Cursing herself and her hormones, Lottie hurled a pine cone at the fireplace. It was the Sunday before Christmas and to say they weren't getting on well was an understatement. Wheelchair or no wheelchair, she really couldn't stay on any longer at Hestacombe House.

It was time to go home.

The door swung open again and Tyler threw her black sweater and cream fake-fur gilet at her. 'Put these on. It's cold outside.'

'Is it?' Affecting surprise, Lottie gazed out of the drawing room window at the garden glittering with frost. 'And there was me, thinking I might wear my bikini.'

'Any more of your backtalk and you will.'

'And I can't wear these two things together. The cream fur moults like crazy.'

336

By this time pushing her at speed out into the hall, Tyler wordlessly reached over, snatched the offending gilet from her grasp and chucked it onto the floor.

'Thanks a lot! Now it's all *dirty*.'

'Will you stop complaining? Do you want more holly or not?'

They'd screeched to a halt on the polished parquet. Lottie fought her way into the black lambswool sweater, dragging it on over her cropped T-shirt. As her head popped out through the hole she said irritably, 'Well, what are you waiting for? Let's go.'

The sun was yet to melt last night's heavy frost. As the wheelchair jiggled over the path leading down to the lake, Lottie's breath formed opaque puffs that hung in the air before being whisked behind her. Tempted though she was to complain about the jiggling she didn't want to be turfed out of the chair and left on the stony ground to die of hypothermia.

'Not those. That's where the last lot came from.' Dismissing the inferior specimens on their left, she pointed instead to a holly tree closer to the water's edge. 'We'll try that one.'

Wordlessly Tyler steered her down to the beach. The swans glided across the water towards them, then figured out that they hadn't brought anything edible and promptly lost interest.

Rather like Tyler with me, thought Lottie as he reached up for the first branch.

Hmm, was that a pair of secateurs in his pocket or was he just pleased to see her?

No, it was a pair of secateurs. She watched him clip through the branch and give it a shake to check the berries were hanging on by more than just their fingernails before handing it to Lottie.

Lottie looked at the holly, glossy-leaved and still sparkling with frost. 'Actually, don't bother. I'd rather go home.'

He shook his head in disbelief. 'Don't be such a wimp, we'll be done in five minutes.'

'I mean there's no point in me decorating that room. I want to go back to my house.'

And exhale. There, she'd said it. At last.

Tyler surveyed her levelly. 'Why?'

'Because we've imposed on you long enough. It's almost Christmas. After putting up with Nat and Ruby for the last fortnight you must be desperate for some peace and quiet.'

'Is that the real reason?'

No, Lottie wanted to shout at him, of *course* it isn't. But I'm hardly going to tell you the *real* reason, am I?

337

Am I?

Oh God, *am* I?

Tyler's gaze was still upon her. To her absolute horror Lottie heard herself saying, 'Actually, I'm just a bit confused. The thing is, I don't know if you even remember this but back in the summer you seemed really keen on me and things between us were getting quite, well, you know. Until Nat and Ruby made things impossible and we agreed that we couldn't see each other any more.'

'Go on,' said Tyler.

Go *on*? Good grief, hadn't she already said enough? Oh no, and here *was* more, bubbling up and out of her mouth as uncontrollably as if someone had slipped her a truth drug.

'So that was fine, we were adults, we knew we had no other choice,' Lottie babbled on. 'Then I met someone else and not long after that Liana turned up, but deep down I was still crazy about you and call me stupid but I suppose I hoped that deep down you were still crazy about me.'

Tyler raised an enquiring eyebrow. 'And?'

'And?' Her voice spiralling, Lottie said in exasperation, 'But they're out of the picture now, both of them, and you even managed to change the way Nat and Ruby felt about you, which has to be some kind of miracle, but what it means is that there are now precisely *no* reasons why we . . . why we shouldn't . . . um . . .'

'Shouldn't what?'

He sounded mildly interested. This was awful, *worse* than awful. Flushed with embarrassment Lottie blurted out, 'Look, all I'm saying is that if you've gone off someone it's only polite to tell them, then they can stop wasting their time wondering if you still like them or not.'

Tyler nodded, absorbing this pronouncement. At last he said, 'You're right, that makes sense. OK, I'll do that.'

Lottie waited, her fingers gripping the wheelchair's armrests.

And waited.

Finally, light-headed with waiting – and forgetting to breathe – she managed to get out, 'You aren't saying it.'

'I know.' Tyler shrugged and at long last Lottie thought she detected a glimmer of a smile around his mouth. 'That's probably because I haven't stopped liking you.'

It was a jolly good job she was sitting down. 'So you still . . . ?'

'Oh yes.' Tyler nodded again, this time with undisguised amusement. 'I definitely still . . .' He waited. 'Go on then, your turn. Do you still . . . too?'

'You bastard!' Lottie flung aside the branch of holly that had been lying across her lap. 'You absolute *bastard*. You know I do!'

'I thought you might. I hoped you did. But I didn't know for sure,' Tyler pointed out. 'You haven't been giving me any clues.'

'That's because you haven't said anything!' Out of her chair now, hopping furiously on her good leg, Lottie yelled, 'You didn't give *me* any clues. I thought you weren't interested in me any more, so why would I want to make a complete wally of myself?' As she said this she lost her balance in the sand, wavered wildly on one foot for a couple of seconds and almost went crashing to the ground. Again.

Tyler caught her in the nick of time. As, deep down, Lottie had kind of hoped he would.

'Heaven forbid,' he drawled, 'that you should ever make a complete wally of yourself.'

He smelled wonderful, just as she remembered. The heat from his body was drawing her towards him like a magnet but there were still questions to be asked.

'So were you *ever* planning to do anything?' Lottie's eyes blazed with a mixture of indignation and lust. 'I mean, if I hadn't said all this today, would we have just carried on the way we've been carrying on for the last fortnight?'

'No.' Tyler shook his head thoughtfully. 'Of course I would have said something eventually. I just didn't want to jump the gun.'

Jump the gun?

'Are you mad?' Lottie blurted out. 'I've been waiting so hard for you to jump the gun that I've been ready to *burst*.'

'Maybe, but this isn't only about you, is it?' He gave her that maddening look again.

'Isn't it?' Her stomach gave a lurch of alarm. 'So who else is it about then?' If he told her Liana was on her way back over here . . .

'There are other people to consider. Like . . . *two* fairly important people?'

Oh *phew*. 'Ruby and Nat? But they love you now!'

'They've loved me for nine days. Possibly nine and a half.' Tyler shrugged. 'Before that they hated me with a passion. Who's to say they won't change their minds again tomorrow?'

'They won't. You've won them round completely.' Joyfully Lottie exclaimed, 'We can be together!'

'I hope so. But I still think it's better to ask them how they'd feel about it, rather than just presenting them with a fait accompli.'

'That's so thoughtful. And you're right. We'll ask them as soon as they get back.' Nat and Ruby had been taken Christmas shopping in Cheltenham by Mario and Amber. Checking her watch, Lottie said, 'They won't be home for a few hours yet.' She frowned. 'Gosh, I wonder what we could possibly do to pass the time?'

'Stop that. Not until we know.' Tyler removed her wandering hands from the front of his shirt before she had time to undo even one button.

Spoilsport.

'They're my children,' Lottie protested. 'Trust me, they'll be fine about it.'

'All the same.' Taking his phone out of his jacket pocket Tyler said, 'Just give Mario a call.'

'Mario?'

'Say, have you asked them yet?'

'You mean you . . . ?'

'Just do it,' prompted Tyler.

Flabbergasted, Lottie keyed in Mario's number. When he answered she said, 'Tyler's asked me to ask you if you've asked them yet.'

Moments later she said, 'OK, thanks,' and switched off the phone.

'Well?'

'He asked them. They said it's cool.'

A slow smile spread from Tyler's mouth to his eyes. 'Cool. Well, that's a relief. Cool is more than I dared hope for.'

'See? I knew they'd be OK about it.' Triumphantly Lottie wrapped her arms round his neck and kissed him. 'I'm always right.'

Tyler kissed her in return, until she was tingling all over. 'All that trouble, solved by one little word,' he drawled. Then, as Lottie launched herself away from him and began hopping backwards: 'What are you doing now?'

'You're taking me back to the house.' Lowering herself into the wheel-chair Lottie said, 'It's way too cold out here for what I have in mind.'

'Really? Oh well, in that case.' Tyler swung the chair in a homewards direction. '*Cool.*'